TO WEAR A CROWN

MARILENE LOUISE BLOM

Marilene Louise Blom t/a Gentle Sea Publishing, Cape Town, South Africa

First published in May 2022 by

Marilene Louise Blom t/a Gentle Sea Publishing

www.marilenelouiseblom.wixsite.com/author

ISBN

978-0-620-97294-9 (print)

978-0-620-97295-6 (eBook)

*No matter how many times the fight for freedom is won,
it remains to be fought…*

CHAPTER ONE

THE GRAVEL STREETS WERE QUIET, the lanterns in Yaekós' western slums extinguished hours ago and the full moon well past its zenith. Markham looked around. Once. Twice. He pulled his black cloak tighter around him and continued east. The next alley would lead him to the Crest, would take him home. He was almost there. Almost safe. He just needed to remain unnoticed for a while longer and he'd make it.

He could already see the story forming in his mind: *A dashing, young hero completing his valiant mission with sure steps and pride in his eyes…*

He heard the footsteps split seconds too late, turned into the alley to find two men already waiting—the maroon of their capes unmistakable. Guild members.

He froze, muscles tense as he closed his hand around the dagger hidden in his belt. They would be well-trained, ruthless. They had to be if they were wearing the red.

They advanced slowly, with the swagger of those who had nothing to fear. Markham's grip tightened around the dagger's hilt, but he straightened nonchalantly.

"Gentlemen," he offered, flashing them his most charming smile. "Enjoying the Rooks' bustling nightlife?"

One of them grinned at him, a crooked grimace that forced Markham to clench his jaw. "Let's not play coy, son."

He was tall and broad-shouldered, the lower half of his face marred by an old burn wound. The other, a scrawny troublemaker with blackened stumps for teeth, had stringy orange hair that sagged against his scalp—a creature that would crawl from the sewers and poison you with one bite. His voice was a piercing rasp, barely more than a whisper.

"I can see you fondling that knife. Why not make this easy and give over that pretty purse at your side without trouble?"

"Oh, this?" He patted the crimson velvet purse with his free hand, the one embroidered with his initials–the golden *MA* that would give him away. "Sure. I just don't know what you're going to do with it, since it's empty. I, on the other hand, attach strong sentimental value to this particular purse. See, it was a gift from my mother–"

"Don't play us for fools. The fine material of your cloak gives you away," Burnedface growled.

Markham chuckled. "Oh no, I'm not denying that I am scandalously rich. I just don't have any money on me at this moment. See, I spent it all on your mother earlier… Lovely woman, very experienced. And she has this beautiful, pink– "

Ginger lunged, his hunting knife out for blood.

With a roar, Markham dove into action and became the embodiment of every combat lesson he'd had. Duck. Slash. Block. Kick. Parry. Side-step.

Ginger pounced. Markham smirked. With an expert feign and a well-timed stab to the thigh, the Red Cloak crashed to the ground, letting out a satisfying grunt.

He didn't have time to retrieve his dagger from the Red Cloak's leg. A fist slammed into his chin, had his jaw go slack. *Burnedface.* Markham staggered. His skull met the wall and he gasped.

Not going down that easily, asshole.

Fighting a spell of dizziness, he surged forward. Knee to groin. Followed up with a boot to the gut. Fists met the enemy's jawline, one blow after another. Kick. Shove. Punch to the nose. Shoulder. Kneecap. He was winning. Winning. Forward. One more blow. Just one more.

Pain ripped through his side.

He roared and looked down to find his own dagger embedded in the flesh between his ribs. If his reflexes hadn't pulled him to the side the moment the blade had struck, it would've torn through more than muscle. Still, every breath spread an inferno through his chest, and he shuddered.

Shit.

Both thieves were on him in an instant. He clenched his teeth together, whimpered as he pulled the dagger out of his side, and held it in front of him with shaking hands. He faced them with a wounded growl. He would fight them. Goddess be damned, he would fight them, and he would win.

Ginger dove forward and Markham snarled. The dagger, still dripping with his own blood, found its mark. The Red Cloak yowled, gaped at the blade now impaling his palm.

Markham attacked, even though he wheezed with every movement. All he knew was survival—a frenzy that bubbled in his veins. Defend. Strike. Growl. He took hits without slowing. Pushed ahead against his own failing body.

This doesn't end here. I will not *end here.*

With speed he didn't know he possessed, he slid to the side, slammed an elbow into the enemy's throat, and gouged his fingers into eye sockets. Burnedface was down.

Markham turned, watched Ginger's eyes widen. The assailant's hand hung limply at his side. He had little chance when Markham struck, crashed his fists into the prick's face. Neck. Chest. Cheek. Again. Again. Again.

The Red Cloak collapsed into a bloodied pulp.

Markham snarled and pressed a hand to the wound at his side. He gulped air into his lungs, whimpering.

Come on.

He limped further down the alley. He was almost there. Would make it. He just needed to slip through those two shacks at the end and he would be free of the Rooks. He hobbled forward, clutched at his wound. He was almost there. Almost there. Right there.

Then, he heard boots on the gravel behind him. A third Red Cloak had swooped from a nearby roof. Markham spun, blinded by the glint of steel as a sword pommel slammed into his brow. He blinked and stumbled backward. The world went in and out of focus. Blurred. Turned black.

Markham's eyes flew open and he gasped. Pain crawled across his body. His cheek. His chin. His head. And Goddess, his chest was screaming.

He was alone in the alley, the shacks around him even more grotesque in the graying light. His attackers must have finally discerned that he was telling the truth and let him be. His purse was still missing though, and his hood had fallen from his face. Even bloodied and bruised as he was, he didn't doubt that they'd gotten a good look at him. Recognized him.

Damn it.

Hey, what's a good story without some hardship for the hero?

A sharp sting from the wound at his side reminded him that there were bigger things to worry about. He was bleeding out quickly and felt the light-headedness of it already. It was almost dawn and, come sunlight, his presence in the west of the capital would be difficult to explain. So, he took as deep of a breath as he could manage and pushed himself off the ground. He had to pause mid-way, but with a cry and a surge of willpower, he rose into a standing position. He swayed, let out a tortured roar. He didn't care who heard him. These people were too accustomed to life down here to leave their homes for the sounds of dying men.

You're not dying.

With a few shuffling steps, he was at the end of the alley. He slid in between the last two dwellings and squeezed through, followed the steep climb up to Coinsgain Plateau. It took ten minutes instead of the usual two.

Being found on the Plateau would be better, but not ideal. He needed to get to the hill that loomed over the city from the east.

His hands were stained and overflowing, couldn't contain the blood seeping from his wound. He gasped as he removed his shirt, then bunched up the fabric and pressed it into his side to prevent leaving a crimson trail. He silenced his moans as best he could, limping through Yaekós' middle-class neighborhood.

Golden streaks started to caress the sky and Markham cursed. Panic flooded through him, his breath shook and the blood spurted from his side. He started jogging. He had to go faster. Faster.

Just breathe. Almost there. Almost there. Almost—

A wave of nausea swept over him and he toppled forward, heaving slime and blood onto the paved road. His eyes shuttered, his abdominal muscles quaked. Every spasm sent a fresh wave of crystallized agony through him until all he wanted to do was lie down and give up.

When his body finally stilled, he rose slowly, swaying like a sailor on the docks. But he kept pushing forward. Looking up, he found the Temple of the Goddess rising over him, a white and green signal that he was nearly at the Crest, nearly home.

And so, struggling onward one step at a time, he made it to the base of the hill. Collapsed. Grass and rough patches of soil met his face and he surrendered, closing his eyes. Then, something touched his forehead so gently that the antithesis woke him up.

A young man was kneeling over him, his hair jutting out at various angles, as if he'd run his hands through it repeatedly. His golden eyes were wide, the skin underneath thin and veined with lack of sleep.

Markham smiled, feeling more exhausted than he'd ever imagined possible, and croaked, "Amile."

His friend helped him up with a level of strength disproportionate to his lean frame. "Shhh. It's okay. You made it."

When Markham was on his feet, they shuffled further up the hill, one man carrying the weight of two. Markham chuckled, coughed up blood. "I did it."

Amile nodded, his lips pursed. "Yes, Markham, you did."

†

The training dummy snapped back on its handmade stand as Staella sent blow after blow, kick after ferocious kick, its way. She sucked in a breath, leaped out of her crouch to vault her body off the ground. Rotating mid-air, she hit the dummy with a spinning kick that sent its hay stuffing flying through the air.

The sun was beating down on the open field she'd chosen as her training ground, her family's farm ever too big for the amount of cupa beans they had. She stepped away from her target, chest heaving with effort and skin slick with sweat.

"You can stop staring at me now. My performance has reached its climactic end for your purposes," she called to the young man she'd noticed sauntering onto the field a few seconds ago. She spun to grab her water bottle, cocked an eyebrow at him.

He leaned against the gate, arms crossed over his chest, and golden-brown eyes trained on her with eerie intensity. He had well-groomed hair, the same dark color as his heavy eyebrows, and sandy skin. His wide lips spread into a smile that didn't reach the corners of his eyes. She stepped up to him, realized that he was taller than she'd gauged.

"Amile Qarvette," she observed. "You are far from the capital."

He untangled his arms, opened the gate to come closer. "You know who I am."

She shrugged, unwinding the protective covers from her knuckles. "Your brother is the High Ruler. That puts you high on the list of recognizable people."

He shook his head. "I doubt many in Avetown would've identified me as easily."

Staella met his gaze, didn't wither under the subtle challenge she found there. "What are you doing here, Mister Qarvette?"

The corner of his mouth twitched upward. "If you know who I am, you must be familiar with the name Markham Aesher."

She scowled at him. "Lad Aesher. He's one of the Representatives in this year's Election… I'm still failing to see what this has to do with me."

"I'm here to offer you the esteemed position of being his protector," the young man announced.

"Why would Lad Aesher need a protector?"

"To protect him."

Staella rolled her eyes and turned away from him to pick up the bow and quiver of arrows waiting in the grass. She lined herself up two dozen feet from her hay target, nocked an arrow, and aimed, pulling the drawstring as far as it could go.

"I take it then that Lad Aesher's little riding accident wasn't horse-induced at all." She fired. The arrow zinged through the air, found its mark in the dummy's eye.

Amile, who now stood next to her, spoke again, "You're quite well informed, Miss Thenos. And you assume correctly. Markham was attacked in the Western Rooks."

She paused, eyebrows inching up her forehead. "The Western Rooks? What was Lad Aesher doing in the Rooks?" She loaded another arrow. This one landed barely a hair's breadth to its predecessor's right.

Qarvette cleared his throat. "I'm afraid I'm not at liberty to discuss that."

She turned to face him, planted a hand on her hip. "If I'm supposed to be Lad Aesher's protector I'd like to know exactly what I'll be protecting him from."

He sighed and glared at her in frustration. "He was…visiting a friend."

She retrieved her arrows and ambled back to his side. "Lad Aesher has many friends in the Rooks, does he?"

His jaw clenched. "It was a, uh, lady friend."

Staella snorted, flashing him a look of contempt. "Ah, so I'm to protect him against prostitutes then?"

He sighed. "Look, the attack in the Rooks was just a wake-up call. It's not of that much significance. Markham has various political threats. He is a favorite to win the Election, after all."

She narrowed her eyes at him. "It's interesting that you would put your faith in him and not your little sister. I wonder whether it's sexist or personal."

He seemed taken aback at that and blinked a few times. "What? No… Look, do you want the job or not?"

She crossed her arms in front of her. "Why me?"

He shrugged, his shoulders too broad for his lean frame. "You're the best fighter not currently in the employ of my brother."

"That's because your brother's Lorde of Security doesn't employ women."

"He doesn't employ criminals either," Qarvette retorted.

Staella froze, gulped. "What?"

His eyes seemed to come alive at that, the brown sparking golden. It was gone in an instant, though, behind the years of buried emotion clear in his every gaze. "Two years ago, a teenage girl won Yaekós' illegal cage fighting tournament. She called herself the Crimson Jackal and she was unstoppable. Too bad that when the city guards showed up after the finals, she was nowhere to be found."

She clenched her teeth together. "You're going to blackmail me."

He shook his head. "No, Miss Thenos. I'm going to offer you a job at good payment."

"What?"

"Yes. If you accept, you'll receive a monthly salary of fifty gold pieces."

Staella's eyes nearly popped out of her head. "*Fifty* gold… I could buy a house on the Plateau in three months with that."

He sighed dramatically. "I could make it less if that would suit you better." She glared at him, lodging her tongue against the inside of her cheek. He huffed. "Markham's safety is very important, and his father does own the gold mines."

Staella chewed at her bottom lip, shook her head. "I'm not for sale."

A muscle feathered in his jaw. "I can make your criminal record disappear…"

She froze. The two years after fleeing the capital had been soul-crushing. She was not made for being idle, for hiding away in a small town with nothing but straw dummies to fight.

She looked up at him, hesitated. Then, with a final shake of her head, she held out a hand. "Well, Mister Qarvette, it seems you have yourself a deal."

He shook her hand, offering the first semblance of a real smile.

CHAPTER TWO

A WEEK LATER, A GORGEOUS stallion-drawn coach carried Staella Thenos up the slope of Goldvinger Crest. She'd never been up the eastern hill before, had only been in Yaekós for a few months, and had stuck to the darker areas of the capital. Until now, the Crest had remained a jewel to admire from afar.

She peeled back the drapes at her side, staring in awe at the palaces that surrounded her, one after the other. Sure, the Thenos family did alright, but this place… These people were aristocrats cultivated in their social superiority since before the existence of the People's Monarchy. These were the homes of gods who deigned to engage in human politics.

Staella thought she'd never get used to it, to the absolute wonder yet striking insignificance she felt every time she saw it. The scalding sunlight reflected on the bronze streets, bathing the Crest in perpetual, brilliant light—a phenomenon which had led to the redubbing of the area from Hayvinger to Goldvinger.

The coach continued its ascent, past the Qarvette castle with its crown-patterned flags, past the Temple of the Goddess with its three triangular towers, and past the colossal estate at the peak of the rise that belonged to those legendary Hayvingers.

After a short decline to the east, the coach halted at a mammoth, gold-wrought gate. Staella's breath caught in her throat, and she stuck her head out of the window to marvel at the entryway as they started moving again. The ground was laid with pristine, white marble. The entire path was lined by scarlet-flowered haletayl trees in full bloom and the house was more marvelous still, its front porch the same polished marble, its walls so white they shone. A further two haletayls framed the entrance all the way up to the third story, matching the cherry-colored roof and shutters. The smell of those blossoms drifted towards her, the sweetness nearly eliciting a moan.

There were two men on the front steps. The first was Amile, looking polished in an ivory shirt that billowed at the sleeves. The other she knew only from his gold-clad image on Aldahad's coins. He was shorter than Qarvette, but still stood more than a foot taller than she, had shoulders that would be excellent for swimming. Sun-kissed skin highlighted a defined bone structure with a sharp nose and a chin that delved in ever so slightly at the center, forming an artwork completed by full lips and bright, pear-colored eyes. As he stepped down into the light, the rays of the afternoon caught the honey streaks in his tawny hair and Staella blinked. He was lazy, summer days come to life, and despite the bruise on his cheek and the cut on his jaw, he was stunning. Lad Markham Aesher.

The coins didn't do him justice…

Suddenly, her driver was there, pulling open the coach door to reveal her to the estate.

†

The girl was everything you'd expect a warrior maiden in an adventure tale to be. She had dark red hair pulled back tightly, wore close-fitting black pants that shamelessly failed to hide the power contained in her short frame, and her lips were set in a perpetual, sensual pout. Oh, he could see her on battlefields already.

Markham cocked an eyebrow and whispered to Amile, "Why didn't you tell me she's beautiful?"

Amile frowned at that. "She's not… It's not of significance."

"How long have we been friends?" he quipped. With that, he grinned and sauntered down the steps to her, hiding the wince of pain at every movement. The wound in his side was still an annoyance at best.

Upon reaching her, he took her fingertips in his and planted a kiss on the ivory knuckles. She didn't blush. "Staella Thenos, it is my sincerest pleasure to meet you."

She kept her hand in his and curtsied. "Lad Aesher. Thank you for welcoming me to your home."

When she straightened, their gazes met and Markham found himself looking into eyes nearly black in their darkness, alight with intelligence and defiance. Those eyes plucked at some string deep in his chest and it was only after a few seconds that he managed to turn away and clear his throat.

He faced the hoary driver. "Thank you, Felis. Please have Miss Thenos's things taken up to the northern suite on the second floor." He took the heavy pouch of coins from his pocket and dropped it in the man's hand. "For your boys. I know how Markis has been eyeing those bows. This should get him the best one on the market and some baking supplies for Parrick."

Felis grinned, bowed low. "You are too good to us, my lad."

Markham faced the girl again and motioned for her to enter. Once inside, he led her through the foyer to the lower living room, enjoyed the way her face lit up at the white lace curtains and glass furniture. Amile walked past her to take his usual seat in the corner chair. Staella took the pillowed couch and Markham opted for the loveseat opposite.

He smiled, holding the tray of finger snacks out to her. She took a tiny croissant and nodded in thanks. "First of all, Staella, I would like to thank you for uprooting your life to join us here in the capital to become my protector."

She grinned wryly. "Don't thank me too much. I'm mostly here for the fifty gold coins."

Markham scowled at Amile. "I thought we agreed on seventy."

The latter shrugged, poured himself a glass of apple cider. "I started low, expected her to bargain. She didn't."

Markham just raised his eyebrows. "Thank you for protecting my interests, Amile, but we really don't need to haggle." Turning back to Staella, he announced, "You'll be getting seventy."

Staella nearly choked on her food. "My lad, no. That's an outrageous amount. I couldn't—"

He chuckled. "You know, Staella Thenos, you're the first person I've ever met who would decline more money. If only you could run in the Election. But alas… Now, the more you protest, the more inclined I'll be to give you more."

She opened her mouth to retort, but then simply smiled and said, "Thank you, my lad." The challenge hadn't disappeared from her eyes. He had a feeling it never would. "So, I haven't really received much information about what my job entails…?"

Amile answered promptly. "You are to keep the estate safe from any and all threats, as well as accompany Markham any time he leaves the estate, in the most discreet manner possible."

"You see, having a bodyguard may raise unwanted questions. So, for now, you'll just be one of my old friends visiting."

"Yeah, okay, like you and I being childhood friends is a plausible story."

"Miss Thenos, you wound me."

Amile cleared his throat loudly. "Your background will be adjusted to fit the narrative. I have also spoken to the Lorde of Security. He has agreed that you train with his guards and perhaps even work for him when you are not required here."

Staella blinked at him. "What?"

Amile nodded. "It was the condition to having your name cleared of all charges. And you will be the first woman in the Lorde of Security's service… I thought you might appreciate that."

She beamed, nodding. "Yes. Yes, I do. Thank you very much."

"And, even though you will be one of the guards, I couldn't stand having my protector living in those filthy barracks, which is why I prepared one of the best suites in the house for you," Markham added.

She nodded at him, the corners of that pouting mouth lifting slightly. "So, I'm at the barracks during the day, keep an eye on you when you go out and come back at night. Sounds simple enough. I'll need to talk to the existing guards, to set up a perimeter check, and also your schedule at least three days in advance so as to plan my movements accordingly."

"Yes, ma'am. You'll have it in your room by tonight."

She looked around the open-plan area, scowled. "Where are all the other people?"

"Other people?"

She shrugged. "It would be absurd to have a mansion like this with only one person living in it."

He chuckled. "Staella, if you're calling out the absurdity of life on the Crest on your first day, we are going to get along very well. Sadly, you are very close to the truth. There are servants about, of course, but my mother has been with the Goddess for some years now and my father lives on the estate at the gold mines. It's only Amile and I here."

She cocked her head at Amile, a curious little fox. "You don't live in the palace?"

His gaze was as flat as his voice as he said 'No' and took a long gulp of his cider.

Staella pursed her lips and nodded. "Well, thank you for the hospitable welcome, Mister Qarvette, Lad Aesher. If there is no more business to discuss, I'd like to retire. I have a long journey to wash off."

Markham nodded. "Of course. Take the stairs to the second floor and turn left. It's the last door in the corridor. I hope it suits your taste."

She nodded, chuckling softly. "My lad, if it has a bed and hot water it'll do marvelously."

When she'd started towards the staircase, he added, "Staella…"

She spun to face him. "Yes?"

"It's just Markham."

She grinned crookedly and cooed, "Markham."

Once she'd disappeared upstairs, he threw Amile a pointed glare. "You were very forthcoming there."

His friend stared at him flatly. "Well, the role of the flirt was already taken. So, I figured I'd take nice-but-mysterious-guy-in-corner."

Markham threw his head back as he laughed, stood to look out the window. There was a moment of silence before he sighed and asked, "You took care of the other night?"

"Yes."

"You're sure?"

"Yes, Markham, I'm sure. Your endeavors will remain a secret."

"Good."

†

Leda swallowed down her meal with nearly half a decanter of water. Steamed vegetables and dry chicken. Again. She watched as her father took his last bite of glistening, beautiful pork neck, the juices dripping over his fingers and down his dark brown chin. Her brother was digging into a particularly crispy piece. She felt the drool gather in her mouth and gulped it down.

"You know," she sighed. "…if I have to suffer through bland chicken and *broccoli*, the least you can do is suffer with me. Is all of this really necessary? I mean, one, little piece of meat wouldn't be a crime, would it?"

He stared her down, dark eyes unflinching. "The Election starts tomorrow. You need to be strong, healthy…"

"Pretty," she finished.

He clenched his jaw, the subtle movement making her wince in anticipation. "Who am I?"

Leda suppressed the urge to roll her eyes. Goddess, they'd had this conversation so many times. "Honiel Hayvinger," she replied flatly.

He smiled at that, an arrogant grimace that stretched his skin tight, made it look like leather. "And who are you?"

Once again checking her irritation, she said, "Leda Hayvinger."

He rose from his seat, hands planted firmly on the mahogany table. "Exactly. What does that name mean, Leda?" He turned, pacing around the back of her chair. In the instant he looked away, she eyed the final piece of pork neck longingly. It was so close she could smell it… But before she could act, his face popped up next to her, growling, "What does that mean?"

She met his eyes, kept that hard gaze. "It means that my family created the People's Monarchy of Aldahad."

"Yes." He rose, gesturing passionately. "Your ancestor wiped out the Salingzer line, freed us from tyranny, and created the very system we have today. Lowena Hayvinger wrote the Core. Our family made the Election possible." His chest was heaving, his voice now only a whisper. "The next few months are very important."

She could smell the barbeque marinade on his breath.

Mighiel, who had finally finished stuffing himself, looked up with that sharp glare of his and announced, "Our line created this world, but three terms have passed without a Hayvinger ruling over it. That number cannot become four. It would be unacceptable."

Honiel nodded, eyes glinting. "See, your brother understands the direness of the situation."

"Maybe all the meat is making him smart." She reached over to that center plate, that wondrous piece of pork neck just sitting there…

Her father's hands slammed down on the table. "*Leda!*" She yanked her hand back, her face paling. He pulled her wrist from her lap, squeezed it—hard. "Do. Not. Disappoint. Me. Tomorrow." He threw her hand down and marched out of the dining hall, shutting the door with a *bang!*

Leda exhaled shakily. Her older brother looked at her with a smirk on his tan face, his caramel hair falling over one cheek. "The Goddess is cruel to have made the incompetent sibling Representative." With that, he left as well.

Leda curled back her upper lip, made an obscene gesture at the door, grabbed the piece of pork neck, and promptly stuffed it into her mouth.

†

Staella couldn't sleep. It was past midnight and she'd been rolling around. It would take some time to get used to the new bed. Yes, the room was stunning, with blackwood furniture and silk linens, but it wasn't home.

She missed the flower-patterned quilt she'd shared with her sister, the creaky floors. Here, everything was quiet. There were no paternal snores or performing crickets to be heard and the night was black as pitch, a new moon invisible in the sky.

She rolled over, sighed, and lit the candle on her nightstand. The light cast the room into a warm glow, elongated shadows flickering across the walls and warping into childhood monsters. Staella suppressed a shiver, padded to the cupa table in the suite's living area to pour herself a glass of water. She brought the drink to her mouth—

A shriek tore through the world, a piercing, tortured scream. The glass fell to the floor, shattered into hundreds of pieces. Her feet were bleeding, her hands too. She stood frozen, eyes wide and breath gasping.

Silence…

Then another roar, a cry that echoed through the house, penetrated her bones, and made her shake.

That sound.

Her heart was beating a furious rhythm against her ribcage.

Markham…

Perhaps her skills as protector would be put to the test earlier than anticipated. Another scream. It was crazed, bloodthirsty, and it came from above. She dashed to the end table, grabbed the candlestick and the knife she kept under the pillow. Leaping over the shards of glass, she flew out the bedroom door and into the corridor.

The cry sounded again. She followed it.

The candlelight cast those monsters on the walls as she sprinted, raising the hair on the back of her neck. She found the staircase and took the steps two at a time. Once on the third floor, she turned the light in every direction, finding nothing but wooden floors, furniture, and shadows. She closed her eyes, tried to calm her breathing in order to listen. The pounding in her ears was the only sound…

You're not in a horror novel, Staella. You're not–

The next scream was twisted. It gurgled and turned into a series of growls. She jumped, heading in the direction of those inhuman sounds. Her hand was aching from its tight grip on the knife hilt and she was lightheaded.

For Goddess' sake, calm yourself.

She continued slowly. Something rattled next to her. She gasped. Spun to find a door. It was like all the others in the house, perhaps a little sturdier, except for the iron bolt and heavy lock on the outside.

On the *outside.*

That chilling shriek sounded again. It came from behind the door.

Staella yelped, found her limbs quaking. She took deep breaths, tried to slow down her raging heart. Every nerve in her body told her to run, but she didn't because her brain so desperately wanted to know what was yelling—growling—behind that door. She could probably pick the lock.

That lock was put there by someone. They know…

Taking a step closer, she called, "Who's in there?" The rattling stopped. Utter silence consumed the hallway.

Bam! Something heavy slammed into the door from the other side. Again. Snarled. Scratched. Screamed. *Bam!*

And then nothing.

Just like that, the onslaught stopped.

Staella shook her head and bolted back down the stairs. At the landing to the second floor, she dashed right, away from her room to the one farthest down the hallway. She stopped at the door, panting. Her candle's flame sputtered in the looming dark.

She slammed her fist into the wood, hammered at it and yelled, "Markham. Are you okay?" She heard shuffling inside, but couldn't wait any longer, so she grabbed the handle. Locked. She banged on the door again. "*Markham?*"

Someone mumbled on the other side, a key turned, and the door swung open. He was safe.

Lad Aesher's hair looked like a bird's nest, his face puffy with sleep. He frowned down at her. "Staella, what's going on?"

Her chest was still heaving as she pointed upward. "Screaming. Someone—some*thing*—is screaming."

He seemed to wake up at that, eyes widening. "Uh, yes, we—" Another howl tore through the manor.

Staella's knuckles whitened around the candlestick. "Now that I know you're safe, I should open the door." She turned away, starting for the staircase. "I should…"

A hand caught her wrist. She stopped and twisted to find Markham with her in the corridor. "No."

She scowled at him. "No?"

He let her go, rubbed a hand over the back of his neck. "Staella… This house is old. It has many secrets. Secrets I cannot share at this time." The breath left her lungs in one *swoosh*, leaving her covered in ice. She just stared at him. He attempted a small smile. "Know that we are all safe. You're safe."

"I've never been a protector before, but I'm pretty sure I'm supposed to be doing something," she squeaked.

He moved closer and took her free hand with gentle movements. His eyes were pleading, soft. "I know you have no reason to, but please trust me."

She really wanted to, felt everything in her tug to acquiesce. "Tell me you're not evil. That you're not keeping someone in that room against their will. That nothing sinister is going on."

He shook his head, squeezed her hand. "No. No. I promise, Staella."

She gulped, looking down at their intertwined fingers. "Then, as your protector, I will respect your secrets."

He sighed with relief, shoulders slumping. "You are Goddess-sent… You're shaking. I'm sorry. Hearing the screams must have been horrifying. I should've warned you. Can I have some tea brought up?"

She huffed a laugh at the absurdity of it all. "I think you overestimate the power of tea."

He chuckled as well, the tension of the moment broken. "I think you underestimate it."

She shook her head, realized she was still holding his hand. She pulled back her arm and cleared her throat. "I'm alright. I'll just head back to bed."

"I can walk you to your room."

"I'm supposed to be the bodyguard here, remember?"

The corner of his lips tugged upward. "Of course… I hope you can sleep well." She nodded, turned to head to her own room. "Staella." She looked around, found him in his doorway. The expression on his face somehow settled her nerves. "Thank you."

The screams had not ended until dawn and had started up again the next night just after midnight and the night after that, haunting the dark hours without end. A part of Staella demanded that she open that door, that she discover what the Aesher manor was hiding. But there were other parts that kept her in bed with closed eyes, desperately hoping for sleep. She was afraid. Staella could face men without flinching, could fight without hesitation. But this… This was something else. And she was a protector now. She worked for Markham. He was a Lad, and he was allowed to have his secrets, and it was only professional of her to keep them. *Just ignore it. Just breathe.*

So, Staella stayed away from that door

CHAPTER THREE

CITY SQUARE, STRETCHING OUT from the foot of the Crest into the Plateau, was packed with people, the air abuzz with conversation. At the back, those from the Rooks were crowded together in the noon sun, squinting to see. The Plateau residents were gathered in the shade cast by Signal Tower, the nobles seated at the front. The inhabitants of the Crest wore the peculiar, darkened spectacles of which Staella had also received a pair.

"It protects your eyes from the glare of the sun," Markham had explained. "It really does help when you live on bronze streets."

She was inside the enormous tower that overlooked that mass of people, in a side room Amile had arranged for them to keep an eye on Markham. Qarvette was next to her now, awaiting the proceedings with a strained expression she'd given up on interpreting.

Staella sighed, crossed her arms, and leaned against the window out of which they were looking. "Why is this taking so long to start?"

Amile gave her a sideways glance. "Because everything here is a ceremony and ceremonies start fashionably late; it's a rule."

She huffed at that and had to resist the urge to punch him playfully. Finally, there was movement.

A man in his late twenties stepped out onto the balcony that jutted out over the square, his suit immaculate and his raven hair slicked back. The family resemblance to the man next to her was undeniable. He had with him his two children, a stoic boy of seven who looked like a miniature version of his father and a younger girl with black curls and her mother's bronze skin. The latter was beaming, her dimples and bright eyes promising later beauty.

They reached the end of the balcony and Staella noticed the cheers that greeted them mainly came from the front half of the crowd. He lifted his hand in a wave, smiled dashingly. "Good afternoon," his voice boomed out over the square and Yaekós quieted. "Good afternoon, my fellow Aldahadi. In case anyone was wondering, I am Yathan Qarvette." This elicited a few chuckles from those on the ground. "As your High Ruler, it is my privilege to welcome you on this blessed day. Thank you for taking the time to be here despite the scalding heat. My father always used to say that the only thing separating Yaekós and the fires of the Realm Beneath is a strip of netting."

Staella chuckled, whispering to Amile, "He seems nice."

He clenched his jaw. "He's charming. He's not nice."

"We are here today to celebrate the history of our People's Monarchy, but also to herald in a new future," Yathan continued, placing a hand on each child's shoulder. "It is, therefore, my honor to read you the laws set forth in our Core…"

A servant scuttled forward to hand his master a scroll, disappearing again instantly. Unrolling that legendary document, Yathan cleared his throat and began. "This Core, written by High Ruler Lowena Hayvinger and her advising council in the Sixth Year of the Panther, henceforth known as the year One After Hayvinger, sets out the manner in which the People's Monarchy of Aldahad will henceforth be ruled. The People's Monarchy of Aldahad will be under the sole leadership, management and control of the High Ruler, who has the power to pass, adapt or abolish any laws or regulatory measures, except those set forth in this Core. The High Ruler will be elected in an open and democratic Election every ten years, this period constituting a ruling term. The candidates in such Election, henceforth known as Representatives, will be the youngest members of those families that can trace their noble lineage back at least seventeen generations and are between the ages of nineteen and thirty years. Each High Ruler will have…"

Staella hid her yawn behind a hand, her thoughts starting to drift. She'd heard the Core read aloud enough times in her life. Her parents had brought them to the city during the previous Election. Even as a little girl, she hadn't found it very interesting. Her elder sister, however, had been mesmerized by the lives of these glamorous aristocrats, the way they spoke and dressed and moved.

An elbow jabbed into her side and she scowled at Amile, who said, "We're not paying you to daydream."

She rolled her eyes. "I don't see how watching your brother talk is protecting Markham."

"It won't kill you to know what's going on in the politics that govern his everyday life," he retorted, and she refocused her attention on the balcony.

Yathan handed the Core back to Scurrying Servant, held out his arms, and announced, "In this, our One Hundred and Sixty First Year After Hayvinger, I welcome you to the start of the sixteenth

Election of the People's Monarchy of Aldahad. Please allow your Representatives to introduce themselves."

Once again cheers erupted from the gathered crowd and Yathan bowed slightly, taking his children's hands and heading back inside. The first Representative to take his place was tall and lean, her skin paler than her brothers', her eyes blue and eerily alert to her surroundings.

"I am Zandi, Representative of the line Qarvette and I am honored to run in the Election."

Next was a man with sand-colored skin, narrow eyes, and arrogant cheekbones. Amile leaned into her. "That's Aedon Blomehill, he's—"

"I know the Representatives, Mister Qarvette."

"You know *of* them. There's a difference."

She smiled slightly, looked up at him from the corner of her eye. "Alright, enlighten me."

His lips twitched upward. "Aedon is Markham's cousin on his father's side and he is the biggest asshole I have ever met." She giggled, shaking her head at him. "Honestly, I've never heard anything from his mouth that hasn't offended someone."

A few Representatives later came the dark-skinned and beautiful Neke Vardan. "He has a horrible drinking problem, much to his elder sister's dismay. She's Cala, the High Companion."

"Your sister-in-law, then."

"In theory… That's Rayn Valanisk." He pointed at the woman now on the balcony. She was statuesque and powerful, with a waterfall of black hair cascading down her back and charcoal skin that glowed in the sun. When she spoke, even her voice dripped with majestic poise.

Amile had a wry smile on his face. "Rayn is quite extraordinary. She looks like a goddess, has the strength of one too. She's very sophisticated whilst simultaneously having quite a reputation as a serial lover."

Staella cocked an eyebrow. "You sound like you have personal experience of this reputation of hers."

He snorted and shook his head. "She prefers women… Ah, this is Chrisjon Damhere."

"I don't remember that name."

"That's because this is the first time the Damhere family is eligible for an Election. At twenty-six, he's also the oldest Representative, and it's blindingly obvious to everyone that he's the only one who doesn't know his way around politics."

"Isn't the Vaekish line also new?" Staella asked.

He nodded. "Yes, but the Vaekishes have been mingling with royalty for generations. The Damheres, on the other hand, have most certainly not."

Chrisjon was built like many of the fighters she'd faced in the cage: hulking shoulders and arms like tree trunks, but his face was certainly much more attractive than those she'd bloodied years ago. A high-set brow sat above warm, almond-shaped eyes that complemented his russet skin and long, black hair. He stepped up to the edge of the balcony, waving somewhat over-enthusiastically at the crowd. "Hello, everyone. I'm Chrisjon from the line Damhere and I'm honored to, uh, be a Representative in this year's Election. Thank you."

A few more Representatives stepped forward before it was Markham's turn. When he grinned and winked at the people, Staella noticed that the cheers he received were mostly female.

Can't really blame them…

After him was another young woman and Staella had to blink. Once. Twice.

How are all these people so damn hot?

The woman was tall and lean but had enough curves to fill out her white chiffon dress, which seemed to dance around her defined legs as she moved. She had skin that glowed as bronze as the streets of the Crest and golden-brown waves of hair that seemed tousled and perfect at the same time, and her bone structure was extraordinarily feline.

Staella said the name before Amile could. "Leda Hayvinger."

He nodded, looking at the Representative with fondness. "Yes. A good friend and an amazing person. She bears a striking resemblance to her ancestor Lowena. Her father is a horse breeder, treats her like one of his animals."

The reaction she received trumped even Markham's, but she seemed wholly unaffected, merely stepping forward to produce the generic introduction before retreating inside.

Eleven Representatives had appeared before the people of Aldahad and it was finally time for the last candidate to introduce herself. She addressed the crowd with a warm smile, her molten-lava eyes inviting. "You know who I am, because I know many of you by name. Today, I want to urge you to support the Representative who knows you, who actually does something for you. This is the *People's* Monarchy. This is your country, and you deserve to be served by those you put in power."

The tower vibrated with the cheers and stomping that came from the masses in City Square. She stayed on the edge of the balcony, soaking up the applause. It only quieted when she returned into Signal Tower.

Staella turned to Amile with wide eyes, and he nodded. "The one and only Delilah Haltstone. The Election is nothing more than a pageant. Whoever becomes a silver idol for the people to worship wins. Delilah has a less subtle approach. She works amongst the people and does a lot of charity."

When Yathan returned, the crowd was completely silent. "People of Aldahad, these are your Representatives. The sixteenth Election of the People's Monarchy of Aldahad is now officially underway."

The cheers were few. And then, at the back of the square, fists were raised in silence, one by one, until nearly all those in the Rooks bore the sign of defiance. Almost in slow motion, a single arrow born of that crowd flew forward, zinged just pass the High Ruler's head. It found its mark in the tower's wall. Attached to the shaft was a flag. A black background delved through by a white lightning bolt.

The symbol of the Rebellion.

CHAPTER FOUR

"HALT."

The two guards at the front gate of the barracks barred Staella's entrance the next morning, their hands on their weapons and their faces young under the brown caps they wore. The one who had stepped forward, said, "State your identity and your purpose here."

She sighed. "Staella Thenos reporting to Lorde Knoxin on the orders of Amile Qarvette."

The guard cocked an eyebrow, but nodded at his companion, who scurried inside and returned moments later with another guard. This one didn't wear the customary cap, had two red and two green stripes on his breast pocket. He was the second-in-command. His beige face was set in an annoyed grimace, and he ran a hand through his short blond hair before bearing down on her with the force of a tornado.

She opened her mouth to introduce herself, but he didn't give her the chance. "Stella, is it?"

She blinked and straightened. "Actually, it's Staella, but Miss Thenos will suffice, sir."

His glare was less than impressed. "Why are you here, Stella? Are you mad or are you just looking for attention?"

Her eyes widened at that. "Excuse me?"

"You heard what I said. You're distracting my men and you claim that you are reporting to Lorde Knoxin. I am his deputy and I have no knowledge of your business here. Please go back to where you came from. I don't have time for delusional little girls."

Staella lodged her tongue against the inside of her cheek and crossed her arms. "Firstly, if your guards get distracted by one girl coming up to the barracks, I can't imagine that they'd be very effective in battle. Secondly, you must have a flawed perception of the effectiveness with which your organization communicates. I…"

"I must admit that I am at fault, Miss Thenos," another, raspier voice said from behind her.

She spun to find a cluster of guards standing at attention, their leader inches from her. She could smell him: steel and sweat that mingled to become a surprisingly pleasant scent. His uniform bore one white stripe more than the conceited pig's at her back. His skin would have been pale had it not been sun-kissed and his eyes were a fascinating kaleidoscope of blues. His dark hair curled into the curve of his neck as it spilled out from under his cap.

Staella gulped. "Lorde Knoxin…"

He grinned. "It's a pleasure, Miss Thenos. Deputy Caven, Thenos is here to train with us and will be a valuable part-time asset to us. I trust that you will respect that."

Caven nodded with a tense jaw. "Yes, my lorde."

Saul Knoxin turned to his men then. "At ease. Take the afternoon's in-camp leave." The guards dispersed immediately, and he faced Staella again "Please follow me."

She nodded and they entered the barracks together. It was nothing more than a square clay building hollowed out to make room for a grassy quad. The place was bustling with activity, guards doing everything from washing windows, to jogging, to sparring, to taking off shirts to fight the heat.

Staella found herself jumpy watching them and had to convince herself that she didn't need to run anymore. A few years ago, the sight of one of these men would have sent her dashing to find a hiding place. Now, she was following their leader deeper into their home.

They eventually ended up in a spacious office with a desk, an armored mannequin, and a colossal table with a map of Aldahad engraved in it.

He unstrapped his weapon belt, threw his sword down on his desk, and sighed. "I apologize for not being here when you arrived, but I was in the Rooks, hunting rebels. Yesterday's fiasco has turned me into quite a busy man, but I'm happy to do it. Such an outright display of insolence is unacceptable, and the culprits must be rooted out."

She pursed her lips. "I hadn't realized that the Rebellion was quite as mature already."

Saul removed his cap, shaking out that mane of raven hair. He looked up at her with eyes that could pierce your ribcage and stab at your heart. "We didn't realize it either. That arrow was quite the wake-up call. These insurgents are rejecting everything Aldahad is built on. If we allowed every baker and shoemaker to stand for High Ruler, the Monarchy would descend into chaos." She offered him no reply. He huffed, shook his head. "Sorry, here I am rambling on about matters that don't concern you… I must say, Thenos, I'm quite pleased to have you in my office. I've been searching for you for a long time—the Crimson Jackal… Ironic that when I finally find you it's to grant you amnesty. But if you won that horrible cage fighting competition, you can't be bad, and we are in desperate need of more manpower. I have a report to write before lunch, but why don't we go out back and you can test those skills of yours against a professional soldier?"

She smirked at him. "It would be my absolute pleasure to educate you on the skill level of an illegal fighter, my lorde."

He chuckled. "Oh, I bet it would."

After he grabbed his blade, they headed to a private training ground behind the office. Staella, who had strapped her blade to her hip that morning, unsheathed the weapon and took up her stance.

Saul did the same. "Good form. Tell me, did you use weapons in the cage?"

She shook her head. "No. The real thrill lies in disabling your opponent with nothing but your body. But don't worry, I've had extensive training."

"I won't go easy on you, then."

"I would be offended if you did."

He lunged forward and their dance began, a complicated series of parries and blows and expert maneuvers. Staella found herself having to duck and dash out of the way as he anticipated even her best tricks. But he never caught her, never landed a blow. They wove their bodies and their swords around each other in an intricate choreography that became less about winning and more about the exhilaration of discovering a partner that could match every movement. She found her heart beating wildly, her breathing shallow, and her cheeks flushed. He was grinning at her, and she beamed right back, sidestepping the arc of his sword.

Finally, she glimpsed her chance. She ducked into the space between his arm and chest to pull herself up against his side, weapon pointed right at his heart. She cocked an eyebrow at him, feeling his chest heave against her body. His heart-shaped lips really did complement his wide-tipped nose.

Staella waited for him to acknowledge her victory, but he just winked, eyes trailing down. She followed his gaze to find his own blade angled over her abdomen. Double checkmate.

She chuckled, stepping away to sheath her sword at her side. Saul mimicked her movements, his expression equally as amused. "Well, Thenos, there are few who can match my swordsmanship. I'm interested to see what you can do with just your hands…"

Her eyes met his and she leered. "Well, thank you, my lorde. Your opinion is, of course, of the utmost importance to me."

He just rolled his eyes, which made her laugh.

†

Leda made her way down the quiet corridor, strides slow. She came here often, but the heaviness in her heart hadn't lessened. Reaching the farthest door in the hallway, she took a final steadying breath before knocking. Voices sounded from inside and soft footsteps approached. The door opened and Veress was there, her black hair pinned back tightly, and her face worn out despite her youth.

She smiled. "Leda, it's good to see you," she said, as if it hadn't been only a week since the last time.

Still too long, though.

Leda nodded. "Yes, you as well… How is she?"

"She's quite pleasant this morning," the olive-skinned nurse replied. "She's telling me about a field of flowers."

The corner of Leda's mouth twitched sadly at that, and she stepped into the room, hearing the *click* as Veress shut the door to leave her alone with the grand bedroom's occupant. The woman she'd come to visit sat on the bed, her body turned as she stared out the giant window, topaz eyes unblinking. The sunlight cast her tanned skin bronze and made the blonde strands of her hair strings of gold.

Leda sat down next to her and whispered, "Mom?"

Audrey Hayvinger faced her daughter with a docile smile, taking her hands. "Leda."

That single word was filled with so much joy Leda nearly sobbed. "Yes, Mom, it's me."

She beamed wider, then looked back at the window. "Oh, Leda, isn't it beautiful? The world is so beautiful. Look at all the flowers. The violets and those little blue flowers whose name I keep forgetting."

Leda glanced at the window, at the flowerless view, and nodded with a tear slipping down her cheek. "Yes, Mom, it's lovely."

Audrey turned to her once more, taking her daughter's face in her hands. "And you, my dear, are the most radiant of all. I am so glad that you've come to visit, that you can share this glorious morning with me."

She leaned into her mother's touch and placed a kiss against Audrey's palm. "Of course."

"You look troubled, darling. What is bothering my sweet girl?"

Leda shrugged, pulling away from the woman's hand. "I think it's probably this whole Election." Audrey froze, her entire body going still as the dead. Her eyes rolled to the side slowly, boring into Leda's own. The latter gulped. "Mom?"

A moment of absolute silence. Then, Audrey leapt forward, snarling, hands clamping around Leda's throat. "Leda, no, you can't."

The grip around her neck tightened and Leda gurgled, "Mom. Mom, please." She tried to pull free, but her mother's grip was like a vice. "Mom, *ah*, you're hurting me. Mom!"

"You can't—They'll—They—" Leda was left heaving, desperately gasping for air. "The—Election—You—No—"

Veress was suddenly in the room, slamming her elbows down on Audrey's arms. Leda broke free with a gasp. "Go. Now," the nurse screamed.

Audrey was growling like an animal, thrashing in Veress' arms. "No, you don't understand. She's in danger. Leda, you can't—"

But Leda was already running out of the chamber, clutching at her throat. Tears rolled down her face, staining the front of her dress. When she finally reached her own bedroom, she slammed the door shut and sank down against it, sobbing once again for the heartbreak that had been with her for nine long years.

†

Markham grinned at the confused expression on Staella's face, the way her eyebrows arched. "We're in the stables," she said.

He nodded, leaning over the lower half of a door to run his fingers through a chestnut mare's mane. "Keen observation. See, stables are where horses are kept…"

She flashed him an unamused glare and he chuckled, putting up his hands in surrender. "Alright. We're here because I would like to go for a ride with you."

She shook her head. "Oh no, I don't know how to ride."

His eyes widened in disbelief. "You don't know how to ride a horse?"

"No."

He huffed, shook his head. "Sorry, I just need some time to process the fact that the great warrior Staella Thenos is incompetent at something."

She crossed her arms over her chest, rolling her eyes at him. "Well, it's not like I have an extra arm growing out of my ass. I just never had the need to ride."

He threw his head back in laughter. "An extra arm growing out of your ass… I must admit that that would be quite exciting." She let out a soft giggle at that and he found himself enjoying the sound quite a bit. "Well, since your defect is quite fixable, it's not a problem. I'll just teach you how to ride."

Her black eyes flicked from horse to horse nervously and she pursed her lips. "You know, I'd rather not."

"Oh, come on. If a miner's son can do it, so can you." He winked at her, and her lips formed a grin against her will.

She sighed. "Fine."

He rubbed his palms together mischievously. "Excellent. So, I thought you'd be more compatible with a stallion and Agung here is our most gentle-mannered."

She took in the black beauty with apprehension. Markham shook his head at her, placing a hand on the animal's forehead, cherishing the way it leaned into his touch. Smiling gently, he took Staella by the wrist and rested her hand against Agung's cheek. She tensed but calmed after a few seconds as wonder took over her features.

"See, he's not that bad, right?"

She shook her head, but said. "I'm not sitting on him, though."

He found himself leaning just a little closer. "Oh, I can't imagine why he'd object to that."

She stepped back as he opened the stall to lead Agung into the aisle and reached for the bridle hanging from a nearby hook. He placed the bit in the stallion's mouth and tied the horse to a wooden post before strapping on the saddle.

"Alright, now you get on. You get up from the left side, this foot in this spur. Yes. Now, lift yourself up. Swing over the other leg. There we go…" Her entire body was strung tight. "Staella."

"Yes?"

"Don't look now, but you're on a horse."

Her eyes opened and a magnificent, child-like grin lit up her face. "Oh Goddess, I'm on a horse."

He hopped on a tan mare, a young thing called Bínal, and brought his animal up next to hers. "Okay so, a few basics…"

He carefully demonstrated how to use the reins for various actions, how to kick in your heels to go faster. Soon, they were out on the lawns behind the house, slowly trotting around the estate. He nodded at her. "See, you're doing well."

She beamed at him. "Yeah, I am feeling a little less terrified."

"Now, if you really want to get it right," he added, "you need to move with the horse, up and down with it. Otherwise, your ass is going to feel it tomorrow, extra arm or none."

She adjusted to the stallion's rhythm quickly, the visible muscles of her upper legs guiding her movements. Then, in a sudden flurry, she dug her heels into Agung's sides and flew forward. She raised herself up from the horse's back and leaned her face down close to its neck. Staella dashed around the estate's perimeter at a pace Markham had rarely tried himself and he reined in Bínal just to watch.

The green of the lawn formed a stunning contrast with the clear, cerulean sky, and right there on that line between the two was a galloping stallion, the afternoon sun transforming the beast's coat into velvet stretched tight over unleashed power. Then, there was Staella, clothed in all black. Her body was a tightened bow as she streamlined herself into the animal's back, her fair skin a spot of light against the horse's darkness, her hair a red flag that billowed out behind her.

She raced towards the trees at the southern end of the estate, and when Markham broke from his trance, he rushed his mare to meet her there. She'd come to a halt where the line of shade began, chest heaving with exhilaration and eyes bright.

She laughed and threw her arms out behind her and he couldn't help but shake his head. "You know how to ride, don't you?"

She glanced at him over her shoulder. "Of course, I do."

He simply huffed and led her deeper into the haletayl forest to a small stream. Here, they dismounted, tying the horses to a tree near the water. Markham sat down on a white boulder, motioned for

Staella to join him. He inhaled deeply, enjoying the sweetness of the blossoms that surrounded them.

Staella pulled her knees to her chest and rested her arms on them. "So, why did you bring me here?"

He frowned. "Am I not allowed to take my protector out for a ride simply for the pleasure of it?"

She raised an eyebrow at him. "You are, but you didn't."

He looked at her for a moment, at the slight curl of her lips. "I haven't known you for a very long time, Staella, but I've learned that you might be too smart for your own good."

The corner of her mouth crooked upward. "For my good or for *yours*?"

Markham lied down, crossing his ankles over each other and propping himself up on his elbows. "To most of the people outside these walls, you won't be my protector. You'll be a friend I've known since childhood. I suppose that if you're such an old companion of mine, you should know some things about me. So, here I am, at your disposal. Ask me anything about myself and I'll give as honest an answer as I can."

She sat back. "So, can I ask you anything?"

"Anything about me."

"Why are screams coming from the third floor of your house at night?"

He huffed. "Nice try."

"Fine. What's your favorite color?"

He chuckled, dipping his head back. "Come on, Staella. You can do better than that."

She feigned offense, shrugged. "Alright. I know that it's green anyway… If you want me to ask something more significant, here goes: what's your biggest fear?"

"You must be an excellent friend of mine to know that."

"I'm offended, my lad. When we were children, you used to call me your best mate…"

This girl… Goddess, this girl.

He took a deep breath and slowly released it. "Alright, Staella, my biggest fear is that my outlook on life, my beliefs and opinions, will be assumed based on the privileged nature of my childhood."

She was silent for a few long seconds before she said, "I suppose the fact that I didn't expect that answer only validates the legitimacy of your fear."

He looked up at her, at the understanding in her eyes, and it nearly took the breath out of him. He finally managed to clear his throat, to regain the capacity to speak. "Next question."

"What happened to your mother?"

The question hit him like a blow, and he felt that all-too-familiar dark hand closing around his heart. Breathing felt more difficult, but he answered her. "Uh–Well, when I was fourteen, the Silver Guild, the Red Cloaks' predecessors, targeted my father's business. They stole large amounts of gold from the mine, sabotaged his transportation wagons, and caused a lot of damage. My father, never one to back off easily, continued to mine and set traps for the thieves. He drove the Silver Guild to near extinction, which is when their actions became driven by revenge. They butchered our horses, our dogs… And then my mother."

He had to stop for a moment, had to try to breathe around that heavy hand. Images flashed through his mind… His father's horrified eyes. The mahogany bedroom door.

"My father found her. He wouldn't let me see the body, but I honestly think my imagination has conjured up something much worse than reality." He cleared his throat. "Needless to say, the Silver Guild was completely eradicated a fortnight later and it took two years before the Red Cloaks thought it safe to emerge."

His gaze was fixed forward, on nothing in particular, and the natural scene before him blurred with the memories of that day and the days after. He hadn't realized he was crying until Staella's hand touched his cheek to wipe away the tears.

"I'm so sorry," she whispered. He sniffed, sat up straight and pulled away from her touch. She drew back her hand, as if shocked by her own actions, and cleared her throat. "I'm sorry. I shouldn't have—"

"Next question."

"Markham…"

"Next question."

He met her gaze again, eyes pleading as he nodded. She tugged at her bottom lip with her teeth, asked, "Why does Amile live with you?"

Shit.

"Because he's my best friend."

"Yes, but why doesn't he live with his family?"

Markham did a striking impersonation of a dying fish for a few seconds, thoughts racing to find some truth he could divulge. In the end, he merely said, "Because he doesn't want to." She opened her mouth to retort, but he cut her off. "Alright, I think that's enough difficult questions for one day. We should get back."

They rode back to the stables in silence. All the while, Markham was trying and failing miserably to erase the ghost of a touch on his cheek.

CHAPTER FIVE

STAELLA SPENT THE NEXT FEW weeks mainly at the barracks, since life at the Aesher estate was fairly routine. Markham fought boredom by playing polo with the servants or chess with Amile, the latter always more prone to seclusion than conversation.

So, she'd head out on the morning run with the troops under the scrutiny of Deputy Maron Caven, who'd proven himself to be as big of an oaf as she'd predicted. Then, she would head out to sparring practice with her training partner, Graegg, a man not much older than she who had an easy disposition and a remarkably kind manner. Sparring was followed by lunch with the men, who had finally stopped treating her like an alien and could tell jokes that made her roar with laughter even as she blushed bright red. And finally, for her favorite part of the day, she would accompany Saul to his private training ground to practice any and every skill she'd need to keep Markham safe. Today, however, Saul did not take her to that little training area. He summoned her directly to his office.

Entering, she found him bent over the table with its giant map and it was only when she cleared her throat that he looked up. "Thenos. Welcome."

She smiled, stepped further into the room. "Saul."

He straightened and drew a hand through his dark hair. "You're probably wondering why we're here today."

"No, my lorde, I have unquestioning trust in you," she crooned.

"You're toeing a dangerous line, Thenos." His expression hardened, but his gaze flashed an invitation.

Her mouth crooked into half a grin. "It's only dangerous because it's so alluring."

He kept his eyes on hers for a moment, long enough for her to make out the midnight tendrils in the cobalt, before he asked, "How much does Lad Aesher value you?"

Staella blinked, frowned. "I suppose he values my skills. Otherwise, he wouldn't have hired me as his protector. Why?"

"If Lad Aesher should win this Election or the next, there's a strong probability that he'll appoint you as his Lorde of Security. You could very well be my replacement."

The idea hit her like a blow, and she stood gaping for a few seconds. *I could be doing this for over a decade.* She shook her head, but said, "I guess so, yes."

He smiled at her, motioned to the table. "Then I had better show you the ropes. When I was appointed, there was chaos. I had to figure out everything on my own, since my predecessor was an absolute—"

"Grant Vikan," she interrupted. "Didn't he have a heart attack six years into his term?"

"Yes. Anyway, when I was appointed by Yathan, the systems in place were nowhere near efficient. Probably because Vikan's favorite advisor was a mute girl who thought herself a spy," he scoffed. "I had to figure out everything on my own and I refuse to leave my successor to the same fate… Here, come closer."

She stepped up next to him and watched his thickly-veined hands move over the map. "There are a hundred thousand men under my command. Two thousand are guards here in the city, ninety-five clusters and a hundred and seven officers. Then, there are ten thousand guards dispersed across the Monarchy who answer to one of my secondaries, Chief Harsan. They have headquarters here." He pointed at a spot a few leagues north of Yaekós, between the city of Kahlan and the Loridian mountains. "Five thousand patrol the borders under Captain Calrandin. There are twenty-five outposts on our boundaries. Vateya, here on the east, is the most well-manned and Vista on the southern edge is smallest. The remaining eighty-three thousand men are military, all under General Vaekish."

His jaw clenched at the name. Before he could continue, Staella cocked an eyebrow. "You're not particularly fond of the General?"

"He's the most difficult of the secondaries. Hardly even acknowledges my authority. But don't worry, I manage him well nonetheless."

"Of course."

"The base is to the west near the desert."

Staella let him continue his explanation, her thoughts far from the organization of Aldahad's security forces. She knew most of the facts already, anyway. When running from the authorities, one tends to educate oneself on their manner of working. So, she didn't feel bad at all for making herself notice the way his hair curled into the nape of his neck or how his lean fingers glided over the table or the way his jawline moved…

She'd always had a weakness for attractive men.

He looked up and rested his hands on his hips in anticipation of her response. She blinked, meeting his gaze with a smile. "If you're looking for flattery, you've come to the wrong place."

He nearly growled at that. "Just an opinion then, Thenos."

Oh, I'm pushing all his buttons…

She surrendered with a playful sigh. "Alright, I must admit that it is quite impressive what you've built in four years, especially considering that you had to figure it all out at twenty-one."

"I figured that if Yathan could run a country at nineteen, I could protect it. Besides, it's not that much more impressive than being a Representative's protector at twenty." She curtsied dramatically and he chuckled. "See, Thenos, when you're nice to me, I'm nice to you."

She dared to take a step closer to him, to smell that steal and sweat as she kept eye contact. "Oh, I can be *very* nice…"

His lips parted slightly as he too took a step forward. The corner of his mouth twitched upward, and he reached out a hand to cup her cheek. She bit her lip, closed her eyes as he leaned closer.

Bang!

The knock on his office door echoed through the room, through Staella's bones. Her eyes flashed open, and a wave of annoyance swept through her. He merely stepped back and ordered, "Enter."

A guard rushed inside, saluting with a flushed face. "My lorde, Deputy Caven discovered a rebel hideout on the corner of Baker and Malley. He and his men were met with resistance. They're under attack, my lorde."

Saul sprang into action like an arrow fired, strapping pieces of armor to himself as he talked. "Ready all the men. Have Barton's two clusters stay to protect the barracks. The rest are with me. Meet in the quad in three minutes." The guard nodded and dashed out the door.

Lorde Knoxin turned to Staella when he was done suiting up. "Do you have some sort of protective gear?"

Eyes wide, she shook her head. "No."

"Do you need it?"

"No."

He nodded, squeezed her shoulder. "Welcome to His Highness' City Guard, Thenos. Don't die."

She put on a grin, saluted. "Yes, my lorde."

Staella, sprinting after Saul and with the larger part of the city guard behind her, reached the scene of the fray moments later. She hadn't been to the Rooks in years and wasn't this quite a way to return: an army at her back and a sword clutched in her hand.

The hideout in question was no longer a driftwood shack near the edge of the city but a raging inferno, a beast that breathed smoke in loud gusts and devoured the house with its tongues. Soot-stained women and children fled with leaking eyes and sleeves pulled over their faces. Staella saw a young girl dash out through a crumbling side door. She was clutching a baby to her chest as she dived down an alley. She wailed, coughed, and sank down against a wall.

Staella looked away.

Not far from the entrance, the rebels who were able to fight did so unyieldingly. There were so many of them, a horde to double Caven's guards, who were desperately defending themselves on three sides.

Noticing the arrival of reinforcements, Maron knocked down the teenage boy in front of him with a blow to the jaw and ran to meet his commander. The next few moments Staella experienced almost in slow motion. She saw the rebel at the deputy's back leap forward, hatchet raised as he closed in. The man's face was weathered by suffering and sun, his snarl missing more teeth than it had. He was angry. He was miserable. Catching up to his target, he bore his weapon down. She wondered what sound the blade would make as it lodged into Caven's skull.

Will it be a crunch, a crack? Or perhaps something wetter, stickier…

The rebel froze, let the hatchet tumble to the ground. He looked down, gaping at the javelin that had skewered him from behind. Blood gurgled from his mouth. He coughed and sank to his knees. Died.

Time sped up again and Staella had to force breath into her lungs, had to swallow down the bile that rose in her throat while blinking away tears.

Death-spared Caven was in front of them, a gash across his left eyebrow leaking crimson drops into his eye. Saul grasped his arm, seemed much too calm for the situation. "Caven. Are you alright?"

Maron nodded and grinned. "Yes, my lorde. Just a nasty hag with a cleaver." He motioned to what was left of the building. "It was one of the headquarters. It had inventories, letters, everything we needed. But the bastards burned it down before we could get in. Attacked us like a legion of under-creatures. We've lost two men. Four were injured badly. But we got them out with O' Brigan."

Saul nodded. "You did well." He turned to the men behind him, transformed from friend to commander in a heartbeat. "Cage formations. Cage formations."

Staella's training with the guards kicked in and she moved with them, finding herself in the second row of a block of offense that was five men wide and twenty men deep. Graegg was next to her, gave her a reassuring nod.

"Shields," Saul ordered from her left.

On the outside of the block, shields the size of carriage wheels were raised, the third row on every side lifting theirs to the sky. The shell was complete. They were a single, impenetrable monster. She knew this maneuver, knew how this clash would end. Caven's men scattered at the sight of the formation, because they knew too.

The monster marched into the plebeian group without making a single move to attack. Thumping, hacking sounds struck at the shields around Staella, but the shell was impenetrable. They continued forward, then stopped.

It was dark within the monster, the sounds of rebels screaming, growling, clawing coming from all around it. Suddenly, there was a slip of light as the shield above her shifted. A girl's face appeared there, beaten purple. She tried to tear into the block of guards, a crying snarl ripping from her throat. Her blue eyes met Staella's, wide and wild and pleading. Staella opened her mouth, found no words, no help within herself. The shield jutted into place, hitting the girl against the forehead. It was dark again. A lump settled in Staella's throat, a deadness in her limbs. But she had no time to think about her actions, as Saul shouted, "Now." She moved with the monster.

The block came loose into a single-file circle within seconds as the guards moved with practiced precision. As planned, the ring was opened at four points and, fueled by rage, the rebels poured inside. Screaming victory.

Staella…

I can't.

"Close and turn," came the dooming command.

The circle closed. The guards turned inward. And there was the enemy, ringed in by armed fighters with no way to escape.

It was like being in the cage, only a thousand times worse.

A final order: "Attack."

Her first opponent was on her, a colossal man with a black beard who'd clearly pegged her as an easy target. He wielded an ax, a big beauty with a polished, haletayl shaft. He swung his weapon forward in a powerful arc and Staella ducked. The tightness in her stomach eased. Her heart pumped pure adrenaline and the instincts of battle took over.

With a familiar exhilaration, she slashed out. Blocked, side-stepped, stabbed. The next adversary had impressive hunting knives dripping with blood. Her lips curled into a snarl. Blades met sword. Somewhere, her body screamed with pain. She leapt forward, slipped underneath, and struck. Next challenger. She lashed out with her fist.

Parry. Block. Strike. Another enemy. Next. Duck. Kick. Hit the ground. Roll over. Up. Slice. Next.

She was a weapon come to life, a mindless force of destruction. The world rippled with energy, the sounds of dying men a distant roar in her ears. She was good at this. She could do this.

A glint in the corner of her gaze caught her attention. A woman bellowing, her sword aimed at her eye, inches away and coming closer. Staella's body froze. There was no time to dodge, no time to out-maneuver. All she could do was watch as that sword neared. Everything but that imminent death was a blur. She noticed how the light flickered on the blade, the spots of scarlet that littered it. The golden pommel.

A *golden* pommel…?

A cry ripped her from her trance. She didn't have time to scream as a body was thrown between her and the fatal blow. The man landed at her feet, that beautiful sword buried in his chest.

Graegg.

Graegg.

His hazel eyes stared up at her—lifeless.

The man she'd trained with every day. The friend who'd never done anything but praise and accept her. And now he'd died for her.

An inhuman growl tore from her and she was a jackal again. The fear in the woman's eyes was nothing to her as she broke her neck in one swift twist. Next enemy. Next. Next.

Until she found herself faced with an old man whose ornamental staff had been shattered by the battle. He was bent and shaking, but he stood his ground, stared down the girl who'd so brutally killed his companions. She met his eyes, golden and wise and brimming with a calm sort of panic.

Staella stopped. She lowered her weapon, felt the air *whoosh* out of her. She shook her head. "Stop," she heard herself scream. "*Stop!*" No one listened.

She spotted Saul to her right and dashed to tug at his arm. He spun to face her, eyes murderous. Recognizing her, his gaze softened. "Thenos, what is it? Are you okay?"

"We have to stop. We have to…We've won. We don't need to keep killing them." His brows knotted into a scowl.

You have to speak his language, Staella.

She took a deep breath and straightened. "If you kill them, you lose all the information they have as well."

He hesitated, but nodded eventually. The order was bellowed, and the killing stopped.

Rounding up the remaining rebels didn't take long. They were tired, wounded, and diminished in size. Staella started towards where her cluster was getting into formation when someone pulled at her sleeve. She turned, found the old man. He didn't say anything. He just looked at her with those golden eyes and she nodded.

The Aesher estate suddenly seemed very far from the barracks as Staella made her way back home later that day. She was exhausted and filthy, crusted with dirt and blood. There was a nasty cut across her collarbone, a bruise on her hip. But it was her mind that bothered her, that kept bringing to the surface the details she'd overlooked in her killing stupor, that kept making her insides twist with emotions she didn't dare try to name. Every step she took became emphasized by a vivid memory:

The golden eyes of a rebel. The strangely ornate sword of a woman. Graegg's lifeless body.

Golden eyes. Gleaming sword. Unmoving Graegg.

Gold. Sword. Graegg. Gold. Sword. Graegg. Gold. Sword Graegg.

Goddess, please stop.

When she entered the mansion's living room, Markham and Amile were with a guest, lounging and chatting. The woman was tiny, probably in her late twenties, and had a mane of spice brown hair. Her sandstone skin was flawless, her cheekbones slanted sharply, and her eyes distinctly angular.

She was in the process of stealing a sweet from the bowl in Amile's lap when she froze, gaping at Staella. "Good Goddess."

I suppose I don't exactly look ready for tea.

Markham leapt up from the couch and approached her. "Staella, what happened?"

She'd managed to keep her emotions inside, but now she felt tears stinging her eyes. She looked away, clenched her jaw. "Rebels happened."

Markham froze, face paling. "Rebels?"

The other two were still silent, the woman staring at Staella, whilst Amile's eyes remained trained on Markham.

"Yes."

There was a strained, pregnant silence before he snapped. "Well, are you going to elaborate on that?" She flashed him a glare that made him lift his palms in surrender. "I'm sorry. It's just… You come in here looking like war and I'd like to know the circumstances surrounding my protector's weathered state."

Her eyes flicked to the girl, who had proceeded to pop the stolen sweet into her mouth. "I'm afraid that's confidential information, my lad."

The tense expression on his face disappeared too quickly, replaced by one of his charming smiles. "Of course… Forgive my rudeness. Staella Thenos, this is my cousin, Maci Blomehill."

"Aedon's sister?"

She shot up from her seat and swayed over to the grime-covered protector. "The one and only." She shook Staella's hand eagerly despite the blood. "And you are my cousin's new protector. I must say, you're prettier than I imagined a bodyguard would be. In fact, I dare say you'd be striking when cleaned up." She padded back to her seat, right next to Amile's corner chair. Her legs, which were clad in black tights, were pulled up against her chest and she sank back down. "But then again, Markham has never been known to spend time with unattractive women."

Markham didn't bite. He just nodded and said, "You can talk. She's trustworthy."

"Except when it comes to other people's food," Amile muttered, his voice light as he reached for the piece of candy now in Maci's hand. Giggling, she threw it into her mouth and stuck her tongue out at him. She wiggled her eyebrows and he laughed.

Staella felt like throwing up. She turned to Markham. "The guards found one of the rebel hideouts in the Rooks and were attacked upon trying to enter. Violence ensued. Lives were lost. The remaining rebels were taken for questioning."

There was an emotion in his eyes that she couldn't quite place. "How many casualties?" Markham asked.

She suppressed the image of Graegg's lifeless body being hauled back to the barracks. They were to wrap him in a sheet, send him to his family. She cleared her throat. "Three of ours. Just under two dozen of theirs."

His throat bobbed and it took a few deep breaths before he could ask, "Are you alright?"

She shrugged. "It's just a scratch. I've had much worse."

He shook his head, gaze softening so compassionately she felt it in her chest. "That's not what I meant."

Something in her begged to give. How easy it would be to be the damsel, to let her tears flow and throw herself into his arms, to have him comfort her with that warm voice.

"Yes. I'm fine."

He sighed with relief, shoulders relaxing less than they should have. "Good."

She did not smile at him. She couldn't even think about trying, though a part of her wanted to. "Is it okay if I retire to my room? I'll come down for my patrol tonight."

He nodded and replied softly. "Of course." But before she could reach the staircase, he called, "Staella, wait."

She headed back. "Yes?"

"There's a ball tomorrow night."

Maci beamed. "Ah, yes. The Representatives' Ball. The social event of the decade," she exclaimed dramatically. "Literally."

Amile turned to her. "Are you going?"

"I suppose that if someone asked me to go with him, I would."

Markham nodded at Staella. "The Representatives' Ball gives the nobles the chance to decide which candidate will receive their vote, and having the support of an aristocrat always helps with the lower classes."

"I take it I am to go to this ball to keep you safe."

"Yes. You'll be accompanying Amile, if that's alright with him." Amile looked up with his lips parted in surprise. He recovered quickly though and nodded.

"Who will you go with?" she asked Markham.

It was Maci who answered. "Oh, he'll take Leda like he always does."

Staella froze at that. "Leda Hayvinger? Are you…?"

"Goddess, no," Markham replied quickly. "Leda would probably punch me in the face if I tried to touch her… But we are engaged, an arrangement we made as children. So, we go to public events together, solidify the image that we'd be an excellent High Ruler and High Companion. See, Leda's family—"

"Markham, she's exhausted," Amile intervened.

Markham blinked and nodded. "Of course. Yes. Thank you, Staella. You may retire for the day. I'll let one of the guards do the patrol and have dinner sent up to your room."

She managed a half-smile. "Thank you."

She was tired, yes, and she probably needed rest, but she needed answers more. She needed to wrap her head around what this city had become in her two-year absence. Had to get away from life on the Crest and being a guard in order to understand her own thoughts.

So, that evening when everyone had gone to sleep, she used a rope she'd made from her bedding and clothes to sneak out of her bedroom window. Knowing the guards' patrol route by heart, she managed to dart out of the estate without being seen, ignoring the dull ache in her hip. They didn't need to know what she was doing. It wasn't about them.

The Rooks at night were so familiar that her feet found the way to the Burly Bear without much help from her mind. This was good, since the latter found itself preoccupied with things she hadn't seemed to notice as starkly on her last visit.

The gravel streets ran with waste, the smell of urine standing out above all. The shacks were smaller than she recalled, built nearly on top of each other and wholly insufficient to hold the elements at bay. She remembered how hot it could get in those hovels, how Yaekós' suffocating heat drove everyone outside during the day. There were huddling figures at nearly every door, their bony bodies wrapped in on themselves in a desperate attempt at safety. No one chased them away, because here everyone had experienced at least one homeless night—one night of trying to sleep on dirt and praying that you'd be left unscathed until morning. There was a dog dying in one of the alleys she passed, its body nothing but skin over a skeleton, its mouth foaming with whatever poison it had tried to consume to ease the churning hunger.

As she neared the old tavern, she spotted a group of men loitering outside, yellow tayl smoke rolling up into the air around them. There were more of them now, more youths who had resorted to the escape of intoxication, who had chosen a life of meaninglessness because the alternatives weren't much better.

Staella hurried past them, into the Burly Bear. The place was dimly lit as always, the tables glistening with spilled alcohol. In the corner, a couple was sucking at each other's tonsils. A man was throwing up into a bucket. The big table hosted a bunch of rowdy men singing a vulgar rhyme. Three women sat nearby, playing cards and getting drunker by the second.

Staella pushed her way through until she reached the bar, took a seat on one of the high stools. The barmaid turned to face her and went completely still. "Staella…" She looked exactly the same, her graying hair pinned up messily and her breasts barely contained in her dress.

Staella smiled, sighed. "Hello, Jacline."

The woman's pale eyes lit up and she reached over the counter to envelop Staella in a hug. "Goddess, girl. I haven't seen you since you disappeared that night of the final match. They could've gotten you and I wouldn't have known."

She nodded. "I'm sorry I never contacted you again, but I went home. I had to put those few months behind me."

Jacline snorted. "Yeah, but now you're back, though. And in what a way…"

"What?"

"News spreads fast in the Rooks. I heard there was a red-haired girl in the city guard. Heard she sliced through rebels like something from the Realm Beneath. Should have known it was you. Only, I never imagined that Staella Thenos, the infamous Crimson Jackal, would be working for Lorde Knoxin."

Staella couldn't ignore the contempt in her old friend's voice, felt it like a blow to her stomach. "Jacline, I… I'm not supposed to tell you this, but I guess you'll find out anyway. I'm in the city on business for Lad Aesher and the only way my name could be cleared was to join the guard. I—"

"I knew some of the rebels you killed."

Staella looked down at the counter, lips trembling. "I know."

"Why are you here?"

"Because today caught me off guard. The last time I was here, the Rebellion was a minor movement that I barely knew of and now they're firing arrows at the High Ruler and fighting the city guard. I don't want to be unprepared again. I want you to tell me what you know… I knew you'd know."

Jacline sucked at her front teeth, her lips curling. "You think I'm going to tell you anything? I'd be informing the enemy."

Staella's jaw clenched. "Come on, Jac, it's me. I don't want any inside information. I just want to know what it's about."

The barmaid sighed, poured Staella a shot of whisky, and leaned forward on the counter. "Look around you, girl. The people 'round here are barely surviving and no one up there gives a damn. You think someone who grew up on a hill with bronze streets knows anything about the struggles of the majority of the folks in this city, in this country? They've never even been here. They call it the People's Monarchy, Staella, and tell us we're lucky to have a vote. But what's the point of a vote when they get to choose all the options? It's a bunch of rich kids having a beauty contest. If this is really the country of the people, we should be able to vote for one of *our* people. The Rebellion has been going on for a long time, but they've started gaining momentum these past few years, even when you were here, but I reckon you were a little busy playing hide-and-seek with the guards. They've gotten benefactors, better weapons, more guts. A storm is coming for Yaekós and you'd better decide on which side of it you're going to be standing."

Staella shook her head and downed her drink. "I should have stayed on the farm."

Jacline chortled. "You? Please… The Jackal never cowered from danger before."

She pursed her lips, pressed her tongue against the roof of her mouth. "I'm not the Jackal anymore. I'm sorry that you were expecting her and found me… It was good to see you again, but I should get back to—"

"—the Crest."

Staella gulped, turned away, and started for the door.

You have to do something. Who are you?

She froze, spun, and marched back to the bar. She gripped her old friend by the front of her dress, pulled her closer to whisper, "I'm not getting involved, but… The supply wagons come into the city from the south tomorrow night, guarded by five rookies. Just tell the rebels not to kill them. Please."

The woman's eyes were wide as she stepped away, but she soon grinned. "You know, it would really help to get information from the very top…"

"I'm not informing on Markham. Never him."

Staella left the tavern with quick strides, perhaps more confused than before she'd come.

CHAPTER SIX

STAELLA WAS TIRED AND SORE, staring with contempt at the ball gown that had been hung up against her closet door sometime before dawn. There was a note attached, a rose-scented piece of paper that she ripped from the hanger.

Staella,

The bodice functions as armor, but the dress will ensure that you fit in with the guests. Be ready tonight at six.

Amile.

"Well, isn't that romantic?"

She yelped at the voice that came from behind her, turned to find Maci there, leaning against a bedpost. Staella shook her head, scrunched her eyes shut for a moment, and sighed. She had to still the tumult in her mind. She was getting sloppy, hadn't even noticed an untrained noblewoman coming into her room.

Staella clenched her jaw. "Does everyone in Yaekós have the key to my room?"

Maci shrugged and plopped down on the unmade bed. "No, but Markham does, and he sent me."

"Sent you to do what?"

"I thought that might be obvious." She motioned at the awaiting gown. "To help you get ready for the ball. Not that getting dressed is such a challenging activity to do on one's own, but he insisted and I didn't object. Now, we should—"

"Okay, I understand that, but why are you here?"

The girl cocked an eyebrow. "Markham said that you're smart, but I guess he's somewhat prejudiced. Like I just said, my dear cousin sent me to—"

Staella lodged her tongue against the inside of her cheek, clenched her fists to keep them at her sides. "I meant why are you here *now*? It's six in the morning."

Maci paused, as if she expected more of an explanation. When it didn't come, she scowled. "And your point is…?"

She let out an exasperated sigh. "My point is that I have twelve hours to be ready."

The brunette's cheekbones became even sharper when she laughed, a low, genuine chuckle that made her all the more captivating. "You've clearly never prepared for an event on the Crest before… Perhaps Markham wasn't as idiotic to send me as I thought. Besides, the pampering beforehand is half the fun. Why would you want to rush that? So, we'll start with a nice, hot bath.

I'll call the handmaiden and—" She was up from the bed in an instant, her see-through sweater billowing around her as she headed for the door.

Staella's mouth was still slightly agape, but she managed to call out, "Wait. Wait." The girl paused, facing her with a questioning expression. "I can't take a bath now. I have to be at the barracks in fifteen minutes for the morning run."

Maci waved a hand matter-of-factly. "Amile took care of it. Trust me, there isn't a thing in this world that Amile hasn't taken care of." Staella opened her mouth to protest but was cut off. "Lorde Knoxin knows that your duties at the Aesher estate take preference. Fortunately, getting dolled up is one of those duties."

Staella snorted. "Fortunately? First you force me into an entire day of mollycoddling and then you take away my training. Forgive me for failing to see the good fortune in that."

Maci rolled her eyes, crossed her arms over her chest. "Please don't do that."

"Do what?"

"That whole I'm-a-badass-fighter-chick-so-I-don't-like-being-pampered-and-looking-pretty thing. It's annoying. And the two aren't mutually exclusive. Just admit that a part of you is excited."

Staella stepped forward, ready to retort, but she stopped at the girl's cocked eyebrow. She sighed. "Fine. Maybe I'm not entirely opposed." She offered Markham's cousin a tentative smile and received a beam in response.

"Well, now that we have all of that hostility out of the way, I'll get us started on that bath." With that, she floated out of the room.

Nearly an hour later, Staella was reclined in the tub with lavender-perfumed water and mountains of bubble bath surrounding her. Her legs were thrown over the sides and Maci sat on a wooden stool to paint the protector's toenails a deep blue. Staella studied her face, the polished lines and easy beauty. She didn't look anything like Markham, but they shared that warm allure that drew one in almost involuntarily.

"I still can't believe that you're doing this yourself," Staella commented.

Maci's lips tugged upward. "Why? Because you assume that I have everything done for me?"

She shrugged. "Yes. Your brother's a Representative. Your father used to be High Ruler. And here you are, working on the feet of a farmer's daughter from an obscure little town."

"Avetown, yes? It's a nice place to grow up. Plenty of open spaces, but plenty of close-minded people."

Staella gawked at her. "You've been there?"

Maci nodded, shifting her stool to get closer to the other foot. "I've been to most places in Aldahad and a few beyond."

"You've been outside Aldahad?" Staella had heard of some of the countries and kingdoms outside the borders of the People's Monarchy, had heard stories of the strange terrain and the outlandish customs, but she'd never dreamed of traveling there.

Maci smiled down at her. "I have. Since my father's term as High Ruler came to an end, my parents go from one exotic destination to the next. They've been on one of the Vallanah islands for their eighteenth honeymoon for three months now and they always leave ample resources for our own travels."

Staella huffed incredulously. "I take it you've been on quite a few adventures with your brother, then."

Maci paused her work, throwing her head back in laughter. "Aedon and I? Goddess, no. I travel to get away from him. The servants are excellent company; they've become more like friends over the years. Besides, once you're at your destination it never takes long to meet new people."

"Tell me about the places you've been to," Staella blurted. "Please."

She could almost see the memories flicker behind the girl's brown eyes. "To the west of Aldahad are the islands. Vallanah's cluster is in the south and Bringham in the north…"

Staella closed her eyes and leaned her head back against the lip of the tub, allowing Maci's soothing voice and stunning tales to lull her into brief relaxation. The woman had been on adventure after adventure. She had danced with the Ketannan tribes, dined with the Havinaki royals, weathered the Bringham ice storms, kissed Vallanahn barmaids… She'd lived things Staella had barely read of.

When she finished, Staella opened her eyes and smiled. "The more time I spend on the Crest, the more the life of its people amazes me. It's so..."

Maci stood up, stretched out her back. "I know. But tonight, you take a big step into becoming part of that life." Staella only gulped at that.

After the bath, manicure, and pedicure, Staella was subjected to the uncomfortable experience of having servants rub fragrant lotions into every inch of her skin. Then, Maci started on her hair, pulling combs and clips from a drawer Staella hadn't even known existed. After hours of having her auburn mane pulled this way and that, about five layers of cosmetics were plastered over her wounded collar and face, causing her to sneeze and then grunt as her eye was nearly poked out by a stick of kohl.

"Goddess, Maci, do you want me to be blind?"

"Oh, shush. I'm not even close to your eye."

When Staella was finally deemed presentable, Maci helped her into the dress from Amile, pinned jewelry on her and led her to the suite's full-length mirror. "This is why we needed almost twelve hours."

The dress was more impressive than she'd judged it this morning, boasting a tight-fitting bodice that was a latticework of dark metal and beads. The skirt was midnight blue and hugged her hips before flaring out delicately. It was everything Amile had promised.

What caught Staella's eye, however, was the girl staring back at her. Her hair looked more vibrant, like she carried flames around her shoulders. Her eyes seemed bigger, darker, and her lips more sensual than she knew they could be. She still looked like herself, but a version who'd grown up next to these people, who'd been attended to by servants her whole life. Who'd traveled to other countries and went to balls and played polo every day on manicured lawns. She looked like *them.*

"A storm is coming for Yaekós and you'd better decide on which side of it you're gonna be standing."

Staella managed to make herself smile at Maci Blomehill.

†

Markham checked his hair one last time in the mirror at the bottom of the staircase, pulling at his scarlet petticoat. He turned to Amile with a sigh. "Did they have to choose red this year? It's probably the worst color for my complexion."

Amile shrugged, disinterested. "It must be so hard to be a Representative."

His friend was dressed in dark blue, a white-and-gold medal pinned to the chest of his blazer, marking him as a member of the ruling family. Markham knew he hated it.

Heels clicked above them, and Markham looked up to find Staella at the top of the stairs. She was stunning in her ballgown. How many times he had read a scene like this: a beautiful girl in formal attire floating down a staircase to leave those waiting for her breathless. Yet the cliché of it didn't take away from the experience. The dress suited her, striking yet practical, and he found that his feet moved toward her of their own accord. That heartstring she'd pulled on that first day was being tugged and all he could do was follow.

He met her on the third step, taking her hand to help her down. The corner of her mouth twitched upward and he responded with a full-blown beam. "I must admit that those black leggings of yours remain my favorite, but you… You look like you just slew the monsters in my nightmares and waltzed straight into my dreams."

She cocked an eyebrow at him, snorted. "Would you like some bread with that cheese, Markham?"

Amusement sparkled in those dark eyes, and he chuckled, running a hand through the hair he'd just spent an hour perfecting. "You are something else. But seriously, I predict that you'll break many hearts tonight."

Her hand slipped from his as she stepped to the floor and she half-curtsied. "Thank you. You also look quite regal in the red."

He grimaced at her. "Now I know you're just trying to be nice. I don't pay extra for flattery, Staella."

She sighed dramatically. "Well, I suppose I'll have to retract every nice thing I've ever said to you, then." She maintained eye contact with him, and they just stood there smiling at each other.

Amile cleared his throat loudly and they snapped out of the moment. Staella straightened, lifted her chin. "Leda is a very lucky girl."

Markham opened his mouth, closed it, and nodded. "Yes. Of course. And Amile will be the envy of every man there."

Staella stepped forward, bowed to Amile. He nodded politely, reaching forward to brush a kiss over the knuckles of her left hand. "Staella."

"Thank you for the dress."

Amile's eyes lifted to the stairs, and he frowned. "Where's Maci?"

"Oh, her brother sent for her a while ago. She mentioned something about an emergency, but she didn't seem very concerned."

There was a quick knock at the front door and a guard stepped inside, bowing. "My lad, Lady Hayvinger's coach is here."

Following the two men outside, Staella asked, "Where is the ball, by the way?"

She should probably have asked earlier. *Not very good at this whole protector thing, am I?*

Amile's voice was tight when he answered. "The Representatives' Ball is always hosted by the High Ruler."

She cocked an eyebrow at him. "We're going to your house, then?"

She noticed the wary glance Markham threw in his best friend's direction before the latter muttered, "To my brother's house, yes."

†

The full moon was already starting to appear, but nighttime offered only a slight reprieve from Yaekós' scalding heat, a breeze caressing the haletayls that guarded the mansion. The waiting coach was at the bottom of the front steps, its sides scarlet velvet embroidered with swooping silver patterns. Staella sighed as she curtsied to the driver who opened the door for her.

My legs are going to be sore tomorrow just from greeting people.

She stepped up, nearly hitting her head on the edge of the doorway, and ended up half-tumbling onto the seat next to Leda Hayvinger. The Representative was smiling, eyebrows arched in amusement. Staella gaped slightly at the face in front of her, failing to understand how this woman could be even more striking up close. Her skin glowed as if the bronze of the streets on the Crest also ran through her veins. The lines of her cheekbones were so flawless, the cupid's bow of her bee-stung lips pronounced. And Staella had never known that brown eyes could host so many different hues.

By the time she spoke, Amile and Markham were already seated, and the coach had taken off. "It's, uh, an honor to meet you, my lady."

Leda grinned, shook her hand. "Trust me, I have never done anything to earn that title. Please, call me Leda… So, Staella Thenos, you are Mar's new protector."

Staella's eyes widened, and she turned to face Markham. "She knows? Maci, Saul, Leda… I thought the idea was to tell people I'm an old friend."

"Are you implying that I cannot be trusted?"

Shit.

She hadn't been on the Crest for one month and she'd already managed to offend a Hayvinger. The place was named after them, for Goddess' sake.

Staella gulped and looked around to find Leda cocking an eyebrow. Her mouth was set in a grimace. "I—uh— I—"

Then, as if a floodgate had been opened, Leda and Markham erupted into a fit of laughter, the former even letting out a snort in the process. Amile's lips quirked upward and he flashed Staella an apologetic look.

Leda placed a hand on Staella's arm. "It's alright; I'm just pulling your leg. Shame, Mar, what have you been doing to her? She's as jumpy as a cat taking a bath."

Relief cascaded over Staella's shoulders, and she smiled sheepishly. "Sorry, I'm not very good at politics and these things."

The brunette waved a hand nonchalantly. "Oh, no one really is. The secret is to pretend that you know something no one else does. Makes you look very in control even when you're bored out of your mind."

Markham winked at her. "Wonderful advice, Leda. You should consider running for High Ruler."

She rolled her eyes at him and continued her conversation with Staella. "Anyway, yes, I do know that you are his protector and that you used to be quite formidable in the cage fighting community. There is very little Mar doesn't tell me."

He nodded. "Which means that you might be able to help Staella tonight. She's supposed to be my childhood partner-in-crime. So, tell her something she should know."

A devilish leer took over the girl's face. "Well, if you've been friends since childhood then you're bound to know that Mar still sleeps with his special, fuzzy blanket every night. Can't fall asleep without cuddling Lankie."

Staella's face split into a grin as she turned to see the blush on Markham's cheeks. "What?"

He shot a venomous glare in Leda's direction, but she only shrugged. "Hey, your words were my mandate."

"That blanket still smells like my mother," he confessed, eyes darting to the floor.

Staella's heart stopped and nearly broke. She started to reach out to take his hand, but Leda snorted. "Really? Using your tragic backstory to avoid embarrassment? Why don't you just ask the people for a pity vote?"

Staella gasped, ready to grab the Representative by the throat, but Markham chuckled and shook his head. "Touché… Staella, it's alright. Leda and I are quite used to making fun of the other's crap, since both of us have our fair share."

Leda nodded. "Yeah. Mar's mom is dead; mine's insane. His dad is never home; I wish mine weren't." She pointed an accusatory finger at Markham. "You just don't have an obnoxious older brother to deal with."

"Well, I do live with Amile."

Leda offered him a deadpan glare. "Please, we all know who got the butt end of that deal." She turned to Amile. "He forced you to come tonight, didn't he?"

He sighed dramatically. "He and the ever-present rules of society."

She giggled. "Ah yes, wouldn't we all love to shove those where the sun doesn't shine."

"Staella, you're awfully quiet…" This came from Markham.

She realized that she'd been smiling, basking in the conversation. She shook her head. "Sorry, I—This just isn't what I was expecting. It's… It's nice to see you happy." Markham's lips parted at that, and his gaze locked on hers, sending a wave of warmth through her chest. She blushed despite herself.

Leda lightly cleared her throat, said, "Well, you should see him when the dancing starts."

The coach halted a few moments later, signaling their arrival. Staella had to admit that her chest felt tight with an odd mix of nerves and excitement. She could hear the buzz of a crowd outside, the elated conversations and bursts of laughter that wove around merry music. When the coach door opened, her breath caught in her throat.

The Qarvette palace was formidable, easily doubling the size of the Aesher mansion, but lacking any of the latter's elegance. The fortress was built from gray stone stacked six stories high, its dark roof adorned with emerald banners bearing the crown. There were sharp, menacing towers at each corner of the building, statues of Qarvette ancestors guarding the spires and glaring down at those gathered below.

Staella gulped and leaned into Amile, who had helped her out of the coach and linked their arms together. His expression was even more indiscernible than usual. "No offense, but this place gives me the creeps."

He nodded, teeth worrying at the inside of his cheek. "It does tend to have that effect."

There were two rows of tuxedoed guards lining the deep red carpet that led up to the entrance. The men were familiar to her, which eased the tightness in her gut somewhat.

Since when does the presence of guards set you at ease?

She shoved away that voice and raised her chin. *Just let me have tonight.*

Behind the guards, a throng of spectators in outrageously bright outfits waved at them with beaming, powdered faces. There were two young girls at the front who elbowed each other and pointed at Amile in a fit of giggles.

Staella offered him a wry smile. "I think you have some fans."

"They're fans of the High Ruler's brother, not of me."

"Who are all these people?"

"The upper-class inhabitants of Coinsgain Plateau. They don't have a high enough status to be invited, but they have enough money to secure a spot outside. The impression the Representatives make on them tonight could have a big influence on their vote in the Election."

She cocked an eyebrow at him. "Just watching them walk inside? Wow, this Election is getting more ridiculous by the day."

His eyes met hers for the first time since they'd arrived. He watched her for a moment before his face broke into a strange smile.

The walk up to the door felt endless, marked by nodding and waving at the crowd. Finally inside, they were ushered up two flights of stairs. They paused before the double doors to the ballroom as one of the guards stepped forward. "Are you ready, sir?"

Amile nodded. "Yes, thank you, Elix."

The doors were flung open and Staella blinked. The room was colossal, stretching out to almost the length of City Square and encompassing three stories, a stone-railed mezzanine running along the top. Mammoth black chandeliers lit up the waxed dancefloor and created reflections on the mahogany dining tables that lined the walls. At the opposite end of the hall was a raised dais with six ivory seats and two thrones, occupied by what seemed like ants from where Staella stood. In fact, there were ants everywhere, filling the ballroom with movement and sound.

Elix bellowed, "Mister Qarvette and Miss Thenos."

Every head turned to watch them descend the steps. Staella kept her eyes on the opposite wall, a smile plastered on her face as she muttered, "I've had this nightmare before. At least I'm wearing clothes this time."

Amile huffed. "Yes, fortunately for that."

When they at last reached the foot of the stairs, they headed straight for the dais. They bowed at the first chair, which was occupied by a statuesque blonde woman. Amile reached out to kiss her hand. "Lorde Malano, may the Goddess bless and protect you."

The woman inclined her head. "You as well, Mister Qarvette. Miss Thenos."

Staella was surprised to find Saul in the next seat. He flashed her a quick wink before anyone could notice and she felt excitement bubble in her stomach. "Lorde Knoxin."

Next to him sat the Lorde of the People, a man with hazelnut skin and eyes the color of oceans: Arav Haltstone.

Barely a second after they'd greeted him, another voice boomed, "Amile Qarvette. You have grown up quite a bit. Become a man. Now all that's left is to become a decent one and support your family."

Amile's jaw clenched, but he managed a smile. His eyes betrayed him, though, flashing lightning as he gritted, "Majesty Advisor Karmazuhn." The man was in his mid-forties, with wide features and brown skin. His suit was too small for his mountainous frame and beads of sweat gathered on his forehead. "It has been too long."

"Yes, it has. Because you never deign to visit your own home," he sneered.

Staella felt her fists clench at her side, and she suppressed a snarl. Amile, however, merely moved on to the throne on the man's left.

Cala Vardan grinned at them in all her royal glory. Her dark hair ran in waves down her sandstone skin, framing a cunning face. Her dress was unlike anything Staella had ever imagined possible for clothing. It started white at her collar, ombre cascading downward to the hem at her feet, where a stunning illusion of flames licked up the skirt. When she addressed Amile as "brother", his shoulders tensed.

He bowed. "High Companion Qarvette."

That feline gaze turned on Staella. "Miss Thenos, I see that you are wearing a Cruzan. Fitting choice. It seems that my brother-in-law possesses the Qarvette men's good taste."

Staella gaped, smiled. "Th—Thank you, Your Highness. From you, that is indeed a compliment."

The royal children were next. Yohai had his hair pulled back, his little face so serious it was somewhat ridiculous. Neka was grinning from ear to ear, deep dimples never disappearing. Even Amile couldn't resist genuinely smiling at her.

After Staella had greeted them, she glanced at Amile to find that his attention was already fixed on the final throne. His body had gone rigid. His throat bobbed.

"High Ruler Qarvette."

Staella curtsied, monitoring the exchange keenly. They looked so much alike, but the difference was clear to anyone who looked close enough. Their golden-brown eyes, guarded and perceptive on Amile, were vivid and inviting on Yathan. The latter's wide, well-defined lips were not tight and delicately vulnerable, but rather relaxed and surrounded by the beginnings of laugh lines. His skin was lighter, his features more mature, and there was a charismatic openness to him that Amile could never possess.

"Little brother, it is so good to see you again, face to face. You have grown up so much… How are you?"

Amile was still visibly tense, his voice utterly neutral as he answered, "I am well, thank you."

Yathan nodded and reached out to pat him on the shoulder. He shook Staella's hand gently. "It is a pleasure to meet you, Miss Thenos. Please take care of my brother tonight."

She curtsied again. "Of course, Your Highness."

As they stepped away from the dais, the High Ruler leaned over to whisper something to his daughter. She giggled, squeezed her father's hand.

Amile steered them towards a table with refreshments, sighing with relief. He handed her a large cup of ale and finished his own in three greedy gulps. She took that as a cue to leave him be. After their own exchanges, which took a considerably longer amount of time, Markham and Leda joined them, chuckling at some inside joke.

Markham grinned at Staella and filled up her cup with more ale. "So, how is your first Goldvinger Crest ball going?"

She shrugged. "So far I've walked down stairs and curtsied, so not all that terrifying."

"Ah, well at least we've progressed from terrifying to neutral. I'm sure we can move to pleasant by—"

He was interrupted by Leda pulling on his arm excitedly when the music changed. "Mar, this is our song."

He beamed, offering Staella an apologetic shrug before taking Leda's hand and nearly skipping towards the dancefloor. Watching them, it was obvious that they'd been partners for years. They moved together flawlessly, steps in perfect synchronization and faces glowing with elation. An unsettling emotion churned in Staella's gut, and she looked away, spotting Yathan and Cala swaying to a rhythm about three times slower than the one actually playing. The intimacy of their locked gazes had her averting her eyes once more.

She turned, expecting to find Amile, but he had resorted to leaning against the refreshments table with his arms crossed over his chest. His eyebrows were knotted into a scowl. Staella groaned and decided to indulge in the pastries.

It came as a great relief when someone poked her in the side, and she looked up to see spice brown eyes and a lacy pink dress that must have cost a fortune. She grinned. "Maci. I didn't realize you'd be here… They didn't announce you."

The girl rolled her eyes, half a cupcake already having disappeared into her mouth. "Apparently they don't announce you if you're more than ten minutes late and this," she gestured at herself theatrically, "doesn't happen quickly. I wasn't planning on coming as a noteworthy guest, but Aedon couldn't find anyone masochistic enough to be his date, so I had to swoop in to save the family name."

Amile's head jerked up and he smiled adorably when his gaze landed on Maci. He reached past Staella to bow and kiss her hand with something that could barely pass as a blush on his cheeks. "It's only you who could look this lovely with two hours to get ready."

She offered him a mischievous grin and gasped mockingly. "Did I just receive a decent compliment from *the* Mister Qarvette? Who are you and what have you done to Amile?"

He cocked an eyebrow, huffed in a surprisingly playful manner. "Contrary to popular belief, I am actually quite a nice person."

That teasing smile was still on her face when she winked at him, finally turning to survey the rest of the hall. "Where are Markham and Leda?"

Staella shrugged. "They were dancing, but now they seem to have disappeared. Charming a vote out of someone, I suppose."

Amile suddenly cleared his throat. "Uh, speaking of dancing… Miss Blomehill?"

He held out a poised hand, but Maci feigned ignorance. The corner of her lips twitched slightly upward as she replied, "Yes, Mister Qarvette?"

The same gleam that lit up her eyes had turned Amile's gold, and his tongue flicked out to taste his bottom lip. Staella felt somewhat awkward. "May I have this dance?"

Maci's resolve shattered and she beamed. "Of course you may."

With that they were off, Maci spinning around the hand Amile had intertwined with hers, giggling all the way. In the flash of a husky chuckle, the grim veil that seemed a permanent feature over Amile's face was lifted.

Realizing that she was now utterly alone and had nothing to do, Staella's own smile vanished. She didn't know anyone else, except Saul, but he was probably busy having an important conversation with someone somewhere. Another helping of pastries would only make her nauseous. Perhaps she should pour another glass of ale and drink until this became fun.

You can't intoxicate yourself. You're supposed to be guarding Markham.

From what? Too much female attention? Too many fake smiles?

Staella…

Oh, shut up.

She sometimes wondered whether other people also had arguing voices in their minds. Perhaps she should have that looked at.

It was then that Markham slid up next to her, a rescuer with a charming smile. "Please tell me you enjoy dancing, because if I have to listen to this beautiful music and see you looking like that all night without the chance to share the floor, I might just lose my mind."

Staella cocked an eyebrow at him, feeling a little less professional in her ball gown. "Lose your mind? Oh dear, what will you do then if I tell you that I can't?"

He shrugged, inching closer. "I'd have to teach you, naturally. If it's anything like horse riding, you should pick it up in no time."

She offered him a sideways glance, letting a giggle bubble out of her. "I'll spare you the theatrics this time… I can dance."

He inclined his head towards her. "Now, tell me, what kind of cage fighter knows ballroom dancing?"

She bit her lip, found her ears already burning at her next words: "The kind who understands that seduction can be as deadly as a sword."

He paused, flicked his gaze towards her mouth. Slowly and enticingly, they made eye contact. "Seduction? Now I'm very curious about the type of dancing you do in Avetown."

The leer she gave him made her stomach bubble with forbidden excitement. She didn't know whether it was the music or the ale or the way he was looking at her, but she took his hand without hesitation.

"Then I suppose I'd have to show you."

She led him to the dancefloor, allowing her hips to follow the rhythm of the song. When his arm slipped around her waist, she placed her palm on his shoulder and let her fingers trace over the supple strength they found there. They started moving, somewhat clumsily at first and then in harmonized abandon.

Staella allowed the moment to take her. She closed her eyes, subtly pulled herself closer to this stunning man and let her limbs move to the pace he was setting. When she looked up at him, there was a crooked smile on his face, a feline curiosity in his gaze.

"Why are you looking at me like that?"

He shook his head and swallowed visibly. "Nothing, I just really like this Staella." Without warning, he spun her into a series of turns that made the room blur, then dipped her so low the ends of her hair were surely on the floor. His face was inches from hers; she could feel his breath on her cheek, could see the freckles littering his nose. They weren't moving. They were staring at each other, the warmth and security of his grip around her body causing desire to settle low in her belly. Her heart jolted when he winked, purred, "She's fun."

When she'd been pulled back into a standing position, she knew her cheeks were flushed, her breathing harsh. She cleared her throat and glanced to the side.

"Don't get used to her."

"Why?"

"Because I am an independent, professional woman who should not be engaging in this type of behavior with the man paying her salary."

"I'll have Amile pay it from now on." He received only a roll of the eyes in response to that. "But truly, Staella, you can be whoever you want to be. I keep seeing glimpses of one of the most intriguing people I've ever met, and then you hide them away again"

She sighed. "Regardless of how amazing my acting skills are, I'm not an old friend of yours, Markham. The only reason I get to experience even a fraction of this world, the only reason you're talking to me right now, is because I was hired to protect you, to do a job. I'm not one of you."

"But you are here. Does it really matter why?"

"Yes, it does." *Because it has to. Because you're not one of them. Because…*

He offered her a sad smile. "Well, can I at least have unadulterated Staella for tonight?"

Her grin was unavoidable. "I can't see the harm in that."

Liar.

Shut up.

Two songs later, he stopped suddenly and started leading her back to the refreshments table. "Sorry, Leda is signaling me. I should probably get back to campaigning."

She nodded. "Of course."

Amile was alone on the southern side of the ballroom. She joined him, grabbing another cup of ale for good measure.

He was smirking. "Enjoying yourself?"

She looked for the sarcasm in his expression, found none. "Does it matter? I'm just here to keep an eye on Lad Aesher, right?"

He cocked an eyebrow at her, crossing his arms over his chest. "Yes, but you're also a human being who can answer when you're asked a nice question."

She huffed, allowed herself a smile. "I'm sorry. Yes, I am enjoying myself. You?"

He shrugged. "As much as I can under the circumstances." She found him glaring across the hall to where Yathan was entertaining a group of nobles with an anecdote.

She studied Amile, teeth tugging at her bottom lip. "I'm going to ask you something personal."

He scowled. "Okay?"

"Why do you hate your brother?"

He was silent for a moment, a struggle raging behind his eyes. "I don't know." His voice was softer, lower than it had ever been. "Yathan and I weren't friends as children and he wasn't there for me when I needed him most, but that doesn't warrant the intensity of the anger I feel when I'm around him. I think that only makes it worse."

She hadn't expected such a vulnerable answer. "It makes you feel irrational even when you know that you're not."

His eyes met hers, the gold lighting up. "Yes."

Taking advantage of Amile's sudden forthcoming nature, she blurted, "There's something else I wanted to ask… Have you—Have you heard screaming coming from the third floor. There's a locked door and I—"

"Stay away from the third floor." His voice was a dagger of ice and he left immediately, seeking out Maci.

The hair on the back of Staella's neck stood at attention and her chest tightened. There was something in that house and he knew about it. Astonishingly, she'd learned to sleep through the nightly screams, but she was aware of them, nonetheless. They came just past twelve, every night like clockwork, except when the moon was full.

Lost in that wonderful thought, she was unaware of Lorde Haltstone's presence at her side until he cleared his throat. He seemed younger up close. She knew about him: the man who had received the second-most number of votes ten years ago and had steadily become the most beloved Lorde of the People in history. When news came that he would visit a specific town, the people would start preparing a feast days in advance. He'd go around to each house, get to know each person by name. It was clear where Delilah had inherited her dedication from.

He beamed, the skin around his eyes crinkling beautifully. "I have met you before, Staella Thenos. I don't remember when and where, but I rarely forget a face."

She gaped at him. "You came to visit my hometown once, but that was eight years ago. If you remember that, then you must know everyone in Aldahad."

He shrugged, his smile never faltering. "I very nearly do." His ocean eyes were fixed on Markham and Leda as they laughed with a group of strangers across the room. "Tell me, Staella, what do you think of Lad Aesher? Do you think your friend is the best candidate to rule the People's Monarchy?"

Honestly, I'm still trying to figure him out myself.

"Your cousin is a very inspirational woman; she cares about the individual well-being of Aldahad's citizens, and she works on the ground to make their lives better. Markham is not that, but he has managed the Aesher estate for years and there have been no hiccups. He's smart and he's even-tempered, and I think the difference between the two might account for why we need both a Lorde of the People and a High Ruler."

He nodded, the corner of his mouth twitching. "Wise words… You saved many rebel lives yesterday, Miss Thenos." Staella gulped at the air, searching for a reply, but he continued, "Are you a sympathizer?"

She gulped, clearing her throat perhaps a tad loudly. "Those, uh, those rebels were spared for interrogation purposes."

"Of course."

She glanced at him out of the corner of her eye, lowered her voice coyly. "Are you a sympathizer, my lorde?"

He turned to face her fully, a whole other conversation sparking in his stare. "No need to fear… I am not an insurgent, but I'm not all for cutting them down either. After all, Lowena Hayvinger used to be one."

The thought made her head spin, and she shook her head, blinking rapidly. "I—I'm sorry, Lorde Haltstone… If you would please excuse me; I need to use the restroom."

Already stumbling away, she didn't hear his reply. She wove her way through people chatting and couples dancing and lovers trying to be subtle in their groping. It was all just a blurry mess to her. Her chest was tight. There wasn't enough space to move, to breathe.

Flashing images were intruding on her thoughts, taking over all else. The glaring, golden eyes of that old man. Graegg's impaled body at her feet. A finely-made sword rushing towards her face.

Golden eyes. Sword flashing. Graegg's body.

Gold. Sword. Graegg. Gold.

She slammed into something at full force, stumbling back to find Lady Rayn Valanisk staring at her with a strange grin on her stunning face.

Staella paled, her thoughts cleared by her shock and embarrassment. "My lady, I'm so sorry."

Rayn's smirk widened, and she stepped even closer. "There's no need to apologize, Miss Thenos. Anyone who looks like you is welcome to bump into me any day."

Staella's lower jaw went slack. "Oh—*Oh*... Uh, thank you?"

The Representative nodded slyly before floating away to disappear in the mass of bodies around them. Staella was left staring at nothing.

Did that really just happen?

Then, the hall was thrown into purposeful movement as the dinner bell rang and everyone made for their tables. She had to look around a bit before finding the one Amile had sat down at. Once all the guests were seated, servants entered with plates of carpaccio starters that made Staella's stomach growl. However, when she looked at the vast array of cutlery laid out before her, she gulped nervously.

"You start from the outside and work your way in." The whispered lifeline came from Chrisjon Damhere, who was seated to her right.

She offered him a sheepish grin. "Thanks."

He shrugged. "It's fine. I'm quite new to all of this too. Had to get a lesson in being a proper noble from Lad Caneille over there this afternoon."

The latter, who was on Amile's other side, looked up at the mention of his name. Staella had to blink a few times before her brain understood that such an ethereally beautiful person could exist. His skin was alabaster, his hair marble and his eyes plucked from Yaekós' cloudless sky by the Goddess herself.

"What gossip are you doling out, Damhere?" he enquired with a playful lilt to his voice.

Chrisjon shook his head. "I was just telling Miss Thenos about our lovely training session earlier."

Those piercing eyes fixed on her and he smiled. "Ah yes, that took up the entire afternoon."

Another head peaked out from behind him, this one dark-haired and bronze-skinned with a benevolence of expression that made up for his lack of beauty. "And that was just for dancing."

The one with the alabaster skin laughed at that, turning his attention back to Staella. "Where are my manners? I'm Daniel Caneille." He bowed his head and then motioned to the man at his side. "And this is my husband, Eran."

She offered a genuine beam, relieved that she didn't have to curtsy again. "It's a pleasure to meet you. So, you're going into this Election with your High Companion already?"

Daniel nodded. "That wasn't a very big part of our reasoning, but yes. It offers some stability, which reassures voters. Of course, we do have Markham and Leda to contend with."

"Of course."

She forced the strange feeling in her stomach to dissipate and elected to enjoy dinner with Chrisjon and the Caneilles. The conversation at the table never dulled, shared memories being recalled jovially and topics flitted between with no effort at all. It was apparent that Chrisjon had been the couple's friend for years. Lad Damhere occupied an entire half-hour telling her about his big family and their farm, his cousin who used to be a spy, his grandmother who took no nonsense, and how he loved hunting and tracking, killed only for food. On that topic, Eran took over. He was obsessed with healthy meals and was apparently one of the best cooks in the city, and never skipped his day's running session. Daniel, on the other hand, spent his days composing music and decorating the walls of their home with masterpieces.

Then, they started talking about camping, about all the trips they had taken together and the adventures they'd shared. Staella had never imagined that anyone on the Crest would enjoy sleeping outside, but she'd been wrong before.

When it was her turn, she spoke of the books she loved to read and how she'd even laughed and wept for the characters on the page. She spoke of the freedom and power that came with knowing how to defend herself, of the sports she'd played as a child and the circus shows she'd attended with her family.

Even Amile seemed to come alive, asking questions and making clever comments. She learned about his love for astronomy and biology, how he'd taken it upon himself to study human and animal anatomy. He'd seemingly forgotten their earlier exchange. Surrounded by light-hearted banter and genuine laughter, Staella finally felt herself relax into this strange world.

†

There was only one thing that had made Leda remotely excited to attend the Representatives' Ball: the light show.

She'd watched High Ruler Karmazuhn's ten years ago, in awe of the flames that danced across the room and the excitement that hung in the air like a drug. She remembered her mother's face when the display had started, cheeks glowing with wonder and blonde hair pure gold under the light.

Now, it was Yathan's turn. And if tradition was anything to go on, his would rival all that had come before.

Leda didn't even try to hide her ear-splitting grin as the crowd was ushered into a side room. It was significantly smaller than the hall they'd just been in, but it still hosted the mass of guests comfortably. Seeing the setup made anticipation bubble in her veins. There was a stage at the far end, slim but high. Dangling from chains in the ceiling were hundreds upon hundreds of metal rings about the size of her calves, wrapped in bloodred, oil-soaked rags. At each corner atop the mezzanine, there was an archer standing ready, their arrow nocked and aching to be set alight.

A nervous servant girl handed Leda a candle and gestured for her to take the steps up to the stage. Her fellow Representatives were already starting to line up, a row of crimson that faced the buzzing audience.

She took her own spot just as Daniel stepped up next to her. "Excited?" he whispered.

She chuckled. "For once, yes."

"I get it. I feel like a five-year-old on Yul."

"Remembering you at parties, I don't doubt that."

"Speaking of, I haven't seen you at our gatherings in a while."

She looked down and cleared her throat. "I haven't had much time for pleasantries since the Election kicked off."

"Your father?"

"Yes."

Yathan ascended the stage and the room quieted. He was dressed in an immaculate black suit, a maroon cape slung over his shoulders. Aldahad's precious ebony crown sat on his head, unaware of the absurd power it wielded over the mortals of the Monarchy. There was a single candle in his hand, the flame at its top waving in a breeze that Leda couldn't feel.

His voice was loud, laced with authority, when he said, "Three days ago, each of your Representatives was asked for which virtue they wanted their family's candle to be lit tonight. I urge you to listen carefully and understand that these values are what they will carry with them should they be elected." He stepped up to Caran, who was closest to him. "The Minyaka line has chosen dignity." Yathan lit the Representative's white candle with his own and moved on. "The Blomehills light their candle for courage." Markham was next, his expression uncharacteristically drawn. "The Aesher family stands for equality."

And so, he continued, lighting candle after candle. Vardan for prosperity. Vaekish for hope. Haltsone for humanity. Qarvette for wisdom. Valanisk for justice.

Leda straightened when Yathan stopped before her with a smile. She made deliberate eye contact with her father as the High Ruler proclaimed, "The Hayvinger line has chosen to stand for freedom." A small rebellion, but a rebellion nonetheless.

Caneille for transcendence. Damhere for integrity. Karmazuhn for fortitude.

The torches along the walls were extinguished, the enveloping darkness barely broken by twelve tiny flames.

"Distinguished guests, it is my honor to present the Lads and Ladies of Aldahad." Applause ripped through the air and Leda felt a surge of power, of secret pride, spread through her limbs. Then, one by one, the candles were extinguished again. Yathan killed the last dancing flicker, and all light left the room.

Everything silenced.

The very walls seemed to be holding their breath, mimicking the guests. No one dared to move, but their excitement did unseen pirouettes through the air. Her heartbeat was thundering in her ears. Her stomach knotted around itself. Her toes curled. She was a firework about to explode.

A split second before the first arrow would be set ablaze, a scream shattered through the silence, tearing through the world, through her excitement, through her bones.

The room lit up. A single burning arrow sailed from the farthest corner. It dashed nimbly through each ring in its path, setting a line of clothed rags on fire. The next arrow launched. And the next. And the next. Swift carriers of light and heat had everyone in awe. Soon, the ceiling was alive with flames, dancing, writhing, caressing each other like living creatures. Tongues of yellow. Limbs of orange. Crimson eyes.

Leda blinked, eyes adjusting enough to find that the fire had painted the shape of a crown on the ceiling, as detailed as the one balanced on Yathan's head. It was unlike anything she'd ever witnessed.

But then she turned to her right. Stared at the empty space, at the abandoned candle on the stage floor, at the fresh drops of scarlet.

Leda sank to her knees.

CHAPTER SEVEN

DANIEL CANEILLE WAS GONE.

Staella's eyes were wide, trained not on the spectacle overhead, but on the spot onstage that was now vacant. There had been a scream, a terrified cry for help, and now there was only a white candle with blood splattered down its sides.

She dove into action before anyone else even thought of moving, dashed for the side of the stage. Nothing on the steps, the ground, the walls. Nothing. There was blood, which meant that he had been taken—forcefully. She bolted up the staircase to the mezzanine and shoved past the gaping archers. She ran the perimeter, darted back to the empty ballroom. Nothing. Nothing.

In desperation, she called, "Daniel? Daniel!"

She clenched her hand into a fist so tight she could feel her nails dig into skin. She threw aside tables and crockery. Something. Something. His captors must have escaped somehow, must have taken him somewhere. But there was nothing. No trail of blood. No footprints. No doors left ajar. He was just gone.

When she went back to the light-show room, Saul's guards had finally dispersed to search the house and estate. Markham had left the stage to stand with Amile.

He's safe.

Maybe you should've checked on that sooner?

Oh, shush.

Yathan was trying to calm his guests with useless words, but no one listened to him. That crown on is head was no match for fear. Leda still hadn't gotten up, was staring at the floor in front of her.

The stage.

Staella gasped, scowling at the platform's surface. Maybe there was a trap door… She stepped closer when a hand closed around her arm.

She turned to find Amile there, his jaw clenching and unclenching rapidly. "We're leaving."

Markham was behind him, eyes glazed over as he stared into space. His teeth gnawed at the inside of his cheek and his gaze flitted around with inner dialogue.

Staella huffed at Amile. "Leave? How can we leave? Daniel was just abducted. We need to find him. We can help. I can help."

His expression was stern, uncompromising. "We need to go home now."

She glared at him with as much fire as she had in her, snapping her arm out of his grip. "Are you really this selfish?"

The sinews in his neck pulled tight and he spat, "Don't talk about things you cannot understand. Just come."

His friend's vexation was seemingly enough to snap Markham out of his daze. His eyes met Amile's and stayed there. There was an entire conversation in that look, a confidential exchange without words.

Markham blinked and faced her with jerky movements. "Staella, we are leaving now."

"But we—"

"Now."

The command was clear, unflinching. A master silencing his disobedient servant.

Trying her best to ignore the stinging behind her eyes, she straightened. "Yes, *my lad.*"

†

"Get up."

Sunlight hit Markham's sleeping face and he groaned as the command was repeated. He sighed through his nose, blinked a few times before his eyes managed to open into puffy slits. Staella was standing in front of the window, suited in black, arms crossed over her chest. Her expression was blank, except for a cocked eyebrow.

He wiped a hand across his face, feeling the exhaustion behind his eyes and in his pounding headache. Worries and plans hadn't allowed him much sleep. "How did you get into my room?"

"Amile gave me the key."

He moaned. "Amile gave…Why?"

"I asked him."

He huffed, drew a hand through his hair. "Oh, okay."

"Now, get up."

He propped himself up on both elbows, the golden sheet sliding down his bare torso to pool at his hips. It didn't escape his notice that her gaze flickered over him, quickly returning to his face. The slight blush on her cheeks made him grin. He hadn't forgotten their conversation of the previous evening, the delicious tension between them. He also hadn't forgotten the way he'd spoken to her after Daniel's disappearance and the title with which she'd addressed him. He knew what she must have been thinking, that he'd played right into her fears. In that moment, he'd wanted nothing more than to tell her all the secrets that were pulling at his insides.

Instead, he tinged his voice with teasing charm and asked, "Since when are you this bossy, Lorde Thenos?"

She didn't smile. "When it comes to your safety, I am the boss. And you have to get out of bed so we can begin with your training."

He almost choked. "Training?"

She nodded, finally taking a few steps towards him. "Sword training. It could just as easily have been you that was taken last night. I cannot be at your side every second of every day. You need to be able to protect yourself."

Falling back into the mattress, he muttered, "I'm fine, thanks."

"This is a necessity."

"What time is it?"

"Five."

His breath hitched into a cough. "In the morning? Staella, nothing is a necessity at five in the morning."

She sighed, planting her hands on her hips. "I need to be at the barracks at half past six. I'm already sacrificing thirty minutes of my time with the guards."

"How will they survive?" He turned his back to her, burying his face into a pillow.

A pillow struck the side of his head. He twisted around to see a challenging spark in her eyes. "Get dressed and be on the eastern lawns in ten minutes."

A quarter of an hour later, they were both outside. His eyes were still too heavy for this, and anxiety continued to scratch at his mind.

Staella eyed his shirtless body with a scowl. "I thought I told you to get dressed."

He shrugged. "It's hot. I put on pants, didn't I?" Stepping inches closer, he purred, "Why? Is it a little distracting?"

She clenched her jaw, expertly kept her glare trained on his face. "I don't get distracted."

He rolled his eyes. "Don't do that."

"Don't do what?"

His expression softened along with his voice. "Pull away from me." Her face was so close to his, close enough for him to study the features he hadn't noticed when they were dancing. The little scar on her jaw. The lighter patterns in her almost-black eyes. The slight crease in her lower lip. "Look, I'm sorry about last night."

She backed away, straightening. "You don't have to apologize for being who you are."

Ouch.

"Fine. If work is the only way to get through to you, let's make a deal. I ask you a question, you give me a truthful answer, and then you get to teach me one thing. Deal?"

She stared him down, her teeth working at the inside of her cheek. "Okay. Ask."

He offered her what he knew was his most shit-eating grin. "How old were you when you started training and why did you start?"

"That's two questions."

"Humor me."

"Thirteen. I wanted to be able to defend myself."

He mocked a bow. "Alright, Master. Teach me your craft."

He didn't miss the miniscule upward tug of her lips. "We'll start with the stance. Take a comfortable step forward with your left leg. Back foot turned to the side. Step it out slightly. And now sink into it." The position was quite familiar to him, but he pretended to follow her instructions. "That's, uh, perfect, actually."

He smirked. "I do know the basics."

"Then, we'll start with real swords tomorrow."

He rubbed his palms together mischievously. "Looks like I get another question." It was her turn to roll her eyes. "Tell me one thing you like to do in your spare time."

"Read."

He beamed at that. "Who's your favorite author?"

"Extend your arm as if you're dealing a one-handed blow." He complied. She studied his arm in silence, brow furrowed in concentration. Gliding forward, she wrapped a hand around his bicep. "You're focusing too much power here. You need to let it flow down." Her grip loosened and she trailed a finger along his inner arm. He shivered under the touch. She stopped, but didn't move her hand. Her eyes were fixed on his forearm, her throat bobbing visibly. His chest tightened. Slowly, her gaze traveled to his face. His own focused on her mouth, her lips slightly parted. When their eyes met again, he smiled, and his head tilted down of its own accord.

She scuttled away. "Aurellis… My favorite author is Aurellis."

The name punched him right in the gut and he laughed. "Aurellis? Really?"

Her face scrunched into a frown. "What's wrong with him?"

He shook his head. "Nothing. He's great—I just like him too."

"Next lesson."

And so, Markham let Staella correct his deliberate fencing mistakes, all the while asking her about anything that came to mind. He learnt of her love for her sister, her obsession with spicy food, her hatred of marketplaces, her love of bonfires. No matter how much he learned, he wanted to know more.

†

In contrast to the already-scabbing cut across Staella's collarbone, the wound above Deputy Caven's eye looked uncomfortably swollen as he tried to scowl at her in greeting. The guards had just returned from their morning run and those who were not getting ready for patrol duty were engaged in drills under Maron's stern supervision.

Staella ignored him, marched straight to Saul's office door, and entered without knocking. He was seated behind his desk, frowning at whatever he was writing so fervently. He wasn't wearing his cap and the sunlight from the windows caught the chocolate streaks in his raven hair.

Finally pausing in his scribbling, he looked up at her. It was really unfair how striking his eyes were, how they managed to transfix her despite her better judgment. However, this time she found herself having to shove away thoughts of a different gaze—green rather than midnight blue.

Saul offered her a crooked grin. "Thenos."

She nodded, a tiny smile tugging at her lips as well. "Good morning,"

He frowned, looking down at the watch around his wrist. "Aren't you a bit early for our session? Have they finished the drills in the yard?"

Moving deeper into the room, she shook her head. "I didn't train with them this morning. I had duties at the Aesher estate and thought I'd report straight to you when finished."

"Well, I can't complain about spending more time with one of Yaekós' finest warriors."

"One of?" she teased.

He just huffed at that, smile widening. "You did well in the confrontation with the rebels the other day. Better than I expected. You really do make an excellent addition to the city guard, Thenos."

She fluttered her eyelashes dramatically. "I am only glad to be of service to His Highness, my lorde."

His tongue lodged against the inside of his cheek. "Oh, I'm sure. I hope you didn't sustain any serious injuries. You disappeared before I could check."

"After surviving the cage, I can assure you that I'm tougher than I look." The flashes of memory from the fray had become a regular occurrence in her thoughts, but they jarred her, nonetheless. Gold. Sword. "Graegg?"

The light in his eyes dimmed. "Like all fallen guards, his ashes and possessions were sent to his family. The parcel left for Norwell yesterday. In my letter, I made sure to mention the valiant way in which he sacrificed his life for Aldahad's safety. He's received a medal of excellence... He won't be forgotten."

When her voice was steady enough, she asked, "Why are the barracks so quiet?" He only scowled at her. "Daniel Caneille disappeared last night, and everything is progressing routinely. I expected a bit more action. A Representative is missing. Are you not utilizing all resources to find him? To figure out what happened to him?"

He sighed, waved a hand over the hurricane of papers in front of him. "I am assembling a small, efficient task force to handle the investigation. They should be operating by Leidsday… But it's only a formality, really. I already know who took Lad Caneille."

"Wait, what?" Staella's eyes had nearly popped out of her skull at that.

"On the night of the Ball, the supply wagons into the city were ambushed. The cargo was looted, the vehicles destroyed beyond repair, and the guards tied and gagged. And *these* were left all over the scene."

He sifted through the pile of documents on the desk, finally handing her a half-crumpled flyer. She straightened it out, heartbeat threatening to consume her senses. A pitch-black background delved through by a single white lightning bolt. Crimson letters: THE REPRESENTATIVES DO NOT REPRESENT US.

Her blood froze in her veins, her movements delayed as she threw the flyer to the floor.

"You think the Rebellion took him."

Jacline...

No.

"I am quite certain they did. This kind of message being sent at the exact same time that one of the Representatives is abducted? I don't believe in such uncanny coincidences. But I need proof before I can report to Yathan, which is what the task force is for."

Staella gulped. "If the rebels have him... "

"He's in trouble," Saul finished for her. "Their entire Rebellion is based on only a select few being able to stand for High Ruler. He is one of those select few. I can't imagine that they'd be very benevolent. You saw what they did to Graegg... And the Rebellion is spread out across the entire Monarchy. He could be anywhere."

Staella shook her head. "No. It's not—it's not a done deal yet. How did they get someone close enough to the Ball to take him? How did they get him out of the palace unnoticed? It could be something entirely different. It–it could be the Red Cloaks. Someone with a personal vendetta. Anyone, really."

Who are you trying to convince?

She wanted to run to the Rooks right now, to crash into the Burly Bear and demand answers. But Jacline would never confess to her.

You're the enemy now, remember?

"Thenos, I know that it might be difficult to accept, but—"

"I'll investigate the disappearance. The task force will only be ready on Leidsday. I can start now."

"Thenos."

"Please."

Saul sighed softly and stood up, placing a hand on her shoulder. "We need someone to go to the Caneille estate. Look around. Talk to Eran. Gather any information that might mean something."

"I'll go right away. Thank you."

He didn't say anything, just squeezed her shoulder and returned to his seat. She had work to do.

†

The silver mare was galloping at full stride, its lean muscles flexing with natural grace, nostrils flaring. The three-tiered obstacle loomed closer. Closer. Closer. Leda dug her heels into the beast's sides. She tensed her legs, bent forward. Relaxed her shoulders, eased her grip on the reins, and murmured in the horse's ear. They leapt, mythicizing gravity as the silver's body soared over the upright like it was but a nuisance. Leda's smile nearly touched her ears as she closed her eyes, cherishing the wind through her hair and the smell of adrenaline surrounding them. Her stomach was in her ribcage, her heart about thrice its usual size.

On the descent, she leaned backward to move with the mare. They landed with a jarring *thud.* Urging them to a standstill, Leda laughed and ran a hand down the animal's smooth neck.

"Good girl, Ezra." She reached into her back pocket to pull out a treat. "There you go. You were amazing today, sweetheart. This is why you're my favorite... But don't tell Marcio." She released the reins and laid down on Ezra's back, sighing.

She'd only just closed her eyes when the mare made a disgusted sound, pawing at the grass. Leda frowned and pulled herself into a seated position to see what the horse was on about.

Mighiel.

Her brother was leaning against the camp's fence with crossed arms and a condescending glare. She pulled a face, whispered, "Ezra, do you think we can trample him and call it an accident?" The mare whinnied and Leda rolled her eyes. "I know. I know. Murder is never the answer. Why do you always have to be right?"

She got a huff in reply and gritted her teeth, leading the horse to meet him.

She remained mounted, quite enjoying the way she could look down on him. "Did you just come to glower at me or is there a point to your presence?"

His hair had been tied back, leaving his face open. The Hayvinger face: sharp features and dark eyes full of familiar hypocrisy. It was unnerving how much that gaze resembled her father's.

When he spoke, his voice was laced with venom. "I didn't miss your little stunt last night. Father may have been oblivious, but I'm not."

She stiffened, staring at him in terror before raising her chin. "I can't say that I know what you're talking about."

He leaned over the fence, yanking Ezra forward by the bridle. The horse neighed indignantly, and Leda gasped as she was jolted towards him. His face was right at her side, too close for comfort. She squirmed.

"Don't be coy with me, little sister. *Freedom*? Freedom from what? From the privilege of running in the Election? From the chance to bring glory to the family name? You've always been an ungrateful brat. You are not worthy of being a Hayvinger."

Tears stung the backs of her eyes. "I get it. You think it should have been you, and you're probably right, but because of a bullshit tradition, it can't be. I can't not be our Representative. I am a Hayvinger, whether you like it or not, and the only thing that makes me unworthy to the rest of you is the fact that I don't believe I'm better than the rest of the world because of my last name."

His glare drove a dagger through her chest. "This family would have been so much better off if you'd never been born."

The breath was knocked out of her. She hurried to wipe the tears from her face and jumped down to meet him face-to-face. She was so tired of keeping her mouth shut, of listening to pompous men rant about glory. When she finally spoke, she let her words shoot lightning.

"You know what I wanted freedom from? From everyone in this house thinking they have the right to control my life. From having to be something I am clearly not. From being looked down on and lectured to in the name of a family who doesn't give a shit about its actual members. If you want to run to Father like the lap dog you are, go ahead. See, I may not have wanted it, but I am the Hayvinger Representative. That makes me the head of this household. There isn't a guard or a servant on this estate who would obey your orders over mine. I'd advise you to remember that the next time you think about coming to me with idle threats, brother."

Her chest was heaving, blood pounding in her ears. He was gaping and staring at her with wide eyes. A thrill ran through her as he spun to sulk all the way back to the manor. There was excitement in her veins, but also dread. What would happen when her father heard? Next to her, Ezra snorted. She could almost hear the "good riddance" in the horse's scoff and burst out in laughter.

†

It wasn't Eran who opened the door to the Caneilles' sandstone château, but a haggard-looking Chrisjon Damhere. His skin was pale, his jet-black hair untied and disheveled. He was still in the shirt he'd worn the night before, but it was unbuttoned over his barrel of a chest and his feet were bare.

"Staella… You came by?"

She nodded, holding out the tray of hot-cakes she'd bought along the way. "I come bearing comfort food. May I come in?"

He blinked, took the package and stepped aside. "Of course. Thank you. These, uh, these are actually Daniel's favorite." His brows knitted as he stared at the cakes for a moment too long.

She reached out to lay a hand on his shoulder. "How are things?"

His eyes snapped up and he led her into the spacious kitchen. "I suppose that we're doing alright under the circumstances, which isn't saying much." She took a seat on a bar stool, keeping her eyes trained on Chrisjon as he made a pot of tea. "I couldn't leave Eran alone after what happened. Daniel's sister is coming tomorrow. I at least have to stay until then. It took some time to get him to leave, to stop yelling at Yathan and Saul to do something. We didn't get much sleep."

Staella had to swallow past the lump in her throat. "Please tell me if there's anything I can do."

They're good people. They don't deserve this.

He poured her a cup of the lemony brew and took the seat beside her. "Thank you, Staella."

"I volunteered to work on the case of Daniel's disappearance immediately. I'm here to look around, talk to Eran, find anything worth looking into. Would that be okay?"

His lips pressed together in a thin line. "I think it would be better if you talked to me. As you can imagine, Eran's not in the best head space at the moment, and I know Daniel pretty well too."

"Of course." She did not hesitate to take his hand in hers and give it a gentle squeeze. "You're a good friend. I hope you know that."

He offered her his best attempt at a smile. "I'd like to think that any decent person would've done the same… So, ask away."

"Right. Well, did Daniel have any rivals, any enemies? Anyone who might've had a motive to do him harm?"

"Goddess, no. I don't think there's a more widely-loved person in this world."

"Would there be anyone who'd want to use Daniel as a weapon against you or Eran or any of the Caneilles?"

He was silent for a few seconds before shaking his head. "No. My enemies are quite unaware of my identity. Asha, his sister, isn't the easiest person to be around, but no one hates her to that extent, and Eran hasn't wronged anyone in his life."

Staella scowled, clenching her fist behind her back. "Would…" *Deep breaths*. "Would Daniel have had any reason to leave of his own volition?"

His gaze bore into her, body frozen. "You're asking me if he ran away?" He raised his voice, harshened his tone. "Yeah, he decided to take a spontaneous vacation right in the middle of the light show at the Representatives' Ball. Because queers are just that dramatic, right?"

The blood drained from her face, and she gaped. "Chrisjon, I… I'm so sorry. I didn't mean any offense. I just need to cover everything."

The sigh that escaped him was jagged, broken. "I'm sorry," he breathed. "I know." Flattening his fingers against the counter to stop their shaking, he closed his eyes. "Daniel would never just leave. He has a good life, with friends and a husband. No, Staella, someone took him."

She clenched her jaw. "I know."

There was a flurry of movement in the corner of her vision. Eran marched into the room, a bottle of cleaning agent in one hand and a dust cloth in the other. He was wearing nothing but a pair of checkered pajama pants and a layer of perspiration. His eyes were settled deep in their sockets, ringed purple and blue, his hair a bird's nest.

He barely looked up as he started speaking. "Oh hello. Chrisjon, why didn't you tell me we had a visitor? Staella it's nice of you to come over how are you." Words tumbled out of his mouth without pause, his attention trained on wiping clean the glass dining table at the far side of the open-plan living area. She had no time to answer. "Sorry I'm a tad busy just getting everything perfect for when Dani comes home you know he hates a mess gets terribly frustrated when one little thing's out of place never would've expected that from an artist right."

He paused at some invisible blemish on the tabletop, working at it with the cloth until Staella could see the veins in his arms bulging. When she tried to catch Chrisjon's eye, he just grimaced and looked away. This was why they hadn't slept.

"That's alright, Eran. I'm here for the investigation." No reply. "Would it be alright if I looked around the house, particularly Daniel's bedroom and studio?"

He waved a dismissive hand her way. "Yes yes sure just please don't move anything he's very particular about where he keeps everything."

"Of course. I'll keep it in perfect order."

Chrisjon rose silently, leading her down the corridor to the right of the living area. They passed two doors before reaching the master bedroom. Eran had obviously already swept through the room in a tornado of cleaning, since the space was neat to a fault. Every piece of furniture was either black or white, the monochrome theme standing out starkly in the morning light that streamed through the oversized window.

Chrisjon leaned against the doorway, arms crossed over his chest. "He's been like this since one this morning. Hasn't eaten or slept. He doesn't want to talk about it or listen. So, I didn't know what to do except let him go on."

Staella stepped further into the room. "He's still in denial. I think you should appreciate it while it lasts. It'll be much worse when reality sets in."

She opened the drawers of each nightstand. Found novels, old love letters, a packet of sweets, a tube of gel, a collection of bookmarks, and a box of matches. The desk was covered in copies of recipes, pencil drawings, and an endless supply of stationery. Nothing remotely significant. The dressers and chest yielded more of the same. She followed Chrisjon to the studio, studying every small detail they passed. If there was something here, she was determined that she would find it.

The step into the studio was a step into another world. Almost every inch of wall had been covered in paintings, each initialed "DC" and each a masterpiece in its own right. A landscape of multicolored flowers. A river flooded in moonlight. Naked bodies engulfed in an embrace. Eran's smiling face. A woman bleeding from her arms. Even the ceiling was artwork, rendering a night sky that made her feel as if she were floating. The floor was a map of the world, as detailed as the one in Saul's office.

In the far-left corner was an easel with a blank canvas mounted and ready. Color-coded containers held paints, brushes, palettes, and sticks of charcoal. Right in the center of the wonderland stood a pitch-black piano, its upper surface cluttered with piles of sheet music.

Staella approached the instrument slowly, afraid that any sudden movement would break the enchantment of the room. A hand-plotted composition waited above the keys and she let her eyes drift over it, wishing that she understood the language. She could see him sitting there, the ghost of his slim form swaying along with the music his fingers made. She imagined the melody starting, slow and heavy. She could almost feel it, as it accelerated progressively, undetected at first and then stark and brilliant. Faster and faster. Higher and higher. Until the notes grew dainty and light. Louder and louder yet. Then nothing.

It stopped in the middle of the page where he'd probably left it to get ready for the ball.

The tip of her nose tingled, her eyes burned, and she reached down to run her fingers along the ivory keys. There was a crash. Something shattered. A cry rang out from the living room. Staella and Chrisjon turned to face each other with wide eyes and dove into a sprint a split second later.

Eran was on his knees next to the cupa table, his head bowed and palms seeping blood.

Chrisjon was at his side in a blink. "Eran, what happened?" A single, raw sob tore from the kneeling man's throat. There were fragments of a shattered porcelain vase on the carpet and Staella understood. Chrisjon sank to his knees, wrapped an arm around his friend. "Eran?"

The latter's mouth was open in a silent scream, his crimson hands trembling. Another sob. "It was his favorite… He's going to be so upset. Oh, Goddess, it was his favorite thing. We got it at a stall in Lukai and he said it reminded him of his parents he's going to be so sad it was his favorite."

Tears spilled across his tan face and his shoulders spasmed under the force of his grief. He buried his face in his hands, not knowing about the blood that stained them, that still flowed from them. Chrisjon embraced him with fierce affection, pressing his lips to the side of Eran's head.

He peeled the red hands from his face and cupped Eran's jaw with his own. "Listen to me. He's not here. He's missing, Eran. We don't know where he is or when he's coming back. But I promise you that we will find him. I promise. And then he'll be so happy to see you he won't care about some stupid vase."

The sobbing stopped, Eran's body stilling ominously. He looked up at Chrisjon and snarled, "It was his favorite." He balled his hands into fists. "Get away from me."

He shoved the Representative away with enough strength to make him fall backwards. Eran shot up, fled down the corridor, and slammed the bedroom door shut with a resounding bang. Staella didn't pause to wipe away her tears as she reached out a hand to help Chrisjon up. He was silent, eyes trained on the floor.

When he finally looked up, it was with a question she had been dreading to answer. "So, any theories on where Daniel might be?"

"I do, but I don't like it," she breathed.

"Tell me." She did. His response, though, was unexpected: "I don't think the Rebellion took him."

"What? Why?"

"They've never given any indication of being violent or cruel," he replied

"They've killed guards."

"Out of self-defense."

"They shot an arrow at the High Ruler," she exclaimed

Chrisjon shook his head. "They shot an arrow at the wall behind him."

"Whose side are you on?"

A muscle feathered in his jaw and he shook his head. "I'm on Daniel's side. If the guards are focused on a single theory, they might never discover the truth. All I'm asking is that you don't blind yourself to other possibilities."

"I'm not in charge of the investigation, Chrisjon. I came here to try to find another explanation, but I found nothing. Saul won't abandon a likely theory on anything but hard evidence."

"You may not be in charge, but you have Saul's ear. Just try to convince him to keep looking… Please."

The desperation in his eyes made her nod. "I'll give him my recommendation. That's the best I can do."

His hand was still splattered with Eran's blood as he took hers. "Thank you."

CHAPTER EIGHT

FROM THE OUTSIDE, THE AREN had always seemed like just another hole in the wall in Yaekós' slums—a low-rise storeroom converted into a hangout for the despondent and the criminally inclined. Now, it was a shell, an abandoned building long ago looted of anything alcoholic. The door was still knocked down, the windows shattered by loitering children. It seemed that no one had dared come here since that night two years ago. The night when the bulk of the city guard had come storming in with the wrath of the Goddess in their fists and Saul Knoxin at their lead. They'd thrown out all the patrons and shut the place down for good. Not for the dubious activities inside, but for the illicit ones underneath.

Everything was still there—the tables, the bar, the dance floor. It was covered in a thick blanket of dust, but it was all the same.

Despite this, the place felt almost unrecognizable to Staella without the buzz of clients and the horrible music by the band Ilan had formed with his friends.

She struggled to swallow past the thickness in her throat as she wiped away the dirt from the hidden door in the floor behind the bar. She wondered where Ilan was, and Fhani, the girl who'd always taken care of her after a particularly nasty fight. She wondered about Penn too, who did the books and hated the noise.

Konje with her charming smile and cheating hands? Roan? Gauln? Trisha…

Maybe they were in the group of rebels you hacked into the other day?

She sniffed, shaking her head in a futile attempt to clear it, and headed down the too-familiar staircase that led underground.

Cobwebs clung to her in the dark, while scurrying noises and disembodied scratching sent shivers up her spine. Landing at the bottom of the steps, she reached out to where she knew a lantern hung. Even that was still there. Pulling matches out of the packed bag slung across her shoulder, she lit each of the nine lanterns down the right wall before turning to take in the cavern that had once been her home.

The dirt floors were soggy and littered with animal droppings, the card tables gnawed into whimsical shapes. But in the center of the room, the cage stood strangely untouched by time.

The cavern was hollowed out in the center and pavilion steps of dirt led down to her old stage. Behind those crooked bars, she'd stood with her wrapped fists in front of her and her clothes stuck to her body with sweat. The jackal mask would have been panting, staring down the much-larger opponent entering on the other side.

Staella breathed in, closed her eyes, and she was there.

"He's undefeated," Fhani exclaimed while checking the straps around Staella's knuckles.

"So am I."

The girl shook her head, big brown eyes brimming with concern. "I don't know why you do this to yourself."

She didn't reply, only squeezing her friend's shoulder and stepping towards the exit of her room. It was one of the chambers set out right next to the club.

Louder than even her own heartbeat was the chanting of the crowd. Jackal. Jackal. Jackal. *Staella grinned behind the mask, clenched her fists tight. She'd made quite a name for herself.*

Why did she do this?

Because she liked doing what she was good at, and she was spectacular at this.

When she slammed open the door, the horde of spectators went wild, having to be held back by Aren's cronies. She walked through the crowd with slow, deliberate steps. Soaking up the attention. The adrenaline. The anticipation.

When she entered the cage, her opponent was already there. The Skullcrusher. *Like his chosen name, he was anything but subtle. With the height of a haletayl, arms the circumference of her thighs, and an uncovered face marred by scars, it wasn't difficult to guess how he'd built up a reputation to rival hers.*

The cage door was locked behind her.

Aren bellowed his show of a speech.

The Skullcrusher made a slicing gesture across his throat.

Staella decided she would toy with him before she won this championship.

The horn blared.

As expected, he leapt forward at the first opportunity, fists swinging at her like wrecking balls. With an easy slide, Staella slipped through the space between his legs, ended up at his back. He looked around in confusion and stumbled. The crowd jeered. She tapped him on the shoulder, gave him a little wave. He snarled, spinning around with a left hook ready. She danced backward. Ducked. Sidestepped. Each one of his blows landed on air and she could feel the frustration roll off him as the laughter around them grew.

She'd played him excellently, but he was undefeated after all. With the next lunge, he was on top of her. Knuckles the size of limes smashed into the side of her face. Blood flew from her mouth. Something cracked. She stumbled back, but still didn't attack.

The next assault was evaded. Then another hit, to her left shoulder this time. She cried out as her entire arm went limp at her side. The crowd was restless, yelling at her to do something. She didn't and her opponent became more and more brash.

He was panting, charging, swinging. Angry. Impulsivity dripped from him. He was tired. And she hadn't done a thing.

Finally, he was swaying, perspiration running down his sallow skin in rivulets.

She planted her feet, put all the strength she had into the muscles of her legs, and kicked up. It was unimaginably satisfying—the sound of his breath wheezing out of him as heel connected with solar plexus. Then, groin and, as he doubled over, jaw. Right elbow to his temple…

She'd won the championship moments later, but had never been able to enjoy the victory. The chaos as the guards descended on their world had made all else insignificant. It was only with speed and Fhani's help that she'd escaped a life of imprisonment.

Her old room was to the right, the door long gone. To her surprise, she found the rest of the space perfectly preserved. There wasn't much dust here and the rats seemed to have kept away. The bed was made, the dresser unchewed, and the couch in the corner barely dusty.

Strange.

She dropped her pack on the floor and headed straight for the punching bag still strung from the ceiling. This was why she'd come. She'd needed to get away from the barracks and the Crest. She needed to come to a place where she'd known exactly who she was. Needed to feel the cold hardness of something inanimate hitting her fists.

She stepped up to the bag and ran her fingers over the surface. Then, sinking into a low stance, she clenched her hands and let everything go.

Every punch was harder than the last, every breath more of a gasp. Right hook. *Graegg.* Uppercut. *Rebels.* Left jab. *Daniel.* Spinning kick.

Chrisjon. Jacline. Leda. Markham.

"What did that poor punching bag ever do to you?"

Staella yelped, spinning to find Saul leaning against the open doorway, his eyebrows cocked.

She pretended to huff a laugh, shaking her head. "Imagining a certain Lorde of Security's face on there does wonders for motivation."

Why are you here? Can the world just leave me alone?

The corner of his lips tugged upward. "You're already a felon returning to the scene of the crime. I wouldn't push my luck if I were you."

She bit the inside of her cheek and crossed her arms over her chest. "If I didn't know any better, I'd say you're threatening me, my lorde."

"What if I were?" He stepped forward.

"I'd warn you not to push your luck."

Laughter spilled from him, and he strolled into the room. "You really are something else, Thenos."

Staella cleared her throat. "May I ask why you're here?"

"You left very quickly after giving me your report on the Caneille case… And the whole thing seemed to upset you. I wanted to check whether you'd prefer to take a few days off. When the guards at the Aesher estate told me you'd left in a hurry and no one knew where you'd gone, I followed a hunch and came here. It seems my intuition hasn't failed me after all these years… So, do I need to worry that you're resurrecting the Aren?"

She huffed, sank down on the bed, and motioned for him to take the couch. "No, I'm not returning to my errant ways, although that might be easier at this point."

He frowned, taking a seat and crossing one leg over the other. "That's not awfully reassuring."

Her breath came out in a coarse sigh. She rubbed a hand over her face, tightened her ponytail, and shook her head. "I just—I don't—I'm just frustrated. I know you're not the ideal person to talk to about this, but the Crest really isn't what I was expecting. This job isn't what I was expecting. And my mind won't shut up. And I don't…" *…know who I am anymore.* "Never mind. I'm just rambling. In fact, maybe I'm just insane."

"You're not."

She looked up to find kind eyes fixed on her, his expression so soft it made his features instantly more attractive. "What?"

He smiled. "You're not going insane. I was a senior guard in Saribi when a bunch of candidates for Lorde of Security were selected. I hadn't had much experience and there really was nothing special about me. But when Yathan came to scout, I guess he saw something in me… Ten men from all over Aldahad were brought here and housed in the Qarvette home. Spending time on the Crest, being introduced to people who seemed to be gods, becoming friends with the High Ruler himself… It was overwhelming. It was a whole other world and I found myself having to become a whole new person. I did and it landed me a position more qualified men envied."

Staella shook her head, eyes starting to burn in frustration. "But you had to change who you were. You had to become something else."

"I became something better."

"That might be debatable."

Saul huffed, scratched the back of his head. "You really can't go five minutes without insulting me, can you?"

Her grin was real this time. "The male ego is so easy to mock, though. It would be a missed opportunity not to." He just rolled his eyes at her, half hurt and half amused. "So, you're from Saribi?"

"Born and raised."

"Seaside or mountainside?"

He leaned back in the chair, allowing himself the memory. "Our house was a few streets from the beach, but I was in the mountains every weekend. My younger brother and I used to go hiking every Tarnday and then spend Cründay lounging in the hot springs at the top of Galinea. We nearly got ourselves killed on those slopes a few times, but none of my mother's warnings stuck."

He chuckled and she found that it was impossible not to smile with him. "It must be amazing to grow up close to the ocean… I've never even seen the sea."

His eyes widened. "Never?"

She shrugged. "Don't look at me like that. Where was I supposed to see the ocean between Avetown and Yaekós?"

He held up his hands in a theatrical surrender. "Sorry. You're just such a confident, world-wise woman. It's difficult to imagine that you've seen so little."

Heat bloomed in her cheeks, and she had to look away. *Really, I've resorted to blushing?* "When I was a fighter, I spent most of my time between these four walls, learned all of my *world-wisdom* here… It's strange to be back. And this room is so perfectly preserved. It's like I could just step over into a different life."

"I'm glad I could keep it to your liking."

"*What?*"

Saul shrugged. "When you first disappeared, I came here many times. I was looking for clues as to where you might have gone. Being the unfailingly neat person I am, I tried to keep it in order. I kept coming here long after we gave up hope on finding you. Something about an abandoned underground cavern seems to relax me."

"Well, you'll just have to find another abandoned underground cavern because this one is mine."

He jumped up and bounded across the room. He held out a hand to her. "Come on."

She scowled. "What? Come where?"

"You will not sit here in your old room and mope all night. There's only one place in this city I can go when I miss the sea and I'm taking you."

"But I—"

"And bring your bag. No one should sleep in a place where there are this many rats crawling around."

He grabbed her hand and pulled her into a standing position. She had little choice but to comply.

The sound of slow-flowing water was the first thing to hit her: the steady *ghurru-ghurru* of river over stone. Then, there were the owls and crickets in their nightly debate, the soft *swish* of a breeze through the jungle.

They broke through a line of large-leafed trees and there it was: the Roccalee River. The body of water formed the northern border of the city and gave way to a stretch of untamed land. The sky was already pitch-black, a half-moon casting the world silver.

Staella closed her eyes and took a deep breath through her nose. She smiled up at the man next to her. "Even I know rivers and oceans aren't the same."

Exasperated, he shook his head. "They aren't, but you have to make do with what you have… Besides, I didn't bring you here to stare at it. We're going swimming."

"What? Now? I'm not exactly dressed for a dip." She motioned down to her linen training pants, trying not to look at the delicious smirk he was sporting.

Without a word, he reached around to the back of his shirt and pulled it over his head, discarding it in the dirt. His boots were next to go. His cargo pants… and there he was—Saul Knoxin in nothing but a pair of black underwear.

Staella gulped. The moonlight illuminated every scar on his body, every muscled curve and hard edge. He was like a marble statue, a perfectly-honed warrior with strength in every pearlescent line.

Shit.

She let out a shaky breath and reached down to her top's hem, going as slowly as her trembling hands would allow. Shivering slightly as the night air hit her skin, she didn't dare look at his face as she bared her body to him.

What are you doing?

When she was left in nothing but her flimsy underwear, she peeked up at him with wide eyes to find his own trailing down her exposed form, unhurriedly consuming her in a way that made her palms tingle. Finally, their gazes met and Staella's mouth dried. His pupils had consumed nearly all the stunning blue. She wondered if her own feelings were as clear. They had to be, judging by the hammering of her heart.

His throat bobbed once. Twice. Then he blinked, cleared his throat. "Since you always try to outdo me, Thenos, I have a proposition for you."

She bit her bottom lip and cocked an eyebrow. "And what is that, my lorde?"

The grin she received in answer was positively devilish. "Race you to that fallen tree." Without missing a beat, he leaped forward, dashing past her, heading straight for the water.

She squeaked indignantly and sprinted after him, eyeing the spot down the river where a log lay suspended over its width. The water was icy as it hit her diving body, but she didn't stop. With a last intake of breath, she was submerged. She kicked forward off a large stone and shot ahead. The muscles in her legs tightened as she swam, her arms moving in powerful arcs through the river. She only came up for breath once before continuing her surge toward the finish line. It was exhilarating—the caress of the water, the thrill of competition, the anticipation of meeting him on the other side.

With a final heave, her hands met tree trunk and she surfaced with a gasp. Saul was nowhere to be seen. Then, a split second later, he rose up next to her, raven hair flipped back from his face.

Chest expanding powerfully, he shook his head. "I was one of the best swimmers in the Ocean City… only to come to Yaekós and be bested by a girl who's never seen the sea."

"I thought we established that rivers and oceans aren't quite the same…" He inched closer and she became achingly aware of the rivulets running down the line of his collarbone, tracing the curve of his bicep to tease the veined lines that made his forearms all the more distracting. Staella gulped. "There, uh, there was a lake outside Avetown and…" Now, he was close enough that she could make out the tendrils of silver in his midnight blue eyes, the way the moonlight sharpened his jaw. The strands of wet hair clinging to the back of his neck. "…and we had a swimming team and I was actually quite…" His steel-and-sweat smell hit her. The heat of his body. "…good…"

She was silenced as he reached out to capture her chin between his fingers, tilting her head up towards him. Her breathing all but stopped. His thumb reached up, brushing the sensitive skin of her bottom lip before pressing down harder to open her mouth slightly. She allowed him the moment of control before wrapping her lips around that finger, sucking gently, all the while keeping her eyes fixed on the whirlpools that had become his.

The sound that came out of him could only be described as a growl. He surged forward, arms wrapping around her naked waist and pulling her flush against that gorgeous, solid body. Grabbing onto the hair at his nape, she pulled his face down and they clashed in a flurry of lips, tongues, and teeth. The ache low in her belly made it impossible not to moan as their tongues fought for dominance, as he pressed his hips against the juncture of her thighs and shuddered.

She would get him back for that moan, for making her mind lose all sense and her knees buckle. Her teeth tugged at his lip and he groaned. She grinned at that, permitting her hands to travel across the broad planes of his back and shoulders. Then, in a superb power move, he lowered his grip, took hold of her thighs, and hoisted her up. She gasped into his mouth, wrapped her legs around him without missing a beat.

His mouth moved lower, latched onto the juncture between her neck and collar. The hitch of her breath had him smirking, laving that spot with teeth and tongue until she dug her heels into the small of his back.

Goddess…

He pulled away, looked down at her with an intensity that set her blood on fire.

With his fingers rubbing circles into the backs of her thighs, he whispered, "I think we should take this somewhere a bit more appropriate?"

The question—the challenge—was clear in his expression and her heart missed a beat. Was she doing this?

Weren't you looking for a place to find yourself again?

He found me.

She grinned, tugged at the hair in her grip. "Only if you think you can keep up with a cage fighter."

His lips twitched upward and the kiss that followed was all the answer she needed.

She was alone in Saul Knoxin's bedroom.

They'd nearly run from the river to the barracks after donning their clothes, sneaking around to his private quarters with hands unable to resist wandering and hearts aflutter. He'd given her a single, dizzying kiss before hurrying out to lock his office and check with the patrolling guards one last time.

Her fists were clenched at her sides as she tried to get her breathing to calm down. She was sure that her cheeks were flushed, her hair a disheveled mess. She couldn't—wouldn't—let him unravel her completely.

Dark eyes roamed over the sparsely-decorated room: a dresser, end-table, and pristinely-made bed. She paused at the bed, wondered whether the sheets would be soft against her body.

Then her gaze snagged on something else. She scowled and stepped closer at the sight of a scrap of red fabric sticking out from under the mattress.

You're invading his privacy.

Oh, he's going to be invading mine soon.

Checking for the absence of approaching bootsteps, she grabbed hold of the patch of velvet and pulled it out. Her blood froze as she beheld the small object in her hands, as she realized what she'd just found. She'd never seen it before, but its significance was obvious. The world spun for a split second and blood hammered in her ears.

Intrusive thoughts popped up once again.

Gold. Sword. Graegg.

Gold.

She didn't have time to make sense of it as the doorknob turned. Gulping, she lunged for the bag she'd discarded in the corner and shoved the thing inside.

When Saul entered, she panicked, surged forward to overwhelm him with her mouth on his. He yelped, but melted into her soon enough, his embrace wrapping around her body. Quicker than she would've liked to admit, he had her gasping again.

His hands slipped underneath her top, teased up her sides, undid her chest wrappings with practiced ease, and then his palms were squeezing, his calloused fingertips tormenting vulnerable flesh until she rolled her head back and let out a treasonous whimper.

Feeling heat singe her every nerve, she pulled away, pressing her palms flat against his chest. She pushed until his back met the wall. He bit down on her bottom lip, undressed her with determined efficiency.

When she was finally, *finally*, bare before him, his hand reached down to the juncture of her thighs, and she had to hold onto him for dear life as her legs nearly gave out. She was panting, writhing, digging her nails into his shoulders.

"Why are you still wearing so many clothes?" she gasped.

With quivering hands, she gripped his shirt and yanked. Buttons scattered across the floor as she ripped the material off him, all the while planting messy kisses against his jaw. She fumbled with the zipper on his pants and pulled his hand away from her so she could concentrate. When she'd eventually flung the breeches to the side of the room, she reached out with eager hands to touch him. But she didn't get the chance.

In one swift move, he flipped their positions. She now had the front of her body pressed against the wall, the cold raising goose bumps on her skin. His hands gripped her hips hard and he pulled her backside against him. He rolled his hips once, twice in a maddening bid to taunt her.

"Saul." Her voice was breaking, but she didn't care anymore.

"Say it," he groaned.

She knew what he wanted, knew what probably got Lorde Knoxin off. "Saul…"

His breath danced over the shell of her ear and she whined. "Say it, Thenos."

"Please, my lorde."

That would do it. When he finally entered her with one powerful thrust, she could do nothing but tip her head back and succumb. He was as good a lover as he was a fighter—kissing, biting, stroking strategically, and setting her on fire in ways she hadn't known were possible. He was almost mechanical in his movements, relentless and unwavering. Yet, as his own pleasure started to overwhelm him, his composure faltered.

His lips were sloppy against her shoulder, his onslaught erratic. He pressed a whispered curse against her hair. And when he snapped, Staella thought she had never felt anything as satisfying as Saul Knoxin losing control.

She was sore the next morning, had bruise marks on her sides and purple blotches across her neck and back. She dressed, left the barracks before the guards woke up. Stopped at Madam Eve's medicinal stall for a contraceptive tonic. She downed it and bought extra. Headed back to the Aesher mansion.

CHAPTER NINE

STAELLA STEPPED INTO THE MANSION to find Markham sitting on the main staircase, hair standing up into a hundred different directions, jaw taut. She cocked an eyebrow at him.

"What's going on with you?"

He looked up at her, eyes slow with exhaustion. "Where were you last night?"

Scowling, she crossed her arms over her chest. "I needed some time away. I informed Amile that I wouldn't be here."

His fists clenched where they rested on his knees. "You don't work for Amile. You work for me."

The words hit harder than they should have, made her feel ridiculous for the way her stomach always seemed to flutter when he came close enough. Swallowing down that unwelcome flood of emotion, she asked, "What is your point?"

He shook his head, clearly fighting the urge to raise his voice. "Where were you?"

She hated the fact that guilt swirled in her chest. *You have nothing to be ashamed of.*

She met his gaze head-on, lacing her voice with venom. "I suppose that since I work for you, I'm obligated to answer that. I went to my old hunting grounds and then I spent time with Saul."

Markham started at that, forcibly having to keep his body seated as surprise flooded his features. "All night?"

She knew the implication of the question and didn't care. "Yes."

He exhaled shakily, rubbing a palm across his face. "Well, I'm glad you had fun. But, while you were out galivanting, there was no one here to do your job. Anything could've happened last night. Someone could've broken in, stolen everything, murdered us in our sleep, and you'd be none the wiser. We were left vulnerable while you were out entertaining Saul Knoxin all night."

Every scrap of emotion in her turned to rage. She stepped closer to him, pointed a finger at his face. "Don't you dare. I may work for you, but I am not your slave, and you have no right to tell me what I can and cannot do with my life. I told Amile I wouldn't be here. I doubled the guards on perimeter duty and checked every inch of this estate before I left.

"And you know what? I am so tired of your seesaw act. You tell me to be comfortable around you, to open up and allow you in, and then you turn around and treat me like a servant. I'm done. The whole time I've been here I've felt like five different people living in the same body, but I'm done. From now on, I'm just going to be whoever the fuck I want and if you don't like that, you can fire me. I don't care."

He opened his mouth to retort, but she didn't give him the chance. Stepping past him, she marched up the stairs and slammed her bedroom door behind her.

†

"I'm sorry, Leda. She just isn't fit for company today… She's been getting worse and I can't figure out why. It's like something is gnawing at her."

Veress gripped Leda's hands in her own, her brows furrowing as she barred the entrance to Audrey Hayvinger's room.

Leda's eyes stung with unshed tears, but she nodded. "I understand. Thank you, Veress."

She turned with a sigh and started back down the corridor. The nurse stopped her, hand clasping around her arm. "Are you… Are you alright? You look like you're carrying the weight of the world on your shoulders."

Her mouth automatically opened with a lie, but the compassion in Veress's eyes made her hesitate. "I just really needed a hug from my mom today. And not the woman sitting in that room… my mom. The woman who raised me, who always knew how to make everything better."

Those tears sprang free and a soft sob broke from her. Veress's arms were around her instantly, one hand rubbing her back as the other stroked her hair. "Oh, Leda. Did something happen? What is it?" Her voice was so gentle, warm with a wisdom beyond her thirty-one years.

Leda shook her head, burying her face in the woman's neck. "Nothing happened, I just… I feel like I'm slowly drowning, like something is sucking me down and soon I won't be able to breathe." The tears were a steady stream now, spilling from a deep well of anger, desire, and despondence. Embarrassed at the spectacle she was making of herself, she sniffed and pulled away to dab at her wet cheeks with her sleeve.

"Mighiel may be right. I'm pathetic. Look at me. I have nothing to complain about. I come from the greatest family in Aldahad. I have everything I could ever need. I get to run in the Election. The people in the Rooks are fighting for everything I have. Yet here I am, a crying mess, an ungrateful little rich girl."

Veress sighed. "Leda, that's not true. Your life hasn't been moonshine and haletayls. Honestly, it's absurd that anyone your age would have to carry the burdens you do."

Leda snorted and turned her head away. "I keep hearing that I'm the spitting image of Lowena. Looks like the similarity ends there. She created this Election and I can't even handle being in it."

A long silence followed before Veress murmured, "Maybe you're not as different as you think…" The woman paused, seemingly arguing with herself. Finally, she breathed, "She didn't like the system she was in. So, she changed it."

Leda froze, heart knocking at her ribcage in a strange rhythm. "Veress, what—?"

"I was looking through your mother's old things last week, trying to find anything that might bring her comfort…" Her voice was so low that Leda had to lean in to hear. "I didn't find what I was looking for, but I did find something that might be able to help you."

"What? What did you find?"

The nurse hesitated one more time before spinning around and motioning for Leda to follow. They headed for the locked door next to her mother's room. It was a storage chamber with all of Audrey's things, filled to the brim with memories of a past life. Leda had spent hours in the room as a child, had rubbed her cheek against old ball gowns to burn her mother's scent into her mind. She remembered holding the leather of a saddle between her fingertips, recalling her mother's laughing face whenever she rode her tan steed.

Her favorite item was the painting mounted against the left wall, a portrait of an adolescent girl with sun-kissed skin and blue eyes gleaming with adventure. She had still been Audrey Espara then, the wildling of the Crest. Leda had heard stories of that girl, heard that she snuck out of dinner parties to go skinny dipping in the Roccalee, had gone dancing in the saloons on the western side of the Plateau.

As a girl, Leda had always wondered why someone like that chose to marry Honiel Hayvinger, who had tried to snuff out her silliness with conceited efficiency.

Twenty-two-year-old Leda understood. She hadn't chosen it; it had been decided for her. Because he is a Hayvinger. Because nothing matters as much as status. Because the Esparas gaining power meant more than whether their daughter was married to a decent man or not.

But Audrey never stopped being wild, never stopped laughing with every part of her body or living life like something extraordinary was always on the horizon. That is, until she'd snapped. Until her mind became her oasis and then her cage.

Maybe it was because of him.

She thanked the Goddess for Markham Aesher.

Veress produced a key from the breast pocket of her dress and unlocked the door. The curtains were drawn, and the room was dark, but Leda could still make out the familiar silhouettes of her mother's things. She coughed as the stench of trapped air hit her. She swatted at the air to dispel the dust.

The other woman hurried over to the far side of the chamber and set aside a jewelry case to dig into a wooden chest. After a few seconds of fumbling and exasperated whispers, she jumped up. There was a journal clutched in her hands, its cover thin and supple, the pages brown and the spine coming apart.

Veress beamed, nearly leaping to hold out the book to her. Leda scowled. "My mother's journal? Thank you, but I don't..."

"It's not your mother's," she interjected, eyes simmering with excitement.

No…

Leda's heart stopped, fluttered into her throat. She huffed, shaking her head. "Veress, you're kidding."

She shook her head. "I'm really not. I was just as surprised when I found it."

Leda took the journal with trembling hands, a dumbfounded grin splitting her face. "You're telling me that this is Lowena Hayvinger's diary? *The* Lowena Hayvinger?"

The nurse nodded. "I read some of it and I think you'll find it quite inspiring."

She giggled, running her fingers over the rough leather of the cover. "Goddess… I could kiss you right now… This is amazing. Thank you."

Veress chuckled and shrugged. "Don't thank me. She's your however-many-greats grandmother."

Leda shook her head once more, dumbfounded. She clutched the diary to her chest, knowing that it was quite probably the most precious thing she'd ever held.

†

I hate men.

Okay, no. I don't hate men. Avery is probably the only thing keeping me sane in the asylum that is the Rooks.

You know, as individuals they can have great potential. Avery, obviously, is the Goddess' gift to womankind. And my father can be quite decent when he wants to be. What I hate is masculinity. That infuriating arrogance of maleness they strive for and that makes them believe nonsense about the "delicate sensibilities" of women.

What a load of crap. Our household would fall apart if my mother suddenly decided that her sensibilities are a bit too delicate for all the work she does. Plus, I'd wager Aldahad wouldn't be in its current mess if the Salingzers allowed their girls to rule too. Maybe then the kingdom wouldn't be stuck with Ankav the Asinine, and its people wouldn't be suffocating under tyranny.

But here we are with no money and no voice. Crowded and unwanted like stowaway rats on a boat. Because if you're not born a royal or a groveling courtier, no one gives a shit about you.

The Resistance leaders met at our house again tonight, my father gathering them around the kitchen table. They discussed King Ankav's new Regulations and what they should do about it, but not before my father ordered me and my mother to go to the bedroom and shut the door. These were not things for women's ears. Of course not. Goddess forbid one of us should faint.

It's not like the Resistance doesn't concern women. It's not like it doesn't concern me.

I, too, live in a criminal-infested pit in a shack that can barely be called that. I bet the men around that table aren't groped by guards in royal uniforms under the pretense of a weapon search. I'm kept away from good doctors, good food, clean water, a good night's sleep, by a select few who look down on me like I'm vermin. My home is turned upside down by military searches.

I am also marked. The red seal on my arm traps me too, making it impossible for me to leave this dump unless I'm traveling to one of the other slums, where the odds of survival are even worse.

Because I was born a peasant, I am doomed to this life. Because I was born a woman, I'm not allowed to talk about change.

I make good points, right? Well, when I tried to argue this with my father, he gave me The Look. The Look could probably tame wild animals, make storms decide to blow the other way. I am a fearless rebel, but I am reduced to a quivering toddler in the face of The Look.

Mister Mandar. Mister Haxton. Mister Rehon. And my father, the stoic and upstanding Mister Hayvinger. They were deliberating around the table while I sat with my ear pressed against the bedroom door, listening. My mother didn't bother to reprimand me. It wouldn't help. We would just get into an argument and she knows that an argument is something I very rarely lose when The Look isn't there to shut me up.

King Ankav is instituting more regulations on the lower classes: curfews, higher tax rates, lower conscription age. They'd heard this from one of their sources: Mister Mandar's daughter who works as a maid in the palace.

These added regulations will kill us. We're dying. I know I sound melodramatic, but it's true. So many of us are dying... Something must be done.

The King will make the announcement in four months, on the palace balcony, and notices will be sent out to all the towns in Aldahad. This is the perfect opportunity for the Resistance to finally make a move. They could finally do more than talk and resist their own bravery.

But, no. Once again, they won't. Because it's not safe.

Since when is offering resistance supposed to be safe? We're getting nowhere by hiding women in bedrooms and closing our eyes to violence. What security is there in our daily lives anyway? We need to stop cowering in our little dens and fight. Damn it! Get your hands dirty. Grow a spine. Do something.

I'll do it.

Shit.

I can do it. I can do it.

This little girl too fragile to listen to the men talk. I'll create my own movement. Not the Resistance that sits in hovels to deliberate their lives away. No, mine will actually make a difference. We'll actively resist our oppression. We'll make the King tremble in his stone castle.

I'm going to do it. I'll assemble everyone who's tired of sitting around as our lives are destroyed. I have four months. I can do this. And I promise that, come the day when King Ankav makes his announcement, the status quo will crumble.

This was the first entry in Lowena's diary. It was as if she'd known that night would be the start of an extraordinary journey.

Leda's eyes roved over the pages, consuming her ancestor's words. She'd heard the bare bones of the story before, but this was something else.

Lowena had bought a cheap mask from a gypsy trader the following day, a distorted likeness of a demon that protected her anonymity and her life as she spread the news of a new organization, one that would attain retribution and transformation. The first meeting would be in the basement of the Colton family bakery. The word had spread like wildfire and dozens showed. Hundreds had been at the next meeting. Thousands at the gatherings that followed. She'd recruited them all, her vexation resonating with those who bore the red seal of the lower class. She'd swept them up into a frenzy, this demon-masked woman with her big plans and her intelligent words. Until her hordes had been ready to take a stand and damn the consequences.

Conscripted soldiers had joined, trained the others, and created an army fighting for freedom. All the while she'd dodged suspicious guards like it was nothing.

On the day of the King's announcement, her promise rang true. The Red Seals had come marching over the open plane of the Plateau, fists raised and faces painted to match their leader's mask. Lowena had been at the front, a banner carried behind her:

FOR SILENCING US. FOR DEHUMANIZING US. FOR DAMNING US.
WE ARE COMING FOR YOU.
WE ARE COMING.
RUN.

Then, the soldiers had come, hacking into the unarmed crowd until hundreds of bodies became carrion for the circling vultures to consume. Lowena had escaped, but she'd come out slightly broken, suffering from nightmares and anxiety attacks that failed to leave her even in Avery Colton's arms.

Only days after the ordeal had it come to the attention of the royals that they'd distributed Red Seal flyers all over the country instead of the King's notices. So, the Red Seals had taken over every slum in the kingdom, deputies doing Lowena's work where she was absent. They'd sabotaged emissary missions, destroyed luxury theater buildings reserved for the rich, and stole from the ridiculous fortunes of the high lords to redistribute wealth…

And the King had truly started to tremble in his stone castle.

CHAPTER TEN

THE EARLY HOUR HAD NOT ALLOWED the heat to set in yet, but Markham's hands were sweaty, nonetheless. The books felt particularly heavy in his arms and his heart was beating just a little bit faster than usual.

It was Yul, the Day of the Goddess—a day for exchanging presents and spending time with family. It was also the official shift of the seasons. Though the breezes had started to cool, the change was almost imperceptible and Yaekós remained Aldahad's hottest city.

Markham took a last emboldening breath before knocking on the door with the tip of his boot, making sure to smile over the pile of novels he cradled.

"Coming," she chirped from inside the room.

There was no sleepy grumbling, of course. Knowing her, she'd probably already run a lap around the estate. However, when Staella opened the door, she was still in her emerald nightgown, silk and lace clinging to her body in a way that had him hiding a gulp. He kept his eyes on her face, noticed how it fell when she saw him. His stomach dropped at that. *Maybe this is a bad idea.*

Her arms immediately crossed over her chest. "Have I neglected one of my duties, my lad?"

He chuckled nervously, tried to keep his expression as charming as possible. "No, no. Everything is up to your usual immaculate standards. Thank you." Goddess, even his ability to produce compliments had gone.

"Then why are you here?"

"I come bearing gifts." She eyed the books, her cocked eyebrow unamused, but she stepped aside to let him in. The room was pristinely neat, save for the unmade bed she went to sit down on. He deposited the books next to her, pulled a chair closer, and cleared his throat. "These are for you… For Yul."

She scowled. "Yul presents are for family."

This was definitely a bad idea.

"Yes, but since your family is in Avetown and you're here, I wanted to give you something so you would at least get… something." Perhaps it was wishful thinking, but he saw her dark eyes soften slightly. She still hadn't touched the books. "Go on, look."

His stomach tightened as she leaned over to examine each of the three titles. His teeth were sawing at his bottom lip, his heartbeat erratic.

"These are all of Aurellis' novels." She reached out to caress the covers and he couldn't help but crave the gentleness of that touch.

He nodded eagerly. "Yes. You mentioned that they were your favorites, right?"

When she flipped them open and beheld the first pages, her eyes widened, and she looked up at him in ecstatic disbelief. "These are signed first editions."

His fingers clutched at the chair's arm rests as he said, "Look at the bottom of the page."

He knew what she would find there—the thing that had made him so anxious to present her with the books. It was printed in a font so small it was barely noticeable: COPYRIGHT - MA.

She was silent for a few agonizing seconds, slowly meeting his gaze and with a gaped mouth. "You're Aurellis." He nodded. "But these novels, they're—they're about adventure and liberation and revolution."

He laughed at her tone. "You don't have to sound so surprised."

She shook her head, burying her face in her hands. When she surfaced again, she was red-cheeked and beaming.

"Markham, this is amazing. You're amazing. These books…" She huffed and grinned even wider. The fist clutching his gut finally released and he gave her a genuine smile. "Why do you use another name?"

He shrugged, shoulders light with the divulgence of a long-kept secret. "When I'm not Lad Aesher, I don't have to censor my words. Plus, the first two books are terrible. I wouldn't want anyone associating them with me." She giggled at that and he couldn't help but chuckle along.

But then her smile disappeared. She cleared her throat, straightened. "I appreciate the gift, but it doesn't change what I said yesterday."

"No, of course not. However, I'm hoping that an apology will." He clasped his hands together and extended them towards her in a pleading gesture. "I was an absolute prick and I know that. I was worried because I didn't know where you were, but I was also just being a possessive asshole…

"And I realize that I've been quite ambivalent in my treatment of you and I'd like to clarify my behavior. Staella, you do work for me. We have a professional relationship, and in that regard, there are certain roles we must play. But we are also twenty and twenty-one years old and get along quite well when we forget about all of that official stuff. There are so many things in which we are alike, in which we are equal, that there is no reason you cannot be my protector and my friend. My outburst yesterday was uncalled for and I'm sorry for that, but there will be times when I cannot share all the information with you, when I won't be able to explain my abrupt change from twenty-one-year-old to Representative. There are powers at work, decisions I have to make, that you cannot understand at this point. Just know that any harsh orders I may give does not mean that I do not value you as a person. So, will you please be my friend, Staella?"

She was looking down at the bed, nails picking at a loose thread on the quilt. When she finally lifted her head, she rolled her eyes and sighed. "Alright. Since you're asking so nicely." Then she pointed a vicious index finger at him. "But if you ever treat me like you did yesterday again, I'm going to kick your ass."

"Agreed."

"Thank you for the books and for trusting me with your secret. I'm sorry that I didn't get you anything."

"The friendship of the lady is more than sufficient. Now, you need to get dressed because we have a Choosing to attend."

She grimaced. "I've never been to one before. I don't really know what to expect."

"It's quite simple, really: wear white and brace yourself for the weirdest hour of your life."

"Weirder than all the crap that's already happened?"

"Oh, you're in for quite a morning."

†

The Temple of the Goddess at the peak of Goldvinger Crest was a magnificent building from the outside–a single triangular tower cast green. Staella wasn't religious per se, but every time she looked at the temple, a part of her believed that the Goddess existed there. That part only grew when they went inside.

The windows were various shades of stained glass, each depicting the same image of the Goddess with the world map on her dress and stars in her eyes. The light shining through dyed the marble pews orange and green and purple and blue. It was stunning. Ethereal. The aisle was made of thick glass, translucent to show the stream of water flowing underneath, water so azure in color that Staella found herself staring.

Her father had told her stories of the magical creatures that had roamed their world millennia ago. He had told her of the last traces of magic that lived on in the haletayl trees that bloomed at all times except when the moon was full. In this moment, Staella could believe that magic had rather been preserved in this tower.

On the back wall, the painted eyes of the Goddess beheld all who entered—one giant orb blue and the other green. Under those eyes stood twelve thrones, each engraved with a symbol of the Goddess: the sword, the outstretched hand, the crown… A few paces in front of that semi-circle of thrones was a stone cathedra that would have towered above Amile.

People had started to file in, not nearly as captivated by the space as she. The balconies of the second and third floors were flooded by Plateau citizens, easily identifiable by their choice of clothing and the way they leaned over the railings to have a look at the nobles below.

Markham placed a hand on her back, leading her to the second row from behind. Sitting down, she opened her mouth to comment on the lack of lower-class attendees. However, she found that his eyes were closed, his brows furrowed earnestly, and his palms pressed against his chest. He was praying.

When he looked up after a few minutes, Staella frowned. "You're religious?"

"Yes."

She shook her head. "But I've never seen you go to a service."

"I have a more personal view of religion. I don't have a problem with anyone who finds comfort in the congregation, but to me it's hypocrisy and politics dressed as a divine mandate."

Staella blinked. "Wow."

The corner of his lips tugged upward. "First, you're shocked to find out I write about liberation and now you struggle to believe that I have a strong opinion on religion. I'm starting to think you thought I was some airhead, pretty boy lounging around on my father's fortune."

She chuckled, ashamed of herself for having believed just that. "Well, it's only the airhead rumor that's been debunked. So, let's not get ahead of ourselves."

He threw his head back with his laugh, a habit she'd gotten used to and come to find rather endearing. "At least you think I'm pretty."

She stuck her tongue out at him and looked away to hide the grin that was consuming her face.

Leda, Honiel, and Mighiel sat in the third row. A chunk of the left block hosted the Qarvettes and the Vardans, with the exception of Zandi, who wasn't anywhere to be seen. Chrisjon, Eran, and Asha Caneille were right at the front, looking tired and despondent. Aedon was sitting alone. Despite what she'd heard of him, his solitude evoked her pity. *Markham would've suffered the same fate if you weren't here.*

"Where's Amile, by the way?" she whispered.

"He and Maci went to visit his parents in Harreen for the day. They left right after she handed Aedon his present. As usual, he just had a casket of wine sent to the palace by carriage."

Staella cocked an eyebrow. "Wait. He took Maci to visit his parents on Yul? Does that mean that they…?"

He raised his palms to the sky. "I don't think even they know. I've learned not to ask."

Dhun! Duh duh. Dun!

A drum had started beating, an ominous rhythm shuddering through the floors, and it reverberated through the chambers of Staella's heart. A violin joined in with whining notes that pulled at the hairs on her arms, making them stand to attention. She shivered.

Twelve emerald-robed priests entered from a side door, hoods obscuring their faces as they took to their thrones. Following them was Lorde Malano in a loose-fitting white dress, her feet bare and her hair framing her face in a blonde mane.

Staella sat a bit closer to Markham. "How does this actually work. How does the Goddess choose her Lorde?"

"She doesn't."

"What?"

"The decision is political. The Lorde is always an influential Representative. If you ask me, they pick a target way before the Choosing and the rest is smoke and mirrors."

"Well, you're awfully optimistic about the whole thing."

When his eyes met hers, they were darker than usual. "Staella, the priests effectively have the power to exclude a candidate from the Election."

It was only then that she noticed the tense set of his shoulders, the way his jaw clenched every few seconds. He was nervous.

Lorde Malano stepped up behind the cathedra. "Welcome, my brothers and sisters to this extraordinary service. Today, we have the privilege of witnessing the Goddess anoint Her new Lorde. It has been an honor to serve Her for the past decade, but now it is time for the blessing to be passed on to another. Let us begin."

Staella held her breath. Aenette Malano turned to face the back wall, extending her arms to those mammoth eyes… Nothing happened.

Silence. Staella frowned and turned to Markham.

Before she could say a word, a screech ripped out of the Lorde of the Goddess. Her arms extended above her head, her back curved in a painful arch. She fell to the floor, kneeling with her hands in front of her and her hair hiding her face. She roared, howled, twitched, stilled and began to chant in a melodic, forgotten language. The beating of the drums intensified, the violin screamed.

Slowly, she rose to a standing position. She turned to face the congregation and Staella gasped. There were bloody gashes down each of her cheeks and her eyes had lost all emotion. Trembles ran like shock waves down her arms and into her fingers. She stepped down from the dais and prowled down the aisle. The water from below tinted her pale skin blue and Staella found herself holding her breath.

She gulped, wrapped a hand around Markham's arm, and whispered, "I didn't know that the Goddess possessed people."

She could feel him roll his eyes. "It's more of a thing to believe than to know."

The Lorde continued, heading back. Her chanting grew louder. Louder. Markham sucked in a nervous breath as she approached their row and let it go again as she continued past. She continued until she froze at the last pew.

Her head jerked to the side with inhuman speed and when she spoke her voice was deep, laced with authority, and not her own. "Zandi of the line Qarvette, I choose you to be My voice among the people. Zandi of the line Qarvette, I choose…"

Staella twisted in her seat to see the youngest Qarvette paralyzed in her seat, lips gaping and skin even more pale than usual. After a few more repeated proclamations, Malano convulsed and clamped her hands into fists. Then, she returned to herself. Rising calmly, the bleeding woman took Zandi's hand and dragged her to the cathedra. The girl followed with the dazed, surreal movements of a wisp, her expression utterly stunned and her raven hair escaping from its knot. As one, those gathered in the Temple sank to their knees before her.

Amile's sister gulped, staring at them with big blue eyes. Staella realized that her upturned nose and the pronounced cupid's bow of her upper lip made her seem much younger than her twenty-one years.

She looked so frail up there, but her voice was steady when she spoke, "People of Aldahad, I am honored to serve you and my Goddess."

Behind her, the twelve priests rose in tandem, shuffling forward to place their hands on her. They bowed their heads, exclaimed, "All hail Lorde Qarvette. All hail the Goddess."

Staella found herself speaking the words along with the rest of the crowd. "All hail Lorde Qarvette. All hail the Goddess."

Zandi straightened, lifted her head, and managed to transform from a shivering lamb to a woman worthy of worship, a woman who hailed from the ruling family and whose position of power was now secured.

Perhaps, for her, exclusion from the Election had been a form of salvation.

Stepping outside the Temple, Markham was pulled aside by Caran Minyaka, who Staella had learned was his maternal cousin. Still in a daze, Staella meandered down the main pathway, staring at the lawns as she tried to wrap her head around what she'd just witnessed.

A tug on her arm made her spin, blinking up at Saul Knoxin. He wasn't in uniform, his hair tugged back and his white shirt tight in all the right places. She hadn't seen him since…

Two nights ago.

She gulped, smiled. "Hey. Hi."

His face tilted into that devilish grin and the memory of his voice in her ear, gravelly and demanding, invaded her mind and sent a shiver down her spine. "Morning, Thenos. I'm glad to see that you can still manage walking this morning."

Her cheeks flushed beetroot before she succumbed to a fit of laughter. "Oh please, don't flatter yourself, my lorde."

He rolled his eyes, trailing a finger up her arm in an uncharacteristically gentle caress. "You'll have to give me another chance to prove my worth, then."

"Uh, I—I'll have to see how I feel at the time."

"I suppose that's fair enough. As delightful as the prospect is, it will have to wait a bit. I'm heading to Saribi for four days to celebrate the holidays with my family. So, you'll have to entertain yourself for a while."

She stepped closer and lowered her voice. "Oh, I have a very vivid idea of how I can entertain myself… All alone. Thinking of you. Wishing you were—"

A throat was cleared loudly behind them. Staella yelped and jumped backward to find Markham a few feet away. The muscles in his jaw were tense and she had to bite the inside of her cheek and look away. He extended a hand, which Saul clasped immediately. They held on for a few seconds, eyes locked and arms straining. Their knuckles whitened. Teeth were grinded. Finally, Saul pulled back. Markham smirked like a cat, making sure she saw.

For Goddess' sake, boys, you're both pretty.

"Lorde Knoxin."

"Lad Aesher."

"I'm terribly sorry, but I need to steal my protector. We have another appointment."

It was Saul's jaw that clenched this time. "Of course, my lad." Then, with the obvious movements of a stage performer, he leaned over to Staella. She turned her face, had her cheek receive the kiss, and patted his head. He wasn't going to claim her to prove a point. "I'll see you in four days."

As Lorde Knoxin walked away, she heard Markham chuckling softly at her side. "Oh, Staella, please never change."

She jabbed an elbow into his side. "Shut up. So, what's this appointment we have?"

"A very important guest is coming for lunch."

"Who?"

He flashed her a boyish smile. "My father."

CHAPTER ELEVEN

My father came to me tonight. He entered the Demon's office in the Coltons' basement alone, the other resistance leaders waiting by the door. It was a strange feeling, having him approach me as an equal, maybe even a superior. But I must admit that it was indulgently satisfying knowing that I had beaten him at his own game, that the fragile little girl he kept behind closed doors now rules Aldahad's slums.

It was also nerve-wracking to see him coming to me without a trace of The Look in his eyes. It's terrifying to see a fiercely independent man who's taken care of me all my life trusting me to decide the fate of our people.

Of course, he didn't know that it was me. He came to offer allegiance and intelligence to the Demon and it was the Demon who accepted. So, I didn't remove my mask when he sat down to pledge fealty to me and my Red Seals.

But stubborn old me still needed affirmation and satisfaction. He made his way to the door, but I stopped him before he could leave, and I took off the mask.

I wanted him to see the truth. I wanted him to know that his daughter is stronger and more cunning than he imagined.

Now, I'll never be able to forget his face when he saw me standing there. In fact, it's vivid in my mind even as I write. It doesn't make me feel like a conqueror. It makes my blood run cold.

His eyes were twice their usual size and his face drained of color. He whispered my name, then bellowed it. He exploded, raging about the risks. He didn't stop talking about danger, filling my head with all the disastrous ways this rebellion could end.

Every word chipped away at me, made me shrink. The Demon disappeared and it was just me, an adolescent girl being scolded by her father.

He gave me The Look and he ordered me to abandon my childish dreams of changing the world, begged me to keep out of the King's way before it cost me my life.

I was beaten down until nothing could be chipped away anymore.

Then, I snapped.

It wasn't the Demon that stood up to him. It was Lowena Hayvinger, with her unfailing perseverance, who stared The Look right in the face and didn't back down.

Maybe this will make me sound evil, but I'm proud to admit that my father didn't stand a chance.

He came to me to declare his loyalty to the movement I raised from the ground. He'd just come to me with pleading words and then dared to tell me to give up.

Well, I will not.

I understand that he is my father, that he wants to protect me. But I will not submit to him again. I have become too formidable a force for that. I created the Red Seals. I defied King Ankav and had thousands of peasants trained to become warriors in mere months. I would not let anyone else decide what I would do with my life and my rebels.

I was unyielding as I growled this at him, and I watched as The Look sputtered into oblivion. A candle trying to keep its flame alive during a hurricane.

Needless to say, the leaders of the former Resistance are now members of the Red Seals, their spies and their resources mine.

My father was silent when I finished, his lips pursed. He hasn't spoken to me since, and at home we move around each other like strangers. Mercifully, he didn't tell my mother.

So, yes, I achieved a long-awaited victory today, yet I feel far from victorious. In fact, I feel like I may be losing my mind, like my heart has decided to try and run away from my body. His warnings jump around in my mind and bounce off my skull. Waves of anxiety flood over me, stronger with every swell.

Those warnings. Predictions, really. Thrown into the dungeons. Tortured by the palace guards. Raped by the overseers. Put on display for the masses. Executed to destroy all hope. Dungeons. Tortured. Raped. Displayed. Executed. Tortured. Raped. Executed. And the Red Seals will probably suffer the same fate.

Executed. They've already been executed. I can still see them, their bodies left to rot on the Plateau after the massacre. Shit, I'm feeling like I can't breathe. Those lives... All of them were lost because of me. I led those people to their deaths.

I think I'm falling apart.

No. Goddess, Lowena, pull yourself together.

Pull yourself together.

I won't stop. It's going to be hard and I'm going to have panic attacks and people may get hurt and I may not make it... But I won't stop.

Not until we are treated like human beings. Not until the Salingzers are removed from the throne. Not until there is no throne at all.

Lowena had been a formidable leader; she had changed the world. But her father's warnings had turned out to be accurate predictions.

Despite her growing success, her identity had slipped from the lips of one of her father's men. She'd been hunted across the Monarchy and, even harbored in Arbada's slums, the King's guards had found her. They arrested her and took her to the dungeons below the Salingzer palace. It was there where her father's nightmares had all come true.

She had been tortured—whipped and sliced up and nearly drowned. She had been raped by the guards and Ankav's younger brother. She had been put on display in City Square and led in chains to the guillotine for her execution.

†

Howell Aesher sat in Markham's usual seat in the living room, one leg crossed over the other. Everything about him radiated leisure and class: his linen clothing, the sun-kissed glow of his skin. Though he looked at that moment to be the epitome of relaxation, Staella knew that he was ardently dedicated to his work, more so than to anything else. He was the richest man in Aldahad, the man who had eradicated the Silver Guild and who had never loved any woman other than his murdered wife.

She could tell that his hair had once been the tawny color of Markham's, but it was now streaked with silver, a perfect match for the salt-and-pepper stubble that accentuated his Aesher chin. His eyes were blue and not green, but the resemblance was uncanny.

He was speaking to a dark-haired servant girl whom Staella had seen plenty of times around the mansion. The teenager had frequently been great company on idle evenings. "My Goddess, Creanda, it feels like yesterday when you were running around the house with pigtails and bare feet. Now you're basically a woman. Tell me, how are Zella and the boys?"

Creanda's full lips parted in a smile and she tugged a strand of hair behind her ear shyly. "My mother and brothers are doing very well, sir."

"That's good to hear." The beam that took over his face was the most benevolent expression Staella had ever seen on a man's face. "And Vinn… Has he finished his studies yet?"

The girl nodded eagerly. "Yes, sir. He's a fully-fledged doctor now. Thinks he knows everything in the world. He thanks you for your contribution, of course. We all do."

"It's nothing. If it makes your family happy, I'm happy. Tell me, have—?"

He stopped speaking when Staella and Markham stepped forward to make their presence known. His piercing eyes shot up, fixing on Markham with such intensity that Creanda took her cue to scuttle out of the room.

Father and son were both moving towards each other instantly, like magnets pulled across the space. When they met, they crashed together. Howell wrapped up his son in his arms and Markham easily sank into the embrace, burying his face in the older man's neck.

"Dad."

That one word melted Staella's heart.

Howell kissed the top of his head. "Markham." He kept his hand on Markham's shoulder even when they pulled away from the hug. The Representative's eyes were silver with tears despite the ear-splitting grin on his face. "You've grown up so much in just a year. So much… You're not a child anymore."

Markham chuckled. "Well, at least not physically. I can't attest to my behavioral maturity."

"I can," Howell huffed. "I've been following the news reports. It seems you're doing particularly well in the Election. I hear my son might be High Ruler Aesher in less than two months."

"Things are looking good, but there's still a long way to go before I get to wear a crown."

His father squeezed his shoulder. "Nevertheless, I'm proud. The estate is well taken care of. I did notice some extravagant spending in the books, but it's nothing we can't manage. You sent the gifts this morning?"

He nodded. "The Minyakas and the Blomehills received their annual jewelry chests. I also took the liberty of buying Leda new riding gear."

"Already impressing the in-laws, I see." Howell winked, which left his son blushing and laughing sheepishly.

Markham Aesher sheepish and blushing. Here was a side to the Representative Staella hadn't seen before. The wide-eyed youth. The son awaiting approval. Suddenly it was so easy to see through his lazy grins and compliments to the raw truth of him. He was a boy—a likeable, motherless twenty-one-year-old with the weight of a household and a country on his golden shoulders. He was a boy who never caved under all that responsibility, who managed the largest estate in Aldahad and could very well win the Election. A boy who had gone beyond what was expected of him, who had developed liberal opinions and written revolutionary books.

She saw him anew. The sunlight through the lace curtains caught the honey in his hair, the soft lines of his smiling lips, and the deep-rooted compassion in his eyes. It was clear to her that Markham had ceased being a boy a long time ago.

She realized that she'd been staring when they turned to her, twin grins on handsome faces. "Dad, this is my lovely friend, Staella."

She blinked and shook Howell's extended hand. "It's a pleasure, Mister Aesher."

"The pleasure is all mine, Staella. Now, please, if a stunning young woman like you calls me 'mister,' I'm going to feel like I have one foot in the grave already."

Staella giggled, nodding. It was quite clear which side of the family carried the charm gene.

Lunch with Markham and Howell had been unexpectedly comfortable, the latter as eloquent and fascinating as his son. However, when it had been time to say goodbye, Staella had to avert her gaze to spare herself from the emotion in theirs. After his father's departure, Markham had been quiet and retired to his room. He remained there for hours.

It was the arrival of Maci and Amile later in the afternoon that tugged him from his melancholy state, his best friend in higher spirits than Staella had ever seen him. But when Maci left after dinner, both men once again retreated into solitude.

Staella felt Markham's absence in her gut and couldn't get that perception-altering image of him out of her head: the golden boy who had grown up too soon. It was seared into the back of her eyelids and kept her from sleep. The clock at the end of the corridor struck twelve. Staella sighed, turned onto her back, and stared at the darkness around her.

Come on. Just sleep.

She spun to her other side, wrestling with the sheets in annoyance. Scrunching her eyes shut, she forced her mind to clear. If she kept pretending to be asleep, it would surely become real soon.

But then it started: the screaming. The pained, otherworldly roar that echoed through the mansion each night at around this time.

Again. A distorted cry. An inhuman howl. The sound traced cold fingers down Staella's spine and hollowed out her bones, causing her stomach to clutch at itself. Yes, the screams came every night, but she had rarely been awake when they started. It was terrifying to face it with an undazed mind.

Another cry.

Then, just because the Goddess had it out for her, there was a deafening crack of thunder.

A demented screech.

Blue-white lightning.

Staella's blood played a rapid beat in her ears, her breath catching in her throat.

It's okay. Just breathe. Just go to sleep. Breathe. Sleep.

Nope.

Thunderstorms were scary enough without the added terror of roars coming from inside the house. She lunged out of bed, fingers trembling as she lit the candle on the nightstand and grabbed it.

She fled down the corridor, going as fast as she could without sprinting. Old ghost stories flooded her thoughts. Imaginary shadows nipped at her back and a bang of thunder had her yelping.

When she finally reached the last door in that endless hallway, she was unnerved and tingling right to the soles of her feet. Her knuckles assaulted the wood. A murmur sounded from inside the room and it opened.

Markham's hair was a crow's nest and his flimsy pajama top rode up to expose a strip of tanned torso. There were dark half-moons under his eyes, but the candles in his room were all still alight.

His gaze widened. "Staella? What are you, uh—?"

"Can I come in?" she blurted. "Please."

He nodded, still a little frazzled. "Yeah. Yeah, okay. Sure."

The sheer curtains were billowing in the draft from the open windows as the sky beyond the balcony lit up with veins of light.

She turned away from that view. "So, you're still up?"

He motioned at the desk in the left corner, its surface overflowing with notebooks and sheets of paper. "I was writing."

She drew a hand through her hair. "I'm sorry. I'm interrupting. If you need to write, I can leave." The hairs at the back of her neck rose at the mere suggestion.

"No, no. I wasn't getting anywhere, anyway. Do you, uh, want to take a seat?" He pointed her to one of the couches in the little living room. "Would you like something to drink? Unfortunately, I only have water, brandy, and ginger ale."

She sat down, placing her candle on the cupa table. She pulled her knees up to her chest. "Some brandy and ginger ale would be nice, thanks."

He frowned. "Together?"

"You've never had it?"

He pulled a face. "No, and I'm glad because it sounds disgusting."

She rolled her eyes at him, felt the knot in her stomach ease slightly. "Come on, I never took you as a coward. Just trust me and try it."

He grimaced apprehensively, but proceeded to mix two of the drinks. After handing her a tumbler, he scrunched his eyes shut, crinkled his nose, and dipped his tongue into the yellow-brown liquid.

He was silent for a few seconds, then opened his eyes and beamed at her. "That's amazing."

She chuckled, took a proper sip of her own drink. "See, I told you. Besides watered wine, this is all Avetown has to offer. Let me save you the experiment on the watered wine—it's awful."

"It sounds awful." He sank down next to her, leaning to the side to make eye contact. "So, to what do I owe this wonderfully surprising visit?"

She clenched her jaw, looked away. "I was… scared of the thunder." Another cry ripped through the walls and Staella gulped. "And of that."

He nodded, his lips a thin line. "It can be unnerving… I wish I could tell you all the secrets contained in this house, but know that you do not have to fear those screams, and even less so the storm. Look outside. It's stunning. Awe-inspiring... The authority in the sound of the thunder and the defiance of the darkness in every bolt. Lightning does not destroy; it enlightens."

Staella's snort pulled him from his awestruck stare. "You're such a writer. Just listen to you."

There was a confused half-smile on his face. "What? Why?"

She deepened her voice and clutched her hands to her chest dramatically. "'Lightning does not destroy; it enlightens.' Only the heroes in books talk like that."

His head dipped back in soft laughter, the lines of his neck bobbing and drawing her attention more than they had the right to. "What can I say? It's a gift. I have been told that every main character I've written has revealed some aspect of my personality. I don't know about that, but I do draw heavily on the people around me."

"Are you going to put me in one of your stories?" She wiggled her eyebrows at him.

"The snarky bodyguard with a criminal past. Hmmm, sounds a bit cliché."

She gasped, sticking out a foot to nudge him in the side. "Well, you seemed awfully eager to be friends with this cliché this morning."

"You make a compelling argument," he mused. "Well, if I am going to use you as inspiration, I need to know more about what makes Staella Thenos tick."

"Fine. You may interview me as your potential muse, but I need another drink first."

He cocked an eyebrow at the empty glass she held out to him. "Look who turned out to be an old drinker. I'll have to try to keep up." With that, he threw back the rest of his drink and poured two more. Flopping down on the couch, he said, "Right, Miss Thenos, question number one… Who is your favorite Representative in this year's Election?" He flashed her a daring grin.

She giggled and slapped his arm playfully. *Stop touching him every chance you get.* "I'd have to say Chrisjon Damhere for the jawline alone."

"Ah, yes. Haven't we all succumbed to the Damhere jaw at some point? Alright, I suppose it's time to dig deeper into the Crimson Jackal's past… So, why illegal cage fighting?"

The corner of her mouth tugged upward. "A couple of reasons, actually. Fighting is what I'm good at, and since the official authorities deemed women too fragile to be guards or soldiers, I had to take the less official route. Also, the farm wasn't doing great at the time. So, I guess I saw it as an opportunity to prove myself useful to my family."

"What made you decide to become good at fighting in the first place? Why train if there were no opportunities?"

Staella's teeth tugged at the inside of her lip and she shifted in her seat. "I wanted to be able to protect myself."

He raised an eyebrow. "That's a very noble answer, Staella, but I'm going to need a little more than that."

She looked away, remaining silent a moment too long. Could she do this? Open the rawest part of herself to the Representative next to her?

Sighing loudly through her nose, she glared at him. "Fine, but you'd better put me in a book for this." He mocked a salute and all she could see was that extraordinary boy she'd glimpsed that morning. "When my sister was three, my mother was walking back from work—she does the books at the butchery in town. She, uh, she took the shortcut past the old silos, as she did every night. But, this time, a man was lying in wait. She didn't know him or why he'd chosen her, but he…" Her breath shook and she felt the heat of Markham's palm on her knee. "He raped her. Right there in the field. No one lives near the silos, so there was no one there to help her, to hear her scream. It was only much later when my father went looking for her and found her half-naked and bloody.

"Apparently, she didn't talk or eat much for weeks after it happened. The people in town started to treat her differently. They saw her either as a pathetic victim or an unclean wife. I know those people. I know they would've whispered amongst themselves about how she shouldn't have taken that shortcut alone. As if any of it could ever be her fault. Some of them even started asking my dad why he didn't leave her. They coined her as a cheating wife, but he wouldn't have any of it. He stood by her and loved her until she became herself again, until she didn't have to take three baths a day just to feel clean. Until she smiled again and went back to work. In fact, she even found out she was pregnant a few weeks later…

"Then I came out looking just like her rapist. My eyes. My hair. My skin. Everything was his. And she hated me. To this day, she can barely stand to look at me. As a newborn, she tried to drown me in the bathtub. My dad, the one who raised me, saved me. I didn't understand her scorn when I was a child, but as I grew older, I came to understand that I'm nothing but a reminder of the worst experience of her life."

Tears were rolling down her cheeks. She sniffed, wiped them away quickly. "So, at thirteen, I decided that I wanted to be able to defend myself against anyone who might try to hurt me. I refuse to end up battered and violated in a field or be crucified by my so-called friends for a crime committed by a spineless animal. I refuse to have a child I hate so much that I want to drown them as a baby."

Her entire body shook. She downed the drink in her hand and focused on the way it made her mind swirl. "The tub incident is also why I learned to swim... so that water wouldn't terrify me anymore."

Markham's eyes were lined with silver when their gazes met. He wore a strange expression on his face as the candlelight flickered over it. "You're extraordinary," he breathed.

She huffed a laugh and sniffed once more. "Yeah, okay, Mister favorite-Representative-slash-famous-author."

He shook his head, scooted closer to squeeze her hand, only briefly before letting go. "I'm serious. You took every bad thing life threw at you and turned it into motivation to become better. To be as amazing as you are after only training at home..."

"I did have help. I only trained myself for about two years before a retired city guard took pity on me and showed me the ropes."

Markham nodded, eyes narrowing. "I think I know of a guard who left for Avetown around the time of Lorde Vikan's death. Bruhel?"

Staella beamed proudly. "Yeah. That's him. He is absolutely spectacular with a sword. Could still beat me with his eyes closed, I'd wager. He became somewhat like a grandfather over the years—a mentor and a friend."

When she looked up, Markham wasn't meeting her gaze, his stare fixed on the cupa table. The muscles in his jaw were twitching, working as he seemingly tried to figure out something.

Eventually, he cleared his throat and said, "Well, now that I have some background information, it's time for question three."

She cocked her eyebrows at him, huffing. Straightening, she turned to swing her legs up and into his lap. The fact that she had the courage to do so could only be blamed on the weightlessness of her head.

"Alright, Mister Aurellis, what deep, dark secret do you desire to know?"

Markham stretched over to the beverage tray and poured each of them another drink, much stronger this time. She could smell the alcohol and stuck her tongue out at the bitter taste, but took another sip anyway, savoring the warm sting that sailed down her throat.

He chuckled at her scrunched-up expression and draped an arm over her shins. "Well, in order to write you realistically, I need a sense of your aspirations, your dreams for the future. So, Staella, what is it that you want from this life?"

She opened her mouth, but found that no words were forthcoming. No answer leapt to mind. In fact, even as she wracked her brain, one continued to elude her.

She blinked at him and shook her head. "I don't know… I don't know what I want."

"There's something I've never heard a woman admit," he teased.

She ignored the remark. "Shit, I don't even know what I'm doing here, really. What I believe in anymore… Markham, what if I'm like this forever?" Her breath hitched and she curled her hands into fists. "What if I always let life happen to me? What if I never know where I fit in, what I want?"

A gentle hand rubbed her calf. "Hey, look at me." She did. She stared up at those green orbs like they were her only lifeline as her foundations seemed to slip away from under her. He smiled, so kindly it made her heart skip a beat. "You will find your purpose. I promise. You, *we*, are so young. There's still time. In fact, right now your only job should be soaking in everything around you. Just keep doing that, and one day something will stand out enough that you'll want to fight for it."

A giggle bubbled out of her, opening the floodgates to have her shaking with laughter. He frowned at her and she sighed. "Sorry, I just—I'm going to be the most depressing character ever."

He chuckled, hadn't stopped rubbing soothing circles into her leg. "Maybe I've just got a penchant for morose questions. I'll get a little liquid inspiration and we'll come up with something less morbid."

After three more gulps of a potent brandy-and-ginger-ale mix, Staella's head had detached from her body, floating. The world turned golden and endlessly amusing as the screams and the thunder faded to white noise.

Markham's face was flushed pink when he beamed at her. "I've got it." He raised his hand dramatically and Staella devolved into a fit of giggles. "What was your impression of me on that first day?"

She smirked at him. "Fishing for compliments, are we?"

He leaned a little closer, the vanilla and brandy smell of him making her head spin faster than it already was. "I'll take whatever the lady offers."

She bit her bottom lip, seeing the way his gaze followed the movement. Her toes curled at the hunger in those eyes. "Well, I thought you were more handsome than your likeness on the coins and that you looked like a good swimmer."

He snorted, nearly choking on his drink before his head lulled back in ecstatic laughter. "Swimmer? I'm a horrible swimmer."

She shrugged. "It's not my fault you have those shoulders." She cleared her throat, had to look away from him. "So, what did you think of me?"

His cheeks tinged red at that. "To be quite honest, I was admiring your backside most of the time."

She gasped, feigning offense with a hand to her chest. "Markham… If I were sober, I would chastise you."

He held out his palms in surrender. "I know, I know. But those pants are really tight."

Mischief bubbled through her as she took another sip of her drink. "Then, I might as well admit that I was doing the same to you."

The Representative sitting with her legs in his lap extended a golden hand. She found fondness in every line of his face. "Dance with me."

She scowled. "Not to be pedantic, but there's no music."

He flipped her legs to the floor and pulled her up into a standing position before she knew what was happening. "I'll sing."

When he opened his mouth, a bouncing, merry melody that she recognized from the ball came out. No lyrics, just Markham impersonating various instruments. His voice was horrible, a breaking, off-tune mess in stark contrast to his excellent dancing.

Staella was swung around the living area with grace, his feet never faltering and his arms steady around her. They were pressed together, their intoxicated state finally allowing them to attain that desired closeness. She marveled at the way he managed to be strong and soft at the same time, hard and warm and stunning.

Her jagged, high-pitched vibrato joined in and his laughter consumed him so fiercely that he tripped over a cupa table leg. They were both sent toppling to the floor, ending up flat on their backs in a heap of tangled limbs and trembling chuckles.

She propped herself up on her elbows and turned her head to look down at him, beaming with unrestricted happiness. His smile changed, became softer as his lips parted slightly. His hand reached out to trace a featherlight thumb over her cheekbone. "Staella, you're…" She waited for it, waited for the word "beautiful" to compliment the face of her mother's abuser. Instead, he whispered, "You're the kind of girl people write books about."

The breath left Staella's lungs. She became weightless, boundless, as she took in his words—his eyes, his hands, his skin, his mouth.

A series of knocks on the front door shattered through the world and Staella snapped out of her dreamy reverie.

She cleared her throat and jumped up into a standing position. "Something serious must have happened for someone to be knocking at three in the morning… and the guards deemed them friendly enough to let them get to the front door."

Markham's eyes were wide as he rose as well. "The screams. Staella, they cannot hear the screams. We have to meet them outside."

He hauled her out of the room, hand at the small of her back as she forced her feet to become steady despite her detached head. She nearly rolled down the stairs, but managed to maintain a sliver of dignity as she clutched at Markham. They passed through the foyer, out the door, and onto the front porch.

Waiting there, tight-lipped and pacing, was Enin Valanisk, Rayn's sixteen-year-old brother. He had the same, glowing black skin and wide-tipped nose, every bit as striking as his Representative sister. His cheekbones jutted out so sharply Staella was sure they would slice like steel.

There was an older girl next to him, with a pale heart-shaped face and a mane of orange curls. The panic-stricken look in the woman's turquoise eyes told Staella that she was more than just Rayn's friend. That horrified look was echoed in Enin's gaze and the haze was instantly cleared from Staella's mind. *This is bad.*

It was Markham who broke the terse silence. "Enin?"

The gangly boy was shaking as he exclaimed, "Rayn is gone." Staella's blood ran cold. "She's missing. She was in her room all afternoon. At least, that's what I thought. Then, Eilee came to see her, but she wasn't there. She never leaves without telling me and now she's gone. Our guards are scouring the western side of the city and we've been all over the Crest but no one knows where she is…" His breaths were too fast, his eyes flickering from side to side. "Was she…have you seen her?"

Markham shook his head, shoulders drooping. "No. Enin, no. I'm sorry."

"Have you alerted the city guards?" Staella asked desperately.

It was Eilee who answered, her voice sharp with contempt. "We went to the barracks first and found Deputy Caven in charge and all he could say was that he'd been instructed not to take any action regarding missing Representatives, that the task force will look into it tomorrow. Needless to say, we didn't leave it there."

Markham's jaw clenched. "So, the guards aren't going to help you at all?"

Staella clenched her fists at her side. "Saul and his bloody task force… I'll help you look for her. I'll grab my weapons and I won't rest tonight until I've found her."

Before Enin could reply, Markham said, "Yes. We'll comb every corner of Yaekós and we'll deploy our guards as well."

She spun, shook her head at him. "Oh, no. You are staying right here where it's safe. And half of the guards will remain to protect the estate. I'm not risking you on this."

His smile was gone and the giddy redness in his cheeks disappeared with it. "I'm not staying home like a shivering child while Rayn is out there somewhere. I've known her my whole life and I won't stand by idly while you look for her."

She crossed her arms over her chest, let out an exasperated sigh. "Markham, I'm your protector."

"I've done much more dangerous things in my life." He was immovable as a wall.

Eventually, she relented. "Fine. But you're taking your sword and you're staying with me." She tried not to roll her eyes at his answering salute.

A hand closed around her wrist. She looked to the side to find Enin staring at her with big eyes. "Thank you. The Valanisk line is in your debt, in the Aeshers' as well."

She smiled thinly, squeezing his hand, and then dashing inside to get ready.

†

"Markham, stop."

The Representative at Staella's side marched past where she'd come to a standstill in the middle of the paved road, jaw clenched as he headed for yet another door. He called Rayn's name again, though she knew he understood the futility.

"We've been down this street, Markham. She's not here. She's not… anywhere. I don't think we're going to find her."

His fist froze mid-air, halfway to the front door of the Plateau home. "Don't say that." His sigh was jagged, his eyes desperate when he said, "We have to find her. We have to. If I can find her, find out who took her, I can..." The rest of his words remained unspoken as he shook his head.

"You can what?"

What are you not telling me?

He clamped his lips together, waving a dismissive hand. "It doesn't matter… We haven't searched the Rooks yet. There's a good chance that she might be there." He started westward immediately, not looking to see whether she would follow.

She huffed, grabbed his arm, and spun him to face her. "Would you just stop and listen to yourself? The Rooks are dangerous—you were attacked there yourself. Besides, the Valanisk guards are already searching that area. We can scour the Crest again."

His hands clenched into fists at his side. "The Valanisk guards don't know the Rooks like I do."

She crossed her arms over her chest and lodged her tongue against the inside of her cheek. "Oh, is that so? How exactly is it,

Lad Aesher, that you came to know the Rooks so exceptionally well?"

His body went rigid, his mouth opening and closing in answerless silence. "I—I have friends there."

"Ah, yes. I've heard all about your *friends*."

His brows scrunched together at that, but the confusion soon gave way to frustration as he pinched the bridge of his nose between his thumb and forefinger.

"Look, we don't have time for this right now. Rayn is missing. It's imperative that we find her and discover what happened to her. She could be in the Rooks, an area both of us know well. So, I'm aware that it's not the safest place in the People's Monarchy, but I don't particularly care at this moment. I have my sword and I have my protector. So, we're going." He once again turned to the west and all she could do was bite her tongue and follow.

It took them just over twenty minutes to cross the rest of the Plateau and edge down the decline to the Western Rooks. Immediately, the difference was startling.

Uneven streets of gravel wound around haphazard dwellings that leaned against one another for support. Their roofs were jagged, made of the sturdiest material their inhabitants could find in the capital's slums, and barely offered a reprieve from the elements. Gutters overflowing with rancid waste hugged dark alleys and rats peeled from the gaps between shacks like pus from a festering wound. On nearly every street corner sat a too-thin figure under a threadbare blanket of paper or old clothes, knees pulled up to form a harsh pillow.

Staella remembered when she'd been one of those figures. It had been her first night in the city. She remembered the hunger, the fear, the dropping temperatures after sunset.

Then, she remembered her most recent encounter with these people, when she'd arrived with a horde of guards to take part in a massacre. She remembered the silhouettes of those fleeing the inferno, the plea in a girl's stare before she was knocked out by a shield, an old man's golden eyes and how close he'd come to death. She couldn't help but understand what they had been fighting for.

"It's amazing, isn't it?" Markham murmured at her side.

"What?"

"The way those who live in the Rooks manage to carry on, raise families, make a life despite their surroundings..." She realized that she hadn't noticed the flurry of wooden ornaments decorating a nearby shack, or the wire-wrought toys that laid outside waiting for daylight and squealing children. "They deserve better than this."

Staella opened her mouth to respond, but the reply came from behind her—a rasping, male voice. "We appreciate your concern, Lad Aesher, but I think we're doing alright."

By the time they'd managed to spin around, a Red Cloak had a dagger at Markham's throat, his accomplice trapping Staella with a sword tip pointed at her chest.

The latter assailant spoke again. "Imagine this. To run into you only two blocks from where we met last time. I was sure we'd killed you that night. Just think how disappointed I was to hear that the man who mutilated my hand was hunky-dory up in his ivory palace... But you've returned, and I must admit that I'm very glad to see you." The man's grin was fiendish, his orange hair splaying over his shoulders to blend into the red of his cape.

Markham grimaced, the blade at his throat digging into golden skin. "To be fair, you also stuck a knife between my ribs."

The ginger chuckled, low and cruel. "We're about to do much worse." He flashed a leer at Staella and leaned forward. "You're going to regret bringing your little girlfriend this time." Her eyes flashed to the hand holding that dagger to Markham's neck and then to the talkative one's sword, gauging the distance between her body and the lethal blade tip. "Why don't you put away the weapon you're clutching so tightly, sweetheart? We both know you wouldn't know what to do with it, anyway. It's not a parasol, dear."

The Red Cloak at Markham's back sniggered. Staella clenched her jaw, but obliged, loosening her grip on her sword's pommel. She unsheathed the blade, squatted down to place it on the ground.

Staying in her low position, eyes fixed on the attacker's shins, she said. "I apologize for the inconvenience this might cause, but Lad Aesher didn't bring his girlfriend…" Her hand closed around the small blade she kept tucked into her boot. "He brought his bodyguard."

The dagger flew from her fist with the flick of a wrist, found its mark in the center of the hand holding Markham captive. Not losing a second, she surged up, slamming her forearm into Ginger's hand and delighting at his gasp when his weapon clattered to the ground. Her leg kicked out, sweeping the man's feet from under him. He landed on the gravel with a grunt, flat on his back. She dove down to grab her own sword, then leapt up. But before she could take a step, Ginger's leg shot out. His heel connected with her kneecap and she cried out. Stumbled back, feeling the sting of tears at the back of her eyes.

Her attacker rose. Her knee screamed in agony as she placed weight on it to face him. A fist lashed out, aiming for her face. She ducked the blow. Stepped forward, ready to slash at his belly. Her knee buckled and she fell to the ground, groaning. Ginger kicked the weapon from her hand. She was unarmed and kneeling.

A white flash of pain surged through her as Ginger grabbed a fistful of her hair, nearly tearing it from her scalp. She clenched her hand around his wrist in a futile attempt to stop the torture.

He grinned, leaned down until their faces nearly met. "You're not a very good bodyguard, are you?"

She smirked at him. "Maybe not, but that just makes your fate even sadder."

"How's that?"

"Because that means you're about to be obliterated by a not-very-good bodyguard."

The hard bone below the palm of her free hand connected with the bottom of his nose. *Crack!* He roared and released her. His hands flew to the bridge of his now-broken nose, eyes watering. She rose, limping forward. Her elbow jabbed into his throat, making him gasp for air. Then, with a snarl, she closed her hands around his neck and dug her finger into a specific spot in the muscle. His eyes widened. *One, two…* He slumped in her grip, his body completely paralyzed. She dropped him onto the street. Hobbling, she picked up her sword and returned to his side, kneeling with a groan of pain.

His pupils were blown wide in fear, but she met that gaze with nothing but ruthless composure. "I bet you're wondering what I did to you. There are pressure points all over the body. A simple press and you'll find yourself unable to move. One of the few magic tricks still left in our world. It'll last about fifteen minutes. In the meantime, I'm going to be removing the fingers from your sword-fighting hand." A whimper echoed from behind his closed lips. "And because I don't want to kill you, I'm going to tie a scrap of your cloak around your arm, keep the limb above your head so you won't bleed out. You should clean it with alcohol and bind it. You should be just fine, but you might have to find another line of work." She went about her task quickly, efficiently, despite Ginger's suppressed screams. When she was done, she pressed her lips to his ear. "If you ever feel the need to become ambidextrous or find anyone stupid enough to exact your revenge for you, I will kill you."

Staella stood up, sheathed her sword, and spun to find Markham staring at her. Blood leaked from his split lip, spilled onto his chin. There was a deep slash on his left bicep and his knuckles were raw. She peeked behind him to find his Red Cloak unconscious, his body slumped against a wall.

She sighed shakily, her knee sending pulses of agony through her. "Must have been some prostitute you visited to get him that riled up."

"Prostitute?" He huffed, shaking his head. "That's what Amile told you I was doing in the Rooks that night? No wonder you thought I was an asshole."

"I never…Let's not have this conversation in this goddessforsaken alley. We're going home. Now."

"Agreed."

She inspected his wound. It was deep but manageable. He hooked an arm around her waist to support her limping side as they made their way back to the Crest.

CHAPTER TWELVE

MARKHAM FLINCHED AS AMILE DABBED an alcohol-soaked piece of cotton against the cut on his arm. His best friend had his jaw clenched in concentration, while his hands worked with precision. After all, his reading on anatomy and healing had not only been for personal enjoyment.

He pursed his lips together, an expression Markham knew meant bad news. "This will need stitches."

Markham groaned. "Great. I passed out for like three days the last time and now I have to do it again. Courtesy of the same bloody Red Cloak."

He wondered where Ginger was now, if he'd survived long enough to get back to the guild. The wet crunching sound of fingers being severed from the crook's body was still vivid in his mind hours later and the memory of Staella's face as she performed her duty sent a shiver down his spine. The chill was not wholly out of fear. She'd been efficient and cold—a warrior in battle with no time for hesitation. Markham knew that he'd write that scene as soon as he was able. He would relive the moment as he described the adrenaline that had surged through his veins, the metallic tang of blood that had permeated his senses, the stony determination in Staella's stunning eyes.

Amile had bound the protector's badly-sprained knee and ordered her to stay in bed for the rest of the day. She'd nearly snarled at him when he'd forbidden any strenuous activity for the next two weeks.

He rose to grab the shirt Markham had discarded earlier, pausing at the bedroom's refreshments tray to tuck the bottle of brandy under his arm, the same one Markham had been sharing with Staella earlier.

"To be fair, you passed out long before I even started on the stitches. Unfortunately, this time, you won't have the luxury of unconsciousness… We could take you to Doctor Folear to get some real anesthesia."

He shook his head, tongue darting out to taste the blood in his split lip. "And tell him I got sprung by a vengeful Red Cloak in an alley in the Western Rooks?"

Amile shrugged and sat down in the chair next to the bed. "You have a legitimate reason this time. You went looking for Rayn."

Markham cocked an eyebrow. "And what normal Representative would've done that in the Rooks at night?"

The brunet started shuffling through his medical kit, pulling out a curved needle and thread. His golden-brown eyes darkened the way they always did when he was doing something important.

"You don't need to be normal. You just need to be plausible. You took Staella and she didn't question you."

Markham's lips tugged upward. "Actually, she did. Quite adamantly. She always does. Even when she doesn't say it, I know she does… I'm mad at you, by the way."

"Not the smartest thing to say to the man who's about to stick a needle in your arm." He didn't enquire further, knew Markham would continue without prodding.

"You told Staella that I was visiting a prostitute that night."

Amile waited, blinked. "I'm still failing to see the problem."

Markham threw his unscathed arm into the air. "The problem is that you could've come up with a more respectable alibi. She must think I'm a complete jerk. A defiler. A disgusting, entitled misogynist."

"It's the Rooks. Nothing but the truth would've been respectable. Besides, the objective was secrecy, not getting her to like you. Or has that changed?" He flashed him a smug smile and Markham punched his leg in the impish way they'd always wrestled as children.

"Well, genius, it might've helped to get her on our side if she did like me."

Amile scooted closer with instruments sterilized and ready. "Had you only told her from the beginning, she'd be on board by now. However, after recent events, I doubt anyone will be rushing to our side soon."

Markham sighed. "If I could've just found Rayn tonight…"

His friend twisted the shirt into a thick rope, gesturing to the gaping wound in Markham's arm. "No one can say that you didn't try. You do enough. You risk enough. Taking everything on yourself isn't going to solve our problems." He held out the brandy. "Down about a quarter of this."

"If I didn't know any better, I'd think you were trying to get me drunk to take advantage of me."

"You caught me," Amile deadpanned, much to his patient's amusement.

Markham proceeded to gulp down the bitter, burning liquid, and his eyes watered. After what felt like a gallon of brandy being poured down his throat, he broke away from the bottle with a shudder and a cough. He made a loud gagging noise, wiped the back of his hand across his mouth.

"Goddess, I'll never drink again."

Amile rolled his eyes at that. "Now bite down on this."

He gave Markham the shirt-rope, and once again dipped the needle into the alcohol. The world tilted as the drink started to do its job. Everything became slower and his mouth turned numb. He was glad for the degree of fuzziness when Amile began. The needle pierced his flesh and tugged at it. This process was repeated, again and again. *Goddess.*

He was roaring, as his teeth dug into the shirt until the veins in his neck bulged and his fingers clawed at the sheets beneath him. Blood thundered in his ears and he was lost to everything that wasn't pain. His head spun and black curled into the corners of his vision. He was nauseous. His ears were ringing. Amile said something, but he couldn't make out the words. Everything swirled. He was going to throw up. Amile stepped away from him, a vague silhouette amidst dancing black spots. Markham curled over the side of the bed and emptied his stomach on the floor. When his head hit the pillow again, everything disappeared.

†

The crescent moon was already at its zenith when Staella left the stables atop one of Markham's stallions. Despite a whole day of bedrest, her knee wasn't ready for a journey across the city on foot.

The guard at the gate knew she was coming, allowing her to exit with a mere nod. She knew that going back to the Rooks the night after their attack wasn't the safest thing to do, but she'd had enough of mysterious disappearances and dancing around the truth.

So, she made sure to tuck her hair back into the hood of her black cape, her face concealed in the shadows as she raced across Yaekós into the slums. Taking a shiny stallion all the way would certainly raise suspicion, so she found a quiet corner of the Plateau to leave the animal, tying him to the tree and futilely commanding him to be quiet.

The descent down into the Rooks was torture, her knee barking at the odd angle. However, when the terrain evened out into a gravel street, her pace was still agonizingly slow. She stuck to the shadows as much as possible, knowing how vulnerable she appeared in all her hobbling glory. She knew the path to the Burly Bear by heart, knew the tavern's layout like the palm of her hand. She also knew about a secret entrance into the pantry at the back, how to sneak in without being seen, and where to hide to remain undetected as she waited for her prey.

Finally, the door from the bar's side opened and light spilled into the room along with the scent of cheap perfume and ale. The footsteps were slow, loud, and punctuated by a sigh. Staella's muscles tensed, adrenaline shaking off most of the ache in her knee.

She lunged, dagger out as she pinned her target to the far wall with the blade at the woman's neck. The fear in the barmaid's blue eyes was like a living thing, threatening to tear through Staella's resolve.

"You're getting sloppy, Jac."

"Staella." Recognizing her attacker didn't dim the terror in Jacline's eyes to the slightest. In fact, she gulped loudly, throat bobbing against the dagger. "Wh–What are you doing?"

"I'm done with this game. Tell me where they are." Her voice was low, edging dangerously close to a snarl. She didn't care.

"Who? What are you talking about?"

"Cut the crap, Jacline. The Representatives—Daniel, Rayn. I know the Rebellion has them. And I know that you're in deep with the rebels." Her blade pressed a little harder against the woman's skin. "So, where are they?"

Blue eyes became gray steel as fear turned to hatred. "You'd attack an old friend for those spoiled children?"

"It's a very stupid move to challenge the person who is an inch away from ending your life. The Jacline I knew was a bit smarter than that."

"I could scream," she bristled. "My men would be through that door in a second."

Staella had to chuckle at that. "You and I both know that I could take out everyone in that tavern unarmed."

Not with this knee, you can't.

She doesn't need to know that.

To her surprise, Jacline laughed at that. "Yeah, okay, you win. So, let me tell you the Goddess' honest truth. The Rebellion didn't take those Representatives."

Her heart stuttered. "I swear, if you're lying to me…"

"I'm not, and not just because you have a knife at my throat, but because I have the basic decency to trust my friends." She gestured to the dagger and then cocked an eyebrow at Staella.

With a sigh, she slowly lowered her weapon, allowing her friend to rub at the scratch on her neck with a grimace.

Little quick to take her word?

Oh, shut up.

"I'm sorry."

Jacline rolled her eyes and huffed. "It's not like you'd be the real Staella without using intimidation to confront your problems."

Staella flinched. "That's a little harsh, don't you think?"

The woman glared at her. "You just threatened to kill me and all my customers, so no."

"The rebels really don't have Daniel and Rayn?"

"No, but their kidnappings have cost us just as dearly. It's quite easy for the blame to be placed on us, especially after your little tip about the supply trains had us launch an offensive on the same night Lad Caneille was taken."

Staella raised her palms at that. "Hey, I didn't tell you to go around spreading flyers that denounce the Representatives."

"Unlucky coincidence, I suppose."

"So, if the Rebellion doesn't have them, where are they?"

"Maybe they decided to run away to a luxury resort. Maybe they bought their own island to escape the pressures of being worshipped. Who knows how the minds of the privileged work?"

Staella shook her head, took a step back. "They're not like that."

Jacline's only response was an exaggerated roll of the eyes. "I should go."

"Wait." Her friend's hand was clasped around her wrist and she glanced up warily. "Like you said, you can take out everyone in that room… You're an invaluable asset, Staella, and we could really use you."

"Jacline… "

"We have another protest planned in a few days, something that makes a statement without spilling any blood… But there's always a risk. If the worst does happen, it would be life-saving to have you there."

Staella felt her heart break as she removed Jacline's fingers from her arm and pulled away. "I'm sorry. I can't. My name just got cleared, and Markham—"

"Oh, Goddess, please don't tell me you've been stupid enough to start caring about him."

"No, I just can't work for him and join a rebellion against him at the same time."

"Staella, please."

"No. I'm sorry, Jacline, but no. Please be safe."

With that, she slipped out of the hidden door and into the night, heading back to where she'd left her steed.

CHAPTER THIRTEEN

THE MORNING SUN FLASHED OFF Markham's sword as it headed for her in a masterful arc. It was blinding and Staella barely had enough time to raise her own weapon in a block. He was lunging again in a split second, aiming for her right side. A quick retreat had her knee screaming at her. She'd only given it a week's rest and anything too strenuous still hurt.

Markham didn't stop. He advanced mercilessly, thrusting his sword at her heart, her throat, her gut. She blocked, stepped back, tried to parry. Blocked him again. Stepped back. Their dance became a rapid flurry of movement and heavy breathing. Staella clenched her teeth against the pain and surprise as Markham's blows grew in power, in intensity, in technique. He pushed her back again, until her feet became a tangled mess and she crashed to the ground, landing on her back with a cry. The air had been knocked out of her and it took a few desperate gasps for her breath to return.

She just laid there, panting and wide-eyed. Markham had beaten her. The man she'd been instructing for only a few weeks had won a sparring match against her. The man who'd admitted to knowing only the basics and whose stance she'd had to adjust frequently had landed her flat on the grass.

His jaw clenched as he looked down at her, his eyes devoid of their usual spark. He'd barely spoken to her that morning and his annoyance had only grown at her every correction of his form. Until he'd snapped.

It's just because of your knee and the element of surprise…

He extended his sword arm to hover the tip of the blade over her throat and spat, "I've been sword fighting since I was ten years old. The only reason there aren't a few less Red Cloaks in this world is because I was ambushed that night in the Rooks."

He pulled back, sheathed his sword, and spun to leave. He took one step, hesitated, then turned back to offer her a hand. She ignored it, grimacing and launching herself into a standing position. His eyes flashed with irritation before he stomped away from her.

Staella's hands clenched into fists at her side. Eleven years. He'd been training for eleven years and he had taken her for a fool every morning.

She shook her head and marched after him. "Markham!" She caught up to him, yanked on his arm with all the force she had. "Hey!" He swiveled to face her, chest heaving with vexation. "What in the Realm Beneath is wrong with you?"

He glared at her as if his eyes held the power to impale. "What's wrong with me? What's wrong with *me*? Your boyfriend butchered one-hundred-and-seventeen rebels last night. That's what's wrong with me." Rage rolled off him in waves. His shoulders trembled and tears spilled onto his cheeks.

Ice encased Staella's body. "What?"

His breath hitched with a broken sob. "One-hundred-and-seventeen, Staella. Go ask him about it. I bet he's proud."

He ripped his arm free from her grip and stormed back into the house, leaving Staella devastated and breathless on the back lawns.

She didn't care about the ache in her knee. She ran.

Past the guards. Down the Crest. Across the Plateau.

The Burly Bear was closed.

Her heart stuttered as she dashed closer, pulled at the tavern's locked door to no avail. She felt her breath quicken and tears stung her eyes.

No.

She slipped around the haphazard building to the secret entrance she'd used only a week ago. It opened. The heavy-set barman sat on a sack of grain, his back resting against the wall of the pantry. There was a half-downed bottle of ale in his right hand and red rings around his eyes. He looked vaguely surprised at her presence, but soon sank back into his melancholy state with a swig from the bottle.

Staella sank down in front of him on her knees. "Where's Jacline?"

"Gone."

"Gone where?"

He shook his head and growled, "Don't you understand? She's gone. She's dead."

Blood turned to ice in her veins and she shook her head. "No. Are you sure?"

"None of them made it, and she wouldn't have run."

The rebels. They'd made their stand, the one Jacline had asked Staella to join, and Saul had killed them all.

I should have been there. Goddess, I should've been there.

Staella sank down against a shelf and allowed herself to weep.

†

I haven't written in a while, haven't spoken either.

It's been three weeks since my execution date, since Avery stormed Hangman's Square with a band of Red Seals and saved me.

I haven't eaten more than a few bites, haven't gotten out of bed for longer than an hour at a time, and that was only to have my bandages changed and to take yet another bath. No matter how many times I scrub myself raw in that bath, the filth crawling under my skin remains. I've scrubbed until rivers of blood trailed down my body, until Avery came to pin my arms to my side and carry me back to bed.

I keep seeing him. The side of Prince Marov's head as he pinned me down. The smell of him is impossible to forget, the sticky marriage of sweat and cigars, and the echoing mock of my own screams. I was in the maws of the Realm Beneath, but it is these small things that haunt me, consume me.

Avery came to me again last night, to sit with me and read to me in his beautiful voice. For the first time, I was able to look at him and to drown in those blue eyes again.

I wish I had it in me to make love to him then, to let his gentle hands and slow kisses replace the hungry clawing of the prince and his men. But I can't. Not yet.

I let him take my hand and pull my body against his chest and whisper comfort against my hair as I fell asleep.

When I woke up this morning, there was some light.

I am not healed yet, but parts of me have started to return, and they have returned stronger. They have returned to tell me that I am done playing children's games with these tyrants. This is a revolution and I know what I must do.

Leda closed the journal, taking a deep breath and a moment to wipe away the tears that had spilled onto her cheeks. In the legends, the Demon had always been victorious, had always dashed off on another crusade to conquer the kingdom and save her people. It was easy to forget that she'd also been a young woman, barely two years older than Leda, that her story had not always been one of adventure and triumph, that she had gone through unimaginable horrors and had also felt broken and lost sometimes. It was these things that made her all the more heroic.

The way Lowena had fixated on the small details from her traumatic experience was more real than any tale Leda had ever heard of the liberator. She, herself, was still haunted by the fear in her mother's eyes the day they'd locked her away. She couldn't remember much else of the day, but those bewildered eyes returned to her thoughts again and again.

Leda froze. The journal tumbled from her hands. Audrey.

She sees flowers.

Since the day she'd started babbling and hallucinating, she'd always seen flowers. Maybe that was her detail.

Maybe the onset wasn't random. Maybe she experienced something so traumatic that she's been reliving it ever since.

Leda leapt up from her bed and dashed down the stairs and corridors like a madwoman. Blood pounded in her ears.

She banged on the door to her mother's room. The rapid *booms* reverberated through the chambers of her heart. "Veress! Veress, please, I need to talk to her."

The nurse opened the door with a scowl. "Leda, what are you doing? You're going to upset her."

"I need to talk to her. Now."

"I'm sorry, but it isn't—"

"Veress."

The brunette glared up at her, but nodded reluctantly. "Alright. I'll be in the hallway."

Audrey was in a rocking chair facing the window, looking out at the lawns with a dazed expression.

Leda approached cautiously and took a seat on the sill opposite her mother. "Hi, Mom."

The woman's golden face lit up. "Leda. Sweetheart, how are you?"

Leda smiled thinly. "I'm well. How are you?" she rasped.

Audrey reached out to squeeze her daughter's hand. "I am wonderful now that you're here."

Leda angled her body to the side to glance at the view. "Are you looking at the flowers again?" Her mother nodded. "Do you have a favorite?"

"Oh no, I love all of them. Except the haletayls." Fear flickered in her mother's eyes, gone in an instant.

"Mom, can I ask you something?"

"Of course, dear."

She took a deep breath and adjusted her voice to be as soothing as possible. "Why do you see flowers?"

Audrey's brows knitted together. "What?"

"Mom, did—did something happen to you?"

Audrey looked up, expression suddenly crumbling as tears ran down her face. "He used to bring me flowers." Her voice broke.

"The most beautiful flowers, but then he—he—" She broke into a sob.

Leda slid to her knees in front of the rocking chair, taking her mother's face in her hands. "Was it Father? Mom, did Father do something to you?"

The woman's upper lip curled back. "Your father never gave me flowers."

"Then, who? Mom, who is 'he?'"

Another sob tore through Audrey's chest. "Yathan."

Leda's hands fell from her mother's face. "Yathan Qarvette? Did he do this to you? Mom? Mom!"

She had recalled more than her fragile mind could handle. She wailed, hands clawing at her own face. "Leda—he's going to—"

Her screams became incoherent roars as her hands latched onto her daughter's wrists, nails digging in until blood streamed down Leda's arms. She tried to pull away, tried to dislodge her mother's fingers. Audrey only gripped tighter.

"Mom, you're hurting me. Please, Mom."

Veress was there in a flash, sliding into a kneeling position in front of Audrey's rocking chair. She gripped the shrieking woman's arms and murmured gentle words until Audrey's breathing evened out slightly. Leda managed to free her bleeding wrists and withered under Veress's hard glare. "Go," the latter mouthed.

She left without objection, pressing down on her wounds. She felt hollow as she made the journey back to her room, and could think of nothing but her mother's confession while the handmaiden bandaged her up.

Yathan Qarvette?

She hadn't even known that they'd ever spoken and now Audrey claimed he'd brought her flowers. Was she more delusional than they'd guessed? Or was there something Leda didn't know about her mother and the High Ruler?

†

The door to Saul's office slammed open with a *bang* as Staella stormed inside. He was seated behind his desk and had the audacity to look up at her with a smile.

"Thenos. It's good to see that you're up and about again. Although, I would have preferred you knocking."

She didn't reply and stalked closer to place her palms flat on the desk. *One-hundred-and-seventeen. Go ask him about it. I bet he's proud.*

"Tell me it's not true."

He cocked an eyebrow. "You'll have to be more specific."

Dread, heavy and sickening, settled low in her belly and she gritted her teeth. "Please tell me you didn't massacre one-hundred-and-seventeen people less than twelve hours ago."

He shrugged. *Shrugged.* "I authorized the execution of rebels blocking the routes in and out of the city."

"You murdered them."

"I was protecting Yaekós."

Staella shook her head and felt her body tremble with rage. "From what? Unarmed innocents standing in the road?"

Saul huffed. "Innocents? Thenos, they were members of a treasonous organization. These rebels are nothing short of terrorists."

Her eyes flashed lightning. "They are freedom fighters. They have more integrity as little children than you have sitting before me, and you butchered them. The blood of one-hundred-and-seventeen people is on your hands and you dare show not an ounce of remorse?"

He rose from his seat, bringing his face inches from hers. "I eliminated a threat. The Rebellion seeks to undermine our Core and it is my responsibility to prevent that from happening. That involves making the necessary decisions. The roads to the capital had to be cleared and I wasn't going to waste resources imprisoning extremists. Not all of us can afford to lounge around in our marble palaces and entertain ideas of world peace."

"Leave Markham out of this," she growled.

"How can I? This is obviously his doing. I've seen enough of the two of you together to know that he's turned you against me."

It took every ounce of Staella's self-control to keep her voice steady. "No. What turned me against you is your heartless, mindless obsession with duty. I thought you were a commander to be reckoned with, but it turns out you're just boots on the ground, another puppet with strings to be pulled by Yathan Qarvette. Do you have no humanity, no beliefs of your own?"

Tears brimmed her eyes and she didn't feel ashamed of them at all. They distinguished her from the monster staring her down. She moved away, no longer feeling any need to be close to him.

"Well, it seems you're not what I thought you were either. An intelligent and honorable woman wouldn't have come in here babbling fantasies about freedom fighters and shedding tears over hard truths. You're just another sentimental fool. Then again, what did I expect from someone who would spread her legs so easily?"

The breath *whooshed* out of her lungs. She couldn't believe she'd ever been attracted to this man, that she'd let him touch her and take her. Silver-painted memories of intimacy and bliss were all tainted now. The sweetness and passion transformed into a bloody crimson that made her want to rip the skin from her body and replace it with something he'd never laid eyes on.

Her voice was hoarse but strong as she spat, "Typical. You don't have any legitimate retort, so you resort to shaming a woman for something for which you'd praise a man. You are a vile human being and I have never been as disgusted by someone in my life, and I won't have any of it. Lock me up if you want to, declare me a criminal again, but I'm done being a part of your guard."

"Honestly, Thenos, you won't leave that much of a gap."

"You're a monster."

"No, I am a Lorde."

She stormed out of the office with her fists clenched at her sides. She shook with vehemence as she headed for the main exit.

"Trouble in paradise?" The arrogant question sounded from behind.

Maron Caven filed in beside her, jogging to match her pace. She hid her face behind a curtain of hair. "Buzz off, Caven. I really don't have the patience for you right now."

She tried to accelerate, but his hand closed around her arm. "Staella, you're seething."

She turned to face him, gasped theatrically. "Wow, it shocks me that they haven't made you an investigator yet."

He pursed his lips and rolled his fair eyes to the sky. "I guess that's what I get for trying to be nice to you."

She cocked an eyebrow. "Since when are you nice?" They stared each other down for a few seconds before she shrugged herself out of his grip. "I'm not in the guard anymore. So, I'll finally be out of your hair."

He nodded slowly. "Ah… Well, the city guard will be at a disadvantage without you, Staella, but I wish you the best."

She tilted her head, narrowing her eyes at him. "Did you get a blow to the head?"

Maron grinned, drew a self-conscious hand through his hair. "Look, I've never seen a woman fight before. I thought you'd be a liability, but you've proven yourself more than worthy. So, we were lucky to have you… Now, please don't make me say it a third time."

She sighed, shook her head, and tried her best to smile. "Thank you."

She spun to continue on her way out. "Staella." She stopped to look back at him. "Remember, a good lorde isn't always a good man."

"Were you there last night when he killed all those people?"

"He didn't kill them. He made his men kill them. I wasn't there, but I can't promise you that it would've been any different if I were… Orders are orders. I'm sorry."

Staella found an unfamiliar gentleness in his eyes and huffed. "You're still a sexist asshole, Caven, but you're alright."

He chuckled and turned back to his training men.

The Blomehill home was a castle straight out of the fairy tales Staella had read as a child. The building was four stories high, built from dusty pink stone and surrounded by sprawling lawns. Two turrets framed the entrance, connecting in an arch above the colossal front door. Staella's knee barked as she approached, but she didn't dare stop now. For reasons still unknown to her, she'd known exactly where she wanted to go after leaving the barracks. The guards had recognized her from the ball and let her through.

Her heart was heavy as she ascended the black marble steps to knock on a massive door. It swung open to reveal not a servant, but Aedon Blomehill himself–tall, broad-shouldered, and smirking.

She bowed her head. "My lad."

His smirk became an arrogant grin, arms crossing over his chest as he leaned against the doorframe. "Markham's little pet… I see you've grown bored of my cousin's affections already. I'd offer to provide more stimulating entertainment, but I'm afraid I'm not all that into redheads or..." His gaze roamed down her body and back up again. "…athletic types."

Staella blinked, raised her chin to meet his eyes. "Wow. I've been in your presence for less than ten seconds and you've already confirmed every despicable thing I've heard about you. I came here for your sister."

"Ah, I should've guessed that you swing that way." Her tongue lodged against the inside of her cheek and she shook her head.

Without another glance in his direction, she stepped past him and into the foyer. "Hey, you can't just barge into my house uninvited."

She met his glare with one of her own and placed her hands on her hips. "Where is Maci?"

He stared her down for a few moments longer. "She's in the garden. It's straight through to the back. I suppose I should show you, considering the female lack of directional sense."

"I'd suggest saving those excellent navigational skills for finding the deflation vent on your ego. In the meantime, I'll be in the garden."

He chuckled lowly at that, a sound that grated against her nerves. "I think I'm starting to see the allure. Markham always did enjoy a little fire. Perhaps I'll reconsider... Should my dear cousin's bed ever fail to keep you interested..." The look in his eyes was enough to finish the sentiment.

She cackled and sauntered a step closer. "Oh, trust me, Lad Blomehill, you'll regret ever finding me in your bed." She glanced downward to what was undoubtedly the reason for his arrogant overcompensation. "I'm very good with a knife."

Much to her delight, Aedon paled. His throat bobbed and she flashed him a vulgar gesture before making her way to the garden.

Maci was difficult to miss. The woman was on a stone platform behind a towering water feature. Her spice brown hair was woven into an intricate braid. She was standing on her forearms, her slim body arching backwards in an upside-down U that had her pointed toes dangling in front of her face.

Staella gawked. "Maci?"

She unfurled herself slowly, gracefully sliding into a kneel. Then, she rose with deliberate movements, stretching from side to side. When she finally stood like a normal person again, she beamed.

"Staella, what a wonderful surprise."

Staella cocked an eyebrow. "What are you doing?"

She scaled down the stone wall effortlessly, grabbed a towel off the back of a tanning chair to dab at her barely-glistening forehead. The tight fit of her pants and the strip of abdomen left exposed by her top revealed that the girl who looked so delicate and breakable in her oversized sweaters had quite a bit of strength.

"It's a relaxation and exercise technique I learned in Ketanna. Supposedly, it connects you to the ever-flowing energy of the world around us. I don't know if it does all that, but it sure does stretch out my back in amazing ways."

She went to lounge on one of those sun-bathing chairs and motioned for Staella to take the one beside her.

She sighed and called, "Alander."

Seconds later, a young man approached, confusion twisting his fair-skinned face. He had tawny hair combed to perfection and was wearing a button-up the same baby blue color of his eyes. He wasn't handsome per se, but he carried himself with enough sophistication to stand out.

"You called?" His voice was deeper than Staella had expected.

Maci fluttered her eyelashes at him. "Yes, I did. Would you be a dear and fetch us some iced tea?"

He arched a sculpted eyebrow. "I'm a librarian, Maci, not a waiter."

Her lips tilted into a cheeky grin. "Ah, but I knew you'd be nearby, since you do so enjoy watching me do my morning stretches."

Alander didn't so much as blink. "I find the observation of a traditional Ketannan practice educational."

She bit her bottom lip. "Educational? Oh, Alander, how you make me blush." They laughed together at that before Maci waved a hand in Staella's direction. "Alander, this is my friend, Staella Thenos. Staella, this is Alander Ivitus, the Blomehill librarian and an excellent errand boy."

He nodded. "Charmed."

"So, about those iced teas?" Maci enquired.

All he could do was sigh. "Would you like them with lemon slices?"

"Alander, you're a saint."

The librarian turned around with a dramatic roll of the eyes and muttered, "Now all I have to do is find the kitchen."

Staella was about to recommend that he ask Aedon for some directions when Maci turned to her, voice low. "Alright, now you can tell me why you came to visit me for the first time looking like your heart has just been ripped out of your chest."

"I quit my job with the guard after a horrible encounter with Saul Knoxin."

Maci nodded. "Ah... Well, I know that the two of you were somewhat involved." *How does she know that?* "As cliché as it seems, I believe you deserve better. And now for my less savory advice: we can always put hair removal cream in his shampoo."

She giggled, shaking her head. "No, it's not just Saul. It's everything. It's Markham and his secrets, and Daniel and Rayn vanishing. Most of all, it's the Rebellion. I fought against them, I watched them kill a fellow guard who saved my life and yet I can't find it in myself to hate them. More than a hundred rebels were executed last night and no one bats an eye. Maybe that's the worst of it, the fact that people are dying and disappearing and planning revolutions and no one seems to care. This shallow Election and who wore what is still all anyone talks about. Meanwhile, I want to scream my lungs out at how absolutely ridiculous this is."

Maci was silent for a moment, pensive as she stared at Staella. "Welcome to the Crest, where everything sparkles on the surface and rots on the riverbed. It's what we've all been cultivated to uphold, to hide every piece of smut under a layer of gold. Markham is Yaekós' favorite son, but his father has all but abandoned him. The Caneilles throw party after party to blare out their happiness to the world, but Daniel's sister can't stay away from a bottle of wine long enough to do anything with her life. Leda is the Representative of the most powerful family in Aldahad and yet they lock up her mad mother in a shoebox of a room, hoping the world will forget about her. Aedon and I used to be the children of the High Ruler. We have everything we could ever need. We get to go anywhere we want, but our parents live as if we don't exist. So, true to form, Representatives disappear and Yathan doesn't even deign to make an announcement. It's all symptomatic of the greater issue."

"Which is?"

"Instability. The Election gives us new candidates every ten years, gives all the power to someone new who is but a child and has no training. We need change. We need someone different leading us."

Staella huffed and smiled wryly. "I didn't know you were this political."

Something hardened in the line of Maci's jaw, in the slant of her eyes. "No one bothered to ask."

There was a moment of awkward silence before Staella cleared her throat. "I, uh, I'm sorry for just showing up at your house and ranting."

Maci snapped out of her daze and flashed a smile. "Don't you dare feel bad. If you need a confidant in the future, you know where to find me, but if you disturb my morning stretches again, I'll have to force you to join."

She gulped. "Contort myself into impossible positions? I'll pass."

"Would a dinner with Aedon be more to your liking?" Maci asked with a flutter of her eyelashes.

"Stretches it is."

Suddenly, Maci shot up into a standing position. "Well, we can't have you leave here looking like you've been to a funeral. I hear that you like to read?" Staella nodded. "We have the second largest library in Aldahad."

"Who has the biggest?"

"The Hayvingers, of course. Alander used to be an apprentice there before Leda's uncle closed it fifteen years ago."

"Closed it?"

"Yes. Nobles from all over Aldahad used to visit it. It was basically a tourist attraction. Then Haviel shut it down. They fired the librarians and banned all visitors. So now, millions of volumes are left to gather dust. But who are we mere mortals to question the Hayvingers? Anyway, come on, you tell Alander what genre you prefer and he'll recommend some titles. You can borrow as many as you like. I'm ordering you to stay in bed and read and have servants bring you treats and let yourself cry all you want."

Staella shook her head. "I have a job, Maci."

She batted away the thought with a hand. "I'm sure my cousin can take care of himself for a few days."

With that, she took Staella's hand and led her inside.

CHAPTER FOURTEEN

LEDA WAS ONLY VAGUELY AWARE of her father's voice as he lectured her on the importance of winning the throne. She had pretended to listen to his reprimand of her placing third in the pre-Election poll, and had half-heartedly participated in their 'who am I?' spiel.

The results of the all-important poll had been released that morning, but Leda's mind was on the journal tucked under her pillow, on accounts of feat and siege, on the political revolution encapsulated in its pages.

So, when her father was finally out of breath, she rushed to read further. She had just finished Lowena's rendering of the final battle, a showdown in which the Demon had slain King Ankav Salingzer and seized power over Aldahad, and she was eager to devour the final pages of the journal.

It turns out that killing the King was the easy part. Sure, Avery and I got a stunning new home and all the nobles have lined up to pay their respects, being the suck-ups that they are. I don't have to be the Demon anymore. I don't have to wear the stuffy mask and fight all the time.

I do miss it sometimes: the freedom of solving problems with violence, the smell of victory on the horizon.

Now that we have the power, we face the daunting task of deciding what to do with it. Now, I have to listen to a bunch of "expert" advisors who were my oppressors only weeks ago and suffer through endless debates, trying to earn the loyalty of people I can't stand.

But I think we've finally reached an agreement. I would like nothing more than to hand over the power to the people, allow votes, open the government and retire to the countryside.

However, I cannot do this, apparently. No, I must remain on the throne for stability. All the advisors agreed that the immediate implementation of a democratic system would result in anarchy. Untrained persons would be left in charge. (Like an untrained one isn't already.) The voters would undoubtedly only elect whoever promised them revenge against the rich and high-born, and we wouldn't want that.

So, compromise it is. This whole Election and High-Ruler business seems a bit too close to a full-blown monarchy to my liking, but I have to remind myself that it is only an interim measure. Fifty years at most. Fifty years to transition. I suppose that's reasonable.

But I'm drafting the true Core, one that should be implemented by my successors as soon as it is feasible, one that will give power to the people and will never again discriminate on the basis of class.

I'm putting all my effort into this final Core. I will leave it and this journal in my new library so that future generations may find it and know what to do.

Those were Lowena's final words. Here, she'd decided to end her story.

Leda closed the journal slowly and realization tingled her palms. *An interim measure. Fifty years at most.* The Election had remained unchanged for sixteen decades. The true Core, drafted by Lowena herself, was stored somewhere in their library.

Why hasn't it surfaced? Been implemented?

I have to find it.

The Hayvinger collection was vast beyond compare. She wouldn't know where to start. But she did know someone who might.

It surprised Leda every time she visited the Blomehill residence that they didn't have a doorman. Instead, Maci stood in the entrance, frowning at her.

"Leda, what are you—?"

"I need to borrow Alander."

Maci's eyebrows knotted further. "The librarian. Why?"

Leda sighed. "I don't have time to explain, but it's really important. Please."

With a look of mild irritation, Maci stepped aside and motioned behind her. "Okay… Well, you know where to go."

She nodded her thanks, dashed down corridors, and turned until she skidded to a halt a few steps into the library. The voluptuous servant girl dusting a nearby shelf startled, clutching a rag to her chest.

"You."

The girl stumbled forward, fair face paling further. "Y–Yes, my lady?"

"Where is Alander?"

The servant blushed at the mere mention of his name and Leda resisted the urge to break the news: she'd have to grow a different set of genitals for the feelings to be reciprocated. "He's at the far-right station, my lady, documenting new arrivals."

"Thank you."

Without another glance at the girl, Leda bolted again past rows and rows of books and tables scattered with reading nobles. *Odd to have so many people in your home.* Finally, she spotted Alander. He stood on the third rung of a ladder, dressed as immaculately as always, his back rigid with scholarly confidence. Before she could open her mouth, he said, "Leda, how may I be of assistance?" His cerulean eyes remained on the volumes in front of him.

She leaned against the bookcase, cheek pressed flush against it in order to see his face. "Please tell me you still remember the layout of our library."

He raised an eyebrow and looked down at her. "I have a perfect memory."

She sighed, slumping her head in relief. "Thank the Goddess. You have to come with me."

"I'm working."

"Come on, Alander, we're childhood friends. I'd hate to have to use my Representative voice on you." She gave him as stern a glare as she could manage.

He huffed. "Fine, but I get to take a book for myself."

"Yeah, sure. You can take a hundred. Just, please come."

He flashed her a grin. "It would be my pleasure."

The Hayvinger library was truly stunning, even after years of abandonment. The three-storied stark white bookcases were embellished with golden vines. It had man-sized windows and bronze statues of the Goddess. A ceiling adorned in murals. And Alander looked utterly at home.

I really should come here more often.

She'd never understood why her uncle had shut it down. She followed the librarian through a giant arch, up the stairs, and onto the mezzanine. His teeth tugged at his bottom lip as he scoured one bookcase after the other.

"You're sure this was written by Lowena herself?"

"Positive."

He increased his pace, his mouth moving as he rambled to himself. He came to an abrupt stop and Leda barely avoided a collision with his back.

"Well, these are all the works by the first Hayvinger rulers."

There were six shelves stocked with scrolls and books. Leda gawked. "Lowena wrote these?"

Alander shrugged, squatting to run his fingers over the spines on the bottom shelf. "Some of them. Hers are mostly battle strategies or pessimistic political commentary. Unfortunately, they're not very riveting. Avery Hayvinger was the real writer."

He got up and turned to face her. "I'm sorry, but the document you're looking for is not here."

She shook her head. "No, no. It has to be. Isn't there another shelf we can search?"

"This library's filing system is flawless. It's not here."

A pang of dread hit her stomach and clenched at her heart. "Could it have been hidden?"

He was quiet for a moment, nodded. "There are certain documents that remain inaccessible because the High Ruler disapproved of them, but even those are well-documented. What you're looking for isn't on that list."

A tight hand closed around her heart. "Are you sure?"

"As I said, my memory never fails me. I'd definitely remember a Core written by Lowena Hayvinger. I'm sorry, Leda, but it's not in this library."

The realization finally hit her, mind reeling with the horror of it. The room tilted and she had to kneel.

The Great Cleanse of 61 A.H. Fifty years after the end of Lowena's reign, when the new system should have been implemented, Ezemiel Hayvinger, the newly-elected High Ruler, had ordered a mass burning of any writing that undermined the idea of the People's Monarchy. *It was all a guise.* It was an elaborate scheme to destroy Lowena's Core, a Core that would've divested him of his power and stripped away the status of her family.

When the Rebellion started growing fifteen years ago, when they started asking for exactly what Lowena had wanted, Haviel banned the public use of the library. Made sure his uncle's deeds would remain a secret. So, her family and those like it had remained on the throne. They had built an empire of wealth and glory on the corruption of her ancestors and the oppression of those who needed their integrity most.

Alander's hand on her shoulder startled her. "Are you okay?" He sounded absolutely mortified.

She nodded, got up. "Yes. I'm better than I've been for a long time. I know what I need to do, but there's something I have to set straight first."

†

It had taken Staella's mind two days to stop being consumed by flashes of Jacline's face, for snippets from her conversation with Saul to stop swirling around in her thoughts. She'd stayed in bed the entire time, had slept in the company of fevered dreams, and woken up unable to face reality.

However, now that her mind was clearing, her mental state wasn't much better. The knot sitting somewhere in her insides hadn't loosened because a single question kept hammering against her skull and she couldn't confess the answer.

Because it's absurd. It's absolutely absurd.

She remembered the way Markham had behaved the morning he'd shared the news of the massacre—the anger born from loss. She still saw the hurt in his eyes. Remembered the emotion in his voice as he'd yelled at her about the rebel deaths. At the time, she'd been too devastated to think about what that meant. Why had he been that upset? Why would Lad Aesher feel so deeply for members of the Rebellion?

Snippets of memories, of confusing conversation, jumbled together in her mind.

"He was...visiting a friend."

She couldn't lie still anymore, kicked the covers off her legs and rubbed a hand over her face.

"Alright, Staella, my biggest fear is that my outlook on life, my beliefs and opinions, will be assumed based on the privileged nature of my childhood."

She sighed and sat up, shaking her head. She needed to stop thinking.

There was an emotion in his eyes that she couldn't quite place.

"How many casualties?"

She shot out of bed. Clenched her hands around the nearest windowpane. No.

"The Aesher family stands for equality."

It all made sense, and yet none of it did.

"Don't talk about things you cannot understand..."

She resorted to pacing, chewing down on her nails in the way her mother had always chided her for.

"But these novels, they're—they're about adventure and liberation and revolution."

The speed of her pacing increased.

"...There are powers at work, decisions I have to make that you cannot understand at this point..."

Her heart was in her ears now, her head starting to ache. It all made sense. It all made sense.

"...If I can find her, find out who took her, I can—"

Her knees buckled and she grabbed the windowsill, shaking her head again and again.

Gold.

Sword.

Graegg.

It all made sense.

CHAPTER FIFTEEN

THE AROMA WAS ABSOLUTELY DIVINE: sticky, barbeque basting mingling with the woodsy tones of smoked pork, piercing pepper sauce fusing with juicy steak. The spread took up nearly the entire table and included trays of meat dishes, fried potatoes, spiced rice, freshly-baked bread, and cheesecake.

Leda's mouth watered. She sat at the head of the table, leaned back against the high-backed chair with her legs crossed and her arms draped over the sides. Two Hayvinger guards in bloodred livery stood at attention behind her. She'd informed them of the plan, and they'd been more than eager to volunteer. So, they waited.

At last, the estate's clock tower struck seven and it was mere minutes before the dining hall doors opened. Honiel entered first and Mighiel trailed behind as usual. The sight of her in his usual seat had a scowl take over her father's face.

His brows dipped further at the sight of the feast. "Leda, what is the me—?"

"Father. Brother. Do take a seat." She kept her voice light, but allowed herself a sliver of rage.

She felt roiling, white-hot rage at every time she'd been treated like a prize mare, at every pompous word that had ever left Honiel's mouth, every day her mother was locked in that room, every Hayvinger who had tainted Lowena's legacy with lies.

The men's faces were twisted with indignation, but the glares of the guards behind her made them sit down near the end of the table.

She smiled. "Today has been a very important day in my life and I'd like to celebrate with a nice meal."

The younger of the guards knocked on a panel at the back of the room and two servant girls entered promptly, hiding smirks as they laid a plate before each of the Hayvinger men. Dry, skinless chicken breasts and steamed broccoli. The girls then proceeded to heap a portion of each dish onto her plate. She thanked them and proceeded to pour herself a glass of wine.

Raising it in salute, she announced, "May the Goddess continue to bless our family name."

Mighiel glared at the food in front of him, his jaw clenched so tightly it looked painful. "What are you doing?" His voice was taut, on the verge of trembling.

She reached forward, gripping the stem of her glass and taking a sip of the warm liquid. Then, she sliced through a particularly succulent piece of pork and brought it to her mouth. The sweet, hearty taste elicited a moan.

"Well, as the Hayvinger Representative and the head of this house, I've decided to adjust your diets a tad. See, it would be awfully damaging to our reputation for the men in the family to appear unfit and unhealthy."

A chair scraped over the floor with a screech. Honiel stood with his fists balled at his sides. "This is preposterous."

Funny how it wasn't so preposterous before.

The guards stepped forward, flanking her now. Leda opened the door to that rage, sharpening her tone. "Sit. Down."

Her father's face paled, then became blotched with vexation. His upper lip curled back. "You should learn to know your place."

"Oh, but Father, wasn't it you who taught me that my place is on a throne? Or did you expect me to rule as nothing but a puppet with you pulling the strings?"

Mighiel refused to look up, opting to remain silent in fear of becoming collateral damage in the power players' war.

Leda leaned forward. "Who am I?" Honiel stared her down. She narrowed her eyes again and motioned to the guards at her side. "I will not ask again."

"Leda Hayvinger," he gritted.

"Exactly. I am a Hayvinger. What does that name mean?"

"It means that your family created the People's Monarchy of Aldahad."

She nodded, felt her anger deepen into sorrow at what their relationship had become, at what he'd made it. "Yes. My ancestor, Lowena, destroyed the Salingzer line, ended tyranny, and wrote the Core… I am the Representative of the most powerful family in Aldahad and I refuse to follow orders any longer. I am Leda Hayvinger and that means something."

"So, what now?" her father spat. "Will you keep us like prisoners in our own home? Are we to bow to your every whim out of fear of our own guards?"

"No. I am not you. If you stay out of my way, I will leave you be. I'm having the west wing prepared for Mother. Oh, and all expenditure of household funds will need my consent from now on."

Honiel stepped closer. The guards gripped the pommels of their swords. He halted, flashed her one last damning glare, and stormed out. To her surprise, Mighiel remained seated. Leda released the breath she'd been holding and collapsed forward to bury her face in her arms. After a few steadying seconds, she looked up at her brother.

"You stayed," she whispered.

He finally met her gaze. There was a strange expression on his face, a raw softness she'd never seen before. "I'm sorry."

Leda blinked. "What?"

"I underestimated you. I thought you were too weak to be the Representative, but I just realized that you might be the one to take our family to new heights."

The corners of her mouth tugged upward. "I will restore the Hayvinger name." Not in the way he desired—by sitting on a bloody throne and wearing a crown of bones—but she would. "I promise."

†

Markham sat at the dining room table, an avalanche of paper spread out around him. He was scribbling on the sheet before him, hands moving in a frenzy as the words bled out of him. His heart was pumping inspiration through his veins and every letter became a dash to convey the tales that milled about in his mind.

With a flash, something landed next to his hand. He stopped. Red velvet with his initials embroidered in gold. It was the purse he'd lost that night in the Rooks.

Shit.

He looked up to find Staella glaring at him from across the table, stance rigid and arms crossed over her chest.

"I believe this is yours."

He gulped. "Wh—Where did you find it?"

Her tongue lodged itself against the inside of her cheek. "Under Saul Knoxin's mattress. Strange, right? I certainly thought so at the time, but now it all makes perfect sense."

She pulled out the nearest chair and sat down with her forearms braced on the table. Her black eyes drilled into him, and he did all he could not to flinch.

Could this be it? Was she ready? Was he?

"Staella," he breathed. He clung to the sound of her name, accepted the fact that this might be the last time he could utter it as her friend.

"Talk."

Where to start?

He started at the very beginning. For a coherent narrative, or perhaps to buy himself time.

"My tutor as a teenager took it upon himself to give me a broad education. I was taken to all the slums in Aldahad and got to witness the suffering of most of the country's people. I was always disguised, always limited to leaving anonymous donations when we left. When he passed away, it came as a shock to me that my lessons would be over. I realized that I was far from ready to rule the People's Monarchy in three years and that made me question the entire system. None of us are even remotely equipped for the positions we hold."

He clenched his hands into fists, shaking his head. "I could no longer be blind to the absurdity of all of it—the Representatives and so-called Elections. Millions of people are living in deplorable circumstances because we make kings and queens of children who grow up with silver spoons and bronze streets, and I couldn't be a part of that anymore… The Rebellion, what it stands for, suddenly made more sense to me than the life I was living.

"So, after months of digging, Amile found the rebel leader and I became the financier and secret co-leader of the movement. I provide the perspective of the other side and help to make important decisions, but only the leader and his inner circle know my identity." He didn't dare to look at her. "Now, it's the Election, and even though I despise it, I must win. Just imagine the change the Rebellion could bring about with the support of a High Ruler."

He kept his eyes trained on the table, unable to look at her quite yet. He couldn't face the potential contempt in her gaze.

"I guess now it makes sense that the rebels didn't kidnap the Representatives." Her voice was much too calm.

"No," he exclaimed. "We would never stoop that low. I've told you everything..." *Not everything.* "Well—"

"What?"

He took a shaky breath. "Your instructor, Aran Bruhel… He's a member of the inner circle. He wrote to inform me that he'd been training a very talented girl with the aim of her aiding the Rebellion. He'd decided that the best way for her to do so would be to keep me safe. I didn't really consider the offer until I was attacked in the Rooks. So, I sent Amile to get you."

She wasn't moving, wasn't breathing. "He trained me to be a rebel?" She shook her head, drew both hands through her hair. "I've been living someone else's script this entire time. Why didn't you tell me? Was it amusing to you, watching me try and figure out this mess while you knew I was being used as a pawn?"

His chair scraped against the marble floor as he shot up to close the distance between them. He took the seat at her side.

"I didn't tell you because I didn't want you to feel this way, that you were being forced into something. Being a part of this is life-threatening. You shouldn't be part of the Rebellion because other people told you to be, but because your heart won't allow you to do anything else. I wanted to give you time to understand the situation and to decide for yourself."

She bit her bottom lip and looked right into his eyes. "And now?"

His hand wrapped around hers. "Now, you can make an informed decision."

Her face was inches from his and his heart ached with how perfect she was. Stunning and smart and strong. Honorable and brave and daring. Compassionate. She was the calm before the hurricane and the force of the storm all at once—the valiant knight and the beloved princess. And it punched a hole in his chest that she might be leaving his story.

He cleared his throat and stood to put some distance between them. "I'll respect whichever choice you make… Well, I might put up a fight if you choose to hand me over to the guards." He chuckled, but it came out strangled and he had to turn away to look out the window.

A chair scraped behind him and he spun just in time to see her storm out of the room. He wanted to follow, but then heard her roar obscenities in the adjacent sitting room. *Best not to interfere.* She was pacing, talking to herself. He heard her stop and he quirked his head. *Crash!* Something slammed into a wall, shattering to pieces. He ran in, stopped in the doorway to find the remnants of a porcelain vase on the floor. She stood in front of it, shoulders heaving with gasping breaths. Then, she straightened and turned to him, her expression composed.

"I'll compensate you for the damage."

He huffed. "Put me out of my misery and you can break anything you want."

She hesitated a moment. Then: "You have to stop paying me."

His blood froze. "Why?"

"Because I'm not your protector anymore." He felt his knees buckle, had to put out a hand against the doorframe to stay upright. "I am your fellow rebel."

He blinked and felt the ear-splitting grin form on his face. A grin that matched hers. And before he knew what he was doing, he was across the room and pulling her into his arms. His hands cradled her head against his chest as he placed a kiss on her hair. There was only a second's hesitation before her arms wrapped around his waist, fingers splayed against his back. His heart skipped a beat as heat rushed through him and he became acutely aware of every point of connection between their bodies. More than anything, he wanted to—

The vibrations of her chuckle rumbled through him. "What am I getting myself into?"

He hummed, tilting her head up so he could look into those eyes. "I ask myself that same question nearly every day, but I already feel better knowing you'll be in it with me."

She smiled again and his mouth went dry. Gulping, he started to trace the line of her cheekbone with his fingers. He reveled at the way she leaned into his touch. Her eyelids fluttered shut and an irresistible force made him bring his face closer to hers. He halted just before they met, thumb inching downward to tease her bottom lip. Her breath quivered and he felt her melt into him, yield to him.

Blood pounded in his ears, in other parts of him, as he imagined what it would feel like to press his lips to hers, to tug at the supple skin with his teeth and hear her gasp. To slide hands down her sides and grip onto her hips. Stroke the roof of her mouth with his tongue and leave her trembling. To go lower and feel her fingers dig into his back as he found just the right spot on her neck to make her moan. To—

"Oh, wow. Sorry. I didn't mean to interrupt anything. Though I should probably have predicted this…"

They jumped apart and he had to take a moment to steady his breathing, a process not made easier by the delicious blush creeping across her cheeks to her throat. He wondered how far down that blush went, if the red would deepen if he…

Goddess, Markham, pull yourself together.

He cleared his throat and looked up to find Amile leaning against the doorframe with an amused smirk. "Uh, good news. Staella just joined the Rebellion. She knows everything." Amile's eyes widened, and Markham added, "About me."

His best friend stepped into the room. "Well, this does make things considerably easier. Welcome to the only fashionable way to commit treason."

The corners of her mouth tugged upward. "Thank you."

Amile started smiling, then froze as his eyes landed on the purse still on the table. "This is the one you lost."

Markham nodded. "Yes, this—" His heart stopped once again. *This day is going to kill me.* "Staella, you said you found this under Saul Knoxin's bed."

"Yes. Why?"

He met Amile's gaze and found his own realization and alarm mirrored in golden-brown eyes.

Amile was the one who answered. "Because this was stolen by a group of Red Cloaks."

"That bastard!" Markham's fists clenched at his sides. "He's been working with those vermin. That's where he's been getting information on the rebel movements."

Staella huffed, shaking her head. "Allying with Aldahad's most notorious criminals to get to some freedom fighters. I'd say I'm surprised, but I'm really not."

"This also means that he at least suspects your involvement, Markham," Amile said.

Markham drew a hand through his hair. "What do we do?"

Staella answered immediately. "Well, the fact that he hasn't acted on his inkling probably means that he doesn't have the evidence he needs to move forward. Luckily, that's even more true now that this isn't in his possession."

Amile nodded. "So, we keep you as clean as possible."

Markham sighed. "Agreed, but I have to meet with Tomhas first. I need to warn him about the Red Cloaks' involvement."

As in most emergencies, Amile jumped into administration mode. "I'll contact Mycah at once."

CHAPTER SIXTEEN

"SHOULDN'T STAELLA BE AT THE barracks?" Leda settled into one of the leather armchairs in Markham's office, cherishing the sunlight that flooded through the large window. She'd never minded Yaekós' heat.

Markham shook his head, flopping down into the seat behind the desk. He drew a hand through his sweat-slicked hair.

"She decided that her presence was more needed here."

She cocked an eyebrow. "Playing polo with her boss?"

He shrugged, his gaze flicking across the room. *He's avoiding eye contact.* "She's actually quite good. Much better than Amile."

"Mar, the horse on its own would be better than Amile." Markham chuckled, tugged the drinks tray closer with his foot. "You know, if you need even teams, I'm not far away."

He snorted. "And be absolutely disgraced two seconds into the first game?"

"Hey, at least you'd be losing to the best. You should consider it an honor."

"Sure," he drawled, voice dripping with teasing sarcasm. "Can I pour you a glass of orange juice?"

She leaned back in her chair, the corner of her mouth tugging upward. "You can pour me something stronger."

He froze. "Since when do you drink?"

"Since my father doesn't dictate my diet anymore."

He frowned, but didn't push her on the subject, silently pouring two drinks. A tumbler full of yellow-brown liquid plopped down in front of her. She took a cautious sip, hated it, but managed to keep her features neutral. She'd get the hang of it with enough practice.

Markham smiled. "I knew you looked different walking in."

"Fatter?"

"Well, I wasn't going to say anything…" She gasped, dipped her fingers in the drink and flicked the liquid at him. He brought up a hand to defend his face, chuckling. "No, dumbass, not fatter. Stronger. More confident."

"I feel different… I stood up to my father."

His eyes widened. "What made you take the leap?"

She took a deep breath, preparing. "That's actually why I'm here." Nerves twisted her gut. "Lowena Hayvinger kept a journal during the time of her rebellion and I found it. I—I discovered something big…" She clutched her hands together. "She wrote a Core, Mar. Not the Core we have now. A different one, one that was supposed to make everyone equal, to give everyone a chance to be represented."

Markham shot from his seat, his chair scraping as he leaned forward. His hands were braced on the desk and his skin had gone pale. "Do you have it?"

"What?"

"The Core, Leda. Do you know where it is?"

She shook her head. "It was destroyed in the Great Cleanse."

His eyes closed and his hands clenched into fists. He sank back in his seat, expression very close to the one he had as a kid when his ice cream would tumble to the ground.

She scooted closer, pressing her chest against the side of the desk. "But it doesn't matter. I know what it contained. I know what Lowena wanted. What Aldahad should be. What it would've been if it weren't for the corruption of those who came before us. That world… Mar, that Aldahad is exactly what the Rebellion is fighting for."

He went still as the dead. She gulped. "Are you saying that you're sympathetic towards the rebel cause?" he asked.

"Look, I know it's a radical idea, and it goes against everything we were raised to believe, but it's the right thing. Aldahad has become nothing but a playground for the rich, a pageant. We're children fighting for a crown that means nothing." Her hands trembled. "We have to join the rebels."

Before she knew what was happening, Markham had moved around the desk. He pulled her into his arms, crushing her in an embrace.

"I have never admired you as much as I do in this moment."

She was paralyzed in his grip, frowning. "Wait. That's it? No questions? No objections? No 'Leda, have you gone mad?'"

He pulled away, hands still resting on her shoulders. "Leda, I have been one of the leaders of the Rebellion for years."

Everything around her went cold, slowed down. Markham was talking, but she couldn't hear him, couldn't do anything but follow the swirl of her thoughts back in time.

"Is there a reason you look like a puppy that's lost its plaything?" Markham teased as he sat down next to her on the front steps of the Aesher home.

Her bottom lip trembled, and she had to bite down on the soft skin to prevent a sob. "My father's going to marry me off soon."

His eyes nearly popped out of their sockets. "You're fifteen.*"*

She shrugged. "I'm also a Hayvinger. It's all because of this bloody Election. It's seven years away and it's already controlling my life. He wants me to be tied to someone with a good chance of winning. So, even if I don't become High Ruler, I can at least be High Companion… What if he's mean? Or he doesn't want to talk to me? What if he doesn't like horses? Or has chest hair…" She quieted, fear closing its grip around her heart. "Mar, what if he hurts me?" Markham took both her hands in his, his eyes holding more compassion than anyone had shown her before.

With a voice still breaking into manhood, he asked, "Would your father think me a popular candidate in the Election?"

"What?"

"Would he deem me worthy of marrying into the Hayvinger line?" he insisted.

She shook her head. "Are you suggesting that we get married?" He nodded. "Mar, I like you, but I don't—"

"Relax. I'm not in love with you. You're my friend. Think about it. We know each other really well. We get along and we like doing stuff together. It's the perfect solution. Then, you don't have to be afraid anymore."

"Don't you want girls?"

"I can still have girls."

She chuckled, bumping his shoulder with hers. "Alright, as long as I get to veto them. They have to be good enough for you."

His stunning eyes met hers again. "Leda, I promise that you'll know everything. No secrets."

She cocked an eyebrow. "Pinkie promise?"

He hooked his little finger around hers. "Pinkie promise"

That had been years ago. Years. He'd been their leader for years.

The world flashed back into focus and his last words became audible. "…and now *we* can."

He looked at her with a wide smile, the smile that had always made her feel safe, but now nearly brought her to tears.

She pulled away from him. "You've been working with them for years," she croaked. "You're their leader?" Her voice found its strength again and she straightened, happy for the height that had her looking down at him.

"Leda, I—"

"Were you ever going to tell me? Or were you just going to transform our entire world and expect me to sing your praises afterwards? You are supposed to marry me. You're supposed to be my best friend. The moment I thought of joining the Rebellion, I needed to come to you, to tell you, but it seems like the feeling is not mutual. Did you not care enough to inform me? Do you not trust me?"

"Leda, please—"

"Who else knows?"

"Leda—"

"Who knows, Markham?"

He gulped visibly. "Amile and Staella."

Tears stung the back of her eyes. "Staella… Your bodyguard, who's been in your life for about a minute knows and yet you kept me in the dark. Wow. You're an even bigger ass than I thought."

He shook his head, eyes pleading. "No. She found out on her own."

"I don't care if the Goddess sent her a personal letter." Her hands clenched into fists. "You didn't trust me enough to share your secrets. You didn't value me enough to ask me to join you. So, clearly you don't know me at all. Did you honestly think I'm anything like *them*? Did you believe I would condemn you for helping those who need our aid the most?"

His arms were outstretched towards her and his expression was utter anguish. "I'm sorry. Leda, I'm sorry. I just—"

She held up a hand to silence him. "Don't even try, Markham. I'll find a faraway faction of the Rebellion that will appreciate my help. That way I can make a difference and still never speak to you again. Oh, and don't worry, I won't rat you out, despite what you might think of me. May the Goddess be on your side."

She saw the way the greeting broke his heart and saw the light dim in his eyes. *Good.* Before she could start bawling, she stormed out of the study and back to her carriage.

†

Late that same afternoon, Markham, Amile and Staella took a nondescript carriage to a tavern on the Plateau. It was closed, but a secret knock from Markham had the keeper opening the door and ushering them inside.

Staella kept her eyes on the street around them, her hand a permanent weight on the pommel at her hip, its sword lurking beneath the folds of her velvet cape.

The keeper was a gaunt man, his smile barely visible among the worried lines that marred his face. Amile took care to lock the door behind them after they crossed the threshold.

Markham apparently knew that the man wasn't partial to small talk and merely handed him a bulging purse. "For your trouble."

So, they swept on, out through the establishment's back door and into a desolate alley. With absurd familiarity, the men dashed toward the green front door of a small, stone-faced apartment across the street. Amile produced the key from his pocket. Staella made sure to check the alley one last time before following them inside.

The building was narrow and two-storied, the upper level a mezzanine-like loft visible from below, with mismatched furniture scattered around the space. It was colorful, warm, made Staella want to curl up on the thick carpet and soak up the last rays of sunlight drizzling in.

Saloon doors to the left swung open and a girl about Staella's age sauntered out into the living area. Her bronze body was wrapped up in a hot-pink bathrobe, her dark, kinky hair still damp as she rubbed a towel over it. She had the fullest lips Staella had ever seen and green eyes that could cut right through you.

"I was wondering when you'd show up," she said by way of greeting. She sank down into an orange loveseat, her robe riding up her thighs.

Markham chuckled, taking a seat on the couch. "Ever the gracious host, Mycah." So, this was Mycah Delaney, Markham and Amile's link to the Rebellion.

Staella gawked as Amile strode to the kitchen, opened one of the cabinets, and pulled out a packet of lollipops.

He popped one into his mouth and Mycah sighed. "Oh hey, Amile. Please do make yourself at home."

He leaned against the counter, crossing his ankles. "Don't mind if I do."

The girl's eyes finally landed on Staella, who was still awkwardly rooted in place at the door. "You are allowed to take a seat, Miss Thenos."

She nodded and moved to settle down next to Markham. "So, you're in the Rebellion…"

She cocked an eyebrow. "That is why you're here, yes."

"Yes. Of course. Sorry, I'm still getting used to the idea."

Mycah tilted her head to the side, a cat studying its prey. "It is rather easy to forget that one is committing high treason."

Staella's jaw clenched, and she itched to smack the smug grin off the girl's face. Instead, she asked, "What made you join?"

Her expression hardened. "My life."

She didn't elaborate and Staella averted her gaze. This was not a cage fight; she had to play nice.

Markham cleared his throat much too loudly. "Well, as delightful as this conversation has been, we should be getting ready."

Mycah shot up. "Yes. I have everyone's disguises. You two can change in the closet upstairs. Staella and I will get ready down here."

She pointed a finger at Markham, a cheeky smile tugging at her lips. "No peeking."

He feigned offense with a hand to the heart. "You know me, My. I would never."

She swaggered closer to him. "It's precisely because I know you that I took care to issue the warning."

His eyes sparked. "You wound me."

Her voice raised in pitch as she crooned, "Oh, I must apologize for upsetting the lad's delicate sensibilities."

Markham opened his mouth to retort, but it was Amile's voice that filled the room. "Not that I don't enjoy your banter, but the sun is setting, and we have a meeting to attend."

Once the men had disappeared up the stairs, Mycah reached under one of the couch throws to pull out various items of clothing. She handed Staella a pair of ripped leggings and a dark, hooded poncho that grazed her knees. It would hide her weapons and her face, all while blending into the night. Mycah had a similar outfit in her arms and wasted no time disrobing. The pink material fell to the floor and Staella had to suck in a breath. Mycah was so thin that her ribs were countable, and her spine's individual knobs pushed against her brown skin. But that wasn't what shocked Staella to her core. It was the brand that covered most of her upper back. A perfect, horrible hummingbird. She didn't know what the image meant, but she knew who got branded like that.

Slaves.

Human trafficking was supposed to be illegal in Aldahad, but it seemed no one took the time to enforce that law.

Mycah looked over her shoulder, saw Staella staring. "Never seen a whore before, Miss Thenos? You can spare your pity. I don't need it."

Before she could stop herself, she blurted, "What happened to you?"

Mycah swallowed visibly. "My parents sold me when I was seven. Long story short, I ended up in the possession of a brothel in Yaekós. Markham bought it and set us all free."

Staella's hands were shaking. "I'm sorry."

She shook her head. "Don't be. It led me here." To Staella's surprise, the girl was smiling. "I was part of the Rebellion from a very young age… I remember the night Markham and Amile came into the brothel. They were disguised, but they'd done a piss poor job of it. You could smell their privilege from a mile away. They asked a lot of questions, but no one was stupid enough to answer them. Still, Markham freed us and gave us enough money to do whatever we wanted with our lives…"

"So, you decided to stay and help him."

"I decided to stay to help girls like me. Only the Rebellion can change this mess."

They were silent for a few moments, putting on the last of their clothes. "Thank you for staying. For being their link to the rebels."

Mycah turned to face her, eyes guarded. "They mean a great deal to me. Markham, especially." She softened. "Yaekós' golden boy who saved my life."

Staella's teeth tugged at her bottom lip. "So, you and Markham…" She gulped. "Are you…?"

The girl cackled. "Goddess, no. Even if I had any interest in men, I would never do that to myself."

She scowled. "What?"

Mycah sighed. "Look, Markham is probably the best man in Aldahad, but I wouldn't go down that road with him. He likes pretty things and then becomes bored of them. I've seen it happen every time—Harper, Asha, Lai, Yzette… It's just not worth it."

Staella's stomach twisted, and she felt as though she'd throw up at any second.

You're the kind of girl people write books about.

He'd written many books, after all.

She took care to compose herself as Markham and Amile came down the stairs. The sun had disappeared to leave the sky blue-black, signaling their departure to the Rooks.

Tomhas Hardin was older than Staella had expected, and she almost snorted at her own naivety for believing the Rebellion was adolescent-run. No, the rebel leader was likely in his early fifties, umber skin slightly crinkled at his brow and gray dotting the black of his stubble. The dark eyes that watched them enter were intelligent and caring enough to have Staella's shoulders relax. He had a presence that filled the room, a formidability that went beyond his height and mountainous frame.

Finally, an adult.

The room was at the back of a Rooks family's shack and was barely big enough for the table and chairs it held. She noticed the furniture's fine make and wondered just how much of his estate Markham was offering. He'd probably compensated the owners for the use of their home as well.

Tomhas smiled when they were all huddled inside. He hugged each of the others—Markham with a slap on the back, Amile with a hair ruffle that made the latter cringe, and Mycah with a kiss to the top of her head. He held her under his arm, grinning the way Staella's father would when he looked at her.

"How's my girl?"

She beamed. "As well as I can be with these two ordering me around all the time." She shot a pointed look at the boys and Tomhas chuckled.

Markham stepped up to Staella, placing a casual hand on the small of her back. She tried her very best to ignore the jolt of heat it sent up her spine.

"Tomhas, allow me to introduce our newest recruit. This is Staella. She's a fierce warrior, an amazing dance partner, and a criminal-turned bodyguard."

She rolled her eyes, extended a hand. "It's an honor to meet you, sir."

He wrapped both his hands around hers in greeting. "The honor is all mine. I wouldn't mind if your companions were as well-mannered, but you can really feel free to call me by my name." He motioned for them to take a seat. "So, what's so urgent you had to see me immediately?"

"Staella brought us some disturbing information," Markham answered. "As you know, when I came down to deposit those emergency funds, I was attacked by a few Red Cloaks. They took my purse. It was empty, but they still could've gotten a decent amount for it. However, Staella found it hidden under Lorde Knoxin's mattress."

Staella ignored the eyebrow Mycah cocked in her direction.

Tomhas sighed and drew a hand over his short-cropped hair. "That's how they knew the location of the safehouse, how they intercepted our protests so accurately."

Markham's fists clenched where they rested on the table. "We can't allow this to go on. If all our plans and information is fed to the Lorde of Security, we might as well surrender now."

"Agreed. Any suggestion as to a solution?" Tomhas asked.

"I would be able to identify the men who robbed me, but I doubt that we're dealing with a few rogues. It could very well be the entire guild."

"I don't think so, but it might be a substantial number of them. Unfortunately, I know their leader personally. Endras would never side with the authorities. Our traitors are working for themselves."

Mycah leaned forward. "Well, we can't kick out all the Red Cloaks. They're some of our best fighters and most of them are only criminals because they have to be."

"We could try to get specific names, send in spies?" Staella offered.

Tomhas paused for a moment. "Are you still close to Knoxin?"

"No, uh, that bridge was burned when he ordered a mass-murder."

"Could you be? Close to him again, I mean…?" This came from Mycah. "You clearly gained his trust before and we could really use that trust now."

Markham stiffened beside her. Staella clenched her jaw. "To aid the Rebellion, I would, but I'm afraid that I don't leave any material to work with when I burn bridges. He's not going to let me in again."

"We could send in someone else," Markham suggested immediately.

Amile shook his head. "Saul is well-trained and well-guarded. We won't get anyone close enough."

"It would be even more foolish to attempt infiltrating the Red Cloaks," Tomhas said.

Silence. A room full of thinking heads with no answer.

Then, Amile perked up. "We change the membership rules."

"What?"

"We don't accept Red Cloaks."

"I literally just explained why that's a bad idea," Mycah drawled

"No. I mean that if you want to be in the Rebellion, you have to leave the guild."

Markham shook his head. "There are severe consequences for breaking the Red Cloak oath."

"Well, that just means that those who stay are truly passionate about the cause. I doubt anyone will risk the guild's wrath just to work for Saul Knoxin. They may be criminals, but they'll value their lives over whatever rewards he's offering."

Mycah chewed at the inside of her cheek. "And those who do desert? How do we protect them?"

"The guild only operates in Yaekós. We get them safe passage to the farthest town with a rebel faction we know, set them up with families, and arrange for jobs."

"I suppose exile is better than death."

"Endras won't be happy about us poaching his men. He might retaliate," Tomhas argued.

"If he becomes a problem, I'll kill him," Staella interjected.

All eyes in the room turned to her. Tomhas frowned and studied her expression closely. She knew what he would find—no doubt, no fear, stone-cold resolve.

His lips tugged upward. "Well, we might lose a few members, but it seems there is no other way. I say we go forward with Amile's plan. Markham?"

The latter was still staring at Staella, his jaw slack. He simply nodded.

The decision was made.

Later, when they were heading back to the carriage with hoods drawn tightly over their heads, Markham fell into step beside her.

"So, you're completely ready to kill the leader of the Red Cloaks?"

She looked up at him, found his expression wavering between pride and concern. "If it comes to that, yes."

His teeth tugged at his bottom lip. "He's a very dangerous man."

She raised an eyebrow. "Are you questioning whether I'd be able to do it?"

"It'll be extremely difficult, and we'd have to plan out the assassination with absolute precision. I would probably have a nervous breakdown… But no, I know you're able. I'm just wondering why."

"Why what?"

"Why you offered to take him out without an ounce of hesitation."

She shrugged. "Because I didn't feel any hesitation. If it has to be done, I'll do it. I dawdled around long enough. I'm dedicated to this cause now." Something strange gleamed in his eyes at her words, something so soft and enticing that her stomach flipped, something she might have recognized had she not thought it impossible. "Besides, if he threatens the Rebellion, he threatens you, and I won't let that stand."

He leaned closer. "Remind me never to get on your bad side."

She snorted. "You've been there more than once. I hope you have another earth-shattering secret up your sleeve, because that's the only thing that saved you last time."

His chuckle danced into the night sky and she decided that she wanted to bottle that sound and get drunk on it again and again.

CHAPTER SEVENTEEN

YATHAN QARVETTE HAD CALLED a mandatory assembly and City Square was packed to the point where it was hard to breathe. The Lordes and Representatives had been afforded seats at the front, where the shade of Signal Tower offered protection against Yaekós' mid-morning heat.

Staella and Amile stood steadfast behind Markham's chair, the former making conversation with Chrisjon Damhere while stubbornly ignoring Knoxin's gaze. Amile, on the other hand, kept his eyes fixed upward on the balcony where his brother would soon make an appearance. His teeth were sawing at his bottom lip and he clenched his jaw. Markham felt that same anxiety tug at his own stomach. Yathan had never called an assembly before. He could be announcing a new royal color or declaring war on Havinaak for all they knew.

Or, as the masochistic voice in his mind delighted in reminding him, the rebels could have walked into a public execution.

Who knows how many names Saul already has.

He had to swallow down the bile that rose in his throat. Then, a small hand closed around his shoulder. He looked up to find Staella's eyes locked on his. *Don't worry*, they seemed to say. *I'm here. Whatever happens, we'll fight our way out together.*

He smiled as much as he could manage, grateful for the slight ease in his tense muscles. She kept her hand there, a reassuring pressure as the Square quieted.

Yathan had taken to his podium. He made no introduction and offered no charming witticism in welcome.

Markham gulped.

"Daniel Caneille. Rayn Valanisk. Now, Delilah Haltstone."

Another Representative.

His hands and feet throbbed with pins and needles, dread coiling in his belly. A quarter of them were gone.

"My men have been investigating these disappearances day and night and have come to a horrible conclusion. All signs point to the insurgents plaguing our city. Those who call themselves revolutionaries and hide behind a flag of white lightning. The Rebellion has taken our city's most-loved, no doubt to torture them, to punish them in unspeakable ways for being Goddess-chosen to lead. We all knew Lady Haltstone. We all revered her passion for Aldahad's people and the way she inspired compassion among all its citizens, but these terrorists don't care about kindness, about virtue or innocence. No, they only care about usurping power by defiling our very Core…"

Now really isn't the time for a dramatic pause.

"But fear not, my people, I will not allow these atrocities to continue."

Markham's heart had stopped. He wasn't breathing. His entire existence seemed suspended, awaiting the imminent blow.

"I am declaring a state of emergency."

Staella gasped and tightened her grip on his shoulder. He looked up. Soldiers in full armor descended on the City Square. They marched in perfect rows from every direction: swords, lances, daggers, and shields glinting in the sun. They had surrounded the people of Yaekós completely.

"It has become essential to preserve each citizen's safety. The military will be present in every corner and alley of this city, keeping order and peace. There will be curfews instituted in the Western Rooks and on Coinsgain Plateau. Anyone who cannot prove their affiliation to a noble family will receive a passbook, and only if this book bears authorization due to occupation or formal invitation, will such individuals be allowed on Goldvinger Crest. There will be unnotified searches of homes in the Rooks in order to root out the terrorists. Understand that refusing our soldiers access to any area constitutes a serious offense. Together, we *will* make Yaekós safe again."

There were no cheers, no applauding hands, only heavy silence as the soldiers all around them raised their right fists to their chests—a unanimous salute to their king.

"Passbooks will be distributed this afternoon. Detailed regulations will be put up across the city and will come into effect at sun-down. I appreciate your attendance here today and your co-operation moving forward. May the Goddess bless and protect you."

People started filtering out, eyes hollow with fear and heads bowed to avoid the soldiers' glares. Markham was still sitting. His mind was spinning. His body refused to move.

This can't be happening. This isn't happening.

Leda was the only other Representative who hadn't left yet. She stood, her fists clenched and eyes wide. He stared at her, wishing he could reach out to take her hand and have her reassure him with a snarky joke or an embrace.

He was suddenly aware of something tugging at his shoulder. Then, Staella's desperate voice.

"Markham, we need to leave."

†

"We need to leave," Staella declared again.

It was the only thought that kept running through her mind. These were also the first words any of them had spoken since the assembly earlier. Markham had been staring out the living room window for hours, growing paler by the minute. Amile had lain down on a couch with an astronomy book, but had never turned the page.

Staella had taken out her frustrations on the punching bag in the garden before queuing with the servants to have a passbook shoved into her hands. She'd had to explain her presence at the Aesher estate one too many times before being allowed one of the little green booklets.

Markham didn't shift from his place at the window. "I'm not leaving them."

"Markham–"

He spun to face her, skin sallow but eyes aflame. "They are my people and they are in more danger than they have ever been in. Armed soldiers are about to barge into their homes unannounced. If they find so much as a weapon, a suspicious-looking document, a stuttered truth, they will burn those homes to the ground. My people are going to be massacred."

"Yes." She inhaled shakily. "Yes, they are, and the only way to put an end to that is for the Rebellion to fight harder than we have ever fought before. The only way to keep our people safe is to take Aldahad. And for that, we need a leader. We need influence and resources and unflinching passion. We need you."

"I—"

"You can still be our leader from somewhere else. You can't if you're dead. I promise that Saul will find a way to get to you, and then we are done."

He shook his head, stubborn to the last. "They need money to continue the fight, to get people out. How will they get it if I'm not here?"

Staella opened her mouth, but it was Amile who answered, "Mycah." He sat up, putting the book down on the cupa table. "Mycah can stay in the city. If there's anyone who knows how to lay low and survive chaos, it's her. I can go to her now, take all the coin we can fit into a carriage. I'll be back before dark and the soldiers will be none the wiser. Once Mycah has the money, she'll find a way to get it to Tomhas."

Markham still hesitated, his jaw clenched. "They think the Rebellion kidnapped the Representatives. The people think we're terrorists. I have to tell them the truth. I'm the only one they might believe."

Staella blinked, gaping at him. "Have you gone completely mad? Yathan will have you gutted in a private display."

The solution once again came from Amile. "We distribute flyers and let the people know that the High Ruler is spreading lies. It might look like a desperate bid to save our asses, but it's better than doing nothing. Mycah can arrange it with Emzin."

"We're putting Mycah in so much danger," Markham argued.

"We're all in danger," Staella snapped. She was tired of debating, of wasting time. She needed to keep him safe, not just for her own sanity, but for the future of the Rebellion. "If she wanted a safe, quiet life, she wouldn't have come to you after you freed her. She wouldn't have stayed. I'm sure she's more than capable of taking care of herself… Markham, please."

He sighed, sank into the love chair. "Where would we even go?"

"My home. Avetown is small, less guarded, and far enough from here that we'll have ample warning if Saul decides to hunt us down. We'll leave tomorrow at dawn. We don't take a carriage, only three horses, and essential supplies. We can make the journey in five days if we ride hard."

After a few seconds of pregnant silence, Markham finally nodded. Staella nearly collapsed in relief.

Then, Amile said, "I can't go with you."

She glared at him, but his eyes were fixed on Markham. Their gazes locked in silent conversation. *I hate it when they do that.*

Amile didn't break the stare as he stated, "Five days of travel. That means four nights. And even when we get there, where would I sleep?"

Staella scowled. "What do you mean where will you sleep? You'll sleep where we sleep."

They wholly ignored her, their wordless conversation now an argument. Eventually, Amile relented. He refused to look at her, his voice barely a whisper.

"Staella, the time has come for me to tell you my story."

THE BOY

WHEN YATHAN QARVETTE BECAME the High Ruler of the People's Monarchy, his younger brother was only fifteen. Though the boy looked so much like him, they were vastly different. Where Yathan could be found sparring with the older boys, drinking, hunting, and tumbling girls, the boy was softer. Quieter.

He liked to read, play the piano, and dance with his little sister, who was a scrawny little thing with big, blue eyes. He never joined on the hunting trips; he preferred to study the deer that came to the forest edge, to gain their trust until they came close enough for him to capture in drawings.

He didn't have as many friends as the High Ruler, but the friendships he had he valued greatly—none more so than the steady companionship he found in the eleven-year-old Markham Aesher.

The golden boy was his sister's age, but he was so bold and full of ideas that the young Qarvette could barely keep up.

When his brother got married nearly a year after the coronation, the boy's parents moved out of the city. The children remained at their beloved home, where servants and teachers took care of them. The boy missed his parents, but he enjoyed life at the estate, enjoyed playing in the kennels and showing his drawings to Markham's beautiful older cousin. He was perhaps overly analytical and unnervingly quiet, but he was content.

However, his life changed completely one night, when the darkness seemed to change him. When the sun departed from the horizon, everything that made the boy who he was gave way to bloodlust. He wasn't animalistic or mindless. He was calculating, which made him all the more terrifying.

The first time, he killed his squire with a broken pencil. The next, most of the Qarvette servants didn't survive.

When the guards finally managed to restrain him, he was locked in his room and chained to the bed. He screamed for the rest of the night, howled to be freed so he could silence the thrumming of blood in his ears, so he could appease the voices calling for death.

When morning came, the boy was gentle and scared. He remembered what he'd done and how he'd felt, but there was none of the bloodlust left.

But it returned that night and every night after, only the full moon offering a brief reprieve.

They tried to sedate him, but no dose worked. He was chained every day at sunset, but the lust only grew until he nearly shattered the bedposts, until his roars could be heard throughout the estate, until he started sawing at his own arms with splinters and nails just to see blood. It was clear that the High Ruler's little brother was very, very ill.

Yathan did not seek help or tell their parents. He made the servants take a vow of secrecy and locked the boy away in the southern tower. His days were spent reading, drawing, crying. He didn't see Markham or Maci anymore, only the petrified guard who brought him his meals.

Then, one day, his sister came. She'd gotten taller, more beautiful, in the year since he'd seen her. The boy laughed and pulled her into his arms. She wasn't afraid of him like the others, but she was cold, and her eyes held a wisdom beyond her thirteen years.

She stood before him, unflinching and unfeeling as she told him to leave. Told him that he had brought his family nothing but suffering and shame. That if he cared for them at all, he would leave the estate and never return, like the disgraced son he was. She left the key to his prison on the nightstand and disappeared.

The boy ran away.

He took his books and his chains, and he went to Markham Aesher, to the little boy who faced everything life threw at him like an adventure. Markham listened and his eyes grew wide, but he didn't run or scream or flinch. He took his friend's hand and told his parents that the boy would be staying. Howell and Lehana Aesher gave the boy a room with a door that locked from the outside with heavy bolts. He would never again be chained to his bed, never again be imprisoned during the day.

The bloodlust still came every night, but he got a little better. At least now, he could sleep until around midnight and didn't harm himself anymore. Because he was safe and loved.

He vowed never to leave Markham's side, even when the golden boy became a young man and learned to charm the antlers off a stag. Even when Lehana died and Howell left and it was just the two of them. Even when Markham decided he would take Yathan's crown and give it to the people.

CHAPTER EIGHTEEN

Leda,

I am leaving Yaekós. I trust you enough to disclose to you that we will be staying with Staella's family in Avetown. I wanted to stay in the city to help the rebels escape this chaos we're in, but Staella and Amile believe that it is important for the survival of the Rebellion that I be kept out of harm's way. Due to the potentially damning nature of this information, I ask that you burn this letter once you have finished reading it. Feel free to do so now if you don't want to know what I have to say.

I know that I hurt you deeply and I cannot possibly convey how sorry I am on a piece of paper... I know it must seem like I do not value our friendship, but I promise you that is not the case.

I don't know what I'm doing most of the time. I'm in this, but I'm so terrified and unsure and incompetent. I didn't want to involve you in the whole mess of it.

Selfishly, I wanted an escape. I wanted a haven where I could just be a kid, to be who I was raised to be without dooming an entire population. I found that safe place with you and for that I cannot thank you enough.

Yes, I must admit that I was afraid of your reaction, afraid that you would be disgusted at my association with the rebels, that you would damn me for rejecting everything we were taught. Now, I realize that I was a complete idiot for even having considered that a possibility. I know that you will always have my back. More than that, I know that you will always choose what is right.

I hope that I can earn your forgiveness one day because it would be truly devastating to live in a world without your wit and daring.

I beg of you not to let my lapse in judgment drive you away from the Rebellion. They need all the help they can get. But I know that, as the reincarnation of

Lowena Hayvinger, you already know that in your heart.

Please be safe. You are always in my prayers.

With all my love,

Markham xxx

Leda glared at the letter, cursed Markham Aesher for his damned eloquence. She held the piece of paper up to one of the candles on her desk. It was infuriating that one person could hurt her so deeply one moment and then melt her heart with a few well-written words the next. She watched the flame lick up the sides of the sheet, turning it to ash.

The reincarnation of Lowena Hayvinger.

No. She wasn't Lowena. She wasn't that fierce, that forceful. She couldn't possibly be all her ancestor had been, because she had never needed to claw her way out of poverty against all odds.

But she didn't need to be Lowena. Because Leda had power and money. She had a lifetime of experience in handling the might-mad nobles who would stand against them. She knew what the other side thought and desired, and how they played their games of power. She wasn't the Demon, but she knew very well that politics could be deadlier than any weapon, and perhaps that was what *this* Rebellion needed more.

She wouldn't go after Markham. She wasn't ready to face him yet and knew that she was needed here.

I may not be Lowena, but I have her name. A name that meant more to the people of Aldahad than *Qarvette* ever would.

Despite the late hour, she rang the little bell to her left. Her handmaiden appeared seconds later. "Natali, please summon Veress."

"Yes, my lady." The girl curtsied and scurried out of the study.

Leda wondered whether the rebels would accept her allegiance, whether they would scoff at her for growing up in a palace with servants to take care of her every need…

There was a knock at the door and then Natali entered with a confused-looking Veress trailing behind her. The nurse was wearing a silver nightgown, the material crumpled and her olive skin puffy with sleep.

"Thank you, Natali," Leda offered with the kindest smile she could manage. "You may retire for the night. And you can sleep in tomorrow morning."

Natali blinked, hesitated before dropping into a quick curtsy. "Thank you, my lady."

Veress stepped forward, sniffing and rearranging the knot of black hair on top of her head. "You wanted to see me?"

Leda nodded and gestured at the chair on the opposite side of the desk. After Veress took her seat, Leda blurted, "You're a member of the Rebellion."

The nurse's face turned near-gray. *At least she's awake now.* "What?"

"Come on, Veress. You gave me that whole speech about Lowena changing the system. You're the one who gave me her journal. I know you read it, which means that you know about the missing Core too. There's a reason you wanted me to know."

Veress' mouth gaped open, closed again as no words came out. Finally, she relented with a sigh. "Yes."

Thank the Goddess.

"So, you know who the leader is, then?"

The nurse narrowed her eyes and cocked an eyebrow. "I assume you're not asking about the Rooks man giving our orders…?"

"You know I'm not."

"Very few people are aware of the other leader's involvement."

"Then, why are you?"

Silence. Veress just looked at her, assessing every breath she took. "Because I am part of the inner circle of the Rebellion, the commanders second only to the leaders."

The breath *whooshed* out of Leda's lungs. "How did you—how did you keep this secret for all these years?"

The corners of her mouth tilted up. "I wouldn't have been in the inner circle if I wasn't good at keeping my mouth shut."

Leda shook her head. "Well… Wow. This is perfect, actually. See, I need you to tell me what to do."

"What?"

"Veress, I'm joining the Rebellion. My resources, knowledge, influence, it's all at your disposal. So, tell me how I can make the biggest possible difference."

The other woman had lost the ability to close her mouth. "You're serious?"

"If that came off as a joke, I really need to work on my communication skills."

Veress was on her side of the desk in a flash, arms thrown around her and tears staining the Representative's robe.

"Oh, you beautiful, wonderful, Goddess-sent girl. I knew it. All those years, I knew that you were better than all of the others put together. I have to convene with the others, but yes. Leda, this is exactly what we need. We'll make it now. We can actually make it."

Leda shifted in her seat. "I'm flattered that you have this much faith in me."

Veress took her hands. "The last time a Representative decided to join us, we got safe-houses, valuable intel, and actual weapons. We went from a back-alley group to a fully-fledged resistance movement. Imagine what we can do with a Hayvinger in our ranks."

Leda could imagine it and it terrified her, but it also filled her with hope. She saw herself, kneeling in front of Lowena, brown eyes looking into brown, black hands intertwined. It had taken more than a hundred years, but there was finally another Hayvinger to take up the fight.

†

It was well past midnight and Staella hadn't slept a wink. Whether the insomnia was caused by the catastrophe the city had become or Amile's tortured screams, she didn't know.

She'd given up on closing her eyes. It just made the images more vivid: an old man's golden eyes, a hummingbird burnt into brown skin, the glint of sunlight on armor, a boy locked in a tower.

She was on the floor, her knees pulled up to her chest and head resting against the bed behind her.

How could anyone kick out their mentally ill brother? How could no one seek help for a child because it would stain the family name? How could one man have enough power to place the entire city in a grip of fear and how would they recover from being called terrorists, from being declared the people's enemy?

She clutched her head in her hands, fingers digging notches into her temples. *I can't wait to leave this place.* But she knew that leaving Yaekós did not mean leaving their problems behind. No, the kindling had been ignited and facing the fire was inevitable.

She startled at the sound of a knock on her door. "It's open," she rasped. And in came the reason she would face all of this insanity over again.

The candlelight cast Markham's shadow across the far wall, tall and thin. His shirt was askew and his hair was a disheveled mess, the skin beneath his eyes dark. Then, silver brimmed his eyes and he started crying before either of them could speak. A quiet sob hunched his shoulders and sent two perfect tears rolling down his cheeks.

She was across the room before she realized she'd moved. As their bodies crashed together, his arms engulfed her completely. He buried his face in the crook of her neck and clutched at her nightgown as if she was a lifeline in the stormy current.

She felt the wet tears on her skin as her body moved with every sob that tore out of him. She wanted it to stop, wanted to hug him until all his tears evaporated. Her left hand slipped under his shirt, traveled up the warm planes of his back to trace soothing patterns on the skin. The right buried itself in his hair. He shuddered as a new wave of emotion crashed over him. She pulled him impossibly closer, pressed her lips to the side of his head, and closed her eyes.

"I'm so scared," he whispered.

It broke her heart. "I know. I am too."

He lifted his head, his hand cupping the back of her neck. "I feel like the worry is driving me insane, and then I feel guilty for feeling scared and that's even worse. What right do I have to be scared? I'm in a fortress surrounded by guards. I'm here with you, but the people in the Rooks… Imagine the level of fear they're feeling. Imagine being down there just waiting for soldiers to knock down your door. They have nothing to protect them and yet I have the audacity to be scared. I have the luxury of running away and I—I can't imagine how they must be feeling… and Mycah–" Another sob. "Oh, Goddess, I wish I could save them."

He rested his forehead against hers, closing his eyes in a futile attempt to calm down. "It is precisely that guilt, Markham, that makes you better than all of your peers. You are going against a strong system, people with power beyond even yours. They're starting to fight back, hard. You have every right to be afraid. But I promise—I *promise*—that I will not let anything happen to you. I promise that we will survive this, that the Rebellion will come out stronger, that we will change Aldahad forever."

For the first time, saying it out loud to him, she believed it. He wasn't crying anymore, but his breath still hitched with the aftermath of the sobbing. His fingers started moving almost imperceptibly, rubbing circles into the back of her head.

"How are you this good at making me feel better?"

The corners of her mouth tugged upward and she shrugged. "It's a careful mix of flattery and sounding really badass. It usually works on you."

He pulled back a fraction of an inch to look at her. "What a mess we're in."

She huffed. "You can say that again. And it's not just the state of emergency." Becoming very aware of their proximity, she stepped away to take a seat on the bed. He joined her without hesitation. "It's—" Right on cue, another scream echoed through the mansion, a cry for relief or release. Staella flinched, pulling the covers up to her chest. "—that. It's so much worse knowing it's him. I keep imagining him up there, tearing at the door or hurting himself. I wish I could help him."

Markham nodded, wiped a tired hand over his face. "When he first told me, I didn't know what to say. I'd thought he'd just gone to his parents for a year. I never could have imagined that my best friend had been locked up in a tower for that long. I don't know why he didn't go to them, why he chose me… but I'm glad he did. At least now someone's helping him. When he first started living here, doctors came every day. They all came to the same conclusion: there was no illness. Not even sedation worked. Eventually, he begged us to give up, to stop trying to save him."

She put a hand on his knee and squeezed. "You've been a good friend to him."

His eyes caught on her hand and lingered before he slowly lifted his gaze to her face. Her heart fluttered. When he looked at her like that—like he never wanted to stop looking—it sent all the heat in her body pooling into her core. Her mouth went dry. She was staring. She didn't care. Her eyes traced the lines of his cheekbones, the little cleft in his chin, the faint dusting of freckles on the bridge of his nose. She wanted to count them, trace her fingers over the constellations they formed, kiss them one after the other. Her focus shifted downward to his slightly-parted lips. They would be soft, she knew. Would draw her in and never let go.

She'd unwittingly leaned in, and before she could stop herself, she blurted, "Stay." His eyes widened. She froze. *Shit.* She pulled her hand away, sat back. "I, uh, you should sleep here. I mean, if you want to. I just thought it would be easier to fall asleep if we weren't alone. If we slept together. Well, not *slept* together. Just slept. In the same room. Together."

He was laughing–the bastard. "I've never seen you this flustered. It suits you." She stuck her tongue out at him.

Wow, Staella, real mature.

"I would like to stay. You know, to sleep." She rolled her eyes and jabbed an elbow in his ribs.

So, they laid down, extinguished the candles, and pulled up the covers. Only, Staella's mind was far from sleep because there he was. Inches away. In her bed. She could feel the heat from his body and smell his vanilla and sandalwood scent. It was masochistic, she knew, to entertain the idea of being with him. He could have anyone he wanted. Even if he chose her, it wouldn't be for long.

But, Goddess, she wanted him. A lot. Would it be that bad if she just cuddled up to him?

"Markham?"

There was a long silence. Then, as if he'd read her mind, he whispered, "Come here."

A breath escaped from her as she molded her body to his. His arm wrapped around her waist, solid and warm as he tucked her against his side. Their legs entwined and she couldn't help but wriggle even closer. His chin rested against the top of her head and she melted.

She was smiling. They were smack in the middle of an apocalypse. Her friend was howling upstairs, yet all it took was Markham holding her and she smiled.

When did I start needing him this much?

Markham's breathing evened out and she found the steady sound of his heartbeat lulling her to sleep.

CHAPTER NINETEEN

DESPITE THE SUFFOCATING HEAT that clung to any skin, the oversized creatures that scurried in the shadows, and the onslaught of insects, the Roäk jungle at dusk was one of the most stunning things Staella had ever seen. Through the dense web of leaves overhead, the last sun rays of the day filtered in honey-colored patches. The insistent humming of beetle-like bugs was interjected by the mocking calls of parrots flitting through the air, their bellies wine red and their wings moving kaleidoscopes.

Her good mood was short-lived. She pulled the chains out of her pack and grimaced at the grotesque shackles at either end. Amile had chosen a tree trunk and sank down against it. He faced away from the clearing where she and Markham had made camp. He couldn't bear them seeing what he became and claimed that the fire only aggravated his savage half.

The smoke set Staella on edge as well, but she feared the jungle life more than the risk of detection. Hopefully, the foliage above would serve as protection.

She wrapped the chain around the trunk, fastened the shackles around his too-thin wrists, and covered his mouth with a rag. His eyes remained fixed on the floor and all she could offer him was a squeeze to the arm when she was done.

Being chained up again worsened his condition. He no longer slept until near-midnight. As soon as the sun set, Amile was no longer Amile.

Markham waited for her by the fire, gnawing at a piece of dried meat with a grimace. It was their third night in the Roäk and the lad was missing his luxuries.

They'd left via Yaekós' northern gate that first morning, under the guise of a camping trip in the Krezín mountains. Staella knew that Saul would be informed of their departure immediately, which is why they'd only turned southwest after about an hour of riding, to follow the narrow paths that led through the jungle to the smaller towns in the south.

The muscles in her thighs and buttocks screamed in protest as she sat down next to Markham. Even miserable and sweaty, he managed to smell like vanilla.

She groaned. "I hate riding."

"Mmm. A carriage would have been lovely. An inn. Some real food."

She rolled her eyes at him. "We'll be in Avetown in less than two days and then you'll be treated to my sister's cooking. She is phenomenal. I can already smell it. Creamy potatoes with cheese. Soft, marinated chicken…" His stomach rumbled loudly and she burst out laughing.

Taking another bite of dried meat, he jabbed her in the ribs. "You are sadistic, Staella Thenos." She could only grin.

Then, with a rattle of chains, it began. Amile's muffled screams engulfed the clearing. The chain pulled taut around the tree trunk. He was trying to escape. Staella gulped and turned her head away.

"So, what topic shall we use to distract ourselves tonight?" Markham asked thickly.

It had become their habit to talk each other to sleep, to keep their minds off the friend roaring for their blood. They'd covered everything from childhood memories, to books, to what they'd want as a superpower.

Clenching her jaw, she murmured, "These nights are ruining him. I feel like I'm inflicting torture."

He kept his eyes on the fire, teeth sawing at his bottom lip. "I know. I wish I could do more for him."

She placed a tentative hand on his knee. "You've already offered him more than his family ever did."

The corners of his mouth twitched upward. "Sometimes, the people we meet later in life come to be more important than family."

His eyes fixed on hers and bore into her soul as silence enveloped them. A part of her would be content like this forever, getting drunk on the affection in his eyes, getting lost in the heat where their shoulders met. There was another part of her that would not be satisfied with as little, that wanted to surge forward and kiss him until his lips were swollen and the only word he knew was her name. Goddess, she wanted him like she'd never wanted anything in her life.

Lost in the idea of his arms wrapping around her, she whispered, "I want to kiss you."

His eyes widened, his pulse becoming visible at his throat. Yet, his words remained smooth as always. "I don't expect you'll be met with much resistance," he purred.

That sound…

He was so close. So perfect. Leaning in would be the easiest thing in the world.

"Markham?"

"Hmmm?"

"I need to ask you about something Mycah told me."

His heavy-lidded eyes fluttered open and he frowned. "Okay?"

Staella looked away, gulped. *Why can't I just leave well enough alone?* "She, uh, well, she said that... That you like pretty things and then easily tire of them. That it's what happened with Harper and Lai and Asha and Yzette."

She hated that she remembered each of those names with perfect clarity, hated that she imagined his lips dripping with each of them. He was quiet. She looked up, hating the twisted hurt in his expression.

"And you believed her, I presume."

Staella opened her mouth. Closed it. Opened it. *Shit.* "No... Yes... I don't know. I mean, I feel like I don't, but then every time we get close enough, it pops up in my head and I can't help but freak out. Come on, Markham, you're you. You can have anyone you want. It makes sense."

Markham pursed his lips together, his voice too calm for the situation. "I suppose I understand how my past relationships could have appeared that way to an outsider, especially one with Mycah's experience of men... but I didn't fall in love with those women because they're beautiful. Sure, I'm not blind and there's an abundance of good-looking people on the Crest. But contrary to popular opinion, my love is not that cheap. I found something in each of those girls that was impossible not to adore.

"Harper was my first in many respects, but also in love. What I found irresistible about her was that she could walk into a room and talk to anyone, could make anyone laugh. I fell for Lai because she was the most passionate person I'd ever met. Her highs made life an instant paradise and her lows completely devastated it. I was always a little out of breath with her, like she lived at a faster pace than the rest of us…

"Asha… I was consumed by Asha's darkness because I believed that I could fix the broken things inside her… And Yzette I loved most of all. She was a servant at the estate, quiet but so strong. She accepted me unconditionally and she became my home."

His eyes were foggy, his teeth working at his bottom lip. "None of those relationships ended because I grew bored. Harper decided I was too young for her, told me I had just been some fun for a few months. Lai decided to denounce monogamy and that didn't sit so well with me. Asha's drinking problem took over her entire life and I had to leave for my own well-being. Yzette…" He closed his eyes, taking a steadying breath.

"Yzette got a marriage proposal from a wealthy merchant on the Plateau. She didn't want to accept, but both of us knew that our relationship was a dead end. I'd never win the Election with a peasant wife. Of course, I told her that I didn't care about any of it, but she was the voice of reason. It would change the course of the Rebellion if I became High Ruler and I'd made my promise to Leda… So, she married him and I never saw her again." He huffed. "I even went looking for her, but they'd moved."

Staella felt like she'd been struck in the chest. "Goddess, I'm an idiot." He gave no reply and they sat in silence for some time before she finally built up the courage to ask, "If Yzette came back, would you want to be with her?"

He inhaled loudly. "Yzette was what I needed then. I was anxious about everything and her stability kept me sane… but a lot has changed in the years she's been gone. I don't need gentle strength now. I need a partner. Someone who doesn't flinch when difficult decisions have to be made. Someone who cuts off the fingers of my enemies, who shackles Amile to a tree every night because I can't bear to do it, who promises to kill the Red Cloak leader to protect me and my people."

Her heart twisted in her chest and her breath caught in her throat. "Markham, you're engaged to Leda."

He shook his head. "You know it's not like that."

"Nevertheless, it means that any relationship with you will always be a secret affair, something to hide from the world. I'm sorry, but I will always want more than that."

"I won't break my promise to her," came his tortured whisper.

Staella looked away and focused her blurry vision on the fire. "I know."

In a sudden burst of movement, Markham stood, his hands fisted in his hair as he paced. "It's all this bloody Election. Without it, no one would give a rat's ass who married whom. Without it, I wouldn't have had to save Leda from her father's ruthless hunger for power. For generations, that family has been obsessed with nothing but winning the Election. So, they marry off their Representatives like pawns. Alliances and public support and—"

"Markham."

"I wish I could grab Honiel by the neck and tell him what a failure he is as a parent. He doesn't even know who his daughter is, how amazing she is, and her good-for-nothing brother has always been an emotionally abusive twat. So, who's the man that steps up? Who sacrifices his chances at happiness before he even knows what that means? Who—?"

"Markham!"

"What?"

Staella's hand trembled as she pointed to Amile's tree. Where the chain lay slack and unmoving. There was no rattling. No muffled screams. She leapt up and dashed to where their friend should have been sitting. There was nothing but shackles, and it looked like they'd been sawed through.

"Friction," Markham muttered over her shoulder. "Rubbing them together for long enough would break them… He's been planning it since the first night."

Staella shook her head. "Amile wouldn't—"

"He's not Amile right now."

She dropped her head into her hands. "I should've checked the shackles every morning. I would've seen the weak spots…"

"None of that is important right now. He's loose in this jungle with the singular intention of killing and we're the only human prey for miles."

She gulped. "We'll split up, find him, and restrain him."

Markham's jaw was clenched so tightly it must've hurt. "But we leave the weapons here. We can't hurt him."

She nodded. "There's rope in one of the saddlebags. I'll take that. You take the chain. Call out as soon as you find him."

They shared a long, heavy stare before setting out with their hearts in their throats.

Staella headed west, squinting into the darkness as she strayed farther and farther from the fire. Not a single frog belched. Not a mosquito zinged. The very jungle was holding its breath. The silence turned her shallow breaths to gasps, the blood in her ears to a thundering drum.

A rustle sounded from behind her.

She twisted around. It was only a breeze through the branches. Clutching a hand to her chest, she took a steadying breath and continued westward. *Maybe I should call his name? I'm just looking for a friend, after all.*

No. She would be giving away her location to a murderous madman. She remembered his story, remembered that he'd killed half the Qarvette servants the last time he was free, and he'd only been a teenager.

She changed course north, south again, and farther west. Nothing. *Maybe Markham found him.* She started back toward the campsite. What would they do if they didn't find him? What would they do if they did?

A hand closed around her neck and she screamed. A body pressed up against her back, breathing heavily.

"Amile."

Fingers tightened around her throat. Tightened even further. She wheezed, but he didn't stop. The hand pressed down. White flashed at the edges of her vision. Everything swam. Tears streamed down her face.

He didn't relent. She was going to die. He was going to kill her.

Desperation made her hands shoot up. Nails raked gouges into his arm. He wailed and loosened his grip. But he didn't stop. He was fearless. Remorseless. Wanted nothing but her death.

With all the strength she could muster, she swung her leg back. Heel met groin and she was free. She stumbled forward, gasping. Clutched at her raw throat. She spun and he was already there. Pain was a mere inconvenience.

His skin glowed pale in the moonlight, his wrists red and arms bleeding. His eyes… *Goddess.* His eyes were devoid of Amile's wit and shy kindness. Golden abysses of purpose and calculation.

Looking into those eyes, she understood that they'd played right into his hands. Separated. Far from the fire. And she'd walked straight into a maze of tree trunks—a dark labyrinth where he could pounce.

Her eyes flashed left and right. *Find an escape.* But the trees were so dense. There was nowhere to run. Clenching her fists and rallying her courage, she faced him again.

Gone. He was gone.

Blood turned to ice in her veins. She spun and scanned the darkness. Her heart fluttered and her muscles tensed. She stepped forward. Nothing. No sound. No shadows. No movement.

Bam! She was on the ground. Body screaming. Head throbbing. Struggling to see, she noticed he'd thrown her down. The rope was discarded somewhere on the ground. She reached for it.

A hand dug into her ankle. She screamed again. He pulled, walked, and dragged her along. Sticks and rocks tore through clothing and skin as her back scraped across the jungle floor. She kicked. Tried to turn. Tried to get up.

Searing pain. Flashes of foliage. Fear.

He pivoted, arm that held her swinging. Her body flew sideways and her waist met a tree trunk. She couldn't help but cry out.

I'm going to die.

Amile stepped into her line of blurry sight, the satisfaction in his eyes a rare show of emotion. He leaned down. Grabbed her hair. Yanked her up. The other hand closed around her throat. His nails dug into skin and she understood. Strangling her would take too much time, would be too clean. He'd rip out her throat instead.

Her instincts screamed: jab his throat, poke out his eyes. But it would kill him, leave him blind.

Her blood ran thick and sticky down her neck.

"Amile," she choked. "Please."

He didn't stop.

With a roar, Staella slammed her fist into his nose. His grip broke and he stumbled backwards. He launched at her with a snarl and she sagged into a fighting stance, growling.

Her kick met his gut, but he grabbed her leg. Slammed her into the earth. Then, he was on top of her. Straddling her. She punched him in the ribs and he didn't flinch. His fist against her cheek. Pain exploded. Another hit.

Again.

Again.

Again.

Blood ran down her face. Her neck.

Pain. Pain. Pain.

Someone shouted and the weight on top of her lifted. No more blows, but still so much pain. Her head lolled to the side and the world devolved into oblivion.

CHAPTER TWENTY

"SHE'S STILL OUT COLD," Markham said to no one in particular.

Amile remained silent as he cleaned Staella's wounds with alcohol. The rag was already soaked crimson and he'd only just started on her back. Her ankle was black with bruises, her scalp littered with cuts. A patch of her hair had been ripped out. Her lip split open. Deep gouges stood out against the fair skin of her neck. Her back was a mesh of torn flesh. And her face… Her face was a swollen, purple mess. She'd lost consciousness as soon as Markham had managed to get Amile off her. It was morning and she still hadn't woken up.

Markham clenched and unclenched his fists compulsively, trying not to look at the man across from him, who still hadn't said anything. Amile hadn't escaped unscathed, had long scratches running down his right arm and a nasty bruise blooming across his ribs.

When the sun rose, Amile had been frozen, like someone had hollowed him out from the inside. Then, he'd started sobbing. He could remember it all, every detail except for his escape. Apparently, the killer Amile was smart enough to hide secrets from even himself.

Markham had simply untied him, giving his shoulder a squeeze. It was the most he could manage for the person who'd assaulted his Staella.

Markham held her hand as Amile worked, and it took nearly all his strength not to just curl up next to her and stay there. It was his best friend's hitched breath that broke him from his daze.

Amile's head was buried in his hands. "I'm so sorry."

Markham gulped. "You don't have to apologize for something that you didn't do."

He shot up into a standing position, threw the rag onto Staella's unmoving body. "But I did it. *I* did it, Markham. I remember it. I remember my hands around her throat—"

"Amile."

"I remember the fear and the pain in her eyes—"

"Amile."

"And I remember liking it."

Markham was trembling, still clutching Staella's hand like his life depended on it. "Please, stop."

"No. Not until you stop being nice to me. Not until you get angry at me."

"I am angry at you, damnit!" That shut him up. Markham shot into a standing position, tears welling in his eyes. "I am so angry that I can barely look at you… But I know it wasn't your fault, and I know you're already beating yourself up enough for the both of us. You are my best friend and that doesn't end now, but Goddess help me, if you keep testing me, I will snap and I will put you in a worse condition than the one she's in. So, please stop."

Amile's shoulders slumped and he whispered, "Okay."

"Now, what's your prognosis?"

He shook his head. "This is way out of my league. I don't know. She sustained quite severe head injuries. A lot of blood loss and shock. If we keep cleaning the wounds, they shouldn't get infected, but I don't know how long it'll take for her to regain consciousness."

Markham's jaw clenched. "All we can do is keep going and get her home where she can rest."

†

"Please tell me this big unveiling isn't a haircut," Maci called from Leda's bedroom. The latter was in the adjacent closet, getting ready.

"What's so horrible about a haircut?" she asked.

She could practically hear Maci's eyes rolling. "Oh, Leda. Girl decides to change her life. How does she declare this to the world? She cuts her hair. It's an awful cliché and I try to avoid the predicted paths."

Leda chuckled. "Says the beautiful, world-traveling princess with chests full of ball gowns and a prince at her side."

"Mmm. Technically by living like a princess but not being one, I'm subverting that stereotype. You should take note, my lady." She snorted. "And I suppose my prince is supposed to be Amile. Call him *that* to his face and he'd probably give you his serial-killer look. Besides, he seems unable to make up his mind about being at my side. I swear, I have never met a more confusing man in my life."

"Well, the only good news I can offer is that it's not a haircut."

She stepped out of the closet and up to the bedroom's full-length mirror. She'd had the outfit made a few days ago, her usual dresses too impractical. Besides, they'd all been chosen for her. They belonged to a girl she no longer had any desire to resemble.

The woman in the mirror now was someone she wanted to be. The leggings were made of black leather and hugged her legs like a second skin right down to the matching knee-high boots. It contrasted stunningly with the loose white top that billowed around her frame, leaving ample room for movement. Her hair was pulled back, her face without a mask of makeup. She looked older, stronger, like someone who could join a revolution.

Maci stepped up behind her, wrapping pale arms around her shoulders. "It's much better than a haircut."

Leda smiled, squeezing her friend's hand. "Thank you. It helps quite a lot with the confidence levels."

Maci stepped away, cocking an eyebrow. "Doesn't seem like it with those trembling hands."

Leda huffed, looking down at her traitorous fingers. "I may be slightly terrified."

"I'd be concerned if you weren't. You are risking your life, after all."

Leda spun away from the mirror, a wave of nausea sweeping over her. "So are you, yet your hands seem perfectly steady."

"I'll let you in on a secret of mine… I've been a rebel at heart for years."

Leda shook her head. "I still can't believe you're so fine with Markham not telling you he's the leader of the Rebellion."

Maci sank down on the bed with a sigh. "I'd be lying if I said I'm not a little disappointed—mostly in Amile, but I understand why they had to keep it a secret and I admire them for being able to do so."

"Well, you're a better person than I am. I was—"

The door burst open and Veress all but fell into the room, hair disheveled and face flushed pink. She curtsied hurriedly in Maci's direction before facing Leda.

"We have a problem."

"With the setup outside?"

The nurse shook her head. "With the soldiers." Keeping her gaze fixed on Leda's, she nodded slowly. "It has begun."

Leda gulped and straightened. "May the Goddess be on our side."

As the three of them headed for the estate's entrance, Maci asked, "Remind me again why they can't just come *in* through the sewers too?"

"Because it sends a message," Leda replied, "…to anyone who is still unsure of their loyalties, to anyone who may have lost hope. Leda Hayvinger is with the Rebellion."

The ruckus from the setup on the back lawns could be heard all the way to the front gate. The servants and guards had been informed of the plan nearly a week ago and none of them had failed to volunteer. She'd sent her father and brother to the villa in Saribi, her mother to the Blomehill country estate with a new nurse, maids, and guards. Only then had the preparations begun—supplies were bought, extra beds were made, and long tables were carried out into the garden.

The Hayvinger mansion would host nearly a hundred rebels. In the next few days, they would all work together to make up supply packs to aid those very rebels in their escape through the sewers. Once free of the capital, they would be on their own until the next mass meeting, a time and place for which had already been set.

"It also sends that message to those who would have your head for it," Maci countered.

Gaining resolve with every click of her boots on the marble pathway, Leda answered, "It does, but it doesn't give them proof. If Yathan Qarvette executes a Hayvinger on a hunch, he'll lose his crown within a week… The two of you should go to the back and help them get ready. I'll take care of the military."

Veress and Maci nodded, the latter giving Leda's hand a final squeeze before turning away. The Representative took a steadying breath and nodded to the guard at the gate.

What greeted her in the street was near chaos. As far as the eye could see, the bronze roads were lined with scrawny, half-cleaned, and poorly-clothed people. They were abuzz with fear and excitement, queued up to enter her home. From the surrounding estates, servants, children, and nobles had rushed out to behold the sight of common folk on the Crest.

Oh yes, her message would be sent.

At the front of the line, a few steps away, was a group of six armed soldiers. Their leader—a lieutenant by the markings on his breastplate—had a young, shivering rebel by the collar.

The soldier's face was red with frustration and spittle flew as he roared, "You're taking a fat chance, kid. I swear, I can't wait til the lot of you are exterminated like the rats you are. Coming here and telling me–"

"Is there a problem, Lieutenant?"

"Yes, there's a bloody problem." The man turned, froze as he recognized her. "Lady Hayvinger, I—"

"What is your name, Lieutenant?"

"Arian, my lady." He raised his arm in a quick salute.

"Lieutenant Arian, I asked you whether there's a problem."

"Uh, yes, my lady. These peasants all want their passbooks signed on the ground of formal invitation. They say they are your guests."

She blinked at him. "I still don't see the problem."

The soldier was probably in his early thirties, had a bad haircut, and perfect teeth. His mouth opened and closed like that of a dying fish.

"My lady, I—This—They cannot—"

"These men and women are my honored guests." Leda cocked her head, surprised at how much she enjoyed watching him squirm.

"But they're—they're from the Rooks."

Leda stepped closer to him, deepening her voice. "It doesn't matter where they're from. Quick lesson on politics, lieutenant. Hospitality goes a long way with potential voters."

Arian blinked rapidly, shaking his head. "This is highly irregular, my lady. I cannot sign all of these people's passbooks."

Leda crossed her arms and gave another step forward, grateful for the genes that made her tall. "I'd take a moment to consider the consequences of denying me the opportunity to campaign."

A muscle twitched in his jaw. "I'll have to report it."

She shrugged. "Report it, then, but sign the damn passbooks. If you disrespect my guests again, I'll be forced to file a report of my own. Whose do you think will carry more weight, *Lieutenant*?"

He stared her down for a few seconds, then nodded. "Of course, my lady. Forgive me."

She smiled sweetly yet venomously. "You are forgiven. Send them in when you're done."

Leda turned and started back to the estate, barely containing her grin at the snickers and cheers that came from the crowd behind her.

It had begun.

For the first time in her life, Leda truly understood how useless her privileged upbringing had rendered her. She couldn't tie a bow. Regardless of the fact that Veress had showed her slowly, her fingers refused to cooperate with her brain.

The back lawns of the Hayvinger estate were flooded with people, all abuzz and hard at work. The scalding Yaekós sun had left Leda sweaty and irritable, but the rebels remained unfazed, their good spirits seemingly in endless supply.

She was stationed near the end of the final table, where the completed, cloth-wrapped packs needed only to be tied up with string.

She tried one more time, murmuring to herself, "Okay, so you keep your finger here and then you loop and just—ugh!"
Leda threw her hands up into the air with an exasperated sigh while the servant girl on her right tried and failed to suppress a giggle. Then, an umber hand appeared on the pack in front of her.

"I can show you an easier way," a low voice said from her left.

She looked up to find an older man with hickory-colored eyes and a close-lipped smile. He towered over her, as broad as he was tall. She gaped at him for a few seconds before finally nodding. Embarrassment heated her face.

"Thank you. I never knew I was such a baby in the real world."

He shook his head, eyes so kind they made her feel at ease immediately. "No one can master what they haven't been taught." He took the string in his calloused hands to demonstrate. "You twist the ends, pull, and make one loop. Then, you make another loop, tuck one under the other, and pull again. Do that twice and it'll be secure."

He showed her one more time before handing over the pack. She followed his instructions closely, gave a pull, and it worked.

"I did it! It's a bow. I did it." She laughed out loud and spun to face him, an ear-splitting grin on her face.

His answering chuckle was deep and soothing. "See, you're doing just fine in the real world."

"Thank you… Sorry, I don't even know your name."

He extended a hand. "I'm Tomhas."

"It's a pleasure to meet you, Tomhas." She handed him the tied-up pack and reached over to the next as he continued working as well.

"I should thank *you*. What you're doing here is invaluable to the Rebellion. I hope you're prepared for the impact your allegiance will have on your future."

Leda nodded. "For years, I suffered under a system I didn't believe in. It was a different kind of suffering, sure, but it was real.

So, I figure I'll be able to suffer for a cause that actually means something to me."

"It's good to know that we have someone like you on our side."

"What are those?" She pointed at the orange pill he was tucking into a side pouch of each pack.

His smile faded. "Skullroot in tablet form. It kills with one bite. If any of us are captured, we cannot risk information being divulged under torture. Besides, most prefer a quick death over what they do to you in the palace dungeons and Aldahad's prisons."

Leda looked around her. There were servants, gardeners, courtesans, builders, friends, lovers, fathers, mothers, and children. They were all willing to give their lives before they gave up the cause. It was precisely the fact that the People's Monarchy had left them with nothing to lose that made them so resilient, so unafraid. It seemed those clinging to power had dug their own graves.

The song came from Tomhas first and quickly spread from table to table. It swelled powerfully, the base notes reverberating through the ground, the melody echoing off the walls:

Goddess, please take your mercy on me
A nameless, peasant soul
My father has gone to the dungeon again
My mother, she's growing old
My lover is off to the Crest to serve
My sister in dark rooms sold
Oh, Goddess, please have your mercy on me
On my damnéd, peasant soul

CHAPTER TWENTY-ONE

AMILE'S SCRATCHES AND BRUISES had started to fade, but the shadows in his eyes were more stubborn. They left him sallow and largely unresponsive as they rode.

Staella's face was still a collage of bruises, her one eye swollen nearly shut, and her back… Markham had had to hold back a cry when he saw it that first morning. He felt sick at the probability of seeing her hurt again before their rebellion was over, and he hadn't let himself forget that he'd brought her here.

She wasn't fully conscious yet, alternating between absolute oblivion and dazed groans. She winced at every movement of their horse and all he could do was tighten her arms around his waist, allowing her to rest against the expanse of his back. She tucked her face deeper into the crook of his neck and a wave of affection rolled over him.

"Staella…" She hummed. Nudging the top of her head with his jaw, he whispered, "We're in Avetown."

Her eyes opened and she managed to lift her head. Her gaze was foggy with the herbal pain mix Amile had concocted, but a relieved smile bloomed across her face. She fell asleep again almost immediately, but that smile had been enough.

Following Amile's lead, they entered through the market district. Small shops lined the streets, each with a jutting awning under which their best goods were put on display. Lady Garteh, the tailor, proudly exhibited her hideously outdated gowns. At Big Loaf's, a suspiciously skinny man was arguing with someone through the window. Yae Dispensary's display consisted of rows of jars with discolored liquids in which mysterious solids floated. Markham shuddered. Big Belly Butchery had small, dead animals dangling from the roof, bloody and still furred. The smell alone made him gag.

People strolled from one merchant to the next, chatting leisurely and living slowly. He counted sixty at most, which was probably a busy day for Avetown.

As the three of them rode past, many of the townsfolk stopped to stare, pointing at him and Amile, then scowling when they saw Staella. What a sight to see: one of their own arriving with the face of their golden coins and a young man who bore an uncanny resemblance to the High Ruler.

We should've disguised ourselves.

He raised a hand to wave. Some returned the gesture with broad smiles, while others only glared. There were guards too, stationed at every fifty paces. They were immaculate in their dark green uniforms. He didn't know how much they knew, whether they were friend or foe, so he waved at them too.

Next, they entered the residential area and Markham was struck by the lack of class distinctions. There was no Rooks, no Crest or Plateau. The houses were small, but they were neat and sturdy. They were also a kaleidoscope—the doors, walls, roofs, and shutters painted different colors.

Staella stirred behind him, mumbling something.

He frowned. "What?"

"Do you smell the air?"

What was in that pain mix?

"I've never loved this town, but I missed the air. No politics and corruption and people dying… Just air."

"I smell it." It was Amile who answered, earning him a grin from her.

Markham pursed his lips. "I'm sorry for having taken you away from it."

She shook her head, words slurring as she replied, "But, Markham, we will make the whole world like this. When we're done, the air in all of Aldahad will smell like this."

A lump rose in his throat. "Yes, it will."

She sighed and leaned her weight against his back again, and the warmth only spread further through his chest,

The houses started to thin out, giving way to fields of breath-taking green interspersed with cattle-dotted pastures. A few of the Avetown farms were giant spots of natural growth, but most were relatively small and crowded.

I wonder what these farmers would have been able to do with the land Honiel Hayvinger uses for his thoroughbreds.

The final farm was of the latter variety, comprising only one field of strange red-cherried plants, a barn, and a humble house. The Thenos establishment was aptly named Two Daughters, its gates wide open as their horses trotted through.

"What do they farm with?" Markham asked Amile.

His friend was clearly surprised at finally being talked to, blinking a few times before replying, "Cupa beans. It's not popular in Aldahad, but the trade to Havinaak and the Vallanah Islands is good."

They headed for the stone house, dismounting as they reached the steps to the front porch. Markham woke Staella up with a gentle hand to the forehead before slowly lowering her down into his arms. She winced but made no complaint.

The house was bigger than he'd expected, maybe thrice the size of Mycah's apartment, with triangle-shaped windows and a green roof. It was quiet, smelled of freshly baked bread and something distinctly bitter. He carried Staella to the front door bridal style, careful to keep his touch on her back light.

Amile only gave one knock before a perky voice called, "Just a minute."

Something fell. Someone cursed quite creatively. Then, there were footsteps and the door opened.

Aside from their shared face shape, it was clear as day that the sisters had different fathers. The woman in the doorway had a mane of blonde hair tied up messily and skin bronzed by the sun. Her teal-colored eyes were stunning and stared at them from above a freckled nose and lips with a defined cupid's bow. She was taller than most, generously endowed, and wore a flour-dusted apron over a loose summer dress that would have been scandalous in the capital.

She stood frozen, her mouth agape. Her eyes didn't know where to land first: the nobles standing at her door, or her battered sister cradled in the arms of one. She gaped, closed her mouth, and gulped. Markham feared she might faint.

Finally, she said, "What the fuck happened to my sister?"

She dove forward, leaning over Staella to touch careful fingers to her face. The redhead gave a feeble smile.

"It's a long story," Staella rasped. "Maybe invite my friends in first… Ellaeya, this is Markham Aesher and Amile Qarvette."

Ellaeya shook her head quickly, expression stuck on disbelief. Then, she dropped into an abrupt curtsy.

"Of course, where are my manners?"

Markham smiled. "You really don't have to curtsy. We are close companions of Staella's and we are honored to meet you."

She looked at him through rapidly-blinking eyelashes, her face turning beetroot red. In a sudden flash of black and white, something hurtled past Ellaeya's legs and crashed into Amile with such a force that he ended up on his backside on the porch. The dog was all tail and tongue as it wormed its way into Amile's lap.

Ellaeya gasped in horror. "Avry, no! Bad boy."

Amile waved her off and laughed—actually *laughed*. "It's alright. Animals tend to have this reaction towards me." He rubbed his hands over the dog's sides with a grin.

Markham cocked an eyebrow. "Have you informed horses of this special relationship?"

He shot his friend a pointed glare. "Fine. Animals I don't have to ride." Avry licked at his jaw and he chuckled, enveloping the ball of fur in a bear hug.

Markham found himself staring a little too long, unable to hide his smile at seeing his best friend so happy. *I really ought to get him a pet.*

He was pulled out of his own thoughts when Staella whimpered. Her body started trembling and her eyes rolled shut. He shouted her name, repeated it over and over, but she was out cold, still shivering in his arms.

Ellaeya jumped into action. "Bring her inside. We should lay her down." They followed her as she moved deeper into the house. "Our room is down here."

The chamber in question was pinker than Markham had ever thought to associate with Staella, but there was no time to take in the soft pastels or the flower pattern on the quilt. He laid her down with slow, careful movements.

Ellaeya was quick to find a thick blanket to wrap around her. "I'll get a bath ready. That will help." Her eyes were moving side to side rapidly as she thought. "And tea. Yes, tea. Father has some special salve that'll work wonders, but I don't know where he keeps it… and you, you must be exhausted. I'll get apple juice and biscuits. Yes."

She started for the door and Amile stepped after her. "Show me what I can do to help." She hesitated, nodded, and they were off.

Markham kneeled next to the bed, wrapped Staella's hand in both of his. She was scowling, probably in pain even in her sleep. His breath hitched.

"I'm so sorry."

Then, he did the only thing he could think of. In his broken, off-pitch voice, he started singing the lullaby his mother had hummed to him when he was sick as a child. It wasn't much, but the stark lines of her brow relaxed at the first notes. So, he kept singing. With everything in him, he kept singing.

†

Her eyes opened slowly, difficultly. The lids were heavy and puffy, her mind a loopy mess. She blinked a few times, despite the pain it caused. She was in her old room, the one she'd always shared with Ellaeya. Her sister was there now, sitting on a chair in the corner of the bedroom. Amile was cross-legged on the floor, Avry's sleeping head in his lap. Markham was beside her, his brows knotted with worry. She distantly remembered him singing.

No, I must have dreamt that.

She groaned, which got their attention. Markham stood up in an instant, his strong hands helping her sit up. Ellaeya rearranged the pillows behind her. She collapsed against them, tired from the small movement.

Amile was suddenly there, bringing a steaming cup close to her face. "Here. Ellaeya made your favorite tea. I also added some of the pain relief herbs we picked up. It will help." She nodded, took the brew with weak hands, and sipped.

"How are you feeling?" Markham breathed.

"I–" Her voice was raw and feeble. She cleared her throat, but it made no difference. "I think I'm okay… Everything hurts, but it's manageable, and my head's a little fuzzy."

Ellaeya sighed, plopped down on the other side of the bed. "Well, now that you're not dying and you can talk, I think it's time you told me what happened. You leave to defend a lad, disappearing for months, and then you come back beaten to a pulp, with the High Ruler's brother and the wealthiest man in Aldahad with you. Why are you here? Who did this to you?"

Staella risked a glance at Amile, who seemed to be making himself as small as possible, retreating into the farthest corner. She swallowed.

"Well, I—uh. I don't really know where to begin. I don't know if you know about the Rebe—"

"El?" Staella's heart skipped in her chest. She knew the voice calling from the living room well.

Not being able to stop herself, she exclaimed, "Daddy."

He came running, rushing into the room with wide eyes. "Staella?"

He was across the space in an instant, arms thrown around her. Hugging him back made the wounds on her back scream, but she didn't care. In his embrace, she melted. Her every hard edge softened, and she was a child again. His blonde hairline had receded even more over the last few months, the crow's feet around his blue eyes more prominent, but the cupa bean and wet earth smell of him remained exactly the same.

He pulled away to cup her cheeks in reverent hands. "Goddess, Kitten, you look like you turned around at death's door. What happened?"

Her eyes flicked to Markham and Amile, who were looking increasingly out of place in the modest home. "It's a complicated story, but we'll tell you everything."

She cleared her throat, signaling for her friends to introduce themselves. When Markham reached out to shake her father's hand, she swore that Yaekós' golden boy suppressed a gulp.

"It's a pleasure to meet you, Mister Thenos. I'm sorry for invading your home unannounced… and using your barn for our horses."

Her father just shook his head, clasping Markham's hand in his own. "Oh, no worries. That old thing's been empty since we took over the farm, and please, call me Staeven. Any friend of my daughter's is a friend of mine."

To Amile, Staeven said, "Well you and your brother are most definitely fruit off the same tree."

Amile pursed his lips at that. "I'm afraid appearance is where the resemblance ends."

"Good," Staeven replied without hesitation. "No offense, but that man has never done anything for us."

"He's never done anything for anyone," her friend muttered.

Staeven suddenly held up a hand. "Salve. I'll go get my special salve for your injuries and then you can tell me all about your trials and tribulations."

As her father disappeared, Markham cocked an eyebrow at her. "What's this special salve I keep hearing about?"

She smiled. "He makes it himself, refuses to give anyone the recipe. But it's amazing. I guarantee all of us will feel ten times better tomorrow if we use it. I suspect the secret may be haletayl sap, but don't tell him."

"We should try to get the formula from him," Amile added from the corner. "With the way our lives are going, a magic healing salve might not be a bad idea."

However, when Staevan returned and the sweet aroma of the salve filled the air, Amile paled. His nostrils flared and his gaze widened as it honed in on the yellow substance.

He shook his head fervently. "I, uh, I wasn't injured that badly. I'm alright. Thank you."

Her father frowned at his reaction, but moved on without a word. He tended first to Staella's many injuries and then to the few scrapes on Markham's hands from restraining Amile with the ropes.

So, they started talking. Staella began, telling him and Ellaeya of her time with the city guard—the brief affair with Saul, Graegg's death, and her later decision to join the Rebellion. Amile spoke of the Representatives' mysterious disappearance. With wary eyes, Markham confessed his involvement and went on to relate the desperate state of the capital and its rebels, and why they had to leave.

Staeven could only shake his head in disbelief and wonder. "From what we heard, the rebels were all terrorists. But now that I know… Of course, you are welcome to stay here for as long as you need. We will not speak a word of this to anyone else."

Then, it was time to tell them about Amile. Markham assumed that responsibility and Staella watched Amile grow smaller and smaller. He was trying to disappear into the wall.

Staevan didn't flinch or gasp or stare. He didn't condemn the young man with the hollow eyes or scream at him for what he'd done to Staella.

No, he simply turned to him and said, "We'll prepare a comfortable space in the barn for you. It has good locks and solid pillars for ropes. I might still have some chains in my work room.

You'll probably scare the manes off your horses, but you won't hurt anyone."

Amile nodded, his jaw clenched. "Thank you."

Staeven rubbed a hand over his face and sighed. "Well, I think after all of that, we deserve a strong cupa. And we need to eat before sundown."

Ellaeya jumped up, but he placed a hand on her arm. "It's alright, darling. Spend some time with your sister. I'll take care of dinner… With these boys' help, of course."

Markham and Amile blinked at each other. "Ah, yes, of course," the former assented.

So, it was only the sisters that remained in their shared bedroom. Ellaeya was the first to speak.

"I can't believe you brought home Lad Aesher and Mister Qarvette." She giggled, pulling at her ponytail. "I wish Dad would let me cook for them. They say the quickest way to a man's heart is through his stomach."

Staella chuckled. "In my experience, the quickest way to a man's heart is a very sharp dagger."

Ellaeya rolled her eyes. "Such a savage."

She stuck out her tongue in response. "It's my savagery that got them here in the first place."

Giving her a despicable glance, her sister said, "I think it might have done more than just that."

"What?"

"Come on, Staella, I'm not blind. Lad Aesher looks at you the way Avry looks at Mister Qarvette, only much more inappropriately."

Staella was suddenly very interested in the pattern of the quilt. "Markham is engaged to Leda," she mumbled.

"Goddess, you throw around these people's names like they aren't gods."

Staella laughed. "That's because they're not. They're just people, Ellaeya, and they're my friends."

"You should have sent a letter in advance."

This did not come from Ellaeya, but from a gravelly voice at the entrance of the room.

Ela.

Staella looked up to find her mother standing in the doorway, her dark brown hair tumbling over her shoulders and cerulean eyes piercing. She'd lost weight, the generous curves of her petite body jutting out from a sickly-small waist.

Staella opened her mouth. Closed it. Said, "I'm sorry. We had to leave in a hurry."

Ela nodded, taking a cautious step into the room. "Staeven told me the gist of the story." Silence settled, long and stifling, before she finally added, "Are you alright?"

The corners of Staella's mouth twitched. "A bit sore, but nothing I can't handle."

The woman murmured "good" and moved to stand at her other daughter's side. She placed a quick kiss on Ellaeya's shoulder. "Well, I'll leave the two of you to catch up while I get to know our unexpected guests."

She was almost at the door when Staella blurted, "Mom." Ela froze. "I—I missed you."

She hesitated and tilted her body to look at her youngest. There were too many unspoken words in that one half-glance.

"I missed you too."

Then, she was gone.

†

Ellaeya would sleep on an extra mattress in her parents' room, and Amile in the barn. Which left Markham and Staella to share the sisters' chamber. He knew they probably expected him to use the bed roll laid out on the floor…

But it's not like we haven't done this before.

So, under the scrutiny of Staella's raised eyebrow, he got into the double bed next to her.

"You know my mother is going to have a heart attack, right?"

"That's why I locked the door," he purred.

She rolled her eyes at him, but couldn't resist a giggle. "You're insufferable."

Her lids were already drooping with the effects of more pain relief tea, and she was lying on her stomach with her head turned his way, nearly asleep.

He side-eyed her. "Come on. I've been sleeping on the floor for days now. At least let me enjoy the comforts of a house while I can."

She huffed. "You're such a baby, but yes, Markham, you may sleep in the bed." After a moment's hesitation, she added, "I think it will actually help me sleep better."

He settled down, turning on his side so he could look at her. "Well, then I am at your service."

She looked at him for a few seconds, her swollen eyes tracing the lines of his face. Even bruised like this, her face entranced him: the round curve of her cheeks, the supple pinkness of her lips. Now that he had seen her truly hurt, he only felt the tether between them tug more intensely, felt the way his heart swelled whenever they could be alone together. Even if they were just lying in silence, staring at each other.

Eventually, she cleared her throat. "Don't even think of cuddling me. My back won't appreciate it."

He found himself slightly disappointed, but knew he wouldn't have tried it anyway. "May I at least hold the lady's hand?" he breathed, feeling his palm tingle at the prospect.

She nodded wordlessly and he wasted no time intertwining their fingers, his thumb drawing slow circles on her wrist. After a few seconds of silence, he whispered, "Thank you."

"For what?" she slurred, eyes starting to droop adorably.

"For caring enough to bring us into your home, to protect us from danger." She pressed her lips against the back of his hand and his breath hitched.

With her last waking words, she said, "Markham, I've never cared about anything as much as I care about this." He squeezed her fingers and turned to blow out the candle on his nightstand.

The lines of her face were serene with sleep as he breathed, "I love you too, Staella."

CHAPTER TWENTY-TWO

THERE WERE ONLY SIX REPRESENTATIVES still in Yaekós, the others either taken or fleeing. It was less than Leda had expected, and her already-knotted stomach twisted painfully.

What has our city become?

Rows and rows of soldiers flanked City Square on all sides, herding the capital's inhabitants together like sheep. Perhaps this assembly would finally be their slaughter.

The Square fell into pregnant silence as Yathan Qarvette stepped out onto Signal Tower's jutting balcony. Leda gulped as her hands clamped around the sides of her seat. He looked so small from where she sat—a miniscule, black-clad speck that could ruin them all with a word. He was a king in all but name and succession.

She clenched her jaw to the point of pain as his honeyed voice rang out, "My people, I thank you for your attendance, and for your cooperation with our city's new safety measures. These measures have been implemented with great success and Yaekós is exponentially safer for it... However, we have not yet located the missing Representatives, nor have we eliminated the rebel scourge."

Leda's insides churned and she desperately tried to keep her heart in her chest as he continued, "We sought to respect those who play an integral role in Aldahad's functioning by confining the residential searches to the Western Rooks and select areas of Coinsgain Plateau. It has, unfortunately, become necessary to extend our investigation to Goldvinger Crest. All homes on the Crest will be searched within the next three days..." She couldn't see the High Ruler's eyes, but she knew they were fixed on her when he said, "*Anyone* who is found to harbor criminals or aid terrorists in any capacity will be apprehended immediately."

Her heart sank and she felt sick. *There are dozens of rebels in my house at this very moment.* They had to get them out. Tonight. Sooner. There could be no doubt that the Hayvinger estate would be Knoxin's first target.

"Furthermore—"

Goddess, what now?

"It has become imperative for us to manage and track Aldahad's citizens more effectively. We must monitor those who are most likely to be corrupted by the insurgents' manipulation. Therefore, all Aldahadis who cannot prove their noble bloodline will receive an inked green stamp on their right arm." Murmurs spread through the Square, and to Leda it felt like the sound of an approaching apocalypse. "Rest assured," Yathan tried to placate, "that it is a relatively painless procedure and that the bearers of this mark will suffer no discrimination on its basis."

The world started spinning and Leda found herself gulping down bile. Yathan's further words were drowned out by the chaos of voices in her head.

Green stamps. Red Seals. It was happening all over again.

But I'm not Lowena. I'm not—

A stone sailed through the air, far above her head, and shattered against the railing in front of Yathan. Two more followed. Leda spun, gasped. Those at the back of the crowd all stood with their fists raised high in rebellion.

A middle-aged woman with a swath of red material around her head marched forward. When she was nearly at the front, she roared, "Lightning does not destroy. It enlightens."

The line had been on Markham's pamphlets.

Chaos descended on City Square.

Commoners and middle class alike started yelling dissent. Some surged forward and threw more stones, while others spat at the nearest military man. There was a strained command. Soldiers stormed forward. Batted people aside like insects. A woman's scream. Someone knocked over. Trampled. People scattered and ran. Blood flew from a crying mouth as an armored fist descended. The dirt turned to crimson mud.

Leda was frozen in horror, the world a swirl of movement and sounds. *This isn't happening.* Something tugged at her shoulder. *This isn't happening.* Harder. *This isn't—* Harder. Leda snapped back to reality.

Maci was standing over her, her tiny frame shaking with sobs and face drenched in tears. Leda shot up, grabbed her friend by the shoulders. "Maci, what—?"

"Aedon's gone," she wailed.

"What?"

Maci's body curved in on itself. "He's gone. Like the other Representatives. They took him. He's my little brother and they… He's gone. I don't—"

Leda pulled her into a crushing embrace, speaking into her ear. "We need to leave now. This Square and this city. And I know exactly where we have to go."

She kept an arm wrapped around her sobbing friend's shoulders as they ran for the estate, leaving the nightmarish dystopia of City Square behind.

†

She hadn't talked to him for days, not since he'd said…

No, small talk and strategy were the extent of Staella and Markham's conversations as she recovered. Because she couldn't stand anything more.

Every time she heard his voice, she heard those hushed words again. *I love you.* And it set her blood on fire. If she spoke to him for too long, saw that smile, allowed herself to savor that vanilla scent… If she looked into those eyes for more than a few seconds, she would lose control. She'd crash into him without restraint and kiss him until his lips were swollen and he craved nothing but her touch.

Her mind conjured up that stunning image: Markham flustered and panting. How his arms would tighten around her… Need burned low in her belly and she gulped.

She glanced up at him walking beside her, his strides easy and his skin glowing in the sunlight. Her palms burned with the desire to touch him. Every part of him.

She cleared her throat quickly, glad of Amile's neutralizing presence on her other side. "So, have you met Bruhel or did he just send you letters dictating others' futures?"

"We've met," Markham answered. The sound of his voice sent yet another tornado of flutters through her chest. "I only spoke to him once or twice over the years, but it was enough to get to know him. He's stubborn and blunt, but loyal to a fault."

Staella chuckled. "That's definitely Bruhel. If *you* thought he was candid, imagine having him as a trainer."

Amile's lips twitched. "I remember the first time we met. He told me to take my hands out of my pockets and stop looking like I didn't belong… He was one of the first to make us feel welcome in the Rebellion."

She shook her head, aware of the fact that the gouges in her neck no longer pulled painfully with movement. *Daddy's salve really is magic.*

"I still can't believe he was a member of Tomhas's inner circle the entire time, that he was training me to be a rebel. He definitely has some explaining to do."

They'd made their way to the southern parts of Avetown's residential area, where the neighborhood was quiet and the inhabitants mostly retired. Bruhel loved the peace of it, since he'd experienced so little of it during his younger years.

His house was nestled between rows of others, small and impeccably maintained. It was all square lines and bare brick, with black shutters. He planned on painting them green one day.

Staella bounded up the steps to the front door, wincing at the pull on the healing wounds on her back. She couldn't hide her grin as she raised a fist to the door and banged out their secret knock.

With the chaos that had descended on her these last few months, she would appreciate her mentor's steady presence and practical advice. Now that she knew all about the rebels and the world of pageant-politics, they had an endless number of things to discuss. She *would* confront him about keeping such big secrets, but she would give him a tight hug first.

She waited for the customary grunt and heavy footsteps that always preceded the door's opening. But they never came. Her knock was met with complete silence.

Staella sighed and turned to Amile. "He always leaves a key if he's out. It's on the doorframe. I'd jump up, but I don't think that's a good idea in my current state."

Amile nodded and stepped forward to feel around on the upper frame. He frowned, got up on his toes to look. When he lowered, he shook his head.

"There's nothing there."

Dread twisted in her stomach. She knocked on the door again, harder this time. She hoped to find the door locked, hoped he'd just forgotten the key. She reached for the brass knob and turned it.

The door swung open.

Staella screamed and pressed a hand to her mouth in horror.

The cupa table was on its side, its glass top completely shattered. One of the couches had been disemboweled, stuffing peeling out like intestines.

Blood.

It was spattered on the furniture, smeared on the walls. Dried drops trailed deeper into the house.

Markham was the first to follow the trail, and Staella stuck close behind. She wasn't breathing.

He froze. "Staella…"

Her heart spasmed at the tone of his voice. She stepped around him, into the small kitchen. The thing on the floor was wearing Bruhel's favorite boots, but it wasn't him. It couldn't be him. *It's not—*

There was more blood than skin and a festering wound in the side. Larvae were at home in rotting flesh. His arm was bent the wrong way and bone jutted out at the elbow. A knife hilt where there should have been an eye.

She tried to deny it, tried to reason it away… but it was him. Her instructor. Her friend. Slaughtered. Butchered.

The breath left her body and she gasped soundlessly. Her hands trembled. Her arms. Her knees. She sank down next to the body and buried her fingers in her hair. She screamed and her world swam in tears. She was crying. Bawling. Shrieking. Each sob spasmed her body like a shock.

No.

No!

How? Why? Who?

A roar ripped from her throat, burning it raw. She couldn't breathe. She didn't know how to inhale anymore.

Warmth wrapped around her. Markham. She collapsed against him, her hands fisting his shirt. Her knees curled up and he pulled her into his lap.

His low, thick voice coaxed, "I know. I know. Just breathe. Staella, please, you have to breathe." With momentous effort, she managed to gulp down some air. Sucked in a breath, then another. "That's it."

One more. One more.

Amile's voice rang out: "Staella."

"Amile, not now," Markham growled, fiercer than she'd ever heard him.

"She needs to see this."

Staella took one more deep breath and rose on wobbly legs. "Don't talk about me like I'm not here." She reached for the piece of paper in Amile's hand.

Staella,

The inner circle is dead. Saul has Tomhas in Hareth Prison. Lad Aesher's involvement with the rebels is known.

Stay safe.

Caven

She huffed incredulously. Maron Caven had come through. Her fist closed around the note and crumpled it. When she looked up at Markham and Amile, her eyes were fire.

"I'm going to kill Saul Knoxin."

†

Leda stood eerily still as she watched the remaining rebels evacuate through the sewers, rushing to escape before the soldiers came hunting. Her mind was spinning with unwanted images: scraps of possible plans and emotions that were too much to handle.

Yathan Qarvette had sunk them so precisely into the horrors of the past that his announcement still seemed surreal. Aedon was nowhere to be found, the fourth Representative to disappear without explanation.

And Veress was dead, murdered in her bedroom at the Hayvinger estate.

Leda scrunched her eyes shut, hoping it would cast away the memory of her friend's broken and lifeless body. She couldn't think about that now, couldn't afford to fall apart.

Maci had stopped crying, had pulled herself together somewhat to help hide the evidence of the rebels' stay. But Leda knew the other woman was constantly on the verge of tears. The rebels worked quickly, but they were frantic and scared. So, someone had to be calm. Someone had to lead them through the chaos.

Leda had run into the estate with orders streaming from her mouth. The rebels had to escape immediately and stick to the sewers for as long as they could. If Saul came knocking at the gate, the guards knew to delay his team as much as they could. Her most trusted guard, Trew, had raced to the stables to retrieve their two fastest steeds and wait at the predetermined exit point.

As much as she had wanted to take Ezra, she knew that the mare was not built for long-distance travel, and they had little time to rest on their flight to Avetown. So, she stood waiting, using her breathing to maintain a veneer of calm that fooled even her own mind. One of the packs she'd made only days before was strapped to her back, and Maci's hand was clutched in her own.

They would be the last to leave.

CHAPTER TWENTY-THREE

THE SKY WAS BAWLING OVER AVETOWN and sleets of rain turned the dirt in front of the Thenos home to mud.

Staella was not deterred. Her focus never faltered as she flung knife after knife at something that appeared to be the scarecrow incarnation of Saul Knoxin. Her aim was true, her movements lightning-fast yet fluid. Her clothes were drenched, the fire of her hair near-black as a few rebellious strands stuck to wet cheeks.

Markham was mesmerized while he watched her through the living room window, in awe of how beauty and brutality could be combined so effortlessly.

"So, are you going to tell me why the two of you have been tip-toeing around each other the last few days?" Amile asked from behind him. His friend was sprawled out on a couch, the dog content in his arms.

Markham couldn't deny that Staella had been avoiding him. In the four days since they'd found Bruhel's body, she'd been even more withdrawn.

"I might have ruined everything," he confessed.

He turned to see Amile cock an eyebrow. "It can't be that bad. You're the one who's good with women, remember?"

"I thought she was already asleep, but clearly she wasn't and I—I told her I love her."

Amile shrugged. "Well, you love me and I'm not all flustered."

He gave Amile a flat stare. "She's not an idiot, and I'm not about to convince her that my feelings were platonic when I said those words."

Amile rose, much to Avry's dismay, and joined his best friend at the window. "Well, you have to say something. Look at her, Markham. She's training herself to near-collapse in preparation of an assassination. From what I know of her, I suspect that's how she grieves when her tears have dried… I think she would appreciate having someone to talk to. Besides, we're sitting ducks in this town and our Rebellion is falling apart. We need to plan our next move, and for that you need to be on better speaking terms."

Markham watched her. She was trembling—from exhaustion or vexation, he didn't know. He wondered what would happen if he simply gave her a hug. Would she stop, go still, look up at him and smile?

The heat hit him as soon as he stepped outside, the rain offering little reprieve. *As if my blood isn't boiling already.* In fact, his pulse was singing in his ears, a song of seduction laced with notes of fear.

Her side was turned to him, but the deadly focus in her eyes was clear. She didn't acknowledge him, loosed another knife. Scarecrow Knoxin was starting to look like a pin cushion.

He gulped and cleared his throat. "It seems you're already good enough at that. No need to practice in this weather."

She grabbed her next knife off a soaked kitchen stool Ellaeya probably didn't know had been liberated. "If I can still improve, I'm not good enough."

He took a steadying breath. "Do you need to talk about Bruhel?"

"There isn't anything to say." She still hadn't looked at him, hadn't stopped training.

His voice softened. "Staella, I think you may be using the prospect of revenge as a coping mechanism." She gave no answer. "Staella." She threw another blade. "Staella." She turned around to grab the next blade, but before she could, Markham curled a hand around her wrist. "Staella, please."

She became a statue, her eyes fixed on his hand, on the spot where their sleek skin met. "Did you mean it?" Her voice was carefully neutral, cold.

His heart stuttered. "What?"

"You know what."

The song in his ears had become a percussion solo. He gulped, unclasped his hand from her wrist to run his index finger down her palm and gently interlace their hands. She couldn't suppress the hitch of her breath.

"Please look at me," he whispered.

She did, slowly. And he was drowning in his own cocktail of emotions, in her, in the vulnerable lines of her face, in the molten darkness of her eyes, and in the stark pink of her parted lips that contrasted so stunningly with the ivory of her skin.

"Of course, I meant it." His free hand reached out, trembling as he tucked a strand of wet hair behind her ear. He let his fingers linger, tracing her jaw, her chin. Her skin was slick with rain, but soft. Warm and inviting. When he cupped her cheek, she leaned into the touch, brushed her lips against his palm. He wasn't drowning anymore. He was burning. Melting. "How could I not love you?"

He didn't have to bend down.

Staella surged up, hooked an arm around his neck, and pressed her mouth to his. Hard, but sweet. His heart stopped. Revived. Sprinted.

She was kissing him. He was kissing her. And it was so much better than his dreams. His arms wrapped around her, pulled her against him. He shuddered at the way her body curved into his, at the way she deepened the kiss and tugged at his hair. The way she seemed to want him as much as he wanted her.

When his hand found a patch of bare skin at her waist, he gripped and she whimpered. *Fuck*. He was engulfed by that sound. By her. By the sweet taste of her lips and the warmth of her tongue. The softness of her skin over hard muscle. The cupa bean smell of her hair and the way she had started rolling her hips against his.

Goddess.

He growled, tugged at her bottom lip with his teeth. Then, he lifted her up, his arms wrapped around her, and her legs hooked around him. His lips found her neck, her collarbone. She gasped his name and combustion suddenly felt like a good way to die.

He would be hers forever. He would do whatever she wanted just to hear that sound again. And again. And again. But they were still outside. In the pouring rain. In front of her parents' house.

It took an immense surge of willpower for him to pull away. He realized that he was panting, shaking. "We, uh, we should probably stop until we're somewhere more appropriate."

The fog over her eyes took a moment to clear, but then she nodded. He set her down, keenly aware of the fact that her arms refused to let go of him. Then, she giggled and smiled up at him. It was a smile that lit up her entire face and sent the breath rushing out of him. He knew that the image would be burned into his mind forever. She squeezed his hand.

"I'll talk to you tonight. I, uh, I need some time to get my mind working again after… *that.*"

†

She stood with her back to him when Markham entered their shared bedroom after dinner. Closed the door and locked it. She heard the unsteadiness of his breathing, felt the air crackle between them. He didn't come closer. She didn't turn around.

Maybe he'll write a book about us and call it Anticipation.

After trying and failing to slow her racing heartbeat, she started, "I need you to understand that I didn't kiss you because I'm overcome by grief and not thinking rationally. In fact, I think I'm thinking way too much. I miss Bruhel so much it physically hurts, but I am alright. I've just once again been reminded that life can be snatched away at any moment. I kissed you because… Because I love you and I can't not be with you anymore."

Warm arms enveloped her from behind and she sighed, finally allowing herself to melt into him. Markham *felt* like luxury, like coming home and knowing no comfort would be absent. It was in the smoothness of his golden skin and the honey of his voice, the silk of his hair and the vanilla scent that never left him. The solid body that was made for waking up next to.

He hooked a finger under her chin, tilted her face so he could press his lips against hers. It was nothing like the fevered clash of tongues and teeth of that afternoon. No, this kiss was sweet, unhurried, and promised time. There would be time for that devouring hunger, for discovering what made the other gasp and come apart.

For now, though, it was simple closeness they craved. She pulled away and turned to face him. Her hands reached out to cup his face and she ran a thumb over the little dimple in his chin. He was inconceivably beautiful, a sculpture come to life.

"So, it'll be you, me, and Leda," she murmured.

He tightened his arms around her. "I promise you that my heart is and will be yours alone… Leda won't mind."

She nodded, her fingers traveling to play with his hair. As she'd expected, he relaxed into the touch with a purr. "I suppose there are worse things than to be the mistress of the richest man in Aldahad."

Markham chuckled and the sound rumbled through her. "With me for my money, are you?"

She shrugged, failing to hide a smile. "What did you expect from a simple farm girl like me?"

A mischievous glint lit up his eyes. He nestled his face into the crook of her neck and whispered, "I have a confession… I've always had a farm girl fetish."

She giggled, gasped as his lips found her pulse and then her collar. It was ridiculously easy to surrender.

CHAPTER TWENTY-FOUR

THE RAIN WAS STILL BEATING DOWN in steady lines the next morning, the sunlight struggling to breaking through thick clouds to illuminate the Thenos kitchen, where Staella sat alone with her cupa. She leaned her elbows on the table, stomach knotting with a barrage of confusing emotions. Grief still sat like a heavy stone in her gut, but the grin on her face and the lightness in her heart did not subside.

They had decided to stay in Avetown a few days longer, since Markham had already scheduled a meeting with the Rebellion's mysterious weapons master. The risk of staying in one place this long was high, but Staella had assured them that she was unafraid. If Saul came, he would meet an opponent hungry for his blood.

"So, you and Markham Aesher?" Ellaeya swaggered into the room with a wicked smile on her face.

Staella felt her cheeks redden and looked down, hiding behind a curtain of hair. "How did—?"

"Oh, please, you put on quite a show yesterday. Besides, the sounds that came from that room last night were very unambiguous."

She was holding back laughter now and Staella sank down against the table to bury her face in her arms. "Oh, Goddess, did Mom and Dad…?"

Her sister snorted and sat down. "Relax. Those two could sleep through a hurricane. So… Did you… You know?" She winked in a way that made Staella groan.

"No. No, we still have time. I think we'll wait until our *unambiguous sounds* won't be heard next door."

Ellaeya's teeth tugged at her bottom lip. "I can only imagine what it would be like with someone who looks like that. Goddess, his arms alone–"

"Hey, watch it. He's officially taken, sis," Staella interjected with a smile. She knew she just wanted to get a rise out of her.

Ela trudged in, her hair a knotted mane around her face and her petite body wrapped in a robe. "What are you girls gossiping about?" she mumbled, stumbling her way to the pot of freshly-brewed cupa.

Staella shot her sister a warning glare, but it was futile. "Oh, just Staella's new lover," Ellaeya cooed.

Staella hissed and kicked the blonde in the shin under the table. Ela turned, suddenly awake. "Lad Aesher?" Her face hardened into what her youngest daughter had coined the Staella-addressing expression. “Are you sure he has the right intentions? He is a Representative and you’re—”

“Yes, Mom. I’m sure.”

Her mother studied her for a few seconds longer before nodding. “Then, I wish you happiness.” She remained at the other end of the room, fidgeting with the handle of her cup. “How are you feeling after Bruhel?” she asked as she turned her back to make a bowl of porridge.

“It fluctuates.”

The truth was that there were moments in which she felt his absence like a physical blow, in which memories of his lessons made her ache to see him just one more time. The truth was that she woke up in the middle of the night with gasping breaths and tears in her eyes because she couldn’t escape the mangled body of the man with whom she’d spent every day of her youth.

She blinked away her tears, an awkward silence settling over the kitchen. The women in her family were as good at comforting her as she was at admitting that she needed comforting.

Amile strolled into the room with the dog at his heels and Staella could have kissed him for his timing.

Ellaeya looked up and shook her head. “That dog is going to die of grief when you’re gone.”

The corner of Amile’s mouth twitched upward. “I’ll come visit.” He kept her gaze as she offered him a beaming smile. “Staella, the weapons master has arrived, and you’d never guess who it is.” There was an amused glint to her friend’s golden eyes, one she hadn’t seen in a very long time.

She cocked an eyebrow. “Who?”

He just tilted his head in the direction of the front porch and turned, correctly assuming that she would follow.

Markham stood in the door with his back to her. She peeked around him and gasped. On the other side of the threshold, black hair dripping with rain, was Chrisjon Damhere.

She ducked past Markham to dash forward, flinging her arms around the Representative's neck. He chuckled as he returned the embrace.

"Staella Thenos, we always seem to meet in unfortunate circumstances."

She stepped back to take a better look at him. His eyes were hollow, his skin paler than she remembered, but he was unscathed and he was smiling.

"*You're* the weapons master?"

He shrugged. "I have a big family and we're all blacksmiths. It made sense. Trust me, I didn't expect to see the three of you either." He cocked his head, frowning. "Didn't you fight against the rebels?"

She could only offer a sheepish grin. "Life in Yaekós changed my mind. That, and a very persuasive Representative."

She glanced up at Markham, whose gaze now had the ability to turn her insides molten without much effort. He flashed her a knowing grin before stepping forward to extend a hand.

"Lad Damhere, it's good to have you here. We have much to discuss."

Chrisjon shook his hand with a strange scowl on his face. "*Lad*… I suppose that title will be out of use soon."

Markham froze. "What?"

"You haven't heard."

"What?"

"Yathan Qarvette canceled the Election."

CHAPTER TWENTY-FIVE

IT WAS LATE AFTERNOON BY THE time they'd finished sharing their news. They were all gathered in her living room—Markham, Amile, Chrisjon, Ellaeya and her parents—and they were all sitting eerily still, taking in the situation.

Apparently, Yathan had been busy since they'd left, searching Crest estates. He was marking people permanently and postponing the Election until "more stable times." The world was changing quickly, and not in the way they'd intended.

It was Amile who broke the silence. "I always thought my brother stood against the Rebellion and introduced radical measures because he wanted to maintain the status quo." He shook his head and clenched his hands into fists. "It seems it's much worse than that. This can only mean that he's trying to go back... He wants to become King."

Staella wanted to deny it, but she felt the truth of his words in the cold hand that closed around her heart.

"That's a very serious accusation," Chrisjon said.

"These are serious times."

Markham ran a hand through his hair. "This doesn't change our objective. It just speeds up the timeline."

"It speeds it up exponentially," Staella retorted.

"What exactly is that objective?" Staeven asked.

"Complete democracy, but it was supposed to take years of steady reform. Now, the rebels are being hunted. Yathan rules the capital with an iron fist and it's only a matter of time until the trouble spreads to the rest of the country." Markham grabbed Staella's hand and squeezed it. "I wish Tomhas was here."

Amile nodded. "We'll have to break him out at some point, but there's no way that's happening before the big meeting."

Shit. The meeting.

"Big meeting?" Ellaeya enquired.

Markham explained, "Every rebel who is able will be at the Haer Caves two days from now. It's the biggest rebel meeting since Lowena."

There would be thousands of people gathered and afraid, waiting for directions, itching for change.

"Tomhas was supposed to lead it. To give everyone the plan." Staella squeezed Markham's hand even tighter.

His teeth were sawing at his bottom lip mercilessly, even as the skin turned raw. "I suppose now it'll serve to elect a new leader."

"What?" Amile nearly propelled out of his chair. "You're the leader."

"No one knows that. Besides, do you really think the rebels would take kindly to a Representative walking in and claiming to be their savior? Do you think they'd follow me without objection?"

"Technically, you're not a Representative anymore," Chrisjon muttered.

At the same time, Amile said, "If they're told the truth, yes."

"Stop." This came from Staella, whose head was starting to throb. "It doesn't help anyone to argue about this now. We cannot make this decision alone. The rebels will decide at the meeting. If you want democracy, practice it."

"Well, shouldn't we at least have some semblance of a plan when we go to the meeting?" Chrisjon was ever the voice of reason.

"There is only one direction this can go." Everyone quieted at Ela's words. She was staring at them from her perch on the couch arm, her eyes focused and eerie like an owl's. "War."

The word chilled them all, and silence descended on the room–no one had a reply to that.

Ellaeya broke the spell a few seconds later. "Amile, the sun is setting."

"I'll get you settled," Staeven offered, already standing.

Markham pinched the bridge of his nose. "I suggest we take some time to think about the best course of action and reconvene in the morning."

She knew that night would not be an easy one for him, knew that he was prone to anxiety and felt responsible for the world. She leaned her head on his shoulder, hoping that they would find a way to get through this mess together.

†

Markham was sick to his stomach. Fear pounded through his veins and made his hands tremble as he arranged his pillows for sleep. Not being able to contain it any longer, he sighed and sat down.

A sharp breath tore from him and he felt the heat of tears sting his eyes. The bed shifted as Staella took a seat next to him, wrapping an arm around his back.

"Hey," she whispered. He looked at her and he broke, a desperate sob spasming his chest. "I know. I'm scared too."

He shook his head. "I knew that war would come eventually, that we would have to fight eventually, but knowing it and having it show up at your doorstep unannounced are two completely different things."

She smiled sadly. "The world has turned to shit."

He managed a chuckle, leaning forward to rest his forehead against hers. "I don't know what to do. I'm supposed to be their leader. I'm responsible for them, but I have no idea where to take this Rebellion. Should we hide? Bide our time until the worst of the storm has passed? Should we stand up? Risk people's lives and fight against the people I've known my entire life? I know I shouldn't feel sympathy for those in power, but it's how we were raised, Staella. It's all most of them know, and now I'm going to bring a bloody revolution to them?"

She placed a gentle hand on his chest. "One of the things I love about you is that you care about everyone with so much force that it consumes you. But, Markham, the world is not yours alone to save. At the very least, you will always have Amile and you will always have me… That day I decided to join the Rebellion, I took on all your problems, all your worries, as my own. So, I want you to breathe, and I want you to know that *we* will get through this."

He closed his eyes and breathed her in, the cupa and chocolate smell of her that intoxicated him. Calm settled over him in a wave, loosening his muscles and freeing his mind.

"You are amazing."

He leaned forward, brushing his lips against hers. As he surged to deepen the kiss, there was a loud knock at the front door.

Staella pulled away, scowling. "Why has the whole world suddenly decided to come to my house?"

She shot up and he followed. His heart pounded. *Please don't be more bad news.*

Ellaeya had already opened the door and stood frozen. Chrisjon was peeking around her, his bedroll abandoned on the living room floor.

"Can we please come in? I'm drenched in places I didn't even know could get wet."

He knew that voice.

"Chrisjon? Is this the right house? I—"

He knew that voice too. A grin spread across his face as he approached the open door.

Maci and Leda.

They were soaked in rain, their clothes muddy with travel and their faces ashy with fatigue. He leapt forward and enveloped Leda in the tightest hug he'd ever given. *Thank you.* Then, he spun and kissed the top of Maci's head.

Staella greeted them with a frown on her face and invited them in. "Uh, welcome to the official halfway house… Ellaeya, this is Leda Hayvinger and Maci Blomehill."

"Hi," the eldest sister squeaked.

"Could you please make some cupa for them?" Ellaeya nodded and dashed off. Chrisjon followed to help.

Maci shook her body like a wet dog and grumbled. "I was not made for fleeing." Avry bounded toward them, but suddenly stopped. The hair on the back of his neck rose and he snarled at Maci. She yelped, grabbing hold of Markham's arm.

Staella huffed. "I'm sorry. He's never like this. Avry, no!" She herded the dog into their room and closed the door.

Markham was still staring at Leda, and she was staring right back. She hadn't greeted him yet, hadn't said a word. He remembered their last encounter, remembered the hurt in her eyes. He knew that a lot needed to be said between them, but he was grateful for her presence. It was steadying, confident.

Leda will know what to do.

Staella had the uncanny ability to read his mind, saying, "Maci, why don't you join me in the kitchen? There's a fire for you to dry off by, and I know Ellaeya will be dying to talk to you."

His cousin nodded, smoothing out her hair. "Ah, you are Goddess-sent. Please tell me there's some sugar for that cupa. I haven't had anything decent tasting in days."

Staella chuckled, leading her into the other room by the shoulders. "Yes, we definitely have sugar."

Markham cleared his throat and wrung his hands together. "Would you like to talk outside? We can stay under the roof of the porch."

Leda only nodded and headed for the door. Once outside, she took a seat on the steps. He followed. Her expression was neutral, the lines of her face tight and her eyes staring forward. He could see the tension in her body, the way her shoulders hunched and her leg twitched.

"Tell me," he breathed.

She pursed her lips, still not looking at him. Then, she started talking about the announcement and Aedon and the chaos that followed, about the rebels she'd hosted and the struggle of getting them out, about Veress.

He hesitated before placing a hand on her shoulder. "There was another announcement after you left…" She sucked in a sharp breath and he could barely stand to tell her. "The Election has been postponed indefinitely."

To his surprise, her face lit up. She finally looked at him, a weary smile tugging at her lips. "We're finally free."

He shook his head. "I don't think so. We have a long road to go."

She placed a hand over his mouth to shut him up. "I've been shackled by this Election my entire life and now I've been unchained. Yes, Yathan is probably doing this for his own tyrannical motives, but we will end him, and then we'll still be free."

Markham looked at her, his mouth agape. Then, he smiled, which had her lift her silencing hand. "I missed you."

She grinned back at him. "As infuriating as you are, I missed you too."

"So, I'm forgiven?" he asked, heart leaping at the prospect.

She side-eyed him and *tsked.* "Fine." He surged forward to embrace her, already feeling so much more at ease than he had before her arrival. There was a moment of silence before she muttered, "You know what this means, right?"

"What?"

"Now that the Election's canceled, the world is changing… We don't have to get married anymore."

He froze, shook his head. "Are—are you sure?"

"Yes." There was no hesitation in her voice. "The world we're going to create won't force women into political marriages. I'll make sure of that."

He reached out, running a hand through her ponytail. *She never wore it like this.* "I know you will… I would have done it, you know. And we would have been happy."

She smiled at him. "I know. You would have been an exceptional companion, and I can never thank you enough for being willing to take care of me, but that's not what a relationship should be… And I think you may have found the real deal."

"How did you know?"

She huffed. "Oh, please. I could see it on both of your faces the moment I walked through the door."

He was beaming; he could feel it. "I guess this has been a blessing in disguise."

She nodded. "Of course, it is. Yathan just gave us the perfect opportunity to take the country. From what I saw in Yaekós, the people are ready as ever for revolution. I say we give it to them. The big cities should be our first—"

She was interrupted by Staella yelling, "Maci, wait!"

His cousin slammed open the front door and marched across the porch, into the distance. Staella dashed after her, frantic. "What's happening?" Leda enquired.

Realization dawned on Markham and he was up in a second, following the two women. "She's going to the barn."

"What's so exciting about that?"

He didn't have time to answer and sped up to stop Maci before she opened a can of worms that could never again be closed. *Amile doesn't want her to know. He'd never forgive himself if he hurt her.*

Staella had nearly caught up to her, his cousin sprinting faster than he knew she could. "Maci, you don't understand. Please stop. I'll explain. Just don't—"

"This is absolutely ridiculous," she answered. "Why would all of us be sleeping in the house and then he has to stay in the barn? If he's sleeping in there like an animal, I will too."

Before she could be stopped, she pulled at the barn doors, grunting. They didn't give. *Thank the Goddess for locks.*

She spun around, eyes shooting lightning and hands balled into fists. "Open it."

Staella held her arms in front of her like someone placating a wounded animal. "Maci, please."

A roar tore through the world. Maci jumped. Leda gasped. Staella swore under her breath.

Markham inhaled sharply, reaching for the key he kept in his back pocket. *It's too late now.* He stepped forward, placed a hand on

Maci's shoulder. "I'm going to give you this. But, for your own safety, don't open the door."

He knew it wouldn't work.

The moment the key was in her hands, she thrust it into the lock and threw open the doors. Fearless, Staella moved to place herself in front of Maci, ready to protect.

Amile flew at them, teeth bared and eyes locked on his prey. His hands reached out, ready to wrap around Staella's neck. The chains snapped as they went taut, keeping him strained a few inches from her. He was screaming, as if the inability to kill was causing him pain. Markham had to look away and Leda buried her face in his back.

But Maci stepped around her guard, took a few steps in his direction. "Amile?" she whispered.

He was silenced. Markham glanced up, eyes wide in disbelief. Amile was still, no longer rabid to break free. His eyes were still not completely his own, but he made no move to hurt her as Maci stepped closer to him. She moved slowly, kept her gaze trained on his, and then she reached out to rest a hand on his cheek.

Markham held his breath.

Amile leaned into her touch, closing his eyes. Markham's feet propelled him forward of their own accord. He stepped up to them. "Amile."

A switch flipped. His friend's eyes shot open. He roared and leaped forward with murderous intent. Staella grabbed Markham, then Maci, pulling them out of the barn and slamming the doors shut. She twisted the key, which was still stuck in the lock. Then, she placed it in her slipper and backed away slowly. Once the danger had passed, she let out a long sigh.

Maci's eyes were wide as saucers, her body trembling. It was Leda who spoke first. "What was that? What's wrong with him?"

Markham wasn't capable of replying. His head was spinning and his chest ached. It seemed there was only one person in the world who could calm his best friend during his nightly transformation.

And it's not me.

"I think it's best if he tells you himself… Tomorrow. We should get inside, settle down for the night," Staella said.

Leda shook her head. "Our horses. They can't stay out in the rain all night. But we can't put them in there."

"We'll keep them under the roof of the porch for now. Come on."

So, she herded them into the house, keeping a close eye on Markham, who was once again falling apart in silence.

CHAPTER TWENTY-SIX

"WHY DIDN'T YOU TELL ME?"

Amile was twirling a cupa leaf between his thumb and forefinger, watching the green come off on his skin. He studied the field around them, each bush dotted with red berries that would yield beans to be crushed and mixed with boiling water. He'd read long ago that the cupa plant had evolved to contain toxins in its seeds in order to ward off animals searching for a meal. Only, the toxins made humans feel awake. So, that plan hadn't worked out too well in the end.

He knew he was philosophizing about plant life to avoid meeting Maci's eyes. He remembered everything that happened the previous night, knew that she'd seen him consumed by bloodlust. Yet, he hadn't laid a finger on her. Something within him wouldn't allow her to be hurt.

He was still staring at his green-stained hand as he answered, "I didn't want you to hate or fear me."

"Does it look like I hate or fear you?"

He finally looked up. She was sitting on the ground next to him, legs curled up underneath her. She looked dazzling in the newly-returned sunlight, her hair glowing with a reddish hue that made her seem at home in the cupa field.

"No."

She scooted closer and took his free hand in hers. The palm was soft, the bones tiny and the skin warm. He'd always loved holding her hand. "Is this why you've been treating me like a yo-yo all these years?"

He blinked. "I haven't—" She flashed him a stern look and he sighed. "Yes."

She sighed right back at him. "Am I going to get more than one-word answers out of you eventually?"

"Maybe." He glanced at her from the corner of his eye, smiling slightly. She huffed in exasperation before grinning back at him. "I—I've been this way since I was a child. I don't know why and there is no way to fix it. I kept my distance because… Because I will always be this way, Maci, and you deserve more than that."

She shook her head, cupping his chin to turn his face in her direction. "Well, you failed miserably. No matter how many times you pushed me away after pulling me in, I still fell in love with you a long time ago, and my feelings haven't changed."

The breath rushed out of him, and he found himself blinking away tears. "How?"

She rose up on her knees, climbing right into his lap and framing his face with both hands. "How could I not? We've been through most of our lives together. Your parents love me. You steal all my sweets and tease me. You pretend you're all sullen and serious, but when you're with me, I see who you really are. You're mischievous and smart and funny and sensitive… And even in your darkest moments, you couldn't hurt me."

He draped an arm around her waist, still unable to believe her words. "I want to tell you how I feel, but… I don't want to say those words while we're in this mess. I want it to be perfect. I want the world to be better first."

She smiled at him, her eyes crinkling adorably. "Fine, but can we please stop playing games now? Can we just hold hands when we want to? Can you put your arm around me even when other people are there and kiss me whenever you feel like it?"

In answer, he leaned forward and brushed their lips together, slowly and sweetly. They had kissed before, four or five times over the years, but it had never been like this. He'd never taken his time, had never allowed himself to feel this much affection without guilt taking hold.

She pulled away slightly. "No more secrets."

"No more secrets," he vowed in a whisper, kissing her again.

After a while, she sat back, running her hands through his hair. "Do you want to go take a nap now?"

He chuckled, resting his forehead on her collarbone. "That sounds fantastic."

†

Staella had her arms wound tight around her sister as tears stung the backs of her eyes. "I missed you. I'm going to miss you," she sniffled.

Ellaeya patted her back like only an older sister could. "Me too, but when you come back, I'll make you a feast to celebrate a new world."

Staeven was already crying by the time she got to him, his blue eyes swimming. "Oh, Kitten." She fell into his embrace with a little sob. "You are so brave. I am prouder of you than you could ever know."

Ela was looking away, eyes slightly red and nose runny. Staella stepped up to her shyly, clearing her throat. "Mom?"

Her mother paused, then enveloped her in an aggressive hug. "Take care of yourself," she muttered before letting go and dashing inside with a hand over her face.

Staella gave a final wave before heading down the front steps to where the rest of her party was waiting, already astride their horses. She got her own horse this time, with Amile riding behind Maci to sleep against her back.

Markham helped her onto her stallion with a hand and squeezed. "You okay?"

She sniffed, nodded. "Let's go."

And so, they left *Two Daughters* with heavy hearts and light packs. They had two days of travel ahead of them—two days before they reached the Haer Caves and met their future.

CHAPTER TWENTY-SEVEN

STAELLA HAD READ BOOKS ABOUT caves so large they housed entire cities, with houses built into the walls, walkways spanning hundreds of feet, and forests covering the foundation. The Haer Caves were not like that. It was big, yes, but cold and low-ceilinged. They'd had to lead the horses up a steep mountain trail to get to the entrance, which was nearly completely obscured by trees. Then, they had to bow down to get through the low entryway before finally reaching a large cavern.

There were pools of icy water on the ground, sandy stalactites reaching so far down they nearly touched the surface. Staella was grateful for the lanterns she'd managed to loot from her father's workroom, lighting one immediately.

The others followed suit. They tied the horses to the few stalagmites they could find and moved deeper into the mountain. The flames cast shadows against the rocky walls, fluttering with the piercing wind that howled through the caves.

They walked for what seemed like ages, the passageways growing smaller and smaller until they had to crawl in between slabs of stone to get through. Finally, when Staella was just about done with being squished, they entered another cavern.

This one was bigger than the first, its ceiling stretching higher than Signal Tower. There was a small lake in the center, a lake that reflected the thousands of little lights that had been ignited throughout the hall.

There were people in nearly every direction, grouped together around fires. Bed rolls were set up, food was being cooked, and there were even children swimming. *Goddess, aren't they freezing?*

Perhaps Staella had been too quick to judge the Haer. There was an entire rebel city right here. The rebels froze as their party entered, eyes wide. Mothers grabbed children out of the water to clutch them close. Men picked up haphazard weapons. Staella moved closer, taking slow steps and keeping her palms open.

She heard someone whisper, "They found us."

Markham came up next to her, followed by Maci, Amile, and Chrisjon. Then, when Leda stepped into the room, the atmosphere changed.

A voice rang out from the back of the cavern. "Lady Hayvinger! She's one of us. She helped us escape the city."

Leda took her cue and marched forward, head held high and back straight. "I assume you're all here under the lightning banner." The people roared in assent, some raising their fists into the air. However, there were still those who glared at them warily. "*We* are here under that same banner, but we come bearing bad news." The room quieted instantly, Leda's voice echoing off the walls as she continued, "Your leader, Tomhas, has been captured by the Lorde of Security, his inner circle murdered."

Staella heard gasps, a cry of "oh!". She wondered how many people in this room had known Bruhel, had been friends with him.

"However, most of you know that there is another leader, one whose identity has been kept secret. Now, the time has come for that leader to take his place… Markham Aesher."

Buzzing filled the room, some rebels shaking their heads fervently. Markham took up the spot next to Leda, turning on his charm and remembering his eloquence.

"I know this may come as a shock to you, but I have been a part of the Rebellion for years. I provided funds and helped make important decisions. I was never supposed to lead you alone, but now… I know that I am not one of you. I know that I could never understand the tribulations you have faced. If you would have me, I would be honored to help you change Aldahad for the better. But if you would rather elect another leader, that is up to you."

The people didn't cheer. They looked at him with suspicious eyes, grumbling to themselves.

"He's the richest man in the Monarchy. Why would he want change?"

"Mister Golden Spoon walking in trying to play savior."

"Why didn't he reveal his identity earlier? Seems awfully convenient now that Tomhas is gone."

Staella could see Markham deflating, could see all his anxieties boil to the surface. The rebels were only voicing his own doubts.

"Can we please stop this nonsense?" The exclamation came from somewhere near the back. Someone moved forward, the people parting to let the speaker through. A small figure marched up to them, her curls bouncing with each step and her green eyes fierce.

Mycah.

She stopped in front of Markham and turned to face the crowd. "Most of you know me. You know what I've been through, my distrust of all things male and rich, but this man saved my life. He saved all my hummingbird sisters' lives. He's been working with Tomhas for years. Do you remember how the Rebellion used to be? People begging for scraps. A few meetings that never led anywhere. Remember when that changed? When we suddenly got weapons and safe houses and started protesting?

"Well, that was because of him. He gave us his coin, his information, and his heart. He risked his own life to revive our movement. There is no one who will sacrifice as much and work as hard to free us from oppression as Markham. So, let's not waste any more time. All in favor of electing him and his inner circle—" She pointed at each of them standing with Markham. "–raise your right hand."

One or two hands went up immediately. Then, three or four. Slowly, hands were raised. Then, in a wave, most of the room had their arms held high.

Staella let out the breath she'd been holding. Markham smiled. "Thank you. I promise that we will try to free Tomhas as quickly as possible. Tonight, my inner circle and I will strategize. Tomorrow, we will have a plan to transform Aldahad."

†

They had decided to eat lunch first, to spend some time getting to know the rebels who had risked their lives to make it to the Caves.

Markham was weaving through the mass of people like he'd been born to lead. He had that charming smile on his face, the one Leda knew from their childhood days–the one that lit up his eyes and made the whole world like him. He sat down around each fire, making introductions, laughing, then talking seriously. She'd had to champion him, but she knew that the rebels would grow to appreciate him of their own accord before the end of the night.

Leda had followed his strategy at first, taking the time to greet those she recognized from the city, but then she saw the girl that had emerged from the crowd sitting against one of the far walls. She hadn't gotten the girl's name, but there was something undeniably interesting about her. Perhaps it was her skin, only a shade lighter than Leda's own, that glowed pink at her cheeks, or her hair, which coiled so stunningly. Her resolve or her "hummingbird" background. Leda didn't know, but it was time to find out.

She walked over and flopped down next to the girl. "I don't think we've been introduced."

The other's mouth twisted in amusement. *Is she trying not to laugh at me?* Then, she extended a hand. "I don't think we have, *Lady* Hayvinger. I'm Mycah Delaney, the unsung hero of this Rebellion."

Leda cocked an eyebrow and smiled. "Well, then it's an honor, Miss Delaney."

"Some of the rebels seem very taken by you. I wonder if it's because they think you're the new Lowena," Mycah mused.

"You don't seem very approving." Indeed, the girl was scowling, her green eyes piercing and unforgiving.

She chewed on the inside of her lip. "The High Ruler and the nobles in their towers also celebrate her. She was *their* hero. If she'd been ours, we wouldn't be here right now." Leda blinked, shook her head. No one had ever dared to say a bad word about Lowena, and certainly not to a Hayvinger. Before she could retort, Mycah continued, "We don't need another Lowena. I hope you don't lead these people to trust you and then only end up throwing them into oppression under a different name."

Leda huffed. "You're very bold, Miss Delaney."

She flashed a half-grin. "I'm very honest, *my lady*."

"Lowena tried. It was outside forces that thwarted her true plans for liberation." She was becoming annoyed at the girl's insolence.

Mycah snorted. "Always someone else to blame. Look at me. Do you think *I* would've bent for 'outside forces?'" Leda lodged her tongue against the inside of her cheek, sure that her eyes were flashing with rage. Mycah just laughed. "What? Not used to people who aren't fazed by your family name?"

Leda nearly bared her teeth in a snarl, but before she could burst, Staella appeared at her shoulder. "We're meeting in the back room in two minutes," she ordered.

Mycah frowned. "What's going on?"

Staella looked around to ensure that no one else was listening, and whispered, "We have a visitor claiming to bear urgent news."

†

As the last of the new inner circle filed into the small cavern they'd dubbed the "back room," Staella nodded to the woman standing beside her, whose black cloak still obscured her identity. At Staella's signal, the visitor lowered her hood, her sapphire eyes peeking out at them warily. There were gasps all around.

Amile stepped forward and gaped. "Zandi?"

His sister was pale, with deep blue circles blooming under her eyes. Her clothes were stained with mud, her raven hair tied up in a matted ponytail. She hadn't traveled as Lorde Qarvette; that was clear. *She's been running.*

Markham steadied his best friend with a hand on the shoulder, stepping forward to greet Zandi with barely-veiled contempt. "What is it that you want?"

She sucked in a heavy breath, and it emphasized the bones jutting out against her skin. She looked near tears as she said, "I have come to reveal the truth."

Leda walked up to her, placing a gentle arm around her shoulders. "You look like you've been to the Realm Beneath. What happened?"

Zandi closed her eyes, a tear slipping out to roll down her cheek. Trembling, she answered, "I know where the missing Representatives are. I know why my brother suffers every night." She looked up at Leda. "And I know why your mother went mad."

The air rushed out of the room.

THE GIRL

THE GIRL WAS ONLY ELEVEN YEARS old when her brother took the throne and got married to the woman who set free all his inner demons. He'd always snuck off with the older one, the Hayvinger woman with the blonde hair, but he didn't seem to like her anymore, not after his new wife started whispering in his ear.

The girl watched as more and more things around their home started changing. Her parents moved out, left her under the care of her older siblings and the servants. Her eldest brother grew even more distant than he'd been before and she was moved to a far tower of the palace, away from him and his wife. She missed the way her family had been before—before the mean woman had moved in, before they had become the ruling line. Despite this, Zandi adjusted quickly, as most children do.

Her other brother, the boy with the gentle hands and the loving eyes, liked spending time with her, twirling her around in absurd dances and telling her beautiful stories before bed. He also liked spending time alone. She never really understood his need to sit outside and draw little leaves and wild animals. So, she left him be when he got that foggy look in his eyes and said no to playing.

With her parents gone and Yathan preoccupied, the servants had slackened in their duties and the girl was left to her own devices on most days. Yearning to be with her eldest brother, she liked to sneak closer to his part of the house, to see what was taking up most of his time.

The guards or Cala's handmaidens always stopped her before she could get to him. She'd tried to shoo them away, to make them understand that this was her home and not theirs, to make them listen to her, but the authority of an eleven-year-old stomping her foot was not very persuasive.

So, she got smarter instead.

Each time she was caught, she adjusted her plan and improved her sneaking abilities, until she was impossible to catch, until she could tiptoe into the north wing without alerting a soul.

She scurried around their quarters like a mouse, curious and quick. There was nothing really interesting in their bedroom or closet. Their living rooms and gardens were abandoned. She'd come all this way to find Yathan, but he was nowhere to be found. Not the bathrooms or the gymnasium, nor the games room.

Then, with her mouse ears, she heard voices far away. Listening intently, she followed the sound, keeping a lookout for anyone who might apprehend her. She traced the voices to stone steps leading down into the ground. She hadn't even known that there was anything underneath the first floor.

Taking soundless steps, she went down and down the spiral stairs, the voices growing louder. At last, she arrived in a large chamber. Keeping to the shadows, she saw something that she did not understand.

Her brother was there, his wife beside him. They were looking down at a high bed. A light that hung from the ceiling was spinning around and around, flashing periodically and hurting the girl's eyes.

She moved a little to the side, to see what they were looking at. When she did, she had to try her best to silence her gasp.

It was the Hayvinger woman, the one Yathan had always liked so much, but she looked strange. Her eyes were staring out in front of her, not seeing anything. She was humming a broken song. The girl didn't understand what they were doing.

Why had they tied the woman to the bed with leather straps? Why were they injecting her with a yellow liquid that made her writhe and her eyes roll back in her head? Why were they showing her pictures of inexplicable things that had been drawn by expert hands?

She left quickly, scared of being found, but she went back the next day. And the next. And the next. For months. Until they seemed to be done with the blonde woman.

By watching and listening, she realized what they were doing.

She knew that the yellow liquid was sap from haletayl trees that made people's brains act funny. She knew the light was supposed to make her feel dizzy—that was part of the plan. She knew the images were carefully crafted. She knew they were trying to control minds; they wanted to get people to do whatever they said, to lose volition and become puppets. She knew that they were failing, that what they did in that room only made the woman mad. So, they tossed her aside like trash and moved on to another subject.

The girl entered the room one day and was close to screaming when she found her other brother strapped to the bed. Amile had been paralyzed, not struggling or saying anything. She sobbed quietly as she watched them stick the needle into his arm, the liquid a little darker this time. As she watched them show him pictures even as his body started convulsing.

They nearly succeeded with him, but she knew they had failed that first night her gentle brother started screaming and killing.

She never went to that room again and tried to forget everything she'd seen. Her nightmares and tears were disregarded as childish whims, her ever-ghostening state ignored.

Then, when they locked Amile away, she'd used all her stealth to try to get to him, but his tower was too heavily guarded. They had taken him away, turned him into something else, and she couldn't even tell him why.

Along with her body, her sneaking skills grew. It was a year later when she finally managed to slip past all the guards and servants, to steal the key to her beloved brother's cage and see him.

In the year that had passed, she also came to understand the world more clearly than any twelve-year-old should. She understood that it would do no good to tell Amile the truth, that it would only leave him more broken-hearted and frustrated. She knew that if either of them showed any inclination of knowing Yathan's secret, he wouldn't hesitate to take them out. She knew she'd only been spared this long because she was the Representative. But she couldn't stand by as Amile withered away in his prison. So, she steeled herself and told him the biggest lie she'd ever told—that she didn't love him and wanted him gone, that *he* was the shameful one in the family.

Because she knew that it would make him leave.

With his departure, the palace grew even more lonely. She never sought out her eldest brother again, only feigned politeness when they passed each other in the corridor. When Cala had children, she was never truly permitted to spend time with her niece and nephew.

So, she stayed inside her tower, learning to play every instrument she could think of, withering away under the weight of the secret she held. She'd just have to hold on until the Election had passed, then she wouldn't have to stay in Yaekós any longer.

Then, she became the Lorde of the Goddess and Representatives began to disappear. And the girl knew that she couldn't just be a frightened little girl anymore.

So, the Lorde had snuck back into that room, had seen Representative after Representative being minionized under Yathan and Cala's spell. They had figured it out. They were creating puppets.

She finally understood why. As the capital city had been thrown deeper and deeper into chaos, she understood Yathan's plan to dismantle the People's Monarchy and become King, to use the very people who stood in the way of his lifelong reign as his soldiers. Everything was perfectly orchestrated, an expertly-woven web.

So, she ran. She followed the rumors, disguised herself as a rebel, and went to find the brother she'd sent away all those years ago—the one who was now trying to take on their tyrant sibling and change the world.

The Lorde would no longer be a ghost.

CHAPTER TWENTY-EIGHT

NO ONE SAID ANYTHING.

Everyone stared at her. At him.

Amile stumbled forward, steadied himself with a hand to the wall. Everything was spinning, the blood in his ears so loud he couldn't make sense of anything else. It felt strange to breathe and blink. He focused on the veins in his free hand, trying to follow the blue lines with his eyes and recall the names of the bones underneath, but his mind was uncooperative, drowning him in images he didn't want to see.

His brother's cruel face looming over him.

The stab of a needle.

A throbbing headache.

The light flashing again. And again.

He sagged to the floor, landed on his knees, and threw up.

There was barely light in the room, yet it was too bright. Everything was too bright. His blood was too loud. And—

He heaved again. Hands were tucked under his arms and he was lifted up. Markham helped him to stand, supporting him with his body.

"Come on, let's go lie down."

He was faintly aware of being pulled into a different, even smaller room. "Please put out the lamp," he begged as he was lowered to a bedroll.

Markham obeyed before handing him a flask of water. He drank, but it didn't help. His head was still spinning. Spinning. Until he blacked out.

†

Leda gulped, shook her head, started to speak. Stopped. Closed her eyes and clenched her hand into a fist.

"My mother had an affair with Yathan Qarvette?" Zandi nodded, looking even smaller than she had before. "And he's the reason she…?"

"Yes."

She was trembling, her teeth clenched together and her breathing harsh. "We will kill that son of a bitch. Slowly."

†

It was late afternoon by the time Amile was awake and well enough to return to the room. Chrisjon had taken the responsibility of cleaning up where Amile's shock had overtaken him. Staella had held Leda's hand so tightly it hurt, wishing that it could be enough to erase the Hayvinger's years of hurt. Mycah had silently given Zandi some food and water and Maci had disappeared, only returning when the meeting commenced.

They were sitting on the cave floor in a circle. Staring at each other with unspoken words.

Markham was the first to speak. "Zandi… I want to thank you for your bravery in coming here and telling the truth. I want to thank you for saving my best friend and for standing up against your brother."

She shook her head, looking away. "I wish I had done more."

"You still could." Everyone turned to Markham, frowning. "You said you observed Yathan and Cala doing this brainwashing plenty of times… That means you must have some idea of how they did it."

"Well, I don't know all the mechanics, but I watched them do it enough times that I think I understand the basics."

"So, do you think you'd be able to reverse it?"

Staella watched as Amile's eyes widened. He stared at his sister with heart-wrenching hope. She hesitated before answering, "I, uh, maybe with a lot of experimenting I could recreate the process. It's a big maybe, and I don't think I could erase it completely… At the moment, Amile's condition is triggered by nightfall. I could… reroute it, make it subject to some impossible event, I think."

"Could you reroute it to a person?" This came from Amile.

Markham shook his head. "Amile, no—"

"Answer the question."

Zandi nodded slowly. "I guess."

There was no trepidation in Amile's voice as he declared, "I want you to have it be triggered by Yathan."

"What?" Staella gasped. "Amile, we're not using your situation as a weapon."

"You know what I'm capable of when I get like that. Not even you could stop me. I would have killed you if Markham hadn't snuck up behind me." The memory made her flinch. "There is no one with a better chance of taking him out than I, and I think I deserve to be the one to do it."

Markham chewed on his bottom lip. He placed a hand on his friend's back. "If that's truly what you want…"

"It is."

"Then, Zandi, Amile, and Maci will go back to my estate." Markham shifted right into organization mode. "Hopefully Yathan's searches of Crest homes have ended now that Leda left. You should be safe there, and there's plenty of haletayls that can be used." The three of them nodded in agreement.

"Right," Markham continued. "Our biggest problem at this stage is finding a safe place for the rebels to go until we can make our move. It has to be close to the city, but safe from detection."

Silence.

Then after a while, Chrisjon suggested: "We could use the Krezín Mountains."

Mycah shook her head. "It's too far from Yaekós. We'd need another halfway point anyway."

Leda snapped her fingers and looked up with sparkling eyes. "Markham, do you remember how much trouble we would get in when we visited your father as children?"

Markham's gaze lit up and he beamed. "Leda, you are a genius."

"Mind telling the rest of us what's going on?" Maci chirped.

Leda nodded. "The mines. There's a whole world underground and no one would ever think to look there."

Staella grinned. "It's perfect."

"I'll write to my father as soon as I can."

Leda nodded. "Great. So, then we can have the rebels go in small groups at a time, approach the mines from the east… There's another thing we might need if we plan to take Aldahad."

"What's that?" Chrisjon asked.

"Manpower. The rebels have good numbers, but I suspect we may need more. We can contact Lorde Haltstone and tell him the truth. With his niece imprisoned in the palace dungeons, I don't think he'll have much objection to aiding the Rebellion. He can recruit more people from all around the country… But we need people who know how to fight. Most of the rebels are civilians. We need strength and experience."

Staella thought back to a map spread over a large table, a finger pointing to the country's northern border. "I think I can help with that. Saul once told me something I can definitely use to bring some of his men over to our side."

"How long will it take?" Markham enquired.

She shrugged. "If I can go alone, fourteen days max."

He nodded. "Do whatever you need to." He turned back to the group. "Some rebels managed to get out of the city, but there are still many more in Yaekós… The capital is our strongest location. We need someone to go in and rally those members who are still there, to give them new hope and revive their spirits. I can think of no one better than Leda and Mycah."

The two shot each other a venomous look, but nodded. "Whatever the Rebellion requires."

"Good."

"So, what will you and I be doing then?" Chrisjon asked Markham.

The latter grinned. "We're going to break Tomhas out of Hareth Prison."

CHAPTER TWENTY-NINE

THE STALLION WAS ONE OF Markham's best and Staella could feel it. The animal kept its gallop without losing breath for far longer than she'd expected. She would perhaps reach Aldahad's northern border in five days and not six.

Her own body was growing sore, injuries still sending pangs of discomfort through her every now and again. But she pushed on, did not stop until they reached the nearest big town. Darev was always busy, travelers coming and going to sample the market's rare goods and various forms of unsavory entertainment.

She'd never really liked the town. It felt like a cesspool of vulgarity and loose morals, but it was a good place to avoid notice and get a few hours' rest.

It was well past midnight when she stopped in front of a small inn on the outskirts of town, checking that no one had followed her before she knocked at the door. No one answered. She tried again, harder and longer this time. Finally, there were scurrying footsteps inside and the bolted door was opened. It was a woman with unruly gray hair and a long night frock. She squinted at Staella with deep creases in her brow.

"I suppose you want a room."

She nodded. "Yes, please, and a place for my horse."

The innkeeper shook her head and grumbled under her breath, but she stepped aside to let Staella in. "My husband will see to the horse in a minute. You could have come a little earlier, you know."

Staella bit the inside of her cheek and forced a smile. "Unfortunately, that would have meant the death of that lovely animal outside. I apologize for the inconvenience, but I assure you I can make up for it."

She fished a little purse out of her cloak pocket, dropping it onto the woman's hand. The latter's eyes widened as she felt the weight. She gasped upon opening it to find gold inside. Staella smirked.

There are some perks to being with Markham Aesher.

She crossed her arms. "I assume that'll be enough to compensate for my late arrival. I don't need a big room—just a clean one. I'd like my stallion to be fed and watered. Use the best food you have. If there's someone who could massage his legs, that would be great. Don't worry, he's a sweetheart. Any meal you can serve at this hour would be appreciated, and I'll take that in my room."

The older woman nodded tersely. "Of course, madam."

Nodding her gratitude, Staella motioned for the woman to lead her upstairs. She was taken to a corner room with a diagonal ceiling and a single window. It had one threadbare cot, a chamber pot with chipped sides, and a stool-sized table. She'd known the quality of the Darrey when she'd chosen it, but had settled for obscurity rather than luxury—a decision she was sure her better half would not have made.

After a meal of cold porridge and a glass of thick milk, she went to sleep. The single blanket was enough in the Aldahadi heat, and her mind slipped into unconsciousness almost immediately.

†

"You've never hunted before?" Chrisjon cocked an eyebrow at him, hands on his hips.

Markham shrugged. "Once. My father took me when I was about twelve. I found that it didn't really agree with me. I only felt sorry for the animals the whole time."

His companion sighed. "Well, fortunately this hunt will be for survival and not for sport. Would you prefer to make the fire?"

Markham nodded. "Yes, please."

The weapons master only smiled, turning to grab his bow and arrows before he set off into the jungle.

They were back in the Roäk, much to Markham's dismay. He still hadn't become acclimatized to sleeping outside and traveling through the sweltering wilderness, but the jungle was the only way to get to their destination undetected.

The fire was only just starting to rise into heavy orange flames when Chrisjon returned, sweat beading on his forehead and a boar slung over his shoulders. The creature was big, covered in black-gray hair and had tusks the size of Markham's forearms.

He shot up and watched, mesmerized as the other man bent over to drop the animal on the ground, grunting as he did so.

"You killed that all by yourself in the time it took me to make a fire?"

Chrisjon stretched out his arms, rubbing at a spot on his upper back. "The Caneilles and I go camping nearly every weekend. We like going to truly wild places and taking only the bare essentials. So, whilst Eran provides the cooking expertise and Daniel provides the entertainment, I make sure we have meat. It's just practice."

Markham shook his head. "You should have won the Election."

Chrisjon chuckled, crouching down with a knife in his hand to start skinning the boar. "Because I can hunt?"

"Because you can actually do real-world things," he muttered.

"Do you want to learn how to do real-world things?" Markham cocked a suspicious eyebrow, which only made the other laugh harder. "Come here and I'll show you how to prepare an animal for eating."

Markham was hesitant at first, but obeyed a few seconds later. Hunching down next to Chrisjon, he watched and listened intently to the man's lesson. *The way my life is going, I might need this soon.*

After they had finished skinning, cleaning, portioning, and roasting the meat, they sat down at the fire to enjoy their dinner.

"Thank you," Markham said as he finished.

Chrisjon nodded. "Of course. Now, we should probably start planning how we're going to break Tomhas out of the most high-security prison in Aldahad."

Markham sighed. "Yeah, that's probably a good idea. For one, we're going to need more specialized tools and weapons, but I assume our weapons master would be able to help with that."

An idea sparked in Chrisjon's eyes. "Yeah. We can definitely get everything we need at the Damheres'. Plus, there's someone there who might just be able to conquer Hareth…"

†

Mycah flung open the green door, waltzing into the tiny apartment and collapsing into an orange loveseat with a sigh. "Home sweet home. I suppose it's not to your liking, Princess?"

Leda rolled her eyes, setting her pack down on the carpet and moving deeper into the space. Mycah's home was a flurry of color and coziness, reminding Leda of the gypsy caravans in children's stories.

She smiled as she took a seat opposite Mycah. "I actually quite like it. It's much less cold than the estate."

Mycah was stretching out in the sun filtering through the windows, looking like a cat ready for her afternoon nap. "Well, we're not here to bask in the glory of my decorating skills. So, what are your grand plans for the rebels here in Yaekós?"

Leda scowled. "My plans? What about you? We're supposed to be doing this together."

The other's eyes pierced into her as she said, "Oh, I thought you were the champion of the people—the savior of the oppressed. Me, I'm just a poor little ex-slave. What could I possibly know about the people living in the slums?"

Leda shot up. "You know what? I'm sick of this. Why do you insist on tormenting me but not Markham?"

Mycah stood up lazily, a grin starting to tug at the corners of her mouth. "Because he doesn't react so deliciously."

She blinked. "What?"

The girl chuckled, swaggering closer. "You get this adorable little furrow right here." She reached out to touch Leda's brow, which was indeed frowning. "You look like a bird ruffling its feathers every time I say something. It's quite cute."

Leda gulped and pulled away from her hand. She just stared at her companion, her head reeling. *What is happening?* Mycah stood patiently, cocking an eyebrow at her.

When Leda remained silent, she giggled. "Sit down, Princess. I'll make us some tea and we can talk strategy. I've had a few ideas over the years."

Leda only nodded, sitting back down and trying not to furrow her brow. She watched the girl move through the kitchen, featherlight and smiling.

CHAPTER THIRTY

THE DAMHERE HOUSE WAS STUNNING, even to Markham. It was much smaller than any of the mansions on the Crest, but it was beautiful. It stood in the center of a tiny farm, surrounded by sheds and vegetable gardens and various edible animals. The walls were sheeted in stark white planks, matching the massive pillars that held up the balcony jutting from the second floor. The front door was also upstairs and could only be reached via the wide staircase leading from the cobblestone path. The shutters and roof were the color of seaweed, all pristinely painted, and a chimney peeked out above it all.

Markham followed Chrisjon up the stairs, smiling at the blonde cat that lounged on the elaborate wooden railing. To his surprise, there was a woman sitting on the balcony. Her eyes were nearly swallowed by wrinkles, but she still seemed to be looking out over the farm, swaying back and forth in her rocking chair.

Chrisjon beamed and reached to wrap his arms around the lady's shoulders. "Isi."

The woman patted him on the back with a knobby hand and smiled. "Jon. It's good that you are home. Your ma has been so worried. She's starting to take it out on the chickens, you know."

Chrisjon chuckled as he straightened. "Ai Isi, I'll have to tell her you're gossiping about her."

She sucked at her teeth. "You always did like to stir the pot… Are you going to introduce me to your friend or leave him standing there like a deer in a pig pen?"

"Of course. Isi, this is Markham Aesher. He's also a Representative. Markham, this is my grandmother, Chorina, but everyone just calls her Isi."

Markham nodded, shifting his pack to kiss Chorina's extended hand. "It is a pleasure to meet you… Isi."

She eyed him, leaning forward to get a good look at his face. "You should bring more of your polite city friends, Jon. They are much nicer to look at than the pigs."

Both men laughed at that and Chrisjon shook his head. "Unfortunately, Markham is taken, Isi."

She swatted at him. "Stop teasing your elders and go placate that ma of yours."

Just as they turned to head for the front door, it banged open. A toddler ran out on chubby brown legs. He was wearing nothing but a diaper, squealing in ecstasy as he dashed straight for the stairs. Chrisjon leaped and grabbed hold of the child's arm before he could tumble down.

A woman appeared in the doorway, clutching her pregnant belly and breathing heavily. "Jon, thank the Goddess." She waddled forward to pick up the boy and placed him on her hip. "Papoo, you will give your ma a heart attack."

She was pinching her son's chubby cheek, which earned her a gurgle. *She must be Chrisjon's sister*. The resemblance was uncanny—the strong jaw and russet skin, the pitch-black hair and amber eyes.

She reached forward to give Chrisjon a kiss on the cheek. "It's good to see you. You have divine timing, it seems." Then she smiled at Markham. "I know the face on our coins when I see it. Welcome, Lad Aesher. I'm Tana." After they'd shaken hands, she sighed. "Well, I'd love to stay and chat, but this one needs to finish his lunch and Tika still needs to do her reading for the day…" She continued her long list of motherly duties as she turned and went back into the house, her voice eventually fading.

As Chrisjon and Markham also headed inside, the latter asked, "I thought you were blacksmiths?"

The other nodded. "Most of us are, but we don't always make enough coin to sustain this big a family with just that. So, we live off what the farm produces most of the time."

"Yet you still provide weapons to the Rebellion?"

Chrisjon turned to him and smiled strangely. "Of course. You don't need to be the richest man in the world to help other people."

They arrived in a spacious living room with oiled wooden floors and tan couches that looked more comfortable than anything Markham had seen in his entire life. Further down the main corridor was a plethora of rooms, each with more than one bed.

They peeked into these rooms, greeting and meeting family members as they went: a fourteen-year-old brother playing guitar on his bed, two nieces tugging at the same doll, a cousin sweeping, two massive, curly-haired hounds, and a very talkative parakeet. When they finally headed downstairs, Chrisjon swung into an impressive kitchen. Everything was white, tiled, and clean. The space smelled heavenly, aromas of spices and various dishes filling the air.

A woman was standing at one of the counters, her arms moving as she worked. Her back was turned to them, but as soon as she heard someone enter, she turned around. She looked just like Tana, with a few more crow's feet around her eyes and gray strands in her hair. Her face lit up when she saw Chrisjon, and she ran forward to throw arms around his neck.

"Oh, Papoo. You're home."

He smiled and buried his face in his mother's neck. "Hi, Ma. I'm sorry it's been so long."

She pulled away, wiped at her eyes with her apron. "Ai, I heard about all the things happening in Yaekós and I nearly came to fetch you. I am so glad you are out of that terrible city. Now that the Election isn't happening anymore, you can stay right here where you'll be safe."

He cringed. "Actually, Ma, I'm on Rebellion business. I can't stay more than a day."

She sighed, leaning her hands on the kitchen island. "You break your mother's heart, Jon. But I know you will not hide here while others suffer."

"It's not just others, Ma. You know Da would have been a great leader." He clenched his hand into a fist. "This system is ridiculous."

She patted him on the shoulder. "I know, I know. Now, who is this?" She motioned at Markham, who was feeling quite sheepish tucked into the corner of the room. He stepped forward to introduce himself, shaking the woman's hand and answering every question she had about "the horrible people in the capital." "Well, you boys may not be able to stay forever, but you will stay for dinner, yes?"

"Yes, Ma… We also have to talk to Naxa. Is she in the shop?"

"Is she ever anywhere else?"

After placing their bags in the room Chrisjon shared with another one of his cousins, Markham was led to "the shop" on the outskirts of the farm. The blacksmiths of the Damhere family worked in a cavernous brick room that hosted at least three scalding ovens and various wooden workbenches.

There were three men inside, each performing their separate tasks with eagle-like focus. An older man with a beard was pouring orange liquid into a mold. One fire was being stoked by an adolescent boy and a lean, middle-aged cousin was hammering at a piece of metal with expert blows. They were merely spared waves as they passed, heading deeper into the smithy.

They reached an area cordoned off with a flap of canvas. Chrisjon stopped, pulling Markham back to whisper, "You're going to meet my cousin Naxa now… She doesn't speak."

"She's mute?"

Chrisjon shrugged. "Not physically, but… Her parents were murdered in front of her when she was a little girl, and she hasn't uttered a word ever since." Markham gaped, shaking his head. He had no reply to that.

Chrisjon pulled back the canvas. The woman behind it looked up, stopping her work. She'd been painting the hilt of a sword with stunning patterns and Markham couldn't stop staring at the walls. There were various hilts, handles, and lids hung up, each with a unique decoration. The work was detailed and absolutely brilliant.

The woman was probably two or three years older than her cousin, but her eyes seemed to hold a lifetime of experience. Her long, braided hair was only a few shades darker than her copper skin, her eyes a deep hickory. She had one of the most interesting faces Markham had ever seen: long and strong-chinned with a wide nose and pouting lips.

She smiled kindly when she laid eyes on Chrisjon and stood to embrace him. "Naxa, I hope you don't mind us interrupting your work."

Naxa shook her head, made a series of intricate gestures with her hands. Markham felt at a disadvantage. Here was a whole new language he didn't know.

Chrisjon chuckled at whatever she'd replied and gestured to Markham. "I have brought a very important friend."

Her hands moved again.

"Important people only bring trouble," Chrisjon translated. He shrugged. "Well, that isn't untrue. In fact, we're here to ask for your help."

She narrowed her eyes at the two of them, sighed, and motioned for him to continue.

"We need to break someone out of Hareth prison."

Her eyes widened. She threw her hands into the air and shook her head, signifying what Markham was sure meant "no."

"She says it's too dangerous," Chrisjon explained as her hands moved rapidly. "Says that I always bring trouble and that she is done with that sort of thing."

Markham frowned. "What sort of thing?"

She placed her hands on her hips, staring at Chrisjon expectantly. He sighed. "She, uh, she used to be a spy. She worked for the previous Lorde of Security when she was eighteen." He turned to stare her down as she continued, "She was the best—still is, and she is really the only one who would be able to help us break out the leader of the Rebellion."

She remained unfazed. Chrisjon clasped his hands together. "Please, Naxa. Please. The future of Aldahad depends on it."

"I have done enough for Aldahad," she signed.

"Have you ever broken into Hareth?" Markham asked. She eyed him warily and shook her head. "Well, then, how do we know she would even be able to help us?" he asked Chrisjon.

Naxa gave him a deadpan glare. "Try your reverse persuasion tactics on someone a little more naïve."

"Fine, then I'll be more direct." He crossed his arms over his chest. "What do you want?"

"What?"

"In life. Tell me what you want, and I'll make sure it happens after you've helped us."

She laughed at that, the sound of it surprising Markham. She shook her head, looked at him with a pitying glare, and signed, "You cannot buy me, Lad Aesher. All I want is peace and quiet. A space to do my work. And I already have that."

As Chrisjon translated, Markham felt his heart sink. This was no use. "You worked for the oppressors of this country for years… Yet you would not lift a finger to free it now?"

In a blur of movement, she was right up against him. A blade he hadn't known she carried was pressed against his throat, her eyes flashing at him.

She signed with her free hand, baring her teeth. "Don't speak about things you do not understand."

Chrisjon stepped in, placing a hand on Naxa's arm. "Alright, I think he gets the point." She lowered the weapon slowly, never taking her eyes off Markham's. "We're sorry to have disturbed you."

He grabbed Markham by the shoulder and wheeled him out of the workroom, muttering, "I know you're mad right now. I am too. But aggravating her is never a good idea."

Markham shook his head. Mad? He was seething. "So, what do we do now? Our only plan crashed and burned."

Chrisjon sighed, finally letting go of him. "I wouldn't give up on Naxa just yet."

The dinner table was probably bigger than the one in the Aesher mansion, had to be to host all the family members and occasional guests comfortably. Markham was delighted at the feast laid out before them: roasted goose and rice, vegetables loaded with herbs, and a large decanter filled with purple liquid.

He eyed it suspiciously, which made Chrisjon chuckle. "Here, just taste it." He reached over to pour his friend a glass. "It's called chicmora. We make it ourselves from the purple corn out back. It keeps us healthy."

Markham sniffed at the glass and raised an eyebrow. "So, is it medicine or a drink?"

"Ai, just drink it," Isi muttered from his other side.

He closed his eyes and took a tiny sip. It was sour. Very sour, but… *Kind of nice.* He opened his eyes to Chrisjon's expectant face.

"I like it," he announced. To this, the entire family cheered.

As they were eating, the chatter never stopped. Cousins talked over each other. Siblings were teased. Parents scolded rowdy children. Markham didn't contribute much to the ruckus, preferring to sit back and observe. He'd never had a family like this, but it made him miss Amile.

He wondered whether his best friend had made it to the capital safely, whether Zandi was already starting to rewire his brain. If she could do it… Amile would finally be able to live the life he deserved. The idea made Markham smile.

His thoughts were interrupted by Chrisjon's father saying, "So, Markham, my son tells me you are the leader of the Rebellion."

Irnis Damhere was a formidable man, with arms like tree trunks and eyes like a hawk's. When he spoke, his deep voice made everyone listen, and what he said was usually worth listening to.

Markham gulped and gave Chrisjon a glare. "He told you that, did he?"

Irnis smiled crookedly. "We do not keep secrets from our family."

"Yes, I suppose I am the leader. I've been sort of a silent one for years, but now that Tomhas has been captured, the responsibility falls on me."

The man nodded, folding his hands and resting his chin on them. "It is comforting to see that my son keeps good company. When he first joined, it was not difficult for the rest of us to follow. We do not face the brunt of the oppression here on our own land, but we feel its consequences nonetheless."

Markham nodded. "Chrisjon says that you would have been a great leader."

A rueful look washed over his eyes. "Had my family been declared nobility a generation earlier, I could have been. But I do not think I would like being a pawn in the game that politics has become."

Markham gulped, hesitating. "We're going to take Yaekós less than twenty days from now." This resulted in murmurs all around the table. "All the rebels are gathering at the Aesher mines. It would be an honor to have a man like you with us when we change Aldahad forever…" He turned to face the rest of the clan. "In fact, any willing Damhere would be a great asset."

Chrisjon's mother nodded. "We have received the invitation sent to all members of your Rebellion. I think—I think that we would be very ignorant and selfish not to go."

"Well, you'll excuse me if I don't pull out my sword immediately," Isi grumbled. This made Markham giggle and the rest of the table joined in almost immediately.

Then, the room silenced. Naxa came in. Apparently, she often skipped dinner, too entranced in her art to come inside. She had a big canvas bag slung over her shoulder, and she was dressed in sleek black.

She walked over and dumped the bag next to Markham's chair. It flopped open to reveal dry food supplies, canteens, and a myriad of tools: throwing stars, grappling hooks, ropes, a pike, and blades of various sizes.

He looked up at her, her aunt translating this time. "We'll leave in an hour. We should get to Hareth in two days, which gives us enough time to break out your leader."

Markham beamed, bowing his head to her. "Thank you."

"I'm not doing it for you."

CHAPTER THIRTY-ONE

THE HUMAN CHAIN WAS UNBROKEN, stretching around half of Yaekós—from the northern gate, to the western, and ending at the southern entrance to the capital city.

Leda was filled with pride, emotional at the way the remaining rebels stood together, showing no fear in their pursuit of freedom. Traffic in and out of the city was delayed and they had definitely caught attention. Guards tried to get them to move, but they just stared forward, shoulders pulled back and eyes full of unfaltering determination.

Leda had Mycah on her one side, the girl's hand soft and light in hers. A woman who had introduced herself as Trisha was to her right, squinting her eyes against the sun's glare. They had taken up the spot right outside the northern entryway, knowing that this would probably be the soldiers' first point of attack.

"I must say, this is much more peaceful than I thought it was going to be," Mycah mused.

She'd barely finished the sentence when they heard neighing horses and heavy boots. With her back turned to the city, Leda couldn't see them, but she knew who it was. A girl a few feet away cried out as she was pushed to the ground to provide a gap in the chain. Soldiers marched through, manhandling the rebels in their path. They were surrounding a lone rider, a man with a commander's cap and long dark hair.

Leda snarled and let go of Mycah's and Trisha's hands to step right up to him. His military guards stopped her with pointed swords. "That is quite enough. You have no right to treat these people so roughly."

Saul Knoxin's eyes sparked at her. "Lady Hayvinger… We have every right in the world. In fact, this is about to get much rougher. Rebel activities are illegal. High treason is not treated lightly."

Leda cocked an eyebrow, looked around. "Rebel activities? High treason? I think you're mistaken, Saul."

"I am not an imbecile."

Debatable.

"Do you see any rebel regalia? Are there any banners with lightning bolts? Is anyone raising a fist?" He blinked, looking up and down the chain. They had purposefully informed the rebels to appear as innocuous as possible. Leda smirked, not able to contain her satisfaction at the growing frustration on Knoxin's face. "These are my friends, and we have decided that we would like to catch some sun."

"You are encircling the city, preventing people from getting in and out," he countered.

"The eastern gate remains open for all to use."

He clenched his jaw. "I will not stand for this nonsense. Seize her," he barked to his watch-dogs.

The soldier in front of her stepped forward, his hand already reaching for her arm. She pulled away and stared him down. "I wouldn't do that if I were you." The man hesitated and Leda returned her attention to the lorde. "In fact, I'd recommend retreating completely. You have no proof of any wrongdoing. Raise your hand to a Hayvinger and her companions unprovoked and you'll find yourself without a High Ruler to protect." Saul looked at the people behind her and then back down. There was hesitation in his expression and she continued, "You know it's true. Look at all these witnesses. Touch me, Saul, and the country will riot. Even the nobles, the ones you claim to be protecting, will revolt against you."

She was breathing hard now, her feet planted firmly and hands clenched into fists. There was a moment of silence, but she never broke his stare. She was Leda Hayvinger, Goddess be damned. That had to mean something.

Saul's mouth twisted with contempt, but he lowered his voice. "I will get you, Leda. And it will be soon. Your name can only protect you for so long."

She leered up at him. "I'll be sure to sleep with one eye open."

He growled. It caused him immense pain and her complete satisfaction when he exclaimed, "Return to the city." His soldiers obeyed immediately, encircling his steed as they left.

"Goddess, that was amazing." Mycah almost squealed as she entered the little apartment, her face lit up with a smile. "I have to admit, you're pretty scary when you try. The look on that prick's face."

Leda giggled, locking the door behind them. "I confess that I enjoy putting men in their place more than I probably should."

"Good." Mycah danced deeper into the space, heading for the kitchen. "Some tea?"

She sank down on the couch and grinned. "You have anything stronger?"

Mycah stopped, turned to her with raised eyebrows. "You're starting to ask the right questions, Princess."

The girl leaned down to retrieve a bottle with clear liquid from the cupboard. She proceeded to pour a bit of the sharp-smelling liquid into two tumblers. Then, she filled the rest of the glass with some kind of sugary drink.

When she handed it to Leda, the latter frowned. "What is this?"

Mycah chuckled, taking a seat next to her. "This is what us commoners drink. Vodka."

Leda took a sip, eyes widening. "Goddess, that's amazing."

This only made Mycah laugh more. "You really should get out more, Princess… Okay, woah. It may taste like a soft drink but it's not. You might want to take it a little slower."

"Are you implying that I can't handle my liquor?"

"Can you?"

"Goddess, no."

They both chuckled at that, and Leda found herself not really heeding Mycah's advice about slowing down. "Why do you seem so impressed with me? Today was your idea, after all."

"Yes, but the execution was sublime."

Leda clutched at her chest dramatically. "Do my ears deceive me or did Mycah Delaney just say something nice about me?"

Mycah shrugged. "If you want, I could come up with a few insults."

"Oh, I'm sure."

They chuckled again, diving deeper and deeper into the bottle of vodka until Mycah was slightly tipsy and Leda absolutely beside herself. She snorted as she laughed at an impression the other girl did of Saul Knoxin on his horse.

When they had quieted down, there was a moment of comfortable silence. Leda took this time to lean back and stare at her companion, once again feeling a strange sort of fascination at her bronze skin and huntress eyes. She'd never noticed someone as acutely.

Mycah's top had been sliding down her shoulder progressively throughout their conversation, and now the edge of a hummingbird's wing was visible. Leda found herself reaching forward. Mycah watched with big eyes as a finger traced the patterns of the brand.

Leda gulped. "I know what this means."

Mycah's jaw was clenched tightly. "Good for you, Princess."

"But I don't know how you got it." She met the girl's eyes, finding herself unable to look away.

Mycah did, her eyes flitting to the floor. "A slave merchant gave it to me when I was seven, a few days after he'd bought me from my parents."

Leda felt the breath catch in her throat. *Seven.* She was shaking with rage. "How could any parent do that to a child?"

Mycah's eyes flashed. "Not all parents live in palaces."

She shook her head, clutching her hand into a fist. "Need is a powerful thing, but it does not overrule character. My own father was ready to exchange me for a political alliance, but slavery…"

Silver now lined those beautiful green eyes, but they refused to meet Leda's gaze. "At least they were crying when they did it. The merchant was cold when he pushed a scalding rod to the flesh of my back and watched it sizzle a life sentence onto me. It was just another thing he had to do that day. Sign some papers. Check the locks on his cages. Hire cleaners. Mutilate a child."

Tears were rolling down Leda's cheeks silently. "If only that had been the last man to hurt you."

Mycah finally looked at her, still refusing to cry. "The next one was an old farmer. He bought me at my first auction. He had a whole host of us, prepubescent little girls. We worked in the house during the day, sometimes in the field. At night…" Her breath shuddered out of her and she closed her eyes. Leda couldn't even begin to imagine the memories she was calling up. Then, she let out a sharp laugh, a single tear finally slipping. "I bit him."

Leda's eyes bulged. "You what?"

"Two years in, I didn't care about anything anymore. I only knew that I wanted to hurt him even just a fraction of the amount he'd hurt me. He was on top of me and I sank my teeth into his old saggy lips and ripped. He almost bled out… I thought he was going to kill me that night, but that would have been a bad deal. So, he sold me."

Leda took the liberty of filling both their glasses, probably mixing the drinks much stronger than was necessary. "You reminded me of a tiger the first time I saw you. It seems I was not so far off."

She shook her head. "Perhaps not, but a tiger can't do much defanged and declawed." Her entire body was trembling, her mouth contorting with emotion.

Leda slid closer, wrapping the girl up in her arms. "I will never let a man touch you again. Your claws have grown back. Your teeth are sharper than before and now you are not alone."

Mycah's hand closed over Leda's forearm and she squeezed. When she could inhale steadily, she sniffed. She turned her head, her face inches from Leda's own.

"You know, Princess, calling a prostitute valued for her 'exotic' looks a tiger might not be the best comforting tactic, and neither is implying that I can't take care of myself." Mycah smiled even as she said this, and Leda knew that the girl was grateful for her words nonetheless.

She tucked a coil of hair behind Mycah's ear and said, "I am still learning. I might not get everything right. I might sometimes sound ignorant or appear entitled, but I am trying."

The other patted her chest soothingly. "I know, Princess. I know."

Leda woke up groggily, her eyes refusing to open to more than slits. Sunlight streamed through the apartment's windows and she shielded her eyes with a groan. Her mouth was dry, her stomach roiling with nausea and her head fuzzy. She sat up slowly and noticed that she'd been sleeping on the couch. There was a note and a glass of water on the cupa table next to her. She reached for the water first, gulping it down and sighing afterwards. Then she eyed the note.

Princess,

You passed out during our game of cards. Despite my tigress' strength, I refuse to carry you up the stairs.

Have gone out to buy food.

Drink the water. Eat some of the ginger cookies on the kitchen counter. Try not to die.

The corners of her mouth tugged upward as she read, hearing Mycah's snarky tone in every word. She looked up to spot the plate of cookies waiting and made the brave decision to stand up. Her head swirled, but she made it to the counter without collapsing. Leaning against its side, she devoured three of the cookies. Her nausea dissipated soon after and her head felt slightly clearer.

She dug through the kitchen cupboards, trying to find that tea she'd been offered the previous night. She'd just found the container when the apartment's door burst open and slammed shut.

Leda jumped up to find Mycah securing about four different locks and peeking out of the window. She took care to stay in the shadows of the curtain. Her hair was disheveled, her chest rising and falling rapidly. Leda swore she could see the girl's heartbeat through her ribcage.

Temporarily satisfied, Mycah spun around. Her eyes were wide. She started heading upstairs, speaking as she rushed. "We have to leave now. Get your things."

"Mycah, wait. What happened?"

"I don't have time to explain."

"I'm not moving until you tell me what in the Realm Beneath is going on."

Mycah growled, stomping back down the steps. She rummaged through her bag and pulled out a piece of paper. She slammed it down on the counter. "There."

The blood left Leda's body. She slammed down a *WANTED* poster with Leda's face on it. Below the uncanny rendering of her features, were the words "contempt of authority," "treason," and "terrorism."

She shook her head. "No. How…?"

"Knoxin apparently works quickly once he's been scorned." She met Leda's eyes with sympathy, worry, and rage all balled into one. "It seems your family name has stopped protecting you."

Leda closed her eyes and felt the dread build up in her stomach like a wave threatening to wash her away. "I didn't think it would happen so soon."

"I know, but we can't linger on that. They've begun to search the Plateau as we speak. We have maybe two hours before they find us."

"I won't be safe anywhere," Leda shuddered. "They'll search every inch of this city to find me. There is nowhere we can hide."

"Then what do you suggest we do?"

"I have to ensure they don't recognize me."

"We'll put you in a cloak. There's a family in the Rooks who will take us in. We'll make it work."

Leda reached over the counter to grab Mycah's hands. "We're past the point of cloaks. We need something more extreme. Most of the soldiers in Yaekós have never gotten a good look at my face. They only have this drawing." She used one hand to turn the poster so it faced Mycah. "What is the first thing you see?"

She looked afraid to answer, but eventually whispered, "Your hair."

Leda nodded, pulled back. "We'll shave it, right down to the scalp, but I need something that will make them ignore me even when they look right at my face."

"What are you saying?"

"I need a distinctive mark."

"A mark?"

Leda took a deep breath, already reaching for the kitchen scissors. "A scar on the face will do."

Mycah's eyes nearly popped out of her head. "You want to take a blade to that gorgeous face and mar it forever?"

She shook her head. "No. I want you to do it."

"What?"

"Come on, Mycah. I'm determined, but I won't be able to cut up my own face."

"So, what makes you think I'd be able to do it?"

Leda slinked around the counter to stand in front of her. "You are the strongest person I know."

"No. I'm not. Just stop, okay. No."

She was turning away, but Leda grabbed her wrist. "I don't care about my face. I care about my life. I care about the people I could still help. Mycah, please." Every fiber of Leda's being was begging.

Mycah looked down at where their skin met, her lips pursed together until they whitened. Finally, she gave in with a nod. "Alright, but if I'm going to do this, we're not going halfway. The scar will stay and it will be big."

Leda squeezed her wrist in gratitude. She grabbed the scissors and headed for the bathroom with her heart thumping in her throat.

She was still pressing a bandage to the right side of her face as Mycah sheared off her hair. The caramel strands landed on the bathroom floor one after the other until there were none left on her head.

Leda had never really thought about the shape of her head before, but now she noticed the roundness of it in the mirror, the knobs where her crowns had been and the dent near the front where she'd bumped it as a child.

Mycah stepped around her, gently pulled her hand away from her face. Leda winced as the material was pulled away from the wound, sticky with blood. This was the second time the other girl was cleaning it with a saltwater mix. It stung badly, but was more bearable than the first. The blood had finally stopped seeping out, now only leaking through in a few places.

When she was finally permitted to see the damage, Leda did so silently. The cut had been brutal to endure. It began at her hairline, went all the way down her forehead and through her eyebrow. It skipped over her eye socket to continue from her cheekbone to the corner of her mouth. Deep, but not wide. Just enough to be visible and stay that way.

She looked like a completely different person. Her skin appeared a little darker without the hair framing it. Her eyes stood out, her cheekbones too, and the red line she now bore made her seem fiercer than she'd ever imagined. She doubted Mighiel would have the audacity to stand up to her now.

Mycah was also looking at her, with eyes full of sorrow as they met her own in the bathroom mirror. Leda gave her a crooked grin, ignoring the pain the movement induced.

"At least I don't look like Lowena anymore, right?"

Mycah didn't smile back. She just looked away to start cleaning the mess they'd made. "Come on. The soldiers will be here at any moment. We need to be long gone by then. I have no doubt they've been monitoring your movements. They know you're somewhere near the western side of the Plateau. I chose this apartment to be difficult to find, but that won't protect us for long, and I'm not placing all our hope in your new look."

She had bloody rags in her arms and was heading for the kitchen with deliberate steps. Leda reached out to catch her wrist.

"Please look at me." The other obeyed with gritted teeth. She refused to let her eyes settle on the wound. "Thank you," Leda whispered.

CHAPTER THIRTY-TWO

HARETH PRISON LOOKED LIKE a stone-wrought demon from the outside. It sat on an island near the western edge of the Roccalee River, where the current was dangerously strong and the banks far enough apart to deter most escape attempts. The building had black walls all around it, twenty feet high and fortified with hexagonal watch towers at its six edges. Guards milled on the balustrades like insects in a hive, their red uniforms standing out starkly in the twilight.

Markham was on his stomach, his face pressed close to the ground as he peeked through a big shrub. His teeth were worrying at his bottom lip, his eyes trying to absorb every detail about the notorious gaol.

Chrisjon was next to him, lying with his back to the scene and eating dried meat like it was going out of fashion. "You can stop worrying. She knows what she's doing."

They were waiting at the edge of the forest, not far from the southern bank. "How could I possibly not be worried? Look at the place. There is no way she's getting in unnoticed."

Chrisjon just rolled his eyes. "She was trained by Lorde Vikan himself from the age of sixteen. She's killed people others thought were impossible to touch, discovered secrets that had been hidden for decades. She once retrieved a prisoner from the Havinaak royal dungeons single-handedly and they didn't even know he was gone until they were safely across the border. I promise you that she'll be fine."

Markham sighed in concession, but kept his gaze fixed on the prison. When she'd disappeared somewhere downstream, her swimming form beneath the water had been imperceptible, and he'd known to be looking. He hadn't seen a form emerge onto the island, hadn't seen anything to betray her presence. Would he see her coming out as a tiny dot slipping out of the water, a woman appearing on the riverbank?

Chrisjon poked him in the ribs and he looked up in annoyance. "What?" The other just pointed to the forest behind him.

Markham turned and there she was. Naxa Damhere's wet clothes clung to her like a second skin, her hair dripping and dark. She was nearly invisible in the darkness of nightfall, a shadow that moved without sound.

She beckoned them deeper into the jungle, where they could make a fire without being seen by the guards. Without ceremony, she reached for her bag and stripped. Markham looked away quickly, only daring to peek once Chrisjon assured him she was dressed. She dabbed at her hair with a towel and warmed her hands by the flames. Markham watched as they moved in the orange light, fascinated by the complicated signs they made in such quick succession.

"This is going to be more complicated than I initially believed."

"This is the most secure place in Aldahad. I think 'complicated' is to be expected," Markham retorted.

She ignored him, grabbed a stick, and started drawing in the dirt. Her artistic talents were put to good use as she drew a precise map of what she'd seen inside the prison.

She signed, "I couldn't get into the main building. Just past the walls to see the general layout."

She even titled the rooms with perfect script and Markham wondered how many times she'd done this. *I should commission her to draw some maps for my books.*

The hexagonal fortress contained three main buildings arranged around a courtyard. This area was used for assembling the prisoners to take stock and to inflict public punishments. The two side buildings hosted the guards' barracks, kitchens, and offices. These were perpendicular to the main gate, which was triply enforced and heavily manned. The main building sat at the back, colossal and nearly windowless. That was where the prisoners would be kept.

"It will be nearly impossible to break someone out of the building. We don't know what the inside looks like and it's where they'll be expecting it. The only way to get Tomhas out is to get him to the courtyard and proceed from there."

"How are we supposed to do that, exactly?" Chrisjon asked.

"One of us will have to go in," Naxa motioned.

"Won't that be as impossible as breaking someone out?"

She shook her head. "Not if you're a prisoner."

Chrisjon's eyes widened. "You're saying one of us has to become an inmate?"

"I'll do it," Markham announced without hesitation. "He's my friend and this was my decision. Neither of you should have to face that danger."

"No. You're too easily recognizable. Your face is on our money, and I have a different part to play once Tomhas is in position."

Chrisjon threw his hands in the air. "So, it comes down to me. Fuck."

Markham shook his head. "No. You don't have to. We can think of some other plan."

"You're not the only one willing to sacrifice for this Rebellion, you know. Let someone else be the hero for once. Plus, I'd wager very few people outside the capital know what I look like... Alright, what's the plan?"

The apprehension in Chrisjon's eyes was clear, but he listened to Naxa's strategy without hesitation.

†

Leda was dressed in some of Mycah's old clothes. The brown top was too tight and the pants too short, but they would have to do. She had to look like she belonged.

Lines of soldiers were on constant patrol in the Rooks, eyeing every citizen who dared look out of place. The slums felt like a warzone, and they looked like one too. Fear hung in the air alongside old smoke, and suspicion ran as rancid as the waste in the streets. A few military men were lounging in front of a corner shop, their mere presence chasing away the little business the owner had. A teenage girl was approaching, a basket clutched in her arms, and her eyes wide with anxiety. She stepped up to the shop, trying to ignore the soldiers to get to the entrance.

One of the men stepped forward to grab her around the arm. She yelped and his mouth twisted in sadistic pleasure. Whatever he whispered in her ear made her tremble. From the other side of the dirt road, Leda's blood boiled. She started for the shop, but was stopped by Mycah's hand catching her own. The girl gave her a warning glare and pulled her along. If she kept her mouth shut, they would remain unnoticed. Leda's change in appearance was working spectacularly.

They continued deeper into the Rooks, following a labyrinth of alleys and shortcuts until they made it to a small close of shacks. Each was painted a different color and had a clearly marked number on the door.

"What is this place?"

"The closest thing you'll find to a pleasant neighborhood down here," Mycah answered, heading straight for the farthest home.

Its walls were made of an assortment of planks and corrugated iron, adorned in the brightest yellow Leda had ever seen. There were wire-wrought toys laying near the front door, supposedly where the yard was situated, accompanied by a mangy dog chewing on what closely resembled a femur.

The animal gave a single bark as they approached, tail wagging. Mycah scratched it behind the ears. Barely moving her head, she checked the area to ensure they hadn't been followed before rapping her fist against the door four times.

Something crashed to the floor on the other side. There were obvious whispers. A little whine. The door opened quickly. It was a child of about eleven, her green eyes wide and her umber skin ashen as she brandished a pan in her right hand. She'd clearly been prepared for a fight. An even smaller head peeped out from behind her.

Upon seeing Mycah, the older girl let out a sigh and lowered her weapon. The little one jumped out, her coiled hair bouncing with her every movement. She was a tiny thing, six years old at the most, with copper skin and big eyes.

"Auntie My."

She ran right into Mycah's arms, making the latter chuckle. "Hey, Rossi." She looked up at the other girl. "Sorry to have frightened you. Your mother said we could hide here for a few days." The girl looked wary, but nodded and stepped aside to let them in. "Rossi and Rayla, this is Leda."

Rossi waved at her from behind Mycah's legs, while Rayla offered a tight-lipped smile. "We should close the door before anyone comes."

The shack had two rooms: a kitchen and a sleeping area. The kitchen was just big enough to hold a makeshift hearth and a wonky table. The bedroom had two couches piled with blankets and three threadbare pallets set up on the floor. Leda yelped when the blankets on the nearest couch started to move. Then she saw the rumpled face peeking out from the one end and sighed, clutching a hand to her chest. The woman looked ancient, with more wrinkles than teeth, and eyes that struggled to stay open. Her chest rattled each time she breathed and she seemed to be slightly bewildered.

Rayla flitted to her side. "It's alright, Gran. It's just Mycah and her friend." The woman muttered something in a high-pitched voice before settling back into the couch-bed and closing her eyes. Satisfied that her great grandmother had been calmed, the girl turned to them and motioned to the floor. "I hope you brought bed rolls."

Mycah patted the canvas bag she had slung over her shoulder. "Right here. You don't have to worry about anything. We'll stay out of your way until your parents come home."

Rayla nodded, plopped down on one of the pallets, and pulled out a reading book that was frayed at the edges.

Rossi, on the other hand, came up to Leda shyly and said, "You're very pretty."

She couldn't help but touch the scar on her face. She smiled and knelt down to look the girl in the eyes. "Thank you very much, Rossi. I think you're very pretty too."

"You look like Talia." The child held out a doll with pride. It was made of old pieces of fabric, had no face and was slowly losing its head.

Leda cleared her throat, trying to ignore Mycah's suppressed giggles behind her. "Oh, uh, thanks. She's, uh, she's very charming."

She nearly gasped when Mycah's hand made contact with her newly shaved head, brushing softly against the skin in a way that made her spine tingle.

"Come on, Princess, these bedrolls won't set up themselves."

†

Naxa had slipped off to the nearest village early the next morning to steal clothes from some poor family's washing line. Chrisjon now stood in baggy workman's trousers, a nondescript t-shirt, and bulky boots. His long hair was tied up into a messy bun at the nape of his neck and he had been stripped of all his weapons.

He looked down at himself warily. "So, this is the outfit I die in."

Naxa rolled her eyes. "You're not going to die."

"I'm going to walk right up to the most high-security prison in Aldahad and declare war against the country. Don't tell me there isn't at least a fifty-fifty chance that they will kill me on sight."

Markham shook his head. "You just have to be threatening enough to be taken, but not enough to be executed."

"Oh, yeah, simple as that," Chrisjon mused. "Can't I just dig up someone's body and take the head to the door? Hareth takes murderers, right?"

Naxa shook her head. "Why would a murderer walk up to a prison with his victim's head?"

"I don't know. Why would a rebel walk up to it spewing about terrorism?"

"Because that's what they think we are," Markham answered. "Radicals and fanatics who want to tear Aldahad apart. They took Tomhas because the Rebellion is the biggest threat the current regime faces. A rebel mad enough with revolutionary thoughts to threaten Hareth will scare them, but they won't risk execution until they've gotten information out of you."

Markham remembered the chaos of Bruhel's home, the many wounds the old guard had borne. There was no doubt in his mind that they'd tortured him for intel before they'd finished the job. That was the only reason Tomhas was still being kept—he had too many secrets.

Chrisjon closed his eyes and took a deep breath. "If I get… *interrogated* in there, this Rebellion owes me. A lot."

Markham placed a hand on the other man's shoulder. "We already owe you more than can be repaid in a lifetime."

Naxa waved a hand to get their attention, pointing to the prison. The sun was reaching its zenith and the guards were changing shifts. It was time.

†

Children from the neighboring shacks had started to come out, playing a noisy game in the street with a semi-deflated ball. Rossi had run out eagerly, and even Rayla had put down her book to join.

Mycah threw Leda a coy glance. "Ever played assoc?" She shook her head, squealing as her friend pulled her outside.

It was raining, the *cul de sac* turning into a muddy arena as the children ran back and forth. Their little feet handled the ball effortlessly, moving so quickly Leda only saw a blur. A boy of about eight was running. Children yelled. An older girl tried to maneuver the ball away from him and failed. He kept running, then kicked, and another boy jumped out to catch the ball, missing it by a few inches. It soared through the air between the splintered planks they'd erected as goal posts. There were cheers all around.

Leda shook her head when Mycah tried to tug her forward to enter the game. "You can play. It's fine. I don't know–"

"Shut up, Princess, and come mingle with the commoners."

She got a few wary glances from some of the children, but Rossi pulled her in immediately. The girl started explaining rules and moves and who played what, but Leda couldn't keep up. A few seconds later, they were set to start again. Mycah was positioned on the opposite team and gave Leda a cocky wink before someone imitated the sound of a whistle.

The children were off like horses in a race. Leda followed frantically, trying to spot the ball. Someone kicked. Another child yelled about the rules. Mycah usurped the ball, running quicker than seemed manageable. Leda tried to catch up, slipping in the mud to land on her behind. She laughed as Rayla helped her up, not caring in the least that her clothes would probably never be clean again. Mycah had scored a goal, doing a bizarre dance with the rest of her teammates, letting out a *whoop*.

Leda only started to understand the rules around the third match, and the afternoon passed in a flurry of sprinting children and playful shrieking.

The sun was only just starting to set, turning the world dark orange, when a horn sounded nearby. It repeated the same long note every three seconds, high and grating.

The children stopped playing, as if a switch had been flipped. Four boys quickly grabbed the goal planks and ball, throwing them in the dirt beside one of the homes. The rest dashed for a small wooden shed near the entrance to the close. Mycah grabbed Leda's hand and ran after them.

They all piled into an area as big as a horse stall, with something resembling a toilet in the corner and a tap against the other wall.

Rayla grabbed one of the buckets waiting under the tap and filled it. As soon as she was done, another child with a pail took her place.

She herded Leda, Mycah, and Rossi together. In a swift movement, she dumped the icy water over their heads, leaving a bit for herself. Leda screeched. Then, she realized that the children were all cleaning themselves, hands moving over their bodies and through their hair to use what little water could be gathered in the buckets to dispel the mud. Then, they shared the towels piled in the corner to rub at themselves vigorously. Mycah took extra care to dab at Leda's wound.

Heavy footsteps sounded close by, approaching quickly. Rayla's eyes widened. She swooped Rossi up and flew out the shed's door. Mycah grabbed Leda and sprinted for the house.

Once inside, they locked the front door and dried their feet on a towel they'd snatched from the communal bathroom. They were all breathing heavily, apparently very relieved to be inside.

Leda scowled. "Will someone please tell me what's going on?"

Mycah risked peeking out of the front window. She motioned for Leda to join her. "The curfew."

The footsteps they'd heard were marching soldiers, patrolling the Rooks to ensure that no one was out past sunset. The men entered the *cul de sac* in full uniform, passing by each home. They peeked around corners, their hands firm on the hilts of their weapons.

I hope all the children made it.

Finally satisfied, the line of soldiers filed out, off to terrorize a different part of the slums.

"Only those with passes signed by their employers can still move around now," Rayla elaborated. She was sighing at her sister's unruly hair. "We'll have to braid it tonight."

"Can Miss Leda do it?" the little girl asked.

Leda looked down with wide eyes. "I, uh—" She'd never braided hair that curly, had barely been able to plait her own smooth waves, the ones she'd inherited from her blonde mother.

Mycah stepped in. "How about I do it, kiddo? We can teach Leda."

Rossi nodded without hesitation. "Okay."

†

Chrisjon goes in, causes a fight. The prisoners are taken out into the courtyard. Naxa and I place bombs at strategic places, blow holes in the walls, and cause mayhem. In the chaos, Chrisjon gets Tombas out, and Naxa and I disappear.

Markham had been going over the plan in his head again and again, plotting his every move. It was a crazy scheme, but it could work. Emphasis on *could.*

"Why did you end up agreeing to help us?" Markham asked as they both sat staring at the fire.

Naxa made a series of signs with her hands, but he was utterly lost. Before Chrisjon's departure, he'd shown him the basic symbols for "yes" and "no", "come," "shut up," and "now."

He gave her an apologetic look. She sighed and leaned over to pull something out of her bag of endless supplies. She grabbed a notebook and pencil. She flipped past a few pages that were filled with stunning sketches, and finally settled on a blank sheet. She scribbled quickly and then showed him.

I know what the current Ruler does to political threats.

He frowned. "Did they do something to you? Is that why you stopped working as a spy?"

She shook her head and wrote again.

They killed my mentor.

Markham's eyes widened. "Grant Vikan died of a heart attack."

She flashed him a look that didn't need words to be understood. *And you believe that?*

"I assume Yathan needed someone eager to do his dirty work, someone like Saul."

She nodded, her eyes recalling distant memories as she jotted down her reply.

They took out everyone who showed any inclination of morality. I left for my family's farm before they could do the same to me.

He sighed, wringing his hands together. "I'm sorry for the things I said when we first met."

The corners of her mouth tugged upward.

You're only sorry now because I ended up giving you your way.

"No—I—I didn't—" He stopped trying to stumble his way out of that accusation when she cocked an eyebrow and wrote down another retort.

It is alright to be fierce when you are protecting those who cannot protect themselves.

He smiled at her, nodding. "Thank you for coming. I honestly don't know what we would have done without you here."

She pursed her lips.

Now it is up to Jon.

"At least until two days from now."

She nodded.

†

Rossi and Rayla's parents had come home about an hour after curfew, looking utterly exhausted as they took off their shoes and left them next to the front door.

Palra Yade was a woman of almost forty with deep lines of worry etched into her dark brow. She wore a faded yellow dress and an apron as she greeted them. She embraced Mycah, welcomed Leda, and went straight to the hearth to start on dinner. She was apparently Tomhas's cousin.

Renton was a painter, judging by the white-splattered overalls he wore. His hair was shaved in an imitation of Leda's new style, his green eyes the unmistakable source of Rayla's piercing stare. He acknowledged them quickly before leaving for the bathroom.

Mycah was busy placing tiny beads at the end of Rossi's many braids, talking Leda through the process as she worked. Great Gran was snoring softly on the couch behind them, and Rayla helped her mother in the kitchen.

When the last bead was in place, Mycah beamed, patting the little girl's head. "All done."

"Does it look nice?" she asked, eyes zoning in on Leda.

The latter grinned. "Yes. It looks magnificent. You should show your mother." As she ran off, Leda turned to Mycah. "You're really good at that. Why have you never braided your own hair?"

She narrowed her eyes to slits and purred, "Because tigers like to be wild."

Leda snorted with laughter, swatting at her friend's arm. "Should we be helping with the meal?"

Mycah raised an eyebrow. "You know how to cook?"

She felt her cheeks redden. "No, but I could chop stuff? I don't know… Stop laughing at me."

The other shook her head, chuckling. "Palra will just scold us for crowding the kitchen. Trust me, I've tried before."

"You've known this family for a while."

"Since she became a rebel," a smoky voice boomed. It was Renton entering the sleeping area. His daughters clung to him, trying their utter best to wrestle him to the ground. They squealed as he roared with supposed effort, walking even as Rossi wrapped herself around his leg. "Help me, I'm being attacked by monkeys. They're taking me down. I can't—"

Finally, he fell down with exaggerated movements, landing on one of the sleeping pallets. Laughter rumbled out of him as the girls descended to tickle him and then shower his newly-cleaned cheeks in kisses.

When they'd settled down, he sat up to pull Rossi into his lap and cradle Rayla under his left arm. "No trouble today?" he asked.

They shook their heads. "I almost hit Mycah with a pan, and we were just on time for the curfew, but no trouble," the eldest answered seriously.

Leda cleared her throat, suddenly not knowing what to do with her hands. "Thank you for letting us stay here, Mister Yade. You may be saving our lives."

He smiled kindly, a dimple forming in his sandstone cheek. "Of course. It is an honor for us to host Leda Hayvinger, and we will always help any of Mycah's friends."

It was then that Palra entered the room with a bowl of steaming food in her hand. "Dinner's ready."

As the Yade mother kneeled to wake Great Gran, the others made their way into the kitchen to line up.

Renton took each person's bowl and filled it with watery stew. There was no dinner table big enough to host them and so they all sat on their beds, legs crossed and spoons clinking as they ate.

It was barely more than old vegetables and liquid, but the flavor was stunning and Leda licked her lips. "Thank you so much, Mrs. Yade. The stew is splendid. Much better than the things Mycah has been giving me."

Mycah gasped in mock affront. "Excuse you."

Palra chuckled and shook her head. She'd just finished feeding her grandmother, taking the leftovers for herself. "Shame on you. You should feed your guests."

"She's not my guest," Mycah retorted. "She's a rebel in need of my protection and assistance."

Palra looked strangely sad at that. "So, we're all to gather in the mines, right? For a final stand."

Renton rose, took their empty plates, and headed for the kitchen. "You and the children will not be going."

"I'll take care of Rossi. Mom should go. She's good with an ax," Rayla protested.

"And how will your mother and I get there, hmm? We're not even safe to step out of our front door and you want us to go to a rebel hideout on the other side of the city? It's dangerous enough for one person."

Palra stood up as well. "I am no stranger to danger, Ren." She hesitated, mouth opening and closing as she decided on her next words. "But I will not leave our children to fend for themselves. We will be here, praying for the palace to fall."

Her husband sighed with relief. After he'd deposited the dishes on the kitchen table, he headed over to place a kiss on her forehead. Rayla seemed unsatisfied and Rossi kept quiet.

Leda found herself frowning. This was her job in the capital. She was supposed to rally the remaining Yaekós rebels and get them to the mines in time. *I can't even get myself there.*

There was a knock at the door.

Everyone froze.

Three raps.

No one dared to breathe.

Three more.

Leda's heart was beating in her ears, her stomach twisted.

"This is Corporal Hensh. In the name of His Highness Qarvette, I order you to open this door."

Palra leaped into action. She pulled Leda and Mycah to a spot in the floor behind Great Gran's couch, where a hidden door led to a tiny underground storage area. She crammed them inside, motioned for them to remain quiet, and shut the door quietly. The two of them were now in total darkness, crammed together. All Leda heard was her own frantic pulse and Mycah's heavy breathing. She was shivering slightly, struggling to inhale. Mycah gripped her hand tightly and she managed to take a breath.

Footsteps sounded above them, along with more knocks on the door.

"I will not ask again!" the corporal bellowed.

The door was opened. "Is there a problem?" Renton asked quietly.

"Well, that depends on what we find." Three sets of boots entered the shack. "Under the laws implemented by our High Ruler, we may search all Rooks homes at any given time. Today, we have to search all of them. See, we're looking for a girl."

Leda gulped. She had no doubt they had pulled out her *WANTED* poster and was flashing it around.

"Have you seen her?"

"No, sir." Palra.

"I doubt that you'll find Leda Hayvinger in our home, Corporal."

There was a yelp and a growl. "Don't get cocky with me, boy."

Another set of boots moved. "If she's not here, then you won't mind us looking around."

"Go ahead," Renton wheezed, as if someone had him by the neck.

Leda went absolutely still, digging her fingers into Mycah's hands. The footsteps moved through the shack agonizingly slowly, leaving no corner unsearched. *Crash!* Leda suppressed a scream. They were turning over the furniture. Plates shattered. Great Gran moaned. Couches were swept aside.

"Does this bag belong to you?" one of the soldiers asked.

Leda's heart stopped. Her stomach dropped and the blood in her veins refused to move.

Shit. She hadn't taken her bag.

"Yes."

There was a rustle and the sound of items clattering to the floor. Silence.

"As expected. Rebel regalia."

She had one of Markham's old flyers and a lightning-bolt flag. She'd packed it in case she needed to make a statement. *I'm an idiot.*

"No," Leda breathed.

There was a yell from one of the girls. "Get your hands off my child," Palra shrieked.

"You have been found guilty of high treason... Take the kids. Torch the house."

"No." This time, Leda screamed it.

She broke from Mycah's grip and slammed open the hidden door. Renton was being restrained by a burly soldier, Palra by another, and the girls were hanging from the corporal's hands by their hair.

Leda gulped, rose to her full height to face them. "Let them go, now."

"Who the fuck are you?"

She waved her hand inconspicuously, motioning for Mycah to stay put. "I'm the one you're looking for. I'm Leda Hayvinger."

The soldiers went slack-jawed, then laughed. "You expect us to believe a little street rat like you is Leda Hayvinger?" the corporal sneered.

She stepped closer. "Look at the drawing again."

He let Rossi go to pull the poster out of his back pocket. His eyes widened as he studied the picture, then looked back at her. "Holy... Seize her."

The man holding Palra threw her aside and dashed to pin Leda's arms behind her back roughly. She didn't fight it. "You have what you came here for. Now leave these people be."

"They are terrorists."

She bared her teeth and jerked toward the corporal. The man at her back yanked her by the shoulder. "They are not. I paid them to keep me hidden. They are nothing but a poor family who took a handsome bribe."

Hensh nodded for his men to let the Yades go. The soldiers closed in around Leda, leading her out of the shack.

The moment they cleared the front door, the corporal said, "Burn this place to the ground."

"No," Leda roared. She used all the strength she had to attempt escape, but it was no use.

The man holding her kneed her in the back and she sank to the ground with a cry. The third soldier held his torch to one of the shack's planks and watched as the structure ignited. Leda screamed. She tried to stand. Tried to yank her arms free.

"Bloody bitch."

Something heavy landed a blow against her temple. She gasped. It struck again and she collapsed to the ground. With her face pressed into the mud, all she saw were orange flames before the world went black.

CHAPTER THIRTY-THREE

STAELLA HELD HER BREATH, TRIED to drown out the pounding of blood in her ears. The door to the office opened and heavy footsteps stalked across the room. A chair scraped over the wooden floor and the man sank down in it with a sigh. She clenched her jaw, preparing for her next move.

"I know you're there. So, you might as well come out now."

Staella flinched, biting her lip as she emerged from behind the old bookcase. It had been difficult to slip inside the room unnoticed while he was out, to enter an army base and infiltrate the commander's office. She'd taken great pride in having remained hidden, biding her time until she could talk to the man alone. Apparently, she wasn't as good as she believed.

He was sitting behind his heavy oak desk, his graying hair a mess after he removed his cap. He drew a hand through it, lit a cigar, and leaned back in his chair. General Vaekish was shorter than she'd imagined, with a burly frame and wrinkles etched into his sun-weathered skin. His gray eyes followed her intently as she stepped up to face him.

He was smirking. "Patrol guards spotted you when you snuck by them. I was notified immediately, told someone to keep an eye on you to find out what you're up to. There are men stationed everywhere around us. So, if you're here to kill me, I'd advise you to reconsider."

She gulped, trying not to breathe in too much of the smoke he puffed out. "I just need to talk to you… unofficially."

He cocked an eyebrow. "Well, you can start by telling me who you are… unofficially."

"My name is Staella Thenos. I've been sent by Markham Aesher."

Vaekish huffed. "The little bastard who corrupted my daughter?"

From what she'd heard, it had been the other way around. *But now may not be the best time to make that argument.*

She cleared her throat. "If you'd like something a little more official, I'm here on behalf of the Rebellion."

He froze, his eyes boring into her. He put out his cigar and leaned forward, resting his elbows on the desk in front of him.

"You walked into the private quarters of the general of Aldahad's army to confess treason? You're either very stupid or very brave."

Her mouth twitched nervously. "Why not both?"

"Start talking, Miss Thenos."

Where to begin?

"I know you don't like Saul Knoxin." There was a brief moment of silence before the general broke out in laughter. Taking that as a good sign, she continued, "I worked under him very briefly and he was very clear on which of his subordinates were most likely to defy his authority."

He sucked at his teeth. "I think you'll forgive an old man for sometimes questioning the *authority* of a twenty-three-year-old with a hair complex."

She bit back a grin. "Yes, but it's more than that, isn't it?" No reply. "You know he's not worthy of being a leader. I'd wager that someone who's been doing this for as long as you have, has figured out that there's a snake in the grass. Maybe you've figured that out about Yathan Qarvette as well."

"What powerful accusations you make."

She dared to take a step closer. "I have more than accusations. I have the truth. I know what Knoxin and Qarvette have been plotting. I have the means to confirm your suspicions."

He was picking at his nails now, never taking his eyes off her. "And why would you give me this information?"

"Because I need your help to ensure that this country does not remain in their hands."

He barked dismissively. "You want me to help the Rebellion. You do know that my family is eligible for the Election? That we are part of what your organization is trying to eradicate?"

Staella's hand clenched into a fist. "If you don't help us, your son will be taken as well. I assume you know that the Representatives have been disappearing… Your Lorde of Security and his High Ruler pose more of a threat to Nolan than we ever will."

His face had paled, his gaze wide. "Are you saying…?"

"Yes."

A muscle feathered in his jaw. "I think you should take a seat, Staella Thenos. You have ten minutes to convince me to commit mutiny."

Her shoulders slumped in slight relief and she took the chair opposite his. He poured her a tumbler of whisky, downing his in a few seconds. She sipped at the liquid-courage gratefully, took a deep breath before she started talking.

†

Markham had never witnessed an explosion before, let alone been the reason for one. The sound was terrifying, rattling through his skull and causing his ears to sing. The impact was even worse, hitting him with a force unlike any other.

Plumes of dust and smoke billowed around him as Hareth's southern wall became a battlefield. Stones rained down; guards tumbled from watchtowers; someone bellowed and coughed.

Naxa's makeshift explosives definitely worked.

Markham had just enough time to pull himself together before the enemy was upon him.

"We found him," the young guard yelled before storming forward with his sword raised.

Markham ducked quickly, narrowly escaping the blade's edge. There were more of them coming now, eager to apprehend the man who'd bombed their prison. Little did they know that he was not the true threat.

He unsheathed his own weapon, blocking the assaults of the young guard. In a few swift movements he learned from Staella, he disarmed his opponent and took him out, but there was no reprieve.

Another guard was on him. Two now. Roaring for reinforcements. The prisoners, whom Chrisjon had gathered in the quad, were starting to grow restless, to seize the moment of distraction. At the northern side of the gaol, more explosions sounded. The ground shook. Warning horns sounded. Arrows stabbed through clouds of dust. Naxa had engineered the chaos expertly. No one would even notice Chrisjon and Tomhas's escape.

Now I just have to survive until they get here.

Adrenaline was surging through Markham, pounding heavily in his ears and quickening his movements. A dagger flashed and he blocked it. Parry. Stab. His sword lunged through a chest. Stuck. With a grunt, he pulled it free. Ducked another attack just in time. An arrow missed his shoulder by inches.

A blow landed against his jaw, which made him dizzy. He sidestepped the next blow. Lashed out. Anticipated each new strike like steps to a dance. Pain seared through his thigh and his arm, but he couldn't focus on that now. More and more guards poured from the gaping wound in the prison's side.

All that mattered were the movements. Block. Parry. Stab. Feign. Slice. Repeat.

He didn't keep count of how many guards he executed or the amount of time that passed as the ground became muddy with blood, as he became nothing but a conduit of survival instincts.

Agony bludgeoned through his leg. He roared. Looked down to see an arrow embedded in the flesh of his calf. The edges of his vision flashed white. He was going to throw up. Pass out.

Oh Goddess.

He retreated slowly, crying out every time he had to put weight on the leg. It took every ounce of energy in his body to block the blows that kept coming and coming.

He was bleeding. A lot. He could think of nothing but the pain.

The river was only a few feet away now. He had to get to the water, had to make it off the island before the guards finished him.

Another explosion provided the second's distraction he needed to escape. Gritting his teeth, he leapt into the Roccalee.

Cold water hit him. The current was strong. He kicked out and screamed at the pain of the movement. His arms tried to keep him up, but the water kept coming, pushing at him. He couldn't move his leg. The current was too fast. Water slammed into his nose, his ears, his eyes. His head went under.

He couldn't breathe. Desperate for air, he tried to surge to the surface. But his leg wasn't working. The water was spinning around him, his body moving with the current now. His pulse rushed in his ears. His lungs demanded breath. He struggled against the pain, against the water. But he had to breathe. Goddess, he needed to breathe. His vision blurred. His chest burned. Black spots floated all around him.

Fear. Hurt. Then, oblivion.

Water bubbled out of him. His eyes shot open as his chest spasmed violently. A hand at his back helped him turn to hurl up half the Roccalee River. He shuddered, drenched to the bone and gulping down burning breaths. The dirt of the riverbank clung to him, the fear of death with it.

When he finally had enough air in his lungs, he looked up to find Naxa's amber eyes boring into him. Her expression was devoid of sympathy, and she stood as soon as she was sure he wouldn't die.

He blinked a few times, made out two other shapes near the jungle edge. One was Chrisjon, kneeling between shrubs and pressing a folded-up shirt against a crimson wound at his temple. The other was leaning against a tree trunk, swaying even with the support. Tomhas' eyes were barely open, his chest moving laboriously and his body trembling. Markham's heart leapt. He surged up and took a step toward his friend, but his leg gave out under him. He slammed to the ground with a cry of pain, looking down to find the shaft of an arrow protruding from his left calf.

Now, he remembered why he hadn't been able to keep himself afloat in the current, why he'd been sucked under despite his best efforts.

Shit. Naxa must have saved him.

He crawled closer to his party, finally reaching the cover of the foliage. He grunted as he pulled himself up next to Chrisjon. He reached out to touch Tomhas' leg. The man looked down, his eyes cloudy.

"Are you okay?"

Tomhas breathed heavily, nodded. "They have horrible ways of interrogating prisoners. But I survived—thanks to the three of you."

Naxa already had her pack slung over her shoulder when she marched up to them, once again relying on her cousin's translating skills.

"They won't take long to send out a search party. The chaos will distract them for now, but we need to get moving."

Chrisjon sighed and fell backwards to land on his backside. "In case you haven't noticed, we're not really in the best shape for travel right now. I probably have a concussion. Tomhas has been tortured within an inch of his life, and Markham has a fucking arrow in his leg."

Naxa clenched her jaw and threw down her bag with exaggerated movements. "Fine. Basic first aid and then we move. I can't do much about that leg. We'll have to make a stretcher."

Markham nodded and braced himself as she sank down next to him. He gritted his teeth through the pain as she touched the injured calf. He had to clench his fists when she gripped the shaft.

Trying to distract himself from whatever she was about to do, he asked, "Did you give them any information?"

Tomhas slid down against his tree trunk, eyes closing against pain from some unseen ailment. "Some. When they started using hot oil on my back, my resolve crumbled a little."

Markham's eyes nearly popped out of his head. "When they *what*?" he roared, as Naxa broke the shaft just above the entry wound. Panting, he growled, "Take care of Tomhas."

Hardin waved a dismissive hand. "No. If I were going to die, I would have already. Bind up Markham and Chrisjon and we can go."

Naxa utterly ignored them, continuing to shuffle through the contents of her canvas bag—the one that seemed to have everything they could ever need. Markham had just shaken his head when she pulled out salt and some charcoal-colored dust the day before, telling him that she was going to build bombs.

I have to convince her to make some for the rebels.

"What do they know?" Chrisjon breathed.

A rag dipped in some form of alcohol met the bloody skin of Markham's leg and he shivered. Naxa was much less gentle than Amile in her cleaning of wounds. He shuddered, told her to use sap from the nearby haletayls around the wound. If Staeven Thenos' salve was anything to go by, it could save his leg.

"Some numbers," Tomhas answered. "They were trying to get the names of my inner circle, but I never gave that up… They took great pleasure in informing me that they'd figured it out anyway, that they'd killed and tortured each of them." A tear tracked through the dirt on his face. "They knew about the Skullroot in my pack."

"We found Bruhel's body," Markham gritted. Naxa produced bandages, moved up to wrap one tightly around the spot above his knee. He assumed it would aid in keeping most of the blood inside his body. "I don't know what the circle may have told Knoxin, but we must move forward with caution. The situation is so much worse than we previously imagined."

Chrisjon nodded. "We have quite a lot to tell you."

His words were starting to slur, and Markham could only hope that they would recover fast enough to join the coup in little more than a week.

When Naxa finished tending to their injuries, she set off with a dizzy Chrisjon to gather the materials they would need to build a slapdash stretcher.

They would have to carry him to the mines.

†

Amile was tired—bone-tired and soul-tired. His head throbbed and he felt close to throwing up. He stumbled out of the guestroom they'd set up as a testing chamber, the door feeling almost too heavy to open. Maci was waiting on the other side, her expression a little too pitying for his liking. She stepped forward to meet him, tucked her body into his side, and hooked his arm over her shoulders for support.

"Zandi told me."

The fourth session had failed. Like the three before it. Zandi had been trying to reroute his mind for what felt like years. She'd adjusted the haletayl solution, tried different types of lighting, asked him to draw detailed picture after detailed picture. But they only made him worse, and his body ached so deeply he felt hollow.

"Maybe it was a foolish idea from the start," he breathed.

Maci looked up at him with big eyes. "No. Don't say that. We can't give up when success may be just around the corner… I've been thinking…"

"How horrible," he deadpanned.

She huffed, elbowing him in the ribs. "Even looking like death, you test me. I've been talking to Zandi and reading up in the Blomehill library… I think I have an idea for how to make it work."

"Maci, I don't…"

She stared at him with devastating hope in her gaze. "Please. Try it my way. Just once. If it doesn't improve the situation, we can stop… Please, do it for me."

He gulped. He'd never stood a chance against those fluttering eyelashes. Sighing, he nodded.

"Fine. We'll try one more time."

CHAPTER THIRTY-FOUR

HER HEAD HAD BEEN TRAMPLED by a dozen horses, then filled with all the fog that rolled over the Crest on winter mornings. Leda's tongue was heavy in her mouth, her lips cracked dry and her throat raw. Something hard and cold was pressing against the side of her head. She pulled away, feeling aches in nearly every part of her body. She groaned, opened her eyes slowly, and had to blink a few times to understand what she was seeing.

A straw-covered stone floor. Three dark walls. Thick metal bars.

Her heart stopped as she remembered—the soldiers, the fire, the oblivion after. Mycah. She had to get to Mycah. She had to find her, to make sure she was alive.

She was in a cell. There were no windows, the only light emitted by a lone lantern against the aisle wall. Across the walkway were more cages. She squinted into their darkness and could only make out shadows.

Where had they taken her? Was this Hareth, or some other prison?

And why is my head feeling so weird?

She shuffled deeper into the cell, taking stock of each spot on her body that protested. She'd been bruised in various places, handled roughly by her captors. She'd no doubt been thrown into this cell with much more force than was necessary.

But why can't I remember it?

"Psst."

The sound came through the wall to her right, barely more than a whisper. *Am I hallucinating now?*

The sound came again, louder this time. "Leda," the voice breathed.

"Who's there?" she exclaimed.

"Shhh," it scolded. "If they hear anything, it'll blow my cover… How are you feeling? Please tell me it hasn't started to work already."

She frowned. "What worked?" she whispered this time, heeding the disembodied voice's warning. "And who's they? Where am I? Who are you?"

"It's Daniel."

Relief flooded over her. It was quickly followed by despair. Daniel Caneille had been the first Representative to be taken. *He's probably under their control.* This also meant that she was in the palace dungeons, about to suffer the same fate as her fellow candidates.

"Leda?" he asked at her silence.

"Yeah. I'm here."

She could hear him sigh deeply. "Thank the Goddess you're still talking. Leda, listen. Yathan and Cala are experimenting on the

Representatives. They're brainwashing them. They become these husks. They don't talk or move. Only when they're ordered."

"I know... But how are you still *you*?"

She leaned against the right wall of the cell, knowing that he was pressed up against the other side. She listened for his breathing, needing to know that he was really there, that she was not crazy or alone.

"They use haletayl sap. I don't know if you ever believed the stories about the Goddess trapping the last tendrils of magic in the first tree, but turns out it's true. When I was a child, my mom told me about a single bloodline that was allowed to keep their magic, that the Caneilles still had a little drop running through our veins. I didn't believe her. I thought she was just making up tales to amuse her children. But... Leda, the sap doesn't affect me the same. It doesn't make my brain foggy. It doesn't make me pliable. It feels like coming alive. They inject me and I feel this *energy* surge through my body. It took only three tries for it to start... changing me."

A chill ran through her. "What kind of change?"

"My senses are more alive. It's difficult to explain, but everything around me seems to move slower. It's all brighter and louder. More intense. The way I move... I blink and I've moved to the other side of my cell. I'm stronger too."

"How much stronger?"

There was a moment of silence and then *boom!* The wall next to her shuddered, a crack forming a few inches from her head.

Her eyes widened. "Was that...?"

"One punch," he answered.

She was breathing heavily now, exhilarated. "Why haven't you broken out yet?"

She could hear his sigh through the thick stone. "We're underneath a centuries-old castle. I'm not about to go breaking down walls. The entire place could collapse on us, and even with my newfound abilities, I don't think I'll survive that."

Leda chewed at her bottom lip. "We need a plan."

"I appreciate you including me in your thinking process, but that's not really a revelation. I've tried digging, but to no avail. I tried to manipulate guards, but that's a little difficult to do when you're pretending to be brainwashed. I've tried bending the bars. No luck yet."

"So, why are you appealing to me?"

"I've appealed to every Representative they brought in. They just all faded into their current state before we could get out."

Dread dropped like a rock into Leda's gut. Jagged flashes of memory forced themselves into her thoughts. A bright light. Golden eyes. A needle. She reached down to the left side of her neck, wincing as her fingers made contact with the stab wound. The hole through which they'd pumped haletayl sap into her veins to take over her brain. How many more sessions would it take before she was lost?

I have to get out of here.

"Shit. Someone's coming," Daniel hissed.

A few seconds later, she too heard scuffling falling heavily on stone steps. A single source of light flickered into existence, casting eerie shadows across the aisle between cells. Leda caught glimpses of the other prisoners. Aedon stood near the bars with a vacant expression. Delilah crouched in a corner. The light fell on Leda.

The footsteps stopped and she looked up to find Saul Knoxin looming over her, a sickening smirk on his face. He crossed his arms over his chest. "I take it that little *bang* was you waking up and trying to get out."

Leda reared up to her full height, grabbed onto the bars separating them, and snarled, "You burned that house to the ground, you monster! You will pay for this, Knoxin."

His smug smile only grew broader. "And who is going to make me pay? You?" She could only clench her jaw in response. He chuckled. "I thought so. Face it, Leda, the time of the Hayvingers is over. All your riches and fame mean nothing now. You're at the mercy of a nameless soldier from Saribi. Do you know why you were never going to trump over me?" He had the audacity to step even closer. "Because I've had to claw my way up. Because everything I have, I earned. You? You've never had to work for a thing in your life."

She repressed the urge to spit at him. "Your little working man manifesto might feel empowering to you, but you only got where you are by deceiving and murdering and letting evil kings pull your strings."

A muscle under his eyes twitched, but his expression did not crack. "I have other things to do, *my lady*. Please stop trying to get out. It's causing a terrible noise and I already have a headache. Trust me, you'll stop caring about escape soon, anyway."

She snarled after him as he swaggered away, disappearing around a turn and up the stairs. She sank back down against the wall she shared with Daniel, lulling her head back against it.

"He really doesn't like you," Daniel commented in a whisper.

She huffed. "Yeah. And we're going to use that to get out."

CHAPTER THIRTY-FIVE

STAELLA'S HANDS WERE TREMBLING slightly and her stomach felt uneasy. She was beginning to understand how Markham must have felt at the rebel meeting. *You just have to channel your inner Leda, then.*

She took a deep breath, clenched her hands into fists at her sides, and opened the black doors that loomed in front of her. The room went quiet and every eye turned on her. The mess hall of the army base was brimming with soldiers in fatigues, lounging around dinner tables or leaning against the walls, waiting for her.

General Vaekish was apparently acutely aware of a few rebels in his ranks, had used covert messages sent by servants to get the leaders on board with a meeting. Those who had accepted the call were guaranteed immunity and they had started recruiting.

It had only been three days, but there were nearly three hundred men gathered—three hundred trained soldiers who would hopefully march with her under the lightning banner.

She took up position at the front of the hall, standing tall as she knew Leda would. *I would've been less nervous if I had to fight everyone in this room.*

One soldier stepped out of the crowd to meet her, a thirty-something man with a boyishly handsome face that was currently twisted into a frown.

He took up position a few inches to her left and breathed, "Please tell me this isn't an attempt to sniff out the rebels at this base and apprehend them."

Hushed conversation buzzed around the room as worries were shared and the soldiers sized her up. Nervous energy fizzed off her companion in near-visible waves. Oddly, it made her feel calmer.

She shook her head and whispered back. "I can promise that it isn't from my side… I'm choosing to believe that the General's intentions are pure."

He huffed, stuck his hands in the pockets of his khaki pants. His black hair was cropped short, accentuating the lines of concern deepening on his brow.

"This is crazy."

The corner of her mouth quirked upward. "This whole country is crazy."

He cast her a sideways glance, his blue-gray eyes amused, and he smiled. "I'm Reian, by the way. I rallied most of these men here." She noticed the stripes on his uniform—a captain.

She extended a hand. "It's a pleasure. So, are they all secretly rebels?"

"Most. Some just hate the government. Others have a general rebellious tendency."

"Any tips on getting them to follow me to the other side of Aldahad to usurp a throne?"

He hesitated and offered her a sheepish simper. "Be yourself?" She nearly burst out in giggles at that, which had him chuckling as well.

He gave her a single nod before stepping forward. He cleared his throat and the men in the room were silenced, their attention focused solely on their captain and the short redheaded girl who'd had them summoned.

"Thank you for coming, gentlemen. I trust that you will give Miss Thenos the respect and attention she deserves."

Then, it was her turn. She swallowed around the dryness in her mouth and pulled her shoulders back even more.

You're not going to get taller, Staella.

Shut up.

"Thank you, Captain… I am Staella and I come as a representative of the new leader of the Rebellion, Markham Aesher."

The soldiers immediately started murmuring at that. The murmur grew into bellows of indignation and a shout from the back of the room bellowed, "So the resistance is now being run by a child who grew up with a golden spoon up his ass?" This elicited a few chuckles, a few cheers and nods. "How stupid do you think we are?"

Staella clenched her jaw. "Markham has been the silent co-leader for years. He's the one who provided the resources and information the Rebellion needed to come out of the shadows. Tomhas Hardin, the previous visible leader, has been imprisoned in Hareth. Markham has taken the reins in the meantime."

"Who are you? His lap dog? His whore?" This came from the same dissenter, a man with wide lips and a bald head sitting on one of the tables, his back leaning against the wall.

Reian made a move forward, but she stopped him with a hand to the chest. "I am a member of the inner circle of the Rebellion's leadership. Before that, I was his bodyguard."

That caused even more of an uproar—one marked by degrading laughter that made Staella's blood boil. "The lad needed a little girl to protect him? You're not making a strong case for his abilities, sweetheart," Baldhead added. The sniggering continued.

In a split second, Staella reached for the dagger strapped to her hip and aimed. The blade cut through the air and embedded itself with a loud *thud* in the wooden wall a hair's breadth from Baldhead's cheekbone.

The room went quiet. No one dared to breathe. Baldhead watched with wide eyes as she stalked towards him, the soldiers automatically clearing a path for her. She leaned over the man, gripped the hilt of the weapon and pulled it free. She took her time returning it to the sheath in her belt.

"I am not a little girl and I'm not your sweetheart either. My name is Staella Thenos, but perhaps you'll know me better by my other name." *Pause for effect.* "The Crimson Jackal." There were gasps, a few whispers. The man in front of her paled slightly. She stepped away, turning to face the room. "I am not here to start fights or deal with misogynists. If you came here to look down on me, if you think this is some sort of joke, you should leave right now. I will not spend precious time convincing you of my worth. We have more important matters to discuss. So, do I have to fight every sexist asshole in this room or can we get to business?"

She took the silence as acquiescence, smirked as she made her way back to the front. Reian was clearly trying to hide a grin. "Good, then let me tell you of the horrors the High Ruler has been concocting under the palace."

†

Leda's mind was starting to feel fuzzy. They'd taken her for her second session the previous day. She couldn't remember anything more than flashing light and pain. Now, it was getting easier to lapse into nothingness, to clear her mind of all thoughts and stare at the wall.

She had to surge through darkness and fatigue to pull her thoughts deep out of the recesses of her mind. She gasped when her consciousness broke to the surface, flooding her with jumbled images and screaming words.

Plan. The plan. Saul.

Leda… Leda, please…

"Leda."

Another voice cut through the chaos. "Yes. Yes, I'm here."

Daniel sighed with relief on the other side of the wall. "Thank the Goddess. You're lasting longer than the others."

The corner of her mouth twitched upward as she rested her tired head against the stone. "I've always been more stubborn than people think."

"Please tell me you still remember the plan."

She nodded, even though she knew he couldn't see her. *Maybe the haletayls gave him eyes that can penetrate walls… Wouldn't that be nice.*

"I do," she rasped, just in case his newfound powers weren't as impressive as her imagination.

"Good. Because they'll be bringing our food in about an hour if my wall-scratch clock is remotely accurate."

She took a deep breath, clenched her hands into fists. She still had to cling to her thoughts, her very being, lest they sink away into easy oblivion again, but she would be ready. She had to get this right.

One more session and she would forget herself completely.

The same "guard" brought their food every evening. She didn't think he was even really part of Yathan's security team—just a servant boy sent from the kitchen. He looked a few years younger than she, with shoulders too wide for the rest of his body and skin dotted by hormones.

He was used to the other Representatives, the ones who stared at him with vacant expressions and ate their meals while looking at nothing. As far as Leda could tell, Daniel must have been mimicking them expertly, because the boy didn't even blink.

She unsettled him though, as the others must've the first few days, because she actually looked at him and had emotion in her gaze. She even thanked him, although she only wanted to snarl. He was only executing a shitty task, after all. But tonight, she would not grimace and mumble "thank you." Tonight, she would channel her inner madwoman.

He stopped at Daniel's cell, sliding the tray under the bars. When he moved again, she started chuckling. Low in her throat, as menacing as possible. She heard him pause and he shuffled toward her slowly. Her laughter grew louder. When he came to a cautious standstill, she looked up. A crooked grin spread over her face. She knew she probably looked like something from a nightmare, a filth-covered woman with a jagged scar across her face and her mouth sneering.

He gulped visibly. "I, uh, I brought dinner."

She laughed once again, made sure to let it lower at the end before the sound faded away. "I don't need it. I won't be here much longer."

The boy looked too rattled to even frown. He just uttered a tiny, "uh."

Leda rose slowly, her height towering over him. She gave a single step forward. "You're all going to burn soon," she crooned. "They'll skin you alive, darling." She giggled. "And you have no idea."

"I think you're a little confused," he squeaked.

She paced closer, until she was pressed up against the bars. He was still a foot or so away, eyes wide.

She lowered her voice to a whisper. "Come here, let me tell you a little secret." Despite the trembling in his knees, he stepped forward, close enough for her to smell the sweat on him. She brought her mouth as close to his ear as she could and breathed, "They're coming."

Then, she unleashed every ounce of theatricality she had in her with a cackle straight from the Realm Beneath. The boy jumped, letting the tray of food clatter to the floor, and ran. He was up the stairs in a blink. Leda sighed, huffed with amusement as she let go of the cell bars.

Daniel blew out a breath. "Fuck. You should have been an actress."

"Maybe I'm just very close to crazy."

"Do you think it'll work?"

"It has to."

It was only minutes later that another set of footsteps came running down the stairs and into the dungeon. Leda smirked, rolling back her shoulders in anticipation of her impending performance.

Boots, leather breeches, and a blue shirt came into view. Dark hair. Furious eyes. And the keys to the cells hanging from the left side of his belt, on a little hook that unclipped with one flick. Just as always.

She looked up at him from where she sat cross-legged in the center of her cell. "Saul."

His upper lip was already pulled back in vexation. *Oh, this is going to be easy.* "You scared the shit out of my boy, spewing nonsense about people coming. What game are you playing?"

She grimaced, chuckling deeply. "Poor little Knoxin… Always playing catch-up with the real players."

He only scowled at her.

She shook her head, tipped it back to laugh again. "Real power is always a step ahead, and no matter how hard you try, you will never be one of us. You're too slow, Saul. Always a little too slow."

He crossed his arms over his chest and clenched his jaw. "You're saying this to me from inside a cage I put you in."

She got onto her hands and knees, crawled closer to him. "How long did you think you were going to keep me here? Forever? Oh, you sweet, naïve child… This was part of my plan all along." She bit her bottom lip, flashing him a grin.

Doubt flashed across his gaze. It was gone in an instant, but she'd seen it, and it was all she needed. She grabbed the bars of her cell, pulled herself up until they were face-to-face.

"Your end is coming, Saul," she purred. "Quickly." She steeled her gaze. "And when it does, it'll be slow. All you'll remember in your descent is my face, my voice chanting your failure…" Anger was rolling off him now. "Because you never really had a chance."

In a blur of movement, he surged forward. A fist connected with the side of her face. She heard a crack, careened backward until her back met the far wall. The pain was a spear through her cheek, making her eyes water and her brain scream. Still, she forced herself to laugh and let hysterical cackles shake her shoulders. She turned to look at him, thick liquid oozing from the cut Mycah had given her.

"That only proves my point." She wiped away the blood with the back of her hand, cleaned it on her shirt. "You can't even try to face me without a steel barrier for protection."

He took the bait beautifully. Keys jingled, the cell door was flung open, and he stepped inside. She braced herself. *Now for the hard part.*

He moved fast. Smashed his knee into her stomach. She doubled over, gasping to pull air back into her lungs. His hand gripped her bare head, used it to throw her onto the floor. Pain burst through her shoulder. She cried out and spun just in time to see him bearing down on her. His teeth were bared, his eyes feral. He sank down, his knees straddling her waist. Panic groped at her chest.

The plan, Leda. Remember the plan.

His hands were about to pin her arms above her head, but she acted first. Her elbow slammed into his nose—hard. With the brief moment of distraction, she snatched the keys from the hook in his belt and used the strength in her thighs from years of horse riding to throw him off her.

He roared, nose bleeding, and was up in a split second. She started for the door, desperate to flee, but a hand closed around her wrist and dragged her back. She screamed, pulled. Nails dug into the flesh of her arm and yanked. Her back slammed into Saul's chest, his free hand coming up to wrap around her throat.

She was inches from the door. *Just a few steps and the plan will work.*

His lips brushed against her skin and she scrunched her eyes shut in horror. His grip on her neck tightened painfully, his breath hot and sickening on her.

"Not so high and mighty now, are we?"

She gulped, pulling her face as far away from him as she could. He let go of her throat to grab her chin. She was powerless as he turned her head, made her face him. As victory glinted in his eyes, his mouth enveloped hers. His tongue was heavy in her mouth and his teeth dug into her lip.

Rage surged through her. She brought her heel down on his foot, balled her free hand into a fist, and slammed it into his groin. He groaned, pulled away from her lips. Leda hauled herself out of his arms and ran. Faster than she had ever moved in her life, she took the few steps to Daniel's cell. She threw the key that was still clutched in her hand through the bars. She watched Daniel catch it and start on the lock of his own cage.

Saul was on her again, aimed a heavy blow at her ribs this time. She stumbled forward, was kicked in the back. A sob broke out of her as she fell to her knees. She stared at the floor, holding her breath as she waited for the next attack. But it never came.

She looked around to find Daniel free. She hadn't been able to see him all this time, and the change was striking. His pale skin seemed pearlescent, his eyes even bluer than before. His hair was impossibly longer, his body secure in its every movement. He had Saul by the back of his shirt and hauled him into the air with one hand. In what seemed an effortless maneuver, he flung the lorde into his old cell and slammed the door shut. Locked it.

His eyes landed on Leda and he softened immediately, falling into a kneeling position beside her. "Oh Goddess, are you okay? I'm so sorry."

She shook her head, used the hand he offered to stand up. "All part of the plan, right."

He huffed and rose. *Is he taller too?* "Come on, we need to get out of this estate as soon as possible."

He grabbed her hand, hauled her up the stairs. The world was a blur of movement, her legs straining at their pace. Her body was aching, her bruised ribs barely allowing her to breathe. They broke through a door and sunlight crashed into her. She had to close her eyes and was pulled along by Daniel's demanding grip. Someone yelled from above. Daniel swore. She looked around, trying to understand what was happening. An arrow *swooshed* past her and she yelped.

"We have to go faster," he begged.

She shook her head. "I can't."

Sighing loudly, he wrapped his arms around her and flung her body over his shoulder in a single swoop. Then, he ran. Ran as fast as any of her horses. She bobbed up and down, closing her eyes against the nausea spinning in her head.

"Hold on," he warned a split second before they rose into the air.

Can he fly now too? She looked up and saw that they were scaling the Qarvette estate's walls. She grabbed onto his back, wrapped her legs around his waist. He almost slipped once or twice, and arrows continued to land dangerously close to them. Guards were running out of the fortress, coming closer.

A few seconds later they were over the wall. Leda screamed as they plummeted to the ground, but Daniel landed on his feet. *Like a cat.* He continued running and she gulped around the rawness in her throat.

"Markham. Go to Markham's."

CHAPTER THIRTY-SIX

IT WAS NIGHT. COMPLETE AND UTTER night. A new moon sat invisible in the pitch-black sky. Amile stared down at his hands, at the steadiness in them. Listened to the silence in his mind and heard his own even breaths. He was sitting cross-legged on his bed, waiting for the spell of sanity to break, waiting for the other shoe to drop. He traced the veins of his arm with a finger and closed his eyes to cherish the evening breeze that tickled his cheeks, making an effort to take in every sound: the toads, the lone owl, the patter of light footsteps in the corridor. He looked up, his gaze trained on the door that was still locked from the outside. There was a hesitant knock.

Then, a soft, "Amile?"

His breathing stuttered and he rasped, "Yes."

Locks clicked from the other side. Bolts were shifted. The knob turned. Maci stood in the doorway in a baby pink nightgown that barely covered her pale thighs, a dark braid cascading down her one shoulder. Her eyes were wide, her lips parted delicately.

His heart skipped a beat, resumed working at a much faster rate. He gulped as she stepped over the threshold, as she floated closer. She was beside the bed before either of them had said another word.

He found himself fixated on the angle of her cheekbones, on the expanse of smooth skin left bare at her collar, on the way the silk she wore hugged the curves of her chest. He swallowed around the dryness in his throat and got up slowly.

She kept her eyes on him, followed his every movement as he came to stand in front of her. She was inches away and he could feel the heat of her body, see each individual eyelash that brushed against her cheeks. The bob of her throat. The way her shoulders tensed slightly. He'd been watching for years and now she was inches away.

"Maci," he breathed.

She tilted her head back to look at him. "Is it…?"

He nodded. "Yes. She did it. Zandi fixed me. Thanks to you."

After many failed attempts and nearly giving up, they had somehow done it—his brilliant sister and the gorgeous woman standing in front of him.

A sigh of relief rushed out of Maci and she smiled, smiled in that effortless way that tingled through his palms. He reached out, dragged the tips of his fingers over the backs of her hands, her arms. Up and up until they rested on her shoulders. How could anything be so soft?

Her eyes fluttered, her pulse becoming visible at the base of her throat. "Amile…" The way she whispered his name, like it was sacred, made need burn low in his abdomen.

He stepped even closer and cupped her face as gently as he could. The scent of lavender and expensive soap enveloped him and he licked at his bottom lip.

"Please."

"Yes," she breathed, surrendering against him.

His mouth was on hers instantly, desperate but soft. Quick but tender. He used one hand to free her hair from its braid, to tangle his fingers in the strands. The other slipped down her side, around her waist to press against her lower back. He pushed her flush against him, lapped at the seam of her lips and shuddered as their tongues met.

She hummed sweetly, wrapping her arms around his neck, clinging to him. His hand tightened in her hair and he trailed his lips lower. Brushed over the line of her jaw. Attached to the sensitive skin of her neck. Left marks on her collar.

He mouthed at the line of her nightgown, groaned at the way she gasped. *Goddess.* He'd wanted this for so long. To have her pliant and flustered in his arms, to touch and taste and please.

He gripped the backs of her thighs, pulling until her legs were wrapped around him. As he walked them backward, she started tugging at his shirt, huffing as she struggled to pull it over his shoulders.

He chuckled. "Impatient, are we?"

"Oh, fuck you, Amile Qarvette."

Her back hit the far wall and she sucked in a breath. He reached back with one arm to pull the shirt over his head, tossing it aside. Her hands were on him seconds later, prodding touch exploring the lines of his torso.

He leaned into her, tugged at her earlobe with his teeth, and whispered, "I thought that was the plan."

Then, she rolled her hips against his and his cocky comments were swallowed by a moan. They were kissing again—bodies moving together, hands roving over feverish skin. He was hiking up the hem of her nightgown, his touch teasing at her thighs. Her head fell back against the wall and she purred his name.

A scream tore through his muffled senses. He stopped, straightened.

Maci looked up at him with heavy-lidded eyes. "What? What is it?"

He set her down, her arms still wrapped around him as her feet met the floor. "Did you hear that?"

She shook her head, smile tugging at her kiss-reddened lips. "Trust me, someone could be yelling in my ear and all I'd be aware of is you."

He gulped, fixed a hungry gaze on her. She grinned and rose up on her toes to mouth at his throat. Her hands surged into his hair, tugged. He couldn't suppress the low groan that rumbled out of him.

Another scream pierced the air.

He stopped. "You had to have heard that."

"Amile, please," Maci crooned, her hand reaching down to his groin.

He gasped, tightening his hold on her. Every nerve in his body was on fire and his head buzzed with it—with years of desire and affection, with the bliss of being touched by this woman.

"Help!"

This time it was louder, unmistakable. Someone was screeching. He pulled away and stepped back. Maci prowled closer, but he held out a hand to stop her.

"It came from downstairs…" His eyes widened, heart stopping. "Zandi."

He ran. He moved faster than he had in his life, dashing down the stairs two at a time. Swerved down corridors. As he got closer to his sister's room, the screams turned to whimpers and then silenced.

He stopped in front of the door, knocked fervently. "Zandi!"

No answer.

He pulled at the doorknob and rattled it, but it was locked. Taking a few steps back, Amile rammed his shoulder into the door, again and again. It didn't budge, so he pulled back to kick. It finally gave, flying open to reveal a nightmare. The bedroom windows were open, curtains billowing. The sofa in the center of the space had been knocked over, feet sticking up in the air… and there was blood. Blood splattered on the white bed sheets and forming a steady stain on the dark wood. Blood puddled underneath the body that lay lifeless on the floor.

Her skin was even paler now, her blue eyes staring up but not seeing. There was a gash in her white nightgown and a cut on her arm. A gaping, crimson slash across her throat.

"No!"

The sob propelled Amile forward, forcing him to his knees next to his sister. He pushed a hand flush against the weeping wound and pressed with all his might to try and keep the blood inside. His other hand gripped her shoulder, shook.

"Zandi, please. Zandi, come on."

Heavy tears dropped from his cheeks, adding translucent drops to the fabric of her gown. Blood kept gushing, but there was no life. No pulse. No breath. No sparks behind her eyes. A corpse.

A roar tore through him and he launched into a standing position. "I heard her scream. I heard—" He pulled up to the window and saw a shadowy figure disappear into the trees at the edge of the estate. "The bastard. I'll kill him." He spun, ready to chase the assassin.

Maci stood in his way, her eyes wide. "Amile, please. You won't catch him. If you do… You could suffer the same fate."

"The man murdered my sister. I don't care."

"But I care," she exclaimed. "Amile, your sister is dead. Running after the one who did it and putting your own life in danger won't change that."

He shook his head, slowly becoming aware of the blood drying on his hand and the trembling racking his limbs. "No. No. She—Why?"

Maci stepped forward, took his face between her hands. "I'll alert the guards. You take some time. Then, we'll get help with the body."

He nodded, going pliant in her grip. "Oh, Goddess…"

As Maci turned to leave, there was a loud banging on the front door of the manor. Insistent and accompanied by desperate voices.

"What now?"

She gave his hand a last squeeze. "I'll get it. I'll see to everything. Just… breathe."

†

Leda's dizziness had dissipated just enough for her to yell at Markham's front door as she leaned against it, slamming her fist into the red wood. Daniel had a steady arm around her waist, her saving grace as the door suddenly opened from the inside.

Maci stood on the other side, dressed in a skimpy nightgown, looking somewhat annoyed. She gasped as she took in Leda's battered state and Daniel's glowing transformation.

Leda groaned and pushed past the woman into the house. "It's a long story," she grumbled.

The cut on her cheek was throbbing, split open by the force of Saul's first blow. She was still nauseous at the thought of his tongue in her mouth.

Daniel sighed and turned to their hostess. "Sorry, she hasn't had the greatest time the last few days. We just broke out of the palace dungeons."

Maci's eyes nearly popped out of her head. "Leda, they got you too? How are you not… you know? How are you not brainwashed? And Daniel, you've been in there for months."

Leda sighed. "He has magic powers or something. So, he faked it. Then, I came around and helped him escape. Well, he helped me and—Can we please explain this a little later? I need to try and contact Mycah, and lying down would be nice. Maybe some decent food too. I would also sell my first born for a hot bath."

Maci blinked. She looked to Daniel, who shrugged. "We've been prisoners. Some basic amenities would be nice, and Eran. Please, I need to see my husband as soon as possible."

"Uh, okay," she conceded. "Yeah. You can take any room you want. I'll send some servants for clean clothes, food, a bath, and to get letters out."

Leda heard heavy footsteps descend the stairs. She looked up, froze.

It was Amile, with red eyes and sallow skin. Blood coated his hand and arm, stained his shirt. There was even a smear of it on his face. He didn't speak when he saw them. He looked unable to do much more than breathe.

Leda rushed forward. "What happened?"

Leda was lying on a bed in one of the manor's spare rooms, freshly bathed and dressed in some servant's pajamas. She'd never gone to bed in pants before, but it was kind of nice. She stared at the ceiling, watched the candlelight cast shadowy flickers against the white.

Zandi was dead. She was killed a few corridors away, in this big house with all its guards and fences, with busy servants all around, with Amile and Maci right here. As soon as the news had left Maci's mouth, Daniel had run, but even he couldn't find the killer.

So much for long-lost magic.

She hadn't known Zandi very well. They'd grown up a few yards apart, had both suffered under complicated families without knowing of their shared hardships. *Of course, hers was much worse.* She'd been a hero. She'd kept deadly secrets for years. Had saved Amile now more than once and risked everything to share the truth… But they'd finally gotten her. Someone knew that she carried dangerous revelations. Someone knew that she could undo what their twisted plans had mutilated, and someone killed her for it. Someone would probably kill them all.

Despite the trauma of the last few days—the dungeons, the brainwashing, the assault—her thoughts were haunted by the fire, by that family still in the shed when the soldiers had set it alight: her screams, falling to the ground, Mycah still inside.

She'd sent several guards down to the Rooks and Plateau, had sent servants with letters to every spot she thought Mycah might be. It had been hours and none of them had returned with good news.

She scrunched her eyes shut, refusing to linger on the image of a burnt corpse. *She's not dead.* She repeated it over and over in her mind, but it didn't stop her from crying herself to sleep.

Something gripped her shoulder. It was shaking her, whispering, "Leda. Hey." She groaned and turned away. "Come on, Princess. I didn't come here in the middle of the night to be ignored."

Leda's eyes shot open and she scrambled into a sitting position. "Please tell me you're not a ghost."

Mycah chuckled from where she stood next to the bed, hands on her hips. "I would've made a much more entertaining entrance if I were."

Leda shook her head, huffed. Then, before she even knew she moved, she had her arms around the girl's neck. She felt even skinnier than before, but she was warm. Her heart was beating and she was breathing.

Mycah let out a small noise, a noise so adorable Leda snuggled her face deeper into the curls at the nape of her friend's neck. She inhaled deeply, making sure to commit the coconut scent to memory. Mycah's hands settled on her waist.

"Hey, Princess," she whispered.

Leda allowed herself a sob, pulled back just enough to look the other in the eyes. "How?"

She smiled, a grin that showed off the plumpness of her cheeks and made those green eyes crinkle at the sides.

"I see you underestimated me." She sighed and sat down next to Leda on the mattress. "The shoddy build of that little shack saved us in the end. We broke through the back wall in time to get out…" Her gaze landed on the floor, her bottom lip quivering.

Leda placed a hand on her leg. "What happened?"

Her breath hitched, but she managed to answer, "Gran didn't make it."

Leda closed her eyes, squeezing endearingly at the girl's knee. "I'm so sorry. It's all my fault."

Mycah looked up, expression fierce. "No. They allied themselves with the Rebellion out of free will. You—you were willing to give yourself up to try and save them… You're not a Princess, Leda. You're a fighter."

The corner of her mouth twitched upward. "I've kind of grown to like the nickname."

The other guffawed and spent a few seconds just looking at Leda. The hard lines of her face seemed to soften in that moment, turning into something relaxed and affectionate. *I quite like it when she looks at me like that.*

Mycah brought up a hand to the recently-cleaned wound on her cheek, the light touch leaving tiny sparks in its wake.

"I followed the soldiers as soon as I got the family out. I knew that you were in there, that they were probably messing with your mind. I tried to rescue you, but I could never get close enough. Not alone. I—"

Leda placed a finger over her lips, mesmerized by how soft the pink skin felt. When had she started noticing these things? When had she started to wonder how it would feel to touch bronze legs? To taste that expanse of throat? To see full lips part in a gasp?

Mycah was stock still. "Leda…?"

Leda gulped, her eyes fluttering as she looked up to meet Mycah's gaze. "Sorry. I've never… I've never felt this. Never wanted to do this."

"Do what?" the girl whispered.

Leda slowly removed her finger from the other's lips. "Kiss someone."

Then, with the boldness of the naïve, she dove forward to smash their mouths together. Mycah yelped as their noses bumped forcefully. She pulled back, an amused smile on her face.

"Woah there, Princess."

Leda felt heat rush to her cheeks and she buried her face in her hands. *Oh, Goddess, take me away now.*

"I'm so sorry," she mumbled into her palms.

Mycah scooted closer, tugged her hands away gently and beamed. "Hey, it's fine. I'm flattered that you're this eager. I just don't want you to break your nose. Or mine."

Leda looked up shyly, teeth tugging at her bottom lip. "Will you… Will you please show me?"

Mycah swallowed visibly. "Goddess, help me." She cupped Leda's unblemished cheek and leaned in.

Leda was enveloped in coconut and lime, felt stray curls tickle her face. Then, there were plump, velvety lips on hers, pressing forward slowly, sensually. She sighed into the kiss, felt her body melt. She curved into the beautiful girl, her fingers dancing over toned arms and bony shoulders. Tingles ran down her spine when Mycah parted her lips, started moving them. Leda whimpered, saw white sparks behind her closed eyes, pulled the other closer. Expert hands settled around her waist, gripping and teasing at her body through the pajamas. She had never known that something this simple could make her feel like this.

I'm never going to stop doing this.

Mycah pulled away slowly, Leda chasing after her lips to land another peck before allowing them both to breathe. The former ran a shaky hand through her hair.

"See, much better."

Leda giggled, index finger ghosting over her lips. "And to think, I found you insufferable when we first met."

CHAPTER THIRTY-SEVEN

BEING CARRIED ON A MAKESHIFT stretcher by a mute woman, a concussed young man, and a tortured ex-prisoner while nursing an arrow wound in the calf was even more uncomfortable than it sounded.

Markham roared as one of his companions stumbled, rocking the stretcher enough to have agony shoot through his leg. It had been Tomhas, too tired to continue.

Breathing heavily, Markham said, "Stop." His voice was little more than a pained croak. He swallowed, tried again. "Stop."

Naxa heard him, dropped her handle a little too harshly, and guided Chrisjon to do the same. Tomhas sank to his knees, his palms slamming to the earth to keep him from collapsing completely. He was wheezing, back shuddering with each inhale.

Chrisjon, whose eyes still hadn't regained their full clarity, hovered next to him with a hand on his shoulder. Naxa stretched her arms out above her head and signed with tired movements.

Markham recognized the signal for "rest" in there and nodded eagerly. "Yes. Yes. Rest. Please."

Tomhas shook his head. "We can't stop for too long. We're almost there. There are doctors in the rebel ranks. We just need to get there. We just need to keep pushing a little while longer."

Chrisjon sat down with a *thump*, dust billowing around him. Tomhas was right—they were close. The forest to Yaekós' north-east had been thinning out for hours. There were mere shrubs left, surrounded by drier rocky plains. The mines were not far. Help was not far.

Assuming my father didn't kill them all on sight.

He sighed, shifting his leg an agonizing inch. "We'll take a few minutes and then continue."

No one had any objections to that.

After three more hours of trudging over craggy plains of red and yellow dust, Chrisjon finally called, "The mines!"

Markham was lowered and he groaned as he pulled himself up into a sitting position. There it was.

He'd never liked visiting his father's workplace, had always resented the tiers of carved earth and ugly buildings that took his father away, but now he nearly sobbed when the sound of horns rang out around them.

Markham rubbed a hand over his face, laughing out loud. "They've spotted us. Take us closer and they'll meet us at the gate."

"Will they be friendly?" Naxa signed.

Markham nodded. "Assuming they recognize me under all this filth."

As they neared the gate, the watchmen closed in. They weren't wearing the uniform overall his father required, and they weren't armed to the teeth the way he was used to. These were not his father's men. They were rebels.

So, they have taken over the mines.

Their worried faces relaxed instantly when they beheld Tomhas, then turned to concern again when they took in the haggard state of the party. One broke away and stopped them to put both hands on Tomhas' shoulder.

Markham was transferred to more able hands and his companions bowed under the resulting relief.

"What happened?" the front man asked, deep creases forming on his clay-colored face.

Tomhas tried to smile, but ended up looking pained. "Anders… I'll tell you later over a keg of ale. Right now, we need to get help. Is Paulana here yet?"

They started moving toward the gate, the big iron-wrought structure that announced the mine's entrance. His father had built it to be as imposing as possible, to make it clear that whoever stepped across that threshold was in his territory, not the High Ruler's. It had no doubt irked the various monarchs who had held the position during Howell Aesher's reign, but you could only do so much against the man who controlled your gold.

Markham groaned as the stretcher bobbed with the men's jogging across the various terraced paths that comprised the mine's outer façade, into a squat building to the right, until they finally reached the shaft that would take them into the belly of it all. It took a few painful tries to fit the stretcher into the metal box, the lever boy staring on with a starstruck gape. The lift squeaked with each turn of the rod, the light of the upper world fading until only the illumination of a single lantern was left.

Through a clenched jaw, Markham asked, "My father?"
Anders flashed him an inscrutable look and only said, "Yes."

†

Staella was up before dawn. Except for those who'd been tasked to keep guard, the soldiers were still sleeping, their camp a quiet tent city. She'd always thought military men were vigilant and would get up before sunrise to train and be ready to march at the first sign of light. Turns out, when no one shouted orders at them, they took their sleep very seriously.

She huffed, marched down to the tent Reian had declared as his. Boisterous snoring emanated from it, nearly forceful enough to flutter the entrance flaps. Without preamble, she shucked one flap open and poked her head through. He was half-naked on his bedroll, his head thrown back and mouth wide open. He took another rumbling breath and Staella rolled her eyes.

She scooted forward. "Reian." He didn't even twitch. She kicked at his nearest leg. "Captain!"

With a grunt, his gray eyes shot open. He looked up, swallowed, rubbed a hand over his face. "Wha—?"

"The sun will be up soon. Wake your men and get ready."

He groaned and fell back against his pillow with a *thump*. "Staella, you're evil."

"Be that as it may, we need to get going. We're still two full days' march from the mines and the rebels will be waiting."

He slung an arm across his eyes, took a deep breath, and heaved up into a sitting position. She was afforded a glare. On his face, it was about as threatening as a growling puppy.

"Fine. But we're having a decent breakfast first."

She narrowed her eyes at him, but relented easily. "Alright. But then it's double time for the morning."

He sighed theatrically, threw aside his blanket, and rose slowly. “Slaver.”

After the men had been woken up and told to be ready within the hour, Reian made a fire and took down some of the fowl they’d hunted and strung up the previous afternoon. He plucked and sliced them expertly before he skewered them on their stick-made spit. Staella took a seat next to him as they watched their breakfast crisp.

“I’m still reeling from what you told us.” His gaze was focused on the ground in front of him.

She nodded. “It is quite a revelation.”

“I always knew the system was fucked up, that the Rulers were immoral in their lust for power. But this... They’re actually abducting people and turning them into mindless husks.”

“All the more reason to destroy the thing that gives them power.”

He frowned. “The Core?”

She shook her head. “The crown.”

†

The world was fuzzy, like everything was wrapped in a layer of gauze. A faint, greenish light glowed to his left. A voice muttered close by. A cot squeaked under him. A skew table sat next to it. He blinked a few times, then groaned. A face appeared above him and the person held a glass of water to his lips. He drank, sank back as the chamber around him slowly came into focus. The water-bearer was a woman in her sixties, with a salt-and-pepper bun steepled on top of her head. Her green eyes were keen and observant, her nose hooked above thin lips.

Dr. Paulana Leider was the most capable person Markham had ever met. She ordered men about with precise gestures and short commands, managed patients with careful attention, and patched up injuries with deft movements. Her assessments were quick, her hands soft and her pain killers delightful. She'd given him two every few hours and kept him in a near-coma for a day. Now that he was awake, she hovered over him. Cold fingers danced over his leg, where the wound was no longer painful at every movement.

"Who did the stitching on your old injuries?"

"My friend," he rasped.

Her mouth pulled into an impressed bow. "Decent work. How are you feeling?"

"Like I slept for ten years. I feel a little out of it."

"Hmmm. The leg?"

He moved it slightly and felt a dull ache, but nothing more. "Better."

She nodded, smiled. "Good. Ointment three times a day. Pain medication as needed. You can be glad the arrow wasn't poisoned. What did you use to stop the bleeding?"

"Haletayl sap."

Her eyebrows quirked. "Interesting… A visitor has been waiting to see you. After that, get some rest, Lad Aesher."

He nodded. "Yes, ma'am."

She marched out of what appeared to be his private infirmary in the mines and was quickly replaced with another figure. This one was taller, with broad shoulders and light hair. The lines of his body seemed tenser than usual, his eyes less blue in the cavernous dark.

Markham held his breath as the man neared, unable to read the expression on his face. He approached slowly, pulled out a stool from under the table, and sat down at Markham's bedside.

After a few moments of pregnant silence, Markham said, "Hi."

The side of Howell Aesher's mouth twitched. "Hi."

"So…?"

"So." There was another gape of silence as Markham refused to meet his father's eyes. Eventually, Howell cleared his throat. "If I didn't know your handwriting, I wouldn't have believed that the letter was from you. In fact, I entertained the idea that the rebels had somehow taken you hostage and forced you to write it… My son asking me to host a horde of insurgents, to commit treason. I was not convinced.

"Then, the first of them arrived, and believing that I was looking out for your safety, I had them *questioned*." Markham gulped, eyes flashing with concern. "But even under pressure, all they revealed was a young man showing up to lead a rebel meeting with a group of women at his side. They described him and how he spoke, that he was nervous at first but soon convinced them that they could change the world. And I couldn't deny it anymore. It was all true."

His father leaned forward, resting his forearms on his legs. His gaze was expectant—Markham had to say something.

"Thank you for taking them in."

Howell huffed. "Of course. I thought you were a formidable boy, managing the responsibility of an estate with such grace. Little did I know the extent… Why didn't you tell me? If I'd known just how much you were placing on yourself, with your anxiety and at your age, I could've helped you. I would've stayed."

Markham turned his head away. "You would've left no matter what."

He couldn't refute it, couldn't say anything. This had always been their impasse.

After a few seconds, Howell placed a hand on his son's arm. Markham looked up, saw the fondness in his father's eyes.

"You can always ask me for help."

Markham nodded. "I know."

He squeezed Markham's bicep. "Take it easy for now. You'll be better soon." With that, he stood and left.

Markham only allowed his silent tears to spill once his father had left the room.

CHAPTER THIRTY-EIGHT

STAELLA LOOKED LIKE A WARRIOR goddess as she approached the mines from the east, from the craggy mountains where they would not be spotted by the city. She was leading three hundred men who were trained in combat and armed to the teeth. Men who would give them a semblance of a chance in the conflict to come.

Markham found his heart racing as she marched closer, her fiery hair escaping from her braid to flutter against her pale face. She was magnificent, body moving with efficient grace in her custom black attire and dark eyes sparking with triumph.

He'd gotten into the lift as soon as the horns had sounded, knowing in his heart that it would be her. Now, he couldn't help but move closer. The pain in his leg was a mere nuisance as he made his way across the top tier of the mine, to meet her at the far gate.

When she saw him, she sped up. They were close enough that he could see the smile that overtook her face, the way it traced lines of joy around her eyes and flushed the apples of her cheeks. That smile would one day be the end of him, would have him falling to his knees with no questions asked.

He threw open the gate and beamed. She was there in an instant, crashing into him to wrap arms around his shoulders. He enveloped her in an embrace, buried his face in the crook of her neck to breathe her in.

She giggled. "It was a very bad idea to finally get a taste of you and then leave."

He huffed and straightened so he could look at her. His hand lifted to cup her jaw. "I wholeheartedly agree."

Her eyes roved over him, snagging on the bandage tied around his calf. Her jaw clenched and she leveled a scolding glare at him.

"What did you do?"

He shook his head. "Here I thought you might find my bravery charming."

"Markham."

He sighed and leaned his forehead against hers. "I rescued Tomhas and got acquainted with an arrow. But I'm all good now. Nothing a little haletayl sap can't fix."

She nodded, played with the ends of his hair. "The others?"

"Most of them are safe." Her head shot up at that. "Let's get the men underground and then I can fill you in."

†

They were all gathered in a decent-sized cavern off the main hall—the new inner circle and their companions.

Maci and Amile with hands twined together. Tomhas with arms crossed over his chest next to the cherubic Captain Reian. Eran and Daniel Caneille clung to each other as if their lives depended on it. Chrisjon and stone-faced Naxa Damhere had their arms hooked around each other for strength. Staella and Markham were stoic and focused, but stood barely a hair's breadth apart. Then there was Leda, with her fingers shyly brushing against Mycah's.

She looked around the strategy table with its rough map of the Qarvette fortress. *How did we get here?* She was listening to the planning, offering her own inputs as they became necessary, but all the while, Leda was focused on the people around her, on the group she hoped would not shrink in the conflict to come.

Markham, Tomhas, and Reian would be with the infantry, led by the captain. They would enter the city from the eastern gate—fully visible and challenging. Their assault would focus on the front gate of the palace and draw Yathan's men into combat. The cavalry—with Leda, Mycah, and Chrisjon in its ranks—would hide in the jungle to the north. They would engage from behind once the enemy forces were focused on the frontal assault. Daniel, armed with his favorite crossbow, would sneak into the palace dungeons amidst the chaos to free the imprisoned Representatives and get them to safety—to the Aesher manor, where Maci and Eran would be waiting to help secure them.

"Naxa, you will have a vital part to play," Tomhas announced. "You will leave before any of the forces and infiltrate the estate. Once the fighting starts, we'll count on you to open the gates from the inside." She nodded, her dark eyes not showing an ounce of hesitation or fear.

"Where do I come in?" This came from Amile, whose face was paler than usual, but whose golden gaze finally seemed rid of the wounded animal that had been trapped inside.

Markham's jaw clenched. "Amile…"

"Markham."

The latter shook his head. "You don't have to do this. We have others who can take him out. Staella—"

"No." Leda had rarely seen Amile with this much resolve in the set of his shoulders. "Zandi rerouted my mind for this. It is my part to play."

They stared each other down in that eerie way of theirs, talking with nothing but intense glares. Eventually, Markham sighed.

"Once the gates have been opened, Staella will be responsible for getting Amile into the palace and to the High Ruler, where he will execute the final assassination."

Amile met Staella's eyes with a nod. It would be done. Tomorrow, the People's Monarchy would fall.

CHAPTER THIRTY-NINE

MARKHAM WAS LENDING A HAND to a family sharpening their knives beside a glow-worm lamp. The Damheres had come through with nearly enough weapons and armor for the thousands of rebels gathered in the mines. They had been working towards this moment for years.

The children, two girls with blonde curls, were helping their parents. They would remain here tomorrow, cared for by those who would not be joining the battle. But tonight, they would help with the preparations. They would make sure that their mother and father had everything they needed to overthrow a king.

There was a sudden hand at Markham's shoulder, gentle and small. He looked up to find Staella standing over him. She was smiling, a giddy little grin that sparked heat low in his gut.

"May I borrow you for a moment?" *Oh, she's definitely planning something.*

He cocked an eyebrow and got an insistent glare in response. He rose out of his crouching position, cleared his throat.

"If you'll excuse me." As he turned, Staella tucked her arm into his. She was buzzing with energy. He chuckled and leaned closer. "What's going on with you?"

Her teeth tugged at her bottom lip. When she looked up at him, her eyes were bright, like stars twinkling in the black night. His heart skipped.

"I have a surprise."

She was leading him off to the side of the main hall, where his private infirmary had been a few days ago. Her fingers drew tantalizing circles on the skin of his forearm, which really wasn't helping to quell the anticipation thrumming in his veins. They ducked around the corner and were met by a white sheet that had been strung up over the room's entrance. Staella stepped forward to pull it aside, flashing him a devilish look over her shoulder. He gulped.

Inside, the room had been transformed. A dozen glow-worm lamps occupied every surface, casting the cave in magical light and flickering shadows. In the center, on the floor, bedrolls and blankets had been arranged into a bed that called to him to sink down into its soft luxury.

Staella pressed closer to him, placed a hand on his shoulder, and brought her lips close to his ear. "I wanted to do something about the dank air, but didn't know what. Sorry, I know how sensitive you are."

He huffed, rolled his eyes, and turned to face her fully. His arms wrapped low around her torso and heat spread through him as he pulled her close.

"I just enjoy being comfortable."

She hummed, leaning in to run her hands over his shoulders and upper back. "And… are you comfortable, my lad?"

Markham smiled and brought a hand up to start untangling her braid. "Very…" They came together slowly, Staella on her toes and Markham bending down. Their lips touched lightly at first, teasing. Then deeper, tongues twining together and hands growing less tentative. Staella's teeth nipped at Markham's lip and he groaned. "But I am starting to feel a little confined in all of these clothes."

She grinned against his mouth, let her fingers trail down his chest to undo buttons lazily. "I think we can do something about that." Her voice was low, husky. *Goddess.*

He kissed her again, fierce this time. His shirt was on the floor seconds later, her top soon after. He gripped the naked skin at her waist, shivered at the way she writhed under his touch. Hard muscle and sharp lines under velvet-soft ivory skin. He trailed worshipping licks and bites down the column of her neck as his hands worked lower to bare more of that delicious body to him.

She tugged at his hair and pulled his face up to meet hers. Her pupils were blown wide, her cheeks flushed deep red and lips swollen. This was what he'd dreamed about, only indescribably better for being real.

"Please tell me I didn't make that giant bed for nothing."

He chuckled, rested his hands on the swell of her backside. "Is this because we might die tomorrow?"

She undid the final button on his pants and pulled it down along with his underwear. As she lowered, she kept her eyes on his.

"It's because I love you…" When she straightened again, her hand wrapped confidently around him. He cursed, hips stuttering forward. Let out a groan when her teeth tugged at his ear. "…and because we might die tomorrow."

With a roar, Markham hoisted her up by the thighs, kissed her hungrily as he walked to the bed she'd made in anticipation of this moment. She'd planned this, had been thinking of being with him, of letting him see her completely exposed, feeling every inch of her skin against his, of him touching her, making her chant his name.

He laid them down gently, cradling her head with one hand. She opened for him easily, spreading her legs to make room for his hips flush against hers. She wrapped those strong thighs around him, tugged him impossibly closer with crossed ankles at the small of his back.

Then, he started to make her come apart. With caressing hands and teasing lips. Over her collarbones. The dip between her ribs. The pink nubs of her breasts. The taut muscles of her abdomen, and the sensitive skin at her hips. He shifted lower, marking the skin of her inner thighs with his teeth and tongue.

All the while she sang for him. Sounds he'd fantasized of hearing, of pulling from those lips. She moaned when his palms kneaded at her chest. Rasped his name at every inch his mouth moved lower, and whimpered when his tongue finally lapped at her. Her back arched in a perfect bow, her hands fluttering into his hair.

"Holy fu– *Markham.*"

His body shuddered as he worshipped her with his mouth and hands, trying to keep control, to make this last long enough that she would know. Know how he revered her–how she was the most formidable woman he'd ever known.

Her breath caught in a gasp, her body going taut. When he looked up, he knew that he could spend the rest of his life watching Staella Thenos at the peak of ecstasy. Her red hair was fanned out around her face, a flame against the sheets. Her eyes scrunched shut and her mouth opened in a cry.

When she could breathe again, he pulled up next to her and brushed strands of hair from her forehead. He leaned in, kissed her once—deep and slow.

"I love you," he murmured. "Fuck. I love you. I loveyou, IloveyouIloveyou..."

She crashed her mouth against his, her tongue sloppy as she reeled him in. He rolled back on top of her, whined as her hips bucked up against his.

"Please, Markham."

"Anything," he breathed.

When he finally—finally—sank into her, he couldn't suppress his moan. His gravelly sigh of her name. She was everything. All around him. Consumed him. Heat. And soft. Sighs and pants. Skin and lips. Thrusts. Rolling hips. Cries.

Goddess, was he happy to be consumed.

Somewhere in their frenzy, she flipped them over. She rode him with tormenting movements and hands splayed on his chest.

He watched her through his haze, his warrior goddess lost in lust, and when she fell over the edge again, he was right there with her, holding on tight and repeating his mantra of "I love you."

Until she collapsed against him and he knew that he would never be able to let her go.

†

When Staella woke in the early hours of the next morning, she was enveloped in the scent of vanilla and musky perspiration. A golden hand was settled on her waist, heavy breathing huffing into her shoulder. Markham. She hummed and turned onto her back to look at the person wrapped around her—Yaekós' golden boy with mussed up hair and lips slightly parted. Her hand darted up to trail light fingers across his jawline. He hummed, letting out a groan as he snuggled closer and hiding his head in the nook where her neck met her shoulder.

"Morning," he rasped.

She smiled, already addicted to the way his voice rumbled out of him when he was sleepy. "Good morning."

"I know what you're thinking," he mumbled. He pulled back slowly, his eyes opening to slits.

Her grin widened and she reached out to toy with the nest of hair on his head. "And what is that?"

"That I look dashing in the mornings."

He flashed her a smirk and she couldn't help but giggle at that. At her mirth, his hands dug into her sides, tickling her until she squealed. He ended up hovering over her, eyes twinkling with affection.

She sighed and ran her palms up and down his arms. "Actually, I was thinking about how many times you confessed your love last night."

An adorable blush crept high on his cheeks. "Sorry. I'm a very emotional lover."

She shook her head. "No. You can say it as many times as your heart desires and I'll be here every morning to remind you that I love you too." They stared at each other for a few silent seconds, savoring the moment of silence before the storm. She saw the instant that anxiety gripped his heart, knew it in the subtle darkening of his eyes. She reached out to cup his cheeks. "We'll get through today. Together. And when we see each other again, we'll have changed the world."

"And then we'll be able to smell the air, right?" he teased.

Her eyes widened and she slapped his shoulder. "Don't hold that against me. I was charged up on painkillers."

He shook his head, an affectionate smile crinkling the skin around his eyes. "Those words have given me hope all this time."

Her heart hiccupped and she rose up to plant a searing kiss on those gorgeous lips.

She breathed her words against his mouth: "Then yes, we'll be able to smell the air, Markham."

†

It was not yet dawn, the big clock in the main hall telling Markham that they had less than an hour before they marched on the city. He was in full golden armor, leg bandaged up tightly, and he found Amile exactly where he knew he would.

His best friend was above ground, sitting on the top tier of dry earth facing east, waiting for the sunrise. He was already wearing his bronze breastplate, three knives of varying lengths strapped to the belt at his hips.

He looked up as Markham took a seat beside him. There were deep stains of exhaustion under his eyes.

"Hi," Markham ventured.

"Hi."

"I'd ask you how you're doing, but it's pretty clear what the answer is."

Amile huffed. "The anticipation is killing me. It's not that I'm scared. I just… After everything that's happened, after everything Yathan's done… This has been a long time coming."

"I need you to know that you don't have to do this."

"Markham—"

Markham held up a hand. "Just let me say this. I know you feel indebted to me for giving you a home, that you feel the need to repay me somehow. But, Amile, there's nothing to repay. I showed you the kindness of a decent friend and I never expected anything in return. Even if I did, you've paid your dues ten times over. These last few years—after my mother died—they would've broken me had you not been there. Every time I throw myself into the fire, every time I make promises that are near impossible to keep, you're right there behind me making sure I stay standing. None of this, Amile, *none* of this would have been possible without you."

Tears welled in his friend's eyes, emotion so long hidden that it made Markham swallow down a sob as well.

"Thank you," Amile whispered. He shook his head. "But I need to do this. For Zandi. For me."

Markham smiled, looking back to the horizon. "How does it feel to be free in the dark on a crescent moon?"

The beam that overtook the other man's face could light up the mines by itself. "You have no idea. I never thought I would be just me again, and when today is over, the bloodlust won't return ever again. It feels like we're finally making it."

Markham nodded and turned to throw both arms around Amile's shoulders. He gripped tight.

"I love you so much."

Amile returned the hug with desperate strength. "I love you too, brother."

CHAPTER FORTY

THE FIRST SIGN SHOULD'VE BEEN the extraordinarily small group of soldiers manning the eastern gate to the city, who were dispatched easily by the front line of infantry. The second, the lack of resistance they faced marching through the bronze streets up to the Qarvette fortress.

The uneasy feeling in Markham's stomach finally dropped into dread when they reached the estate's front gate. It was open and unguarded. The infantry slowed, then stopped. A rumble traveled through the gathered force.

Then, a shout rang out. Markham's head shot up and he gasped.

Black smoke rose from the jungle to the northeast, flames licking at the age-old trees. Catapults loaded with flaming rocks came into view on the plain to Yaekós' east, a force of roughly five thousand city guards before them.

"Our cavalry," Tomhas breathed next to him.

Markham's breathing became shallow and he shook his head. "They knew our plan. They knew we were coming. Reian!"

The captain was at his right in an instant. "My lad?"

"We need to move to the Roäk. We have to help the cavalry."

Reian looked down and cleared his throat. "With all due respect, my lad, that's exactly what they expect us to do—abandon our attempt to take the palace."

Markham rubbed a hand over his face. "What do you propose we do? I'm not leaving them to die."

"No. We split our force. Four thousand to the jungle. Eight thousand proceed forward. There'll likely be an ambush inside those walls, and we need to be strong enough to withstand it."

Markham chewed at his bottom lip, feeling nausea pressing at his throat. He nodded.

"Give the order."

†

Leda couldn't see anything through the smoke, coughed every time she took a breath. She led her horse forward, trying to find Mycah or Chrisjon in the mess.

With a mighty crack, the flaming tree to her left crashed down, landing in front of her. She yelped, gripped onto her steed's reins as the animal reared with a whinny. Her hand slipped and she crashed backward, thrown from the mare to the ground. Pain shot through her ankle and head. There was fire at all sides, black smoke burning her eyes and throat. She cried out, used all her strength to stand up. She heard a scream. Someone shouting. A crack.

There they were. Saul's men dressed in pitch black, stalking through the jungle.

There was another howl from behind her. She spun, her eyes growing wide as the smoke cleared. Another group of guards closed in from behind. Leda's heart stopped. She coughed again, wiped at her eyes, and drew the longsword at her hip.

"On me!" the commanding officer bellowed. He was young, barely a lieutenant, but he was the one who would have to get them out.

She gripped the frightened horse, whispered a few soothing words, and got on. With a tug, she followed the order and used the echo of voices to navigate her way to the rest of her men. She quickly slotted into the double-rowed circle they were making, a desperate attempt to defend all sides as the enemy surrounded them.

She didn't know the rebels at her sides, but they stood strong and she was grateful. When the first line of guards was upon them, Leda snarled and used every sparring lesson she could remember to stay alive.

†

Staella used the servants' passages that ambled through the palace to get Amile to his target. The Qarvette, who was now behind her, had described the fortress's inside to her in perfect detail and informed her of the safe room hidden behind the panels of the master bedroom. This was where Yathan, Cala, and the children would go as soon as the attack outside started. And this was where they were headed now.

It was too quiet. There were no kitchen maids or messenger boys, no cleaners or handmaidens rushing through the halls, and the sound of fighting had not yet started up outside.

The mission remains the same.

She halted, signaled for Amile to stop. They were about to enter one of the main corridors, its floors glinting mahogany and its walls tapestried. Staella held her breath as she peeked into the hallway, right then left. She shrunk back into the servant's passage. Amile waited with wide eyes.

"One guard on each side," she mouthed. "I'll take the right first. When he's down, you go. I'll follow when the left is taken care of."

He nodded and she was off.

She pulled a dagger from her boot. Silent as the night, she leaped into the corridor. She was on her first target before either guard noticed her. Her blade slipped through his ribs to find its mark and she covered his mouth until he collapsed. Amile dashed past.

The other guard reached her before she could turn and she just managed to dodge the tip of his sword slashing past her head. He stumbled forward with the momentum of his missed blow and she stepped around him quickly. With a stab to the side of his neck, he was down.

This was too easy.

She couldn't linger on that thought. Amile yelled from the end of the hallway. Another guard was waiting.

†

Leda howled as she tumbled from her steed once more. She hit the ground harder this time, felt something in her leg crack. There was a spear buried in the mare's side, a spewing wound widening with the creature's every buck. Leda tried to reach for her, tried to stand, but as the animal screamed and tried to run, it collapsed and couldn't get up again.

A glint above caught her eye. *Shit.* A guard towered over her, his battle ax arced and ready to swing down. She screamed, shimmied backward, and narrowly avoided being cut in half. Her opponent followed her with slow steps—a hunter who knew his prey had nowhere to go.

She crawled backward through the underbrush, trying to get up. But her leg wouldn't budge. The ax swung down again, a hair's breadth from her groin. She scuttled away. Back. Back.

Then, her back met something hard. A tree trunk. Nowhere left to run. She watched with wide eyes as the man sneered, raising his ax in anticipation of the final blow.

He froze.

A hunting knife protruded from the center of his chest, his mouth open as he started to fall. Leda scurried to the side to avoid being crushed by his body. She looked up and found Chrisjon standing in front of her with an outstretched hand.

His hair was free of its braid, matted and sticking to his skin. His face and body were covered in blood, his chest heaving with exertion. She took his hand, leaned on him until she found her footing. Her leg barked with pain, but she was standing.

"Thank you," she gasped.

His jaw clenched. "You need to get out of here."

"What?"

"We're not going to make it."

She shook her head. "No. We–"

"Leda." He stared her down and she withered.

He was right. Reinforcements from the infantry had joined them what felt like ages ago, but it had not been enough. The guards had decimated nearly all of them.

She let out a half-sob. "I can't just abandon those who are left. We can still fight."

Chrisjon grabbed her by the shoulders. "And then what? You dying here won't help anyone. You are the beacon of the Rebellion, Leda. The people need you." A group of guards had spotted them and broke off with a cry. Chrisjon's grip tightened around the hilts of his hunting knives. "Mycah is waiting at the edge of the jungle. Let me get you out."

The guards were getting closer. Closer. Four of them. Leda nodded. "Okay. Okay."

"Run."

She twisted, moving south as swiftly as her leg would carry her. She was hobbling, clutching onto every tree in her path in a desperate attempt to escape. The forest was still burning, still clouded with smoke, and everywhere there were bodies.

Chrisjon was right behind her, urging her on. He'd exchanged his knives for smaller ones, pulling them from hidden pockets in his sleeves and throwing them. They hit their targets often enough to slow down the assailants.

Leda was now close enough to see the plains beyond the Roäk, to smell fresh air. Chrisjon roared, nearly crashing into her. She spun to find an arrow embedded in his side.

"*No!*" She saw them then, the archers hidden in the foliage to the east—waiting to pick off stragglers.

Chrisjon's voice was feral when he bellowed, "Keep going."

He pushed her forward, stumbling onward despite the blood he was trailing. Arrows rained down around them. They stayed low, trying to move quickly. Pain bloomed through her. Leda cried out, looked down to see a shaft sticking out from her bicep. She gasped and felt her breathing become shallow and rapid.

Oh, Goddess. Oh, Goddess.

Chrisjon rammed into her, physically pushing her on. The edge of the jungle was looming. There was Mycah, waiting under an enemy shield she'd procured. The girl was sooty and bleeding, but Leda had never been happier to see her.

Finally, she broke through the line of trees, sunlight beating down to meet her. She collapsed next to Mycah, letting the physical presence of the woman soothe her.

But Mycah's body had gone rigid. "No," she rasped.

Leda spun. Shrieked.

Chrisjon sank to his knees at the line between jungle and plain. His lips were parted, his body swaying. An arrow was rooted in his right eye. He took a last shuddering breath and crashed to the ground.

Leda leapt toward him, but Mycah caught her arm. "Leda, we have to go." She struggled, needed to help him, to at least hold his hand. "He's gone." She wouldn't believe it, couldn't just leave him. "Leda!"

She stopped pulling and felt her body go lax with the first sob that racked it. So, wailing, Leda let Mycah take her to safety.

CHAPTER FORTY-ONE

BLOOD POURED INTO MARKHAM'S right eye. He cursed and stripped off the sleeve of his armor with a grunt. He leaned back against the wall behind him as he tore at the now-exposed piece of shirt, finally managing to rip off a rag.

He wiped it over his eye and forehead, pressed it to the cut on his brow with a wince. He had deep wounds, cuts that bled, and aches that screamed out for his attention, but he couldn't tend to them now.

Tying his makeshift bandage around his head, he pressed off the wall and into the nearest hallway. Outside, the din of battle still sounded and the cries of his men as they were massacred pierced through him.

Reian had been right—an ambush had awaited the remaining eight thousand men inside the estate's walls. The city guard had decimated the cavalry, but the capital's military force had been waiting for the infantry. Soldiers had peeled from every crevice in the palace exterior and had descended upon them in force from where they'd hidden inside the fortress walls. It was chaos.

Markham had fought his way through and struck down enemy men with a singular purpose: get inside. Because Staella and Amile were in there, and the castle's defenses knew they were coming for the High Ruler.

He had to get to them before it was too late.

†

The lone guard in the palace's master bedroom had gone down without much trouble. He'd been young and inexperienced, fiercely loyal to the throne but not much of a match for her.

Staella frowned down at the body. *One pathetic boy as the High Ruler's last defense.* She shook her head and looked over her shoulder at Amile.

"Something's wrong."

He nodded, his eyes darkening as the gears in his mind whirred. "I know."

She sighed, reached down to her weapons belt to reveal a long knife. She handed it to him, wrapping his fingers around the hilt. He had others strapped to his hips, but they suddenly seemed inadequate.

"We can't go anywhere but forward regardless. Whatever's waiting behind these doors, I'll take care of it. You have one target: Yathan."

Amile's throat bobbed, but his hand tightened around the knife. Staella turned back to the bedroom wall, ran her hand over it until she found the little notch that would open the hidden door. She had the layout of the safe room in her mind—a small antechamber, then a larger hall, and finally a padded panic room.

She took a last steadying breath before pushing down. The hinges of the panel-door creaked as it swung open. A single lantern illuminated the bare space, revealing a solitary figure guarding the next door. Staella's breath caught.

Saul Knoxin.

He was armed and armored, hair tied back and face spread into a vicious grin. "Thenos, what a surprise."

She huffed and tightened her grip around the hilt of her blade, the one stained red with his guards' blood. "If you're the big bad at the end of the story, this is going to be easier than I thought."

His grin morphed into a sneer. "I will lay down my life for my High Ruler."

"You must know what he's been doing. Why are you so loyal to that monster?"

"Because he made me," Saul growled.

He launched forward with a snarl, sword thrust out. She narrowly avoided the blade, spinning to the left and blocking the weapon with her own.

He was not Lorde of Security for nothing. With lightning speed, he twirled the sword away and maneuvered it toward her in an expert slice. She yelped, jumped back just enough to escape a fatal blow. The tip of the blade slashed across her bicep, stinging as it drew blood.

She retreated further, drawing him back inch by inch. Only blocked each attack quick enough to stay alive. She moved back another step. Back. Back. Until she saw Amile slip past and through the far door.

Mission complete.

Now, she could focus on pummeling the swine in front of her. With a smirk, she blocked his blade with the edge of hers. Pushed back. Stepped under the arc of his weapon. Landed a harsh kick to his knee. He grunted and staggered back. Growling, he launched forward again.

And so, their dance began.

The first time they'd sparred, they'd been a perfect match. Met each other blow for blow in a near-choreographed flurry of movement. After years of formal training, he was an excellent swordsman.

He was not a fighter, though. He hadn't survived the cage—where weapons were forbidden, but everything else was fair game. She was the Crimson Jackal and this time she wasn't playing nice.

†

Amile ducked through the door quickly, but once on the other side, he halted. He had turned his back to the larger of the safe rooms, pressing his forehead against the cool wood of the door, breathing in slowly. He closed his eyes, dug his nails into his palms so he could focus on the sting of it, rather than the sting of impending bloodlust. Just a moment of silence, a moment of being himself before he became the monster that killed his brother.

He breathed out through his mouth, counted to eight as Markham had taught him, and finally turned around. He opened his eyes.

He'd only seen the room once, when he was little, and it still looked exactly the same. Concrete floor. Stone walls. Two empty beds. A big chair at the opposite end, which was now occupied by a figure in a well-tailored white suit.

Yathan.

The bloodlust started low in his stomach and rose up in consuming waves. It seared through his chest. Bubbled up his throat. Clawed its way into his eyes, and attached to his mind like a parasite.

Life.

Pulse.

Blood.

Kill.

The man in the white suit's eyes widened. He drew his sword hastily, shakily.

Fear. *Good.*

†

Staella was disarmed and had more bleeding cuts on her body than she could count.

Saul surged toward her again, his blade poised to stab. She ducked, avoided the blade only to have the hilt slammed into the side of her head. She cried out, sinking down to her knees.

"What a pathetic adversary you turned out to be," Saul snarled. His boots were blurry stripes in her vision as he paced closer. She blinked, trying to bring the world back into focus, trying to ignore the throbbing in her temple. "The legendary Crimson Jackal who kept eluding me. The cocky criminal who thought she could save the world." Slowly, her vision cleared. She kept her head down and scooped her shoulders inward. "You and your peasant friends will all die today…"

He raised his sword over her head. She tensed. "And I will always get to remember the little girl who joined the Rebellion because I broke her heart."

He slammed the weapon down. The instant before it hit her, she slid forward and up. Slammed her elbow back into his hand. The blade slipped from his grip, clattered onto the floor. She rose, sank into her stance, and closed her hands into fists. Smiled at the bewilderment on his face.

Finally.

He came at her with arms out to punch, just as she knew he would. She dove into his body, wrapped her hands around his neck. Slammed her knee into his groin. Jabbed an elbow into his jaw. She let him go, letting the momentum drag him backward.

Spun to land a side kick against his ear. He grunted, lifted weak arms to protect his face, but she was on him. A jab to the sternum. Punch. Jab. Head butt. Dance away. Block. Block. Kick.

He was heaving, bleeding, and bowed over. He looked up at her, eyes wide. "Thenos…"

She roared. Grabbed the base of his ponytail to spin him, and slammed his nose against the wall. She heard a *crunch* and snarled in satisfaction. She let him go, only giving him enough time to face her before she pummeled her fist into his face, feeling the flesh beneath her knuckles turn to mush.

She let him go with a shove, rage boiling in her every vein. "Fight back, you asshole."

He swayed on the spot, coughed, and spat blood. "Staella, please…"

She growled, stormed forward. "I said *fight.*"

She had never been this angry, had never clenched her teeth this hard and felt tears run down her cheeks with the force of her hatred. She trembled with it. Wanted nothing more than to make him feel pain.

He threw his hands up in a desperate attempt to seek mercy. She screamed, closed her hands around his throat, and pushed him up against the back wall.

She bared her teeth at him. "Jacline." She pulled forward. Bashed his head back into the wall. "Graegg." Again. *Crack.* "Leda." Again. She sobbed, tasting the salt of her own tears. "Bruhel."

Saul's head lolled forward, his eyes slits as they barely managed to focus on her. He wheezed and moaned.

His words were a mumbled mess as he said, "What, lasht one frrr you?"

She clenched her jaw, tightened her grip around his throat. "Aldahad."

One last time, she slammed his head into the wall. His body crumpled to the floor. For good measure, she picked up his sword and sank it into his chest.

Kneeling with exhaustion, she whispered, "That was for me."

†

The man in the white suit still tried to fight back, slamming weak fists into his head and chest. He didn't feel it. He only saw blood and smelled death approaching. Glorious red coated nearly every inch of that white. It oozed from stab wounds and scratches and a bite to the shoulder. The man was screaming too—moaning and crying out in pain. Pleading.

Yes.

Yes.

His knife raised, slashed down, and found flesh. Again. Again. Again. Until the man stopped fighting. Until the body went limp in his arms.

The bloodlust disappeared much quicker than it had come. It vaporized instantly, as if it had never been there, and left him with perfect clarity.

Amile trembled, looked down at the body he was holding in one arm. Yathan—his older brother reduced to a pulp. The blood was on him. It stained his hands, soured his mouth, made tears flood his gaze. He whimpered, let the body fall to the floor.

Oh Goddess.

He tried to stand, but stumbled and emptied his stomach on the floor. When he could finally get up, he only staggered a few steps forward toward the chair where his brother had been sitting only minutes ago. He rested his back against it, slid down to the cold floor, and clutched at his hair. Torturous images flashed through his mind. Yathan's begging eyes. His shrieks of pain. The weight of his lifeless body. A sob tore through Amile, made his body shudder.

What have I done?

He heard the door open behind him.

CHAPTER FORTY-TWO

MARKHAM FOUND NAXA FIRST, curled up in a corner of the kitchen. She had a shallow wound to her stomach, had stolen an apron to press on it. Her eyes widened when she saw him and her hands started moving desperately, signing an urgent message.

He knelt down in front of her, wrapping his hands around her wrists. "Hey. Shhh. It's okay. We know it's a trap." Her shoulders relaxed at that and she shook her head. He helped her get up. "You've helped us more than you can imagine. Do you think you could get out of here unharmed?" She nodded. "Good. Then go. You should be safe at the Aesher estate."

She hesitated, but acquiesced eventually. Markham watched her slip away before continuing his search. He knew that Staella and Amile would've headed to the master bedroom and the safe rooms behind it. He used the servants' passages, as they had. Dispatched guards were scattered across the path, but there were too few of them.

If they knew Staella was coming, bringing a weapon to kill the High Ruler, wouldn't they have stationed their best men at every turn?

The dread in his stomach churned, turned into full-bodied fear. *Unless the trap only comes later.*

He sped up, navigating the palace corridors at a run until he found the open door of the main room. A young guard's body lay crumpled to the floor in front of the panel door. He ducked through the entrance and gasped.

Saul Knoxin was dead, his body motionless on the concrete floor and his head a broken mess. Staella sat next to him, covered in blood and breathing heavily.

Markham sank down in front of her and cupped her face in his hands. She looked up at him, smiled weakly, and leaned into his touch.

"Hi," he whispered.

"Hi."

"Are you—?"

"I'm fine," she rasped. "I'm fine. I just need a minute. Amile." She motioned at the door behind her. "Go to Amile."

He nodded, squeezed her shoulder before ducking into the next room.

His heart stopped. Yathan's body was barely recognizable as human—a mush of red and blue. And there was Amile, curled into a ball against the legs of a chair, sobbing.

But they were not alone. The door on the other side opened. Cala surged through, a scimitar clutched in her left hand. Markham screamed, leapt forward.

No.

He was too late. She drove her weapon forward with a snarl and buried the blade deep into the side of Amile's neck.

Markham froze. Felt the breath leave his body.

His best friend looked up. Locked eyes with him as blood bubbled from his lips. He coughed, gurgled, then slumped forward.

Markham ran, slid down in front of him. "Amile. Amile. Hey." He lifted the man's head, slapping his cheeks. "Hey. Please. Come on."

No response.

"No. No. Come on. Nonononono."

He kept shaking him, his own body convulsing with emotion.

Please, Goddess.

"No!"

†

Staella heard the scream and ran, ducking through the door. She stopped to take in the scene. Yathan. Markham. Cala. And Amile– dead.

Then, from the final safe room behind the High Companion, they emerged one by one. Aedon Blomehill. Delilah Haltstone. Rayn Valanisk. Their expressions were vacant, their hands curled around daggers. Perfect minions.

Cala's lip curled back into a sadistic grimace. Her command was scarcely louder than a murmur: "Attack."

"Markham!"

Staella's warning had barely left her lips before the Representatives surged forward. Rayn and Delilah bore down on a barely-lucid Markham, who rose just in time to duck a blade aimed at his chest.

Aedon was on Staella in seconds, his arrogant face devoid of emotion as he attacked. His dagger slashed out again and again. At her face. Her neck. Her chest. She side-stepped. Ducked. Sprang back. Cried out as she blocked a blow with the edge of her bloodied sword.

She pushed back, swirled her weapon in a perfect arc, and flicked. The dagger tore free of his hand and clattered to the floor. She stabbed forward, sank her blade into the muscle of his forearm.

Don't kill him, Staella.

The wound would've incapacitated most, but Aedon didn't flinch. Came at her with his other hand clenched into a fist. She danced away from his jabs and tried to block his arm with her weapon.

He grabbed the blade in his bare hand, wrapped his fingers around it in a vice grip. Blood surged from his palm, but he only growled and pulled. She gritted her teeth, tried her best to hold on to the hilt. But he was stronger. He ripped the blade from her grasp, flinging it away like a broken toy.

She barely had time to raise her arms as his onslaught began. Punch after punch headed her way, his slashed arm not slowing him in the slightest. Her arms trembled as they warded off the barrage of blows, as he pushed her back. Back. Back.

She cried out as his fist slammed into her jaw, stumbled back until her spine met the wall. She blinked, landing a jab to his stomach. Her knee met his groin, but it did nothing. He rammed her into the wall with his shoulder. Landed fist after heavy fist against her body and head.

Then, his fingers closed around her throat. She grabbed at his arm, scratched at unfeeling skin. He squeezed harder, his teeth bared. She reached out. Found the spot on his neck that would paralyze him. Pushed.

Nothing.

Fuck.

Through blurry eyes, she saw Markham at the other side of the room. Delilah had his arms pinned behind his back as Rayn pummeled his face and chest.

"Stop," Staella croaked. "Why are you doing this? Why are you fighting? Your king is dead."

The command to halt came from Cala, calm and soft. Rayn's fists fell to her sides. Aedon's hand remained around Staella's throat, but his grip loosened.

Cala stepped forward, her heeled boots clicking on the concrete floor. "They don't fight for the king…"

"They fight for the queens."

The latter came from the woman who emerged from that last panic room. Her hair was tied up into a regal knot at the back of her head, her red cloak billowing out behind her.

"No," Staella breathed.

Maci.

Staella shook her head. "You?"

She grinned ferally and stalked forward to take Cala's hand in hers. "Thank you for bringing all our enemies to one place."

"And for taking care of Yathan for us," Cala added with barely a glance at her dead husband and brother-in-law.

Staella snarled, pushed against Aedon's hold. "You traitor. I will make you pay for this. Both of you."

Maci only leveled a bored gaze at her and ordered, "Kill them all."

Aedon's grip closed and Staella gasped. Choked on a scream. Clawed at his hand. She saw Markham's body go limp. Felt tears run down her cheeks. Tried to breathe. Can't. *Fight.* Can't. *Do something.* Can't.

The edges of her vision blackened. Her body sagged. She closed her eyes.

The hand around her throat fell away. She sank to the floor, gulping for air. Her vision cleared and she saw Aedon collapsed on the ground, a short bolt sticking from his left ear. She looked up to find Daniel standing next to her with a crossbow in hand. He was aiming at something and fired again.

Staella followed the bolt's trajectory, watched it soar through the room until it embedded its tip in Cala's chest. The woman gasped and staggered backward. Staella used the moment of distraction to stand, to dash forward as quickly as her broken body would let her. She grabbed her discarded sword on the way and roared.

She slammed into Maci with all her force, sending her flying back until she met the floor. Staella was on her, straddled the traitor's waist and pressed her blade to a yellow-brown neck. She leaned forward, her words dripping with venom.

"Call them off."

Maci glared at her in defiance. "You're going to kill me anyway."

"No. We're going to lock you up like you did with the Representatives, like you did with your brother. How we treat you while you're there is up to this moment… Call them off."

Maci's eyes widened, but she said nothing. Staella pressed the blade deeper into the woman's throat, drawing blood.

"I swear to the Goddess, Maci, I will skin you alive."

She hesitated a moment longer and felt Staella's thighs tighten around her. Gulped. "Stop. Stop!"

Staella saw Rayn and Delilah still from the corner of her eye, sighing in relief. She looked back at Maci, felt hurt and hatred well up inside her.

"Why?"

Maci bared her teeth. "Because I am the queen Aldahad deserves. I am the only one who can save us. I am the queen," she roared.

Staella shook her head and felt tears run down her cheeks. "No, you're not." Then, she sank her blade deep into Maci's neck and stood up on shaky legs. Daniel was there to offer an arm. She grabbed it gratefully. "I had to. She'd always be able to command them."

He nodded, his cerulean eyes hard. "You don't have to justify yourself to me. I would've killed everyone in this room."

"Fly the flag," she rasped. "It's over."

CHAPTER FORTY-THREE

THE LIGHTNING-FLAG WAS FLYING over the Qarvette fortress—over Yaekós and over Aldahad. Yet, it didn't feel like much of a victory at all.

Staella stared at the destruction surrounding her, the bodies littering the palace grounds. They were barely recognizable, with gaping wounds and lifeless eyes.

Staella's body was weighed down with lead, her chest caught in a vice.

Reian, who had survived despite a nasty stab to the left shoulder, walked at her side. He hissed with every movement, but insisted on giving her the report. Because she was the only member of the inner circle there to hear it.

Six thousand infantry were slaughtered right here. Five thousand died in the jungle, where the cavalry had been ambushed. She didn't know whether her friends had made it—whether Amile's was the only corpse that would haunt her dreams.

Don't think about it. You can't think about it now.

Despite her best efforts, Staella trembled. Tears welled up in her eyes, but she refused to let them spill. "So many families have been broken today," she rasped.

"But so much freedom has been won," Reian said from her left. She looked up at him and saw the light shining in his eyes through the gore staining his face, through the pain tugging down the corners of his lips. She only shook her head at him and turned away. His hand settled on her shoulder. "There are thousands of rebels left. Millions of people who will live better lives because of what has happened here today. The sacrifice is great, but the achievement is greater."

A tear slipped. "Tell that to the man I love, who looks like his soul has been ripped from his body." She turned to face the captain, whimpered, "How do I ever look Markham in the eye and tell him it was worth it?"

Finally, the sobs claimed her.

THE WOULD-BE QUEEN

A WOULD-BE QUEEN LAY ON A stone floor, her hand reaching for Yathan's crown even in death.

She had always been smarter than everyone else. Even as a little girl, Maci's mind baffled her parents and her tutors. She read books that confounded older men, studied history with rapt attention, and even beat seasoned scholars at chess. She was a peculiar child who only ever wanted to play one game: Being Queen.

In fact, the singular purpose of becoming a true monarch consumed her from a tender age. She knew she was smarter than everyone else. She knew more about everything than everyone else. She was fair and efficient. She was the only one who deserved to rule, and Aldahad deserved to be controlled by the best.

So, the Would-Be Queen traveled the world to learn about different cultures, to see how other leaders ruled. She read libraries full of books on political strategies, battle, and administration. She sharpened her mind even further.

And she studied people. She realized that she would have to play their games to get to her rightful place. So, by the age of eleven, she'd become a socialite. A pretty, polite, and unthreatening flower who talked about ball gowns and boys and kept her ambitions hidden behind a carefully-crafted veneer.

When the Would-Be Queen was a teenager, she met the path to her throne at a Crest party she was too young to be at. Cala Vardan had waltzed in with an alcohol-dazed mind and the confidence of the stunningly beautiful.

Through her spying, Maci had learned that Cala was promised to Yathan Qarvette. Because of her political knowledge, Maci knew that the most likely candidate to become High Ruler in a few years was that same Qarvette.

So, the Would-Be Queen put on her most dazzling smile and charmed her way into the bed of the soon-to-be High Companion. Once Cala was married, they wove their web together.

Years ago, in the Blomehill library, she'd found a tome on the secrets of the haletayls—a book that laid out how the Goddess had captured the last drops of magic in the first red-blossomed tree, how the remnants still in the sap contorted the mind, and she'd been holding onto a brilliant scheme ever since.

She could smell Yathan's lust for power—taught Cala how to manipulate it to get Yathan to work for them. He never knew about his wife's affair—about the other queen. He thought the plan was to make him king… Fool that he was. He did the brainwashing for them, arranged the abductions, and offered his lover and his brother on a silver platter. It was sublime, the way he played along.

The Would-Be Queen delighted in her power. In how she orchestrated everything from behind the scenes and controlled Aldahad's mighty like puppets on a string.

When Amile left the palace, she stayed close to make sure their secret was kept, and found out that her cousin was planning a rebellion. She smiled at that, let her chess-board mind use them as pawns. She laughed with Cala about the perfection of it all—how they would use the rebels to kill Yathan. How they would wipe out all their enemies in one day and rule together. How they would become queens.

Now… Now, the Would-Be Queen lay on a stone floor, her hand reaching for Yathan's crown even in death.

CHAPTER FORTY-FOUR

HER CHEST WAS BURNING WITH the force of her panting breaths. Her legs ached, but she couldn't stop running. She fled as fast as her body could. Ran. Ran.

She heard cackling behind her and whimpered with fear. She was running, but the corridor was endless, and the woman was gaining on her, getting closer and closer.

She looked back and the woman was gone. She stopped.

Then, she was right in front of her.

Maci. With a too-wide grin and mad eyes. "You can't run forever, Staella. I am the queen."

Markham appeared in the woman's arms. "Help me," he cried.

Staella tried to reach out, but her arms were dead weights at her sides. She screamed as Maci laughed, drawing a knife and slicing it across Markham's throat.

"No!"

Staella woke with a cry, sitting up and clutching her panting chest. She was drenched in sweat and could feel her heartbeat in her ears. With shaky hands, she reached out to the glass of water on her nightstand and took a sip. When she could breathe again, she looked over to the other side of the bed. Markham's spot was empty. She looked to the right to find his silhouette outlined by the moonlight that filtered into the room. He was staring out the window, motionless.

"Are you okay?" she rasped.

As usual, he didn't respond.

She sighed, lied back down and closed her eyes. The rest was needed. She had a self-defense class to present in the morning.

†

Leda walked out of the meeting hall in Signal Tower with a sigh of relief. Finally, after months of drafting, debating, and redrafting, the Transformation Council had created a new Core—one that would secure each citizen's political, social, and economic rights for generations to come.

Mycah was waiting at home with a bottle of champagne and a closet-full of lingerie in celebration of having her girlfriend's attention again. Leda couldn't get to the estate fast enough.

A hand on her shoulder halted her dash for the stairs. She turned to find Tomhas smiling at her. Her scowl disappeared immediately. It was simply impossible to be irritated with those warm eyes on you.

She curtsied teasingly. "Mister President."

He chuckled and motioned at her to keep walking alongside him. "*Interim* president," he corrected.

Ah yes. They would have another election once all the new systems were in place—one where everyone was eligible to stand.

"Mister Interim President just doesn't have the same ring to it."

He grinned once more, fleetingly, before all traces of that smile left his face. He looked away, cleared his throat. "I… How is he?"

Leda tugged at her bottom lip with her teeth, keeping her gaze on the steps below. "The same."

Tomhas sighed heavily. "I'll have to visit him again, but…"

"I know." She placed a hand on his arm. "It's difficult to see him like that, but I still have hope. He just needs time."

He nodded and patted her back as they stepped into the sunlight outside. "Well, say hello to Mycah for me."

"Will do." She watched him leave, noticed the slump of his shoulders. It seemed all of them struggled under the weight of their win.

With a last shake of her head, she turned towards the Crest and put on her sun-blocking glasses. She had one more stop before she could indulge in any celebrations.

The Qarvette palace had been a wreck after the battle, but Leda had managed to restore it after the royal children had been sent to live with their grandparents in Harreen. Servants and nurses bustled about in the old fortress, smiling to greet her when she passed.

She wove through the hallways, past the rooms that held Delilah and Rayn. She went up the stairs, into the master bedroom, which had been transformed into a laboratory and research chamber.

Dr. Paulana Leider was bent over a high desk, scraping tiny particles off a haletayl petal and examining it with a monocle. Leda knocked on the open door and cleared her throat. The woman looked up.

"Miss Hayvinger. Morning."

She didn't smile, but put down her work, which was a show of immense respect from the healer. "Sorry to interrupt. Just here to check on your progress."

Paulana stood, rested her fists on her hips. "Still no breakthrough, unfortunately, but I am pursuing a promising new idea."

Leda nodded. "And the patients?"

"They have all the luxuries they could dream of, but they remain unresponsive, I'm afraid."

"Mother?"

"Still no change. Sorry, dear."

Leda shook her head and flashed her best attempt at a smile. "It's alright. I'm going to visit her quickly and then I'll be out of your hair."

She turned away, straightening her shoulders as she moved down the corridor. There was a nurse stationed in front of the door, sitting on a bench and reading a book. She smiled and motioned for Leda to enter. Her mother was in the far corner, in front of the big window. An easel was propped up in front of her and she was filling it with color—a field of flowers with every shade imaginable, except red.

She looked up when her daughter opened the door and beamed. "Honey." She set down her paintbrush and bounded over to envelop Leda in a hug.

Leda giggled, returning the embrace. "Hey, Mom." When they pulled apart, she gestured at the painting. "You're getting really good."

"Oh, thank you, dear. I only paint what I see." She stared out the window as if the view offered more than lawn and stone wall.

Leda smiled sadly. After everything that had happened, everything they'd discovered, she wanted nothing more than to talk to her mother about all of it. To tell her that she'd changed the world to be what Lowena had wanted. To ask her about her history with Yathan and seek comfort from her grief and nightmares.

But Audrey would not truly understand what she was saying, and Paulana had given her strict instructions not to mention anything that could upset her patient. So, she came every second day to talk about innocuous flowers and painting and the lovely servant girls.

Every time, as she exited, she muttered, "Don't worry, Mom, we'll find a way to make you better."

Today was no different. As usual, her mother smiled and nodded, as if she knew exactly what Leda meant.

†

Staella hesitated in front of the closed door and let out a shaky breath before she knocked. There was no response. She hadn't been expecting one.

The room smelled musty when she entered and she silently cursed the servant for not having opened the windows on his morning rounds. She did it now, consciously avoiding the blanket-covered silhouette in the bed for a few seconds longer. She was still sweaty from her self-defense class and took a moment to savor the cool breeze.

When that was done, she gulped and turned around. Only his face was visible as he curled up on his side, his hollow eyes fixed forward.

She padded closer, sitting down next to him. Her hand settled on his shoulder. "Markham." He shifted his gaze to her, but didn't say anything. Her heart broke, as it did every time she saw the dark circles under his eyes and the sallow tint to his skin. The emptiness in him. He hadn't truly spoken to anyone since Amile's death. She tried to smile, found his hand under the sheets, and squeezed it. "How are you feeling?"

He looked away, shook his head. She nodded and felt tears sting the back of her eyes. "Alright… Well, I got a message from Leda. They finally finished the new Core."

He nodded and their fingers intertwined.

He is *trying*.

She closed her eyes, breathed in slowly to pull herself together. "That, uh, that's all I came to say. So, I'll leave you now. I'll be back at four to read to you."

She bent forward to place a kiss on his forehead and got up. As she stepped away, his hand caught her wrist. She gasped and looked down at him.

"Markham…?"

The corner of his mouth tilted upward and his eyes met hers. There was a tiny flicker of light in the green and it nearly took her breath away.

He licked his lips, then rasped, "Staella, I can smell the air."

ACKNOWLEDGEMENTS

A book is like a child—it takes a village. And now I have a chance to thank all the wonderful people who contributed to mine.

Firstly, thank you to my mother, Yvonne, for reading every word I've ever written and being the most supportive parent anyone could ask for.

To my dad, Thys: you will always be my us-against-the-world.

To my grandparents, thank you for fostering my love of stories for as long as I can remember.

To my best friend and alpha reader, Anja—you mean more to me than you could imagine.

Thank you to my talented critique partner, Kate, and my lovely beta readers: Lana, Lia, Freda, Merel, Melanie, Annie, Nicole and Christina.

A million thanks to Ryan Jones, my editor, and to my cover designer, Florina Leparda.

To every friend who supported me along this long journey, you are appreciated beyond measure.

Thank you to God for the wondrous creativity of the Universe.

And, finally, to you, reader, thank you for making my dreams come true. I hope we will still share many stories.

ABOUT THE AUTHOR

A corporate lawyer by day, speculative fiction writer by night, Marilene lives at the foot of Table Mountain in Cape Town, South Africa. She reads every fantasy book she can get her hands on and has an herbal tea recipe for any ailment.

Website: www.marilenelouiseblom.wixsite.com/author
Tumblr: @thatwritergirlsblog
YouTube: Marilene Louise Blom
Instagram: @marilenelouiseblom
Twitter: @AuthorMarilene
Facebook: @AuthorMarilene

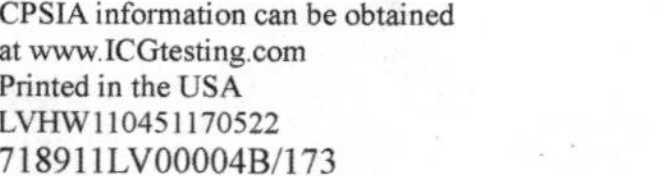

CPSIA information can be obtained
at www.ICGtesting.com
Printed in the USA
LVHW110451170522
718911LV00004B/173